Whispers of Moonlight

LORI WICK

HARVEST HOUSE PUBLISHERS
Eugene, Oregon 97402

Cover by Terry Dugan Design, Minneapolis, Minnesota

WHISPERS OF MOONLIGHT

Copyright © 1996 by Lori Wick
Published by Harvest House Publishers
Eugene, Oregon 97402

ISBN 1-56507-483-1

To Betty Fletcher, LaRae Weikert,
Julie Castle, and all the Harvest House family.
You have turned my dreams into reality. You have
given wings to the stories in my mind and even
been the wind beneath them. This dedication
comes with my love and deepest thanks.

Acknowledgments

So many people go into the writing of every book, and this book is no exception. There are many who touch my world and make me the person and the writer I am. I would like to mention just a few.

Thank you, Carol Middleton, for the friendship you show me. The miles between us don't make any difference. I can feel your love for me no matter where I am. I thank God for you.

Thank you Todd and Becki Barsness. Thank you for the song, but more so for the love you have shown to Bob and me. I praise God for your example in word and deed. You are precious to us.

And to Eoline Hayes, my paternal grandmother. It was wonderful to know you were so proud of me. Hard as it was to see you go, I'm so thankful we had you for 88 years. The reunion in heaven with your sons must have been the sweetest of all.

I also wish to thank my father, who died during the writing of this book. We were closer than ever when God called you home, but I don't think I ever thanked you for the special care you gave to Mom, or told you what it did to my heart to see you smile and caress my cheek. Nothing could have prepared me for the way I would miss you, but I'm so thankful that you're in on that heavenly reunion as well. If the Lord gives you reports on how we're doing, Dad, I hope He can say of me that I've been faithful.

And finally to Bob, at times my toughest critic but also my strongest support. I have no Scripture to back it up, but there must be a special crown for husbands whose wives are authors. Thanks for being there and never wavering in your love for me or the Lord.

About the Author

Lori Wick is one of the most versatile Christian fiction writers on the market today. From pioneer fiction to a series set in Victorian England to contemporary writing, Lori's books (over 700,000 copies in print) are perennial favorites with readers. The Rocky Mountain Memories series brings to life the rugged strength and enduring faith of Colorado settlers in the last part of the nineteenth century.

Born and raised in Santa Rosa, California, Lori met her husband, Bob, while in Bible college. They and their three children, Timothy, Matthew, and Abigail, make their home in Wisconsin.

Prologue

"I'm going, Hannah, and that's my final word."

"But why, Andrew? I don't understand."

Brother and sister, one angry and the other confused, eyed each other across the formal parlor, a dark room to begin with and made even more dim by the blue glass lantern.

"I can't explain it," he said in a low voice, "but the time is right. I feel it. As soon as I'm established, I'll send for my girl."

Hannah's hand fluttered around the lace at her throat and then went to the gray curls at her temple, her voice dropping to a whisper. "The talk, Andrew. What if there really is a war?"

The older sibling watched her brother's face flush with rage. "You'll not talk like that, do you hear me? There will be no war. Are we animals, Hannah? Brother fighting against brother? Preposterous! I'll hear no more about it."

But his sister wasn't cowed. Her chin rose even though her eyes filled with tears.

"If you're wrong, Andrew, you'll be cut off from Rebecca. That little girl whose mother hasn't been dead six months and who worships the ground you walk on will be hundreds of miles away with no way to reach you. She may never see you again."

All the fight went out of him. Andrew sank heavily into a chair, his hand to his brow. He was not an old man, just over 40, but suddenly he felt ancient. Indeed, nothing else his sister could say would have touched him more. He adored his eight-year-old daughter, but if he didn't go west now, he might never get the chance. He believed he could make a wonderful life for both of them, if only he had the opportunity. He had waited years for his now-dead wife's health to improve and felt sure that if he didn't go now, he never would.

7

"My mind's made up, Hannah." His voice was quiet yet resolute. "I'm asking you to keep Reba and see to her schooling. When the time is right, I'll send for her. I promise to write her every week, but I've *got* to do this."

Hannah took a deep breath, knowing she was going to have to accept the inevitable. She guessed she should be happy that he wasn't taking Rebecca with him, but Hannah dreaded the girl's tears and misery when her father left. Her own husband, Franklin Ellenbolt, was a tolerant husband and uncle, but so preoccupied with business that he would never have time for a lonely niece, no matter how precious.

"All right, Andrew, I'll do this," she agreed, "but you need to plan on sending for her no more than six months after you arrive."

The man nodded. "Yes, I think you're right. It will feel like forever as it is. If all goes according to plan, the timing shouldn't be a problem. Keep your eyes and ears open for someone to accompany her. Unless you think—"

Hannah shook her head. "Franklin would never agree, Andrew, and I'm getting too old to be running across the country."

Andrew stood. He would not press her further. "I'll tell Reba in the morning that I'm leaving at the end of the week. That way she'll have a few days to come to grips with the idea."

Hannah's throat felt tight. The end of the week. Four days from now. How would they survive it? How would the little girl sleeping in the next room respond? Rebecca Wagner was the sweetest little girl Hannah had ever known. But then sweet little girls were not always well taken care of. Hannah knew that firsthand.

The 50-year-old aunt had a sudden premonition. Her heart told her at that moment that all would not be well in the days to come. Andrew refused even to discuss the war, but Hannah was not so optimistic. Somehow she knew in her heart that Andrew would not send for Rebecca in six months.

Along with this thought rose a fierce protectiveness: Rebecca's Aunt Hannah was going to take care of her. Having no children of her own, she determined then and there that her niece would never want for anything as long as Hannah was alive. She knew she could never share this with her brother, but in moments Hannah had convinced herself that even if Andrew did send for her, Rebecca would never want to leave.

A door sounded in the other room, and Hannah knew that Franklin was finally home from the office. It was after 9:00, and he would be hungry. Andrew was headed toward the stairs and presumably bed. Hannah determined to tell Franklin of her plans, even if it ruined his dinner.

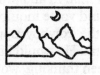

1

**Boulder, Colorado Territory
1870**

The tall cowboy and his buckskin mount drew eyes from up and down the street as he rode into town and stopped in front of the bar. He looped the horse's reins over the rail and worked to push Texas from his mind. No easy task. All the towns in every state he'd crossed since May sported the same sad little cemeteries, starkly reminding him of his mother's freshly dug grave. For years, while his mother was alive, he felt imprisoned in Texas, but now that she was dead, his only thought was to get as far away as quickly as he could.

Not able to remember even half the places he'd been, he now found himself in a small town in the Colorado Territory—Boulder. It was no different from anything else he'd seen. Outside of the church and graveyard, he could see two hotels, a post office, a barber shop, hardware and general stores, and a varied selection of wooden and brick houses. Nothing very special to his mind, but it was already late summer, and he knew if he didn't get settled into work soon, he'd be hungry and cold come winter.

The barroom doors swung open without a sound as he passed into the smoky interior, which he found rather crowded for midday. Small tables with mismatched chairs dotted the room, and without glancing at anyone he moved to a seat at an empty table, one that placed his back to the wall. A moment later, a rotund man in an apron approached.

"What'll it be?" a kind voice inquired.

Hat still in place, the cowboy tipped his head back just enough to order his drink. He would have preferred a tall glass of water, and had he been thinking, would have gone to one of the hotels where such a request would have been common.

"You want the bottle?" he was asked when the drink appeared a minute later.

"No," he said shortly, but without heat.

He reached for the glass, keeping his eyes on his own table and drink, but he had already attracted the attention of several patrons, one of whom was bold enough to approach. His name was Lucky Harwell. Just 17 and feeling quite proud of himself this day, he stood and began to saunter over to the stranger's table.

Lucky worked at the Double Star Ranch. His boss, Andrew Wagner, had known he was headed to town and asked him to keep an eye out for new hands. Lucky, as wet behind the ears as they came, was feeling so pleased with his task that he would have approached a known outlaw. The solitary man at the table looked a bit menacing, but Lucky wanted to return to the ranch and say he'd tried.

"Mind if I join ya?"

The head tipped way back this time because Lucky was taller than average, which gave the young man even more confidence.

"Depends on your business," the cowboy replied.

"Work. I wondered if you've ever worked a cattle ranch."

The chair opposite the seated man instantly slid out and bumped against Lucky's legs. Lucky had to hide a look of awe. He'd never seen such a smooth move; in fact, he hadn't seen that one, but he swiftly recovered and sat down.

"Who are you?" the other man asked before he could say a word.

"Lucky Harwell. I work at the Double Star Ranch, and my boss is looking for hands." He stopped, waiting for the man to show some interest, but received only a stare. The owner of the Double Star had not said much about the position, but Lucky hated to admit this. For some reason he wanted to bring this man back to Mr. Wagner.

"The hands sleep in the bunkhouse." He leaned forward as he spoke. "It's pretty clean, and you have your own bunk. Umm, we have days off, and the cattle drives aren't as long as some I've heard about." He couldn't say that he'd ridden on any, because the Double Star was his first job. He recognized that he was starting to babble and made himself stop. His expression became slightly mutinous, and his chin rose slightly. He was surprised when the other man put his hand out. Lucky shook it without thinking.

"I'm Travis Buchanan," the deep voice told him. "I'd hate to ride all the way to this ranch if your boss isn't really looking for men."

"He is," Lucky told him, all enthusiasm returning. "He talked to me about it just today."

"How many cattle you running?"

"Fifteen hundred head."

"What direction is this ranch?"

"North. Straight out through the center of town and then to the left at the fork in the road." Again, his age and excitement showed on his face and in his movements.

"Well, I'll have to ride out there. Who do I ask for?"

"Grady. He's foreman. Or Mr. Wagner if he's around."

Travis nodded and moved to stand. Lucky saw his intentions and shot up ahead of him. He enjoyed being taller than most men, and the girls liked it too. He didn't want to be caught sitting down. He was certain that if Travis saw how tall he was, he'd also recognize his importance at the Double Star. Unfortunately, his view of Travis Buchanan from across the room had been deceiving. Travis stood to full height until he looked down at Lucky from a difference of at least five inches. Lucky's pride in his six-foot frame all but crumbled at his feet. And if that wasn't enough, the bartender's daughter, Gloria, a girl he had dated a few times, was now hanging over the bar staring at Travis as though her dreams had come to life.

"Thanks for the information," Travis said, and Lucky had to drag his attention from Gloria.

"I'll ride with you," Lucky managed. As disgruntled as he was with the way things had turned out, he had to be at the ranch when this man made an appearance.

Travis, who obviously felt no need for small talk, was headed toward the door. Lucky grabbed his hat and left on Travis' heels.

"You passin' through or here for a time?"

"That all depends on the work," Travis told Grady.

The older man nodded. He was as impressed as Lucky had been. Travis Buchanan was clean-shaven, something he was partial to, and had a calm, professional air about him. In truth, he was foreman material, but Grady wasn't worried about his position. He was more Andrew Wagner's age than this new man, and the two of them thought much alike.

"You can start in the morning, if you've a mind to." He named the wages and mealtimes, and Travis nodded. Lucky was lingering in the background, so Grady called on him to take Travis to the bunkhouse and show him around. From there Grady went inside to tell Andrew they had hired a new hand. He moved toward the office, but the door was shut. It was the only time the boss was not to be disturbed, so Grady left word with the housekeeper and went back out to work.

Inside the office, Andrew was sitting at the desk, his hand to his chest. The awful pain was on him again, this time so intensely that he could hardly breathe. On the desk before him was a letter from Rebecca, and he hadn't even had the strength to open it. His breathing came hard and fast for a time, and he laid his head back on the leather chair and waited for the worst to pass. It crossed his mind, as it did often, that one of these days it was not going to pass. This time the thought drove him to prayer.

"If You're really up there, God," he began, "please bring Reba to me. I need her here. I need to show her the ropes, so this ranch won't go to pieces when I'm gone. In the past it's been my fault that she's not here, but now Hannah has lost her mind, God. I know it. She's keeping my girl from me. I'll make a deal with You. If you get Reba here, I'll go to church every week. I promise I will."

Another pain gripped him and he couldn't think for a time. When it finally receded, he had a terrible headache but still thought of Rebecca's letter. He opened it with a shaky hand, laid his head back again, and read.

It's dreadfully hot here, Papa. I envy you the cool of the mountains. The sentence made Andrew's heart leap, since she had stopped asking to come over a year ago. His hopes were dashed on the next line.

I'm off with friends to the lake this weekend. Marcus will be with us. I told you about him. He lost his arm in the war. I've never met anyone like him. He has such a natural humor. I know he'll have us laughing every minute.

Andrew couldn't read anymore. Clearly she had made a life for herself. How many years had she asked to join him, and he had put her off? It had taken so much longer to settle than he had anticipated. And then the war. Travel had been out of the question. The war had been over for five years, and indeed, he had finally made a home for them.

He had considered sending someone from Boulder to Philadelphia in order to fetch her, but he could tell from Hannah's overprotective letters that she would never allow it. It really was his fault that she wasn't with him already. He'd been a fool concerning the political situation—even Lincoln had been shot—and even more of a fool that he'd wanted Rebecca to come only if she could live in the lap of luxury. Now he was ready to have his daughter join him in one of the most beautiful homes in the state, but his declining health made him helpless to do anything toward getting her there. In the past all of his letters concerning the situation had been to Hannah, but Andrew now wondered if he shouldn't tell Rebecca to make plans herself.

She had a good head on her shoulders. She'd been educated in the finest schools. The thought gave him hope, and he even felt like finishing her letter to him. Rebecca chattered on about her social life and ended with how much she loved and missed him, but Andrew read it absently. A plan was forming in his mind.

Travis rubbed the back of his neck and slapped his hat against his leg in an attempt to dislodge the dust. He was hot and dirty, and all he wanted was a bath, food, and bed—in that order.

"Some of the boys are going into town tonight," Grady told Travis as he threw a saddle over the stable wall. "You goin'?"

Travis' head came up. He looked at the older man from over the top of his mount and then went back to the task at hand.

"No, I'm tired of the saddle."

"They'll probably borrow a wagon," Grady informed him.

Travis turned slowly and looked at him. "What are you really asking, Grady?"

After a month of working together, they knew they could both speak their minds.

"I just thought if you were going in, I wouldn't have to worry about anyone being shot or thrown in jail."

A slow smile stretched across Travis' mouth. "No thanks, Grady. You'll have to get someone else to do your babysitting."

The older man grunted, but he wasn't angry. It had been a long week, and he didn't want to go into town on a Saturday night either. He could hardly blame Travis for sharing the feeling. Lucky had a pretty good head on his shoulders, but he was young enough that none of the other men would listen to him. Nothing more was said, but Grady gave Travis a good-natured thump on the chest when he passed.

As Travis was leaving the huge barn, he noticed the ranch cook, Biscuit, stepping to the bell in front of the mess hall. It was early for dinner, and the dusty hand would have enjoyed a bath first, but he was hungry. He changed directions and moved to the long, narrow building.

The bell rang in his ear as he passed.

"You're always first in line," Biscuit snapped at him in his usual cantankerous manner.

"I don't know why I bother," Travis countered from far above Biscuit's head as he kept moving. "The food is never fit to eat."

"Why you—" Biscuit began, but cut off when they were joined by the other men.

Neither cook nor ranch hand meant any of it. Biscuit and all the men seemed to like Travis enough to give him a hard time. He did his job and was fair and honest. There wasn't a man on the ranch who didn't respect him. Travis himself was well-pleased with the job, feeling as though he'd landed on his feet for the winter. The pay was decent, and the living quarters more than adequate. Travis teased Biscuit about the food, but he'd had worse. He had only met the owner a handful of times, but Mr. Wagner seemed to be a fair man as well.

He would have continued to dwell on Mr. Wagner a little longer had Travis only known he was the topic of conversation in the office right then between the owner of the Double Star and Grady.

"I know it will be a cold ride, but I want you to go."

"All right," Grady agreed. "Are you going to act as foreman?"

"No, I want Buchanan to do it."

Grady nodded. He would have preferred to send Travis on the cattle drive, but he didn't mind going. Coming home was worth the time away.

"Just drive 150 head into the Denver stockyards, see the auction master, and when you have my money in your pocket, get yourself home," Andrew told him. "We should have moved them earlier, but I think you can still make it before heavy snowfall."

"All right. Are you talking to Travis, or am I?"

"Tell him to come see me."

Travis was just finishing his meal when Grady approached. He didn't bat an eyelash when told that Andrew Wagner wanted to see him, but wished again that he'd been given time to bathe. He made the large ranch house in record time, his long legs eating up the distance, and was surprised at how stark the interior was.

Needs a woman's touch. He couldn't figure out where that thought had come from. Unfortunately, it left him scowling when he met his boss.

"I hope that frown isn't for me," Andrew commented, "but you've just come from Biscuit's cooking, and that could make any man scowl." He smiled, and Travis smiled in return.

"Grady said you wanted to see me, sir."

"Yes, I do."

Andrew mapped out his wants for the next few weeks. Travis was more than happy to fill in as foreman and take the raise in pay as well. He would be working closer to Mr. Wagner, which suited him fine. He genuinely liked the man. Travis left the ranch house just 20 minutes later, once again applauding himself for landing on his feet.

2

Ten days later, Travis sat across the dining room table from Andrew Wagner, knowing it was going to be difficult to have Grady return. A foreman's life was one of great responsibility, but it also included a few perks: Dining with the boss and enjoying Lavena's cooking were just two of them.

"How does the south pasture look?"

"Excellent."

"And the stock—it's healthy?"

"Very. No calves left, of course, but the young heifers are already getting fat."

Andrew nodded and took another bite of beef.

"I've got pie," Lavena said by way of greeting. The housekeeper had come from the kitchen to check on them. She was the smallest woman Travis had ever seen, too thin and very short as well. It was impossible to place her age, although her hair was completely gray. She was cantankerous, but Travis still smiled at her. She scowled at him for his efforts, but knowing she was all show, his smile broadened.

"I'll have some," Travis finally said, but Andrew was shaking his head, his face troubled. Lavena frowned at the older man and left them in a hurry. She was back in a few moments. There was no pie plate in her hand, but a tall glass filled with a milky white liquid. She placed the glass before Andrew and then stood at his elbow while he drank.

"That'll put you to rights," she muttered.

Andrew's chest heaved with relief, but he didn't thank her. In a weak voice that was struggling for outrage, he said, "I told you never to do this in front of the men!"

Lavena snorted. "Haven't you figured out yet that Travis is the best man you've got? Even better than that Grady."

With that she stomped from the room, Travis' pie forgotten. An uncomfortable silence fell on them then, and for a moment Travis tried to look anywhere but at his boss. When he glanced at Andrew, however, he found the older man's eyes on him.

"I have a daughter," he stated, his breath still coming a little rough. "She lives back East."

Travis only nodded.

"I'm expecting her soon. If not before winter, then in the spring. She's a good girl."

Again, Travis could only nod, unaware that Andrew had not even heard back from his daughter. The words to his temporary foreman were wishful thinking, but his attacks always drove his mind to the dream of seeing Rebecca.

A painful silence had once again settled, and Travis struggled to fill it in. "I'm sure she'll like the territory once she arrives." Andrew seemed not to have heard him.

"When she comes on the stage I want you to go for her. I want you to take my best buggy and bring her here safely to the ranch. I'll let you know the day."

Travis nodded one more time and watched as Andrew's eyes went to his half-eaten plate of food.

"Are you all right, sir?" Travis asked, although fully expecting to be told to mind his own business. On the contrary, Andrew was pleased with the genuine concern on Travis' face. His chest still hurt, but he managed a smile. His heart had told him this young man was special.

"I'll be fine," Andrew stated. "You just get Rebecca here to me, and I'll be fine."

"Yes, sir, I'll do all I can."

"Excuse me," Andrew said, rising heavily from the table and moving to the stairs.

Travis found that he was no longer hungry. He rose as well and moved through the kitchen to thank Lavena. The tiny woman, her head somewhere below his chest, made him sit down and eat the pie he'd missed. She chattered some while he ate, but his mind was elsewhere. He pictured Andrew's little dark-haired girl, sitting back East and pining for her father. Travis' heart clenched, and he had to force himself to finish the berry pie.

The letter began, *How could you?* and Andrew didn't know when words had done him more good. His sister was outraged, and Andrew felt like dancing for the first time in years. Rebecca was on her way. He swiftly scanned the letter to see what day she'd turned up missing and to his dismay realized that his daughter might be in the area already. Just two days ago he'd told Travis to stand by, and now he must tell him to get to town.

"Lavena," Andrew called as he came from his study. He continued to shout the woman's name until she materialized.

"What are you hollering about?" she cranked at him. "I swear you could wake the dead."

"What time does the stage come into town?"

"I don't know. About 3:00, I guess."

It was just past 4:00. Andrew's heart lurched.

"Find Travis."

"Why, he's out with the men!"

"I don't care. Get him in here now." The man's face was turning an alarming red.

Lavena moved off, muttering under her breath about Andrew putting himself in an early grave, but she did as she was told.

Andrew's chest was beginning to pain him. When he was alone, he made himself sit on the chair in the entryway outside his study and breathe deeply. He had never once asked himself how it would feel to have his daughter traveling across the country. Now the thought terrified him. If she never arrived, Hannah's letter would be right. He would be a no-good skunk. Andrew realized at that moment that he hadn't even read the whole missive, only glanced over it.

Leaving the door open so he could hear Lavena's return, he moved to his desk and sat down to read from the beginning.

How could you? How could you take her from me? I knew you would never come for her, Andrew. I knew it the day you left, and I determined to give her the life I never had. It took a long time, but she finally stopped missing you. She's my girl now, Andrew, and I hate you for what you've done.

A no-good skunk is what you are. My heart nearly stopped when I went to her room and found her letter. Just an hour ago it was, but it might as well have been years.

Andrew paused long enough to look at the date of his sister's letter: 19 September. Rebecca had been on the road for one-and-a-half weeks. With trains beginning to crisscross the countryside, she could nearly be in the territory. Where was Lavena with Travis? The pain came on so suddenly this time that he gasped. He told himself not to panic, but it was no use. By the time Travis arrived he'd lost all color. "Meet the stage," he said in a painful whisper.

Travis took in Andrew's washed-out features and then glanced up to find Lavena scowling at him.

"Get him upstairs," Lavena insisted.

Making a swift decision to do as she instructed, Travis lifted the older man into his arms and carried him upstairs.

Andrew gasped, "Why won't you do as I tell you? You must—" His voice cut off in pain. Travis' heart was pounding by the time he laid him on the bed. No longer able to stand the anguish in his employer's eyes, Travis quickly moved back downstairs to his horse and rode into town, completely forgetting he was supposed to take the best buggy.

Three days later, Travis pulled the buggy up to the hitching post, a little past the stage office, and began his daily vigil. He'd been coming to meet Rebecca's stage every day and had started to give up hope. Andrew became more agitated with every passing moment. Travis wasn't sure if the man would make it if he came home empty-handed again. It would have helped to have Grady home, but he was evidently held up in Denver. The pressure on Travis to be all things to Mr. Wagner was not something he enjoyed.

Travis stepped down from the covered, single-seat buggy and tipped his hat to a woman with a baby, wondering absently if the stage would be as late as it had been the day before. The day was on the cool side, but Travis was sweating. Rebecca Wagner *had* to be on that stage.

The underarms of his dark shirt grew damp, and he paced a bit, afraid to wander far. His black-hatted head shot up when he heard the familiar sound of heavy hooves and jingling tack. Only ten minutes late, the stage, pulled by four horses, was moving steadily down the main street of town.

Four people emerged when the doors were opened. Travis held his breath: They were all men. He saw the stage-office manager speaking to someone inside, and then a small hand came forward to take his. Travis' heart sank when he saw it was a young woman. He waited a moment longer, thinking Rebecca might have been escorted, but the blonde in the small blue hat was alone. Travis turned back to the buggy.

"The Double Star?" the manager's voice carried. "It's out north of town a few miles."

Travis stopped in his tracks and turned back. The stage-office manager had moved on, and the woman's back was to him as she thanked the driver for retrieving her trunk. Travis walked slowly back and stopped a few feet behind her. He removed his hat and said her name in his soft, deep voice.

"Miss Rebecca?"

To his amazement she turned.

"Yes?"

Travis' heart did a flip in his chest as he looked down into the largest brown eyes he'd ever seen. A brown-eyed blonde. Travis blinked.

"Did you call my name?" she asked, looking very unsure.

"Yes, yes," Travis stuttered. "If you're Rebecca Wagner, your father sent me."

"Oh." She was clearly disappointed and then concerned. "Is Papa all right?"

"Yes, ma'am," Travis said, hoping it was true. "I'm Travis Buchanan, and your father asked me to come for you. It's a 45-minute drive to the Double Star."

Rebecca smiled suddenly, and Travis found himself out of breath. "I've done more riding in the last two weeks than I have my whole life. A few more miles won't make any difference."

"The buggy is this way." Travis stepped back and wondered that he sounded so normal. Where was the little girl from his imagination?

"I have a trunk." Rebecca sounded apologetic, but Travis only nodded, put his hat back on his head, and went to retrieve it. He hefted it easily, wondering how she could have traveled so lightly, and loaded it into the back of the wagon. He turned to find her standing and taking in the town.

Boulder's surrounding mountains were far more noteworthy than the town itself, and Travis could well imagine what she might be thinking. He also saw in those moments that she was attracting plenty of attention. It was obvious to anyone with eyes that a lady had come into their midst. Travis swiftly went to her side, his manner unconsciously territorial.

"This way, Miss Rebecca." Travis took her arm and she smiled her thanks, not once having noticed that men were stopped on the street. He tried not to stare at her as he helped her into the buggy, but even in her wrinkled navy traveling suit she was a sight for sore eyes. She accidentally knocked the little hat on her head slightly askew, but that only added to her charm. Travis guessed her to be about 18 and swallowed hard over the emotions flooding through him.

Had she really come all this way on her own? Maybe her sweet smile covered a will of iron or a set of standards that wasn't as high as her demeanor indicated. However, when he climbed aboard and she turned to smile at him, he knew he was wrong. Her eyes were as artless as a child's, and in those eyes he suddenly saw a shyness. But he also saw that she liked what she saw in him as much as he did in her. His heart was misbehaving again.

"I think you're going to surprise your father," Travis spoke, having slapped the reins. He worked at keeping his eyes on the road.

Rebecca turned to look at his profile for a moment and then dutifully put her gaze back to the street.

"Why is that?"

"He never once mentioned your age. I've been waiting for a little girl to get off the stage."

Rebecca laughed, a light, fun sound, her heart soaring because she had heard the compliment and pleasure in his voice.

"I was just a child when he left," she said softly. "He must still think I'm eight."

Travis had to force himself to keep from looking down the length of her. She was anything but a child now, and for the first time in many years the cowboy's thoughts turned to hearth and home. The images didn't last long. Other thoughts were crowding into his mind. For starters, the way Rebecca had come so easily with him. With nothing but his word for who he was, she had climbed into the buggy. Could she really be that trusting? He didn't think he'd been working for the Double Star long enough for Mr. Wagner to write about him. It was something of a mystery.

"Did you say how far it was, Mr. Buchanan?" Rebecca suddenly asked.

"No, but it's five miles, and you can call me Travis."

"Oh, all right. Are there other homes around?"

"No," Travis answered, amazed that she didn't know. "The ranch sits on acres of open range." As he told her this, his heart grew troubled. From the way Lavena had talked, father and daughter were in constant communication.

He fell silent, and it was some time before he glanced at his passenger. She was literally drooping in the seat. Travis slowed the horse just slightly, bringing the reins to one hand and putting the other hand on her arm.

"Lean back, Miss Rebecca, and get comfortable. We have a way to go."

She turned vague eyes to him.

"Put your head back," he instructed her. A moment later she turned slightly toward him, her left cheek against the leather seatback. They hadn't gone 100 yards before her face bounced forward and her forehead lay against his arm. Travis kept the horse's pace slow and steady. He knew Mr. Wagner would be having apoplexy, but right now he had a lovely passenger to see to, and Travis refused to do anything that would disturb her. He also had no trouble admitting to himself that the feel of her against him, even just her forehead, was much too wonderful for words.

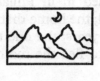

3

"Miss Rebecca," Travis called very softly as the house came into view. "Rebecca," he tried again. She stirred, dislodging the hat completely to tumble at her feet. Travis' face was turned to her, the horse well-knowing the way home, and he watched as she looked up into his eyes and blinked slowly. He was very aware of the way her shoulder leaned against his arm, but Rebecca had only just noticed. Her face red, she pushed upright and looked at the road and beyond. Travis heard her gasp.

The ranch house at the Double Star was a sight to see. They were within 100 yards now, and the lovely home seemed to rise up abruptly out of the prairie. It was painted white, two stories high with an attic, and grand to any eye.

A deep porch with round wooden pillars stretched across the entire front of the house and wrapped around the east side. A large balcony extended from the second floor, and Rebecca instinctively knew this would be off her father's bedroom. The roofline was punctuated by several gables. The roof itself was finished in cedar shakes. Her father's love for the mountains was evident in the large windows that rose from seemingly every room, both upstairs and down.

"This is my father's home?" she questioned softly.

"Yes. This is the Double Star ranch house."

The bunkhouse, cook's shack, and mess hall were all in sight as well, but Rebecca didn't focus on them. She was silent as she tried to take in both the setting at the base of the mountains and the home itself. She kept thinking of the house she'd been raised in in Philadelphia with its small rooms and damp smell; the home that her Aunt Hannah had seldom left in the last years; the one that had made her feel suffocated and ready to flee the moment she found her father's letters.

"It's him," Rebecca breathed. Travis watched as she leaned forward in the seat.

Indeed, Andrew had come onto the porch and was now making his way down the steps. Travis found himself petitioning God, or whoever was in charge, that the man would not die of heart failure before his daughter's eyes.

"Oh, Papa," he heard her whisper, and even though they were far off, he stopped the buggy and let her dismount. Tears he no longer believed himself capable of clogged in the back of his throat as Rebecca ran and was swept into her father's embrace. Travis made himself drive the buggy past them toward the barn. He was certain they would want some time alone.

❧

"Oh, Papa; oh, Papa," was all Rebecca could say for the first five minutes. Andrew had his arm around her, leading her up the steps and into the beautiful home, but she could see only her father's face. He looked old, so much older than she remembered, but it was still him. It was still the Papa she'd adored as a child, and in just a moment of looking into his eyes, she knew that her aunt's words had all been lies.

"Are you all right?" Andrew was asking, his hands on her arms. "Was the trip awful? Did anyone hurt you?"

"No, no. I'm fine. I was on the train for most of the journey. It broke down a few times, but no one bothered me." She smiled suddenly. "The stage was a bit rough."

Andrew hugged her again and took her hand to lead her into his study. He shut the door and turned to watch as she glanced around the room and then moved to look out the window.

Andrew sat on the long leather sofa. Rebecca turned from the glass immediately, a thousand questions coming to mind.

"I waited for you," she said softly, the light to her back. "I waited so long."

Andrew's hand came to his forehead in a gesture of weariness. It hadn't occurred to him that she would want to talk of this right away, but he was more than happy to clear the air. He shook his head a moment. Where to begin?

"I've made mistakes, Reba, dozens of them." Andrew's eyes focused on the dark rug. "But none can compare to leaving you with Hannah and Franklin. Hannah tried to tell me about the outbreak of war, but I wouldn't listen. She said we would be cut off, but I said I had to go."

He looked at his daughter. "I'm sorry, Reba. I never meant for it to be this way. A man should have his child with him, and a little girl should have her papa. I've let you down."

Rebecca went to sit beside him, her hand going to his arm. "It's not all your fault," she told him. "Aunt Hannah's not right, Papa. She doesn't think like the rest of us."

Andrew nodded.

"I'm to blame as well," Rebecca admitted in a soft voice.

Andrew's eyes narrowed, and the young woman could see that he was ready to deny it. She cut him off.

"I am, Papa. I've been living in a dream world. Hannah rarely leaves the house anymore, but she was out the afternoon your letter arrived." Tears filled the young woman's eyes. "Up until then I had no idea. I—"

"What is it, Reba?" Andrew urged her gently. "You can tell me."

"Your letters," she whispered. "I never saw them." She shook her head, so overcome that she couldn't go on. Andrew put an arm around her, his heart and mind trying to deal with what she meant.

How could she have not seen his letters? She always replied to his questions. Had Hannah read them to her? He had a hard time imagining that. After all she was 19 years old.

Surely his sister wouldn't . . . Andrew's thoughts halted. He'd known from her letters that Hannah was not doing well emotionally, and Rebecca had already said as much. The familiar ache came to the region of his chest, and he felt his body sweat. He looked down at his daughter, aching to ask more questions in order to have answers to put his heart at rest. However, the fatigue he saw in her eyes stopped him short.

"How about some supper and then bed? Are you hungry?"

Rebecca smiled at his rescue, but she couldn't help but see the perspiration beading on his forehead and upper lip. Her smile slowly died.

"You're not well. The letter didn't say that, but I know it."

"I'm not as strong as I once was," he admitted, not wanting to talk of his health, "but you're here now, and everything is going to be fine."

Rebecca was not convinced, but she wanted it to be true. Willingly she stood with him and started toward the door at his side.

"Travis usually eats supper with me," Andrew mentioned, "but tonight it can be just us."

"Travis Buchanan?" Rebecca questioned, and something in her voice made him look at her.

"Yes, Travis Buchanan." Andrew said lightly. "He's acting as temporary foreman for me right now." Andrew's voice grew elaborate. "He won't mind eating with the other hands tonight."

Rebecca bit her lip. "I don't mind if you'd like him to eat with us."

They were at the foot of the stairs when Andrew stopped, his gaze tender on her face.

"I take it you didn't leave your heart in Philadelphia?"

Rebecca shook her head.

"What about Marcus from the war?"

"We were just friends."

Andrew continued to look at her. It hadn't been hard to imagine that his pretty little daughter would turn into a lovely young woman, but finally seeing her had done him a world of good. He was not a large man, and Rebecca's mother had been petite, so it was easy to see why she was not very big herself. However, her slim figure still possessed very womanly curves. It passed through his mind to wonder if Travis had been as taken with her as she seemed to be with him.

"You're here now, and we'll have lots of time to be alone together," Andrew replied.

Rebecca smiled and nodded.

"I'll make sure he knows he's welcome," Andrew added. He could see he'd done the right thing when she bit her lip again.

Travis ate his meal from pure habit. He had no idea what was on his plate, or how it tasted. Rebecca had changed from the blue traveling suit to a dress of sunny yellow with white bands on the sleeves, bodice, and neckline. It made her light blonde hair come alive as it lay on her shoulders, and Travis, already captivated, was utterly smitten.

All he'd wanted to do was find a place for the winter. All he'd wanted was to walk away from the pain of the past, but then Rebecca had turned those brown eyes to look at him in front of the stage office that afternoon. Could it have been only a few hours ago?

"I've begun to think that Grady is never coming back," Andrew was saying with no real worry in his voice. "I got word that he gained a good price for the beef, but if I didn't know better I'd say he skipped town with my gold."

"I hope he's not hurt," Rebecca commented. "Is there any way to check?"

Andrew and Travis exchanged a glance and smiled.

"Only if I send Travis out on the trail to look for him." Andrew's voice held a note of laughter. "And something tells me he'd rather not do that right now."

Travis smiled but dropped his eyes. It was true. The last thing he wanted to do was leave, unless of course Rebecca could go with him. The thought made him smile again, and at that moment he looked up to find her eyes on him. She smiled shyly in return and then dropped her own eyes. Neither of the young people was aware that Andrew had sat back in his chair with a contented sigh.

"How old are you, Travis?"

"Twenty-two. How about yourself?"

"I turned 19 in May."

Again the young couple smiled at each other, still keeping a good six feet between them.

Rebecca's plans had been to eat and sleep around the clock, but when the meal was over and her father suggested that she and Travis take a walk, all fatigue fell away.

"It gets cold here at night, doesn't it?"

"Maybe we should go in." Travis was all concern.

"No!" Rebecca said a little too swiftly. Travis smiled. Rebecca smiled in return but looked away when she felt her face heat. Travis studied her profile, his eyes lingering on her lips.

How in the world did a man act when his boss seemed almost to be throwing him together with his daughter? Not that Travis had any complaints, but did Andrew Wagner realize what a temptation Rebecca was? Travis' travels had never been in the fine, big cities. The women he'd met had not been shy and sweet but ready to kiss him before he could learn their names. He'd never met anyone as sweet and genuine as Rebecca.

Rebecca had been protected, that was more than clear, and he'd been anything but sheltered. However, she seemed just as interested in him, and until Travis sensed otherwise, he planned to pursue this young woman with every spare moment allotted to him. Once again he felt torn over Grady's return. He certainly didn't wish the man harm, but it would be difficult to become just one of the hands again.

They had made a large circle of the house, something Travis would have thought his boss would want to do with his daughter, but the older man had been looking pale. Biscuit had come from his small bungalow, a one-room add-on to the cookhouse, and Travis had performed the introductions. Biscuit had been slightly less crotchety than usual for the first few words, but began to complain in less than two minutes.

"Have you seen what old Miller's got in that store? Why I've seen better goods on the back of a wagon, and I swear—"

"We'll see you later, Biscuit." Travis cut him off easily and took Rebecca's arm. She smiled up at him, and his own eyes twinkled with amusement before he dropped her arm.

At that moment he looked up and saw all five hands lined up outside the bunkhouse. They tried to look casual, but with their shirts buttoned to the neck, cheeks clean-shaven as though it were Saturday night, and every hair in place, Travis was not fooled.

"Evening, ma'am." Lucky, always bold with the ladies, was the first to speak when the couple came abreast of them.

"Miss Rebecca," Travis spoke up. "These are the Double Star hands. This is Lucky Harwell."

Lucky smiled charmingly, his eyes not missing a thing.

"Next to him is Race Paulson, Woody Clark, Jud Silver, and Brad Sugars. Gentlemen, this is Miss Rebecca Wagner, and I know you're going to show nothing but courtesy to the boss' daughter."

"Hello," Rebecca greeted them sweetly, unaware of how seldom they saw a lady.

"We'll be moving on now, boys," Travis said, taking Rebecca's arm again. "I'll see you in the morning."

Not a one of the men, young or old, wouldn't have liked to catch the fair Miss Rebecca's eye, but the gaze she turned to Travis spoke volumes. And in truth, as much as they might have liked to get their hands on her, they knew it would cost them their good-paying jobs. Feelings of jealousy for Travis and his position surged through the group.

"That was lovely, Travis. Thank you."

They were back at the house, standing in the entryway. Travis' hat was in his hand, and Rebecca's eyes were on his face.

"Thank you for accompanying me."

"Will I see you tomorrow?"

"I expect, yes." The temptation to linger was strong, but he forced himself to say, "Good night, Miss Rebecca."

"Couldn't you just call me Rebecca?"

The question took the air right out of his lungs. His voice was soft when he said, "I don't know if your father would approve."

Rebecca nodded and oddly enough, Travis was relieved. He hated the thought that all this sweetness hid a rebellious spirit.

"Good night, Travis," she said, turning away.

Travis only smiled at her and let himself back out the door. As temporary foreman he still bunked with the men. He had no intention of answering a single question, so he saddled his horse, Diamond, and took a long ride, hoping beyond hope that when he returned they would all be asleep.

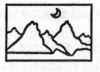

4

"Lavena," Rebecca called to the housekeeper, who had befriended her.

"In the kitchen." The older woman's voice floated to the bottom of the stairs.

Rebecca walked that way, stepped inside, and just stood. Lavena's back was to her, but she still heard the movements. She kept on with her work over a bowl of vegetables, a smile playing around her eyes.

The facts were simple—Rebecca Wagner was at loose ends. She'd been at the Double Star for ten days, searched out every nook and cranny of the large house, tried to help Lavena in the kitchen and with the cleaning, and was now restless. It was a few minutes after 4:00, and Lavena noted that this had become the pattern of the last week. It had taken a day or two to rest from her trip, but now she was raring to go but with little to do. Sunday was the only day she had company other than Lavena's. The housekeeper was thankful that this was Saturday afternoon.

"Has my father ever shown any interest in remarrying?"

Lavena's head spun around as if she'd been stung, all pretense of absorption with her cooking falling away.

"Marrying?" She sounded outraged. "Whatever gave you such a notion?"

Rebecca shrugged, having already learned that Lavena's bark was larger than her bite. "I just wondered. I mean, he's not an old man, and I can't help but think he might be lonely out here."

"He never wrote to you about a woman, did he?" Lavena's voice was sharp.

Rebecca, still so confused about the letters, only shook her head no. Lavena eyed her strangely but refrained from further comment. Rebecca moved from the room. At what point was she going to tell her father how it had really been in Philadelphia? Hannah was a kind, although possessive, woman, and Franklin had never been anything but a gentleman, but Rebecca was convinced that they had both deceived her from the moment her father left. Oh, she'd been happy—very happy. She'd never gone without possessions, time, or attention, but the things she'd been told concerning her father were all lies. And the letters . . .

Rebecca's mind stopped there. Hers had been a happy, secure life until the mail delivery that day. Rebecca's hand went to her pocket. The letter was inside. She knew her father was out with Travis and the hands, so Rebecca moved to his study. She sat at the big wooden desk and read the letter for the dozenth time.

My darling Rebecca,

You have stopped asking when I will come for you. Not recently, but a time ago, and there is no describing the pain I feel. I feel you have given up on me, and I can't say as I blame you. I have never wanted to speak ill of your aunt, but she has not made things easy for us. I want more than anything for you to join me in Boulder, but it is impossible for me to come for you. Please know that were it in my power, I would be there. I ask myself what I will do if we never see one another again. I must then push the thought aside because I can't stand the pain.

You still have not answered my questions concerning this young man Marcus. I have asked about him

for the last several letters. If you do not reply this time,
I will assume that he has hurt you and you do not wish
to speak of it. If anything has happened to your heart, I
will hold your aunt responsible.

Even as I write this, I laugh. Your aunt holds complete control over our situation, and I can do nothing.
But you are 19 now, Reba, and should you ever wish to
come on your own, I would see you here. It's a long
way, but you're your father's girl. Just ask for the
funds, and I will see that you have them—that and
anything else you need.

As ever,
Your loving father

The letter was beginning to tear and wrinkle, but Rebecca
didn't care. She pressed it to her chest and let her eyes slide
shut. She had never heard him talk like this because she had
never read *his* letters. He had wanted her. He *hadn't* been too
busy making a life for himself and forgotten her.

Voices in the entryway, right outside the study door,
brought Rebecca to her feet. She needed to discuss this with
her father but knew that Travis would be joining them for dinner. Had it been anyone else, she would have asked him to eat
with the hands, but for Travis she could put her feelings aside.
Indeed, for Travis she would do anything.

Travis' hand bumped Rebecca's when he passed her a
bowl of potatoes, and their eyes met for just an instant. Just
the night before, when they had taken their evening walk,
Travis had picked up her hand to help her over some rocks
and not let go. Rebecca had not objected, but she had been a
little breathless. Was it too soon? Her heart and body told her
no, but she had so little experience with men. Her aunt had
told her to look at their eyes.

"You can tell a man's thoughts by his eyes" had been her warning, but Rebecca wasn't certain what she was looking for. In Travis' eyes she saw only caring and admiration. Was there something mysterious she should be watching for?

Had Rebecca only known her father's thoughts, she'd have gone to him for advice. Indeed, there was something to be looked for in a man's eyes, and Andrew was already seeing it in Travis'. He didn't object. On the contrary, the whole business was making him feel like himself for the first time in years. Rebecca's presence had been a strong cathartic to his ailing body. No, he didn't object to Travis' courtship of his daughter. However, he hoped that Travis was not in a hurry. Andrew wasn't ready to lose his daughter just yet—not after 11 years of separation.

"You two going to take a walk tonight?" Andrew asked. Travis looked to Rebecca. She nodded, and Travis turned back to his boss.

"Would you care to join us, sir?"

Andrew's heart smiled. Oh no, he had no problem with Travis courting Rebecca, no problem at all.

"I believe I'll retire to the study, but I would like you to come and see me when you return, Travis."

"All right, sir. Are you finished, Rebecca?"

"Yes."

Travis watched her rise and felt his heart constrict. Never had he felt like this. She had been on his mind for days, and he knew it was no passing thing. For the first time in his life, he could envision himself married and happy. For the first time he thought there might be a God who looks down on the subjects of earth to give His blessing. However, his position as foreman was only temporary. What could he possibly offer this woman? He was never a man to worship money, but without it he was at his boss' mercy. Travis realized he could do far worse than Andrew Wagner. It looked as if the older man sanctioned the courting of his daughter, but to what end? Travis was suddenly glad Andrew wanted to speak to him. He had some questions of his own.

"I can't believe the wildflowers here," Rebecca said for the second time. "I've never seen anything like them. What is this, Travis?" She was pointing to a tall-stemmed flower with a bright purple bloom.

"I don't know," he had to admit. "I haven't lived in Colorado Territory that long."

Rebecca looked surprised. "I thought you'd lived here for years, like my father. Where did you come from?"

"I've lived most of my life in Texas, but I was born in North Carolina."

"North Carolina? Why, we were practically neighbors!"

Travis smiled. "I never dreamed I'd be on a walk with the girl next door."

Rebecca's face grew suddenly serious. "Is that what we're doing, Travis, walking?"

It was exactly what they were doing, but he understood the deeper question. He stopped now and stared at her. He'd never seen such huge brown eyes, and her skin made his hands ache to touch her.

"When a man like me meets a girl like you, Rebecca, he asks himself what he has to offer. The answer I had to give myself was not very encouraging."

Rebecca stared back at him. She wanted to say that it didn't matter. She longed to tell him that she'd live anywhere but felt she'd already been bold enough.

"What part of Texas?"

"Amarillo," Travis told her with a certain measure of regret. He too wanted to discuss the other subject, but what more was there to say?

"I've never been to Texas. What did you do there?"

"I worked as a hand, much like I do now." He answered her calmly enough, but the mask that suddenly dropped over his face told her to let the matter rest. If Aunt Hannah had witnessed her conversation with one of the ranch hands, it would have given the woman vapors, but Rebecca was only more fascinated and attracted than ever with the good-looking and mysterious Travis Buchanan. None of the men Rebecca had known in the past had even remotely measured up.

She had never felt this way, so delighted and miserable at the same time. Suddenly she remembered that Travis had been at the Double Star only a short time and asked herself if he might just be passing through. It wasn't that she wanted to leave her father, but she knew how torn she would be if Travis were to leave the ranch.

I'll go with him, she spoke rashly to herself. *I'll go and be by his side. I'll keep his house, cook for him, and*—Rebecca's resolve came to a firm halt. Her aunt had pampered her something terrible.

You're going to have all the things I never had, Rebecca, she would say, and Rebecca, lonely for her father and living in her dream world, would smile and feel content. But now, now that she wanted to be with Travis and take care of him, she wished she'd overridden her aunt's protests and learned to work around the house. She couldn't even cook or bake. Lavena had shown her how to dust her bedroom upstairs, but Rebecca had seen that she was slowing the busy housekeeper down.

"I guess we'd better get back," Travis broke into her thoughts. Rebecca turned without comment and walked by his side. Travis could tell that she was deep in thought, but he had his own musings to deal with.

They were back at the house in less time than either of them expected, and Travis removed his hat to say good night. They stood in the dim entryway and looked at each other for a long time. Both felt that things were unresolved, but neither knew how to fix them. However, one thing was very clear: They both still cared, and emotions were riding them hard.

Travis let his eyes roam her face until his gaze centered on her lips. Rebecca's mouth parted in anticipation, and indeed, Travis would have kissed her had they not heard a noise from behind the study door.

"Good night, Miss Rebecca," Travis said abruptly, turning away.

"Good night, Travis," she answered him, and watched as he turned. Not until he had knocked on the door and disappeared inside did she remember her fears. She went into her room, but didn't ready for bed. She paced until she heard her father's steps in the hall.

"Sit down, Travis," Andrew bade him warmly. Guilt washed over the younger man. *I'd have taken advantage of your daughter tonight if I'd been given half a chance, yet you trust me to keep company with her.* It felt odd to Travis to be contemplating kissing a girl one minute and then sitting calmly with her father the next.

"Did you see the rider who came in this afternoon, Travis?" Andrew asked without preamble.

"Yes, I did. Is there trouble?"

"It's Grady. He's laid up in Denver. He wasn't foolish enough to send money with the man, but I'm starting to worry about both Grady and the money. He didn't take any of the regular hands with him, and anything could have happened. I haven't seen a one of them, and Grady's not a kid anymore."

"What can I do?"

The question was just enough to tip the scales in Travis' favor.

"I want you to ride to Denver. I realize you may get snowed out, but I need you to see after Grady *and* my gold. I don't relish the idea of acting as my own foreman, but I don't trust any of the other hands to go to Denver or act in your stead here."

Travis nodded. He'd rather not leave Rebecca right now, but maybe some time away from her was just what he needed.

"When would you like me to leave?"

"I know tomorrow is Sunday, but I think you'd better hit the trail. I suspect it's going to be a cold ride."

"All right." Travis stood. "If that's all, I'd better get some rest."

Andrew stood as well. "I'm not going to ask you if you'll be back, because I know that that little girl upstairs is worth far more than any gold Grady has for me."

Travis' hat was headed to the top of his head, and its movement slowed only a mite. He carefully put the hat in place and then turned to look his employer in the eye.

"I was hoping to talk to you about that."

"All right."

Travis cleared his throat. He'd been given an opening but didn't know where to begin. He coughed again and stared at the toe of his boot. Rebecca's face swam into view, and Travis found the courage to say, "I don't have anything to offer her."

"That's the least of my worries," Andrew told him. "As much as I worried about my sister spoiling her, she doesn't seem overly concerned with jewels and finery."

Travis still shook his head. "I don't even have a place to live, and my family—"

Travis stopped when Andrew's hand went in the air.

"You're worrying about things that don't exist," Andrew said cryptically. "Go and see to Grady and know that your job is waiting when you return."

Travis stared at the older man for a moment but could read only honest straightforwardness in his eyes. He was forced to take him at his word.

"Good night, sir."

"Good night, Travis," Andrew spoke, and after picking up the lantern, followed him out. He was almost to his bedroom door when he heard Rebecca's voice.

"Papa?"

"I thought you'd be in bed," he spoke softly as he walked to her door. The lantern showed that she was still dressed and worried to boot.

"Is everything all right, Papa?"

"Everything is fine, Reba. I'm sending Travis away, but only for a time."

Rebecca had a sudden fear. "But what if he doesn't return? What if he never comes back?"

Andrew laid a hand on her cheek. "Now there you are, just like Travis, worrying over things that haven't happened."

"Oh, Papa," Rebecca didn't understand what he could be talking about.

"Go to bed, Reba. Your father's not going to do anything to hurt you. Just go to bed, and trust me when I tell you that Travis will be back just as soon as he can."

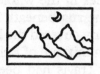

5

Travis turned the collar of his coat up a little bit higher, pushed his hat down a little lower, and asked himself how he'd managed to get into this adventure. His whole plan had been to hunker in somewhere for the winter, yet here he was on the trail. There was no snow, but the temperature made the heat of summer seem like a long-ago dream. And all the time, Rebecca's sweet smile and dark eyes lingered in his mind.

Andrew had been in the stable the next morning, giving him money for the road and all the information Grady had sent him, but he saw no sign of Rebecca. He had no idea which bedroom was hers, but his eyes lingered on every window as he rode from the house. He saw no movement, and it wasn't many yards later that he'd forced himself to look at the road ahead.

Now he was dropping into a small settlement that appeared to have only four businesses and half as many houses. He wasn't even certain he could find a room for the night. He was aching for cleanliness and solitude, things a man usually had to pay dearly for, but tonight he hoped only for a hot plate of food and a place out of the cold. He'd been on the road for only two days, but it was beginning to feel like years.

Rebecca wandered around the room, not really seeing the solid wood furniture or the painting of the Rocky Mountains that hung above the huge stone fireplace. The living room was one of her favorite places in the whole house, but today she couldn't see a thing. The rug beneath her feet had been sent from back East and nearly covered the huge floor. The pattern was intricate, the color a mixture of rich blues and greens, but Rebecca didn't notice. Travis had been gone a month, and Rebecca was convinced that he was never coming back. It hadn't snowed yet, but the air was cold and she just knew that he was frozen somewhere. Rebecca was miserable and had convinced herself that the only thing that could comfort her would be to see Travis.

"Rebecca." Lavena had come to the edge of the room. "Did you want to help me with these cookies?"

Rebecca moved slowly away from the window. "All right, Lavena. I'll help."

The housekeeper rolled her eyes but didn't comment. *You'd think she's gonna die, the way she carries on,* she thought ungraciously, but she wasn't really angry. She led the way into the kitchen and pushed a large bowl across the table.

"Now, just a spoonful at a time, you hear?"

"All right, Lavena."

The live-in cook watched Rebecca load dough onto the pan and then turned away. The week before she'd forgotten Rebecca couldn't cook and left her on her own. The cookies had been the size of horses' hooves and raw in the middle. Not even Biscuit had wanted them, and in Lavena's opinion that man had no taste at all.

"Where's Papa?" Rebecca suddenly asked.

"In his study, just like he told you he'd be."

"Oh, that's right."

"There's no use pining, girl," she added a little more gently. Rebecca only sighed.

Lavena decided then and there to go into town the next day. She didn't need much, but she would take Rebecca with her. They worked in silence, the afternoon stretching on. At one point Lavena turned and caught Rebecca's profile. The line of her chin was more prominent than it had been four weeks ago. She was dropping weight. Turning back to her cutting board Lavena called on Travis, wherever he was, to come home soon.

~~~

Everything she told you is a lie. Andrew read the line again and again and then sat back in his desk chair. What had happened to his sister? He hadn't heard from her since the letter came saying Rebecca had left Philadelphia, and now she opened with this line. The rest wasn't very long, and he now read that again too.

I never tried to keep her from you. I gave her everything you sent. It was Franklin. He's mad but won't admit it. Rebecca is a spoiled child. I gave her everything a girl could dream of and she betrayed me. I tell you it's all lies, Andrew, all of it. God will get you for what you've done.

And that was the end. It wasn't even signed. Andrew shook his head. Should he respond? Would she even open a letter from him? He knew Rebecca had yet to write to her.

And Travis. What could be keeping him for a month? Why, they hadn't even had snow yet. Andrew shook his head. Could he have been that wrong? He'd seen the young cowboy's eyes. He was honest; Andrew was certain of it. And the way he'd looked at Reba . . .

Again Andrew shook his head. He had to be right. He simply had to be. Rebecca had been pushing her food around her plate for over a week now. That man simply had to come back. Andrew pushed himself to his feet and walked to the window. He would welcome the beauty of the snow on the mountains, except that he wanted Travis to return first.

With a hand to the back of his aching neck, he turned to the desk. His sister's letter was as he'd left it. Oh, yes, he wanted Travis to return, not for the money—for Rebecca. But for now, it was time for Andrew to find out from Rebecca what his sister was afraid she would tell.

Denver

"I'm back," the sheriff commented, but Travis remained silent, his feet planted firmly apart, his expression remote. He'd been in a Denver jail cell for over a week and had little to say.

"I talked to your friend, Grady," the sheriff told him. "He's certainly in a bad way."

Travis remained silent.

"He backs up your story about Andrew Wagner." The sheriff spoke as he made himself comfortable in the desk chair. "Says he gave you the money and all, but I still haven't heard from Texas."

Travis sighed; he couldn't take any more. "How many times do I have to tell you that I have never run from the Texas law? There is no wanted poster out on me."

"Then how do you explain this?" The sheriff lifted the handbill from the desktop, and Travis' face stared back at him.

"There's nothing to explain." Travis tried to remain calm as he repeated the same argument. "It says the man's name is Hank Randall. Mine is Travis Buchanan. Grady must have told you that."

"Well, that doesn't make it true," the lawman reasoned. "Even if you did tell Grady that was your name, how would he know the difference?"

Travis dropped away from the bars and lowered himself onto the lone bunk. It was preposterous. He was not Hank Randall. The facial resemblance was striking, but he was not a wanted man. And the man's description was right on the wanted poster—5'8" with a medium build. But Sheriff Turlock was not taking any chances. He thought he had a killer on his hands, and he was going to hold onto him.

Why in the world had he stayed around an extra day? Travis had asked himself this question a dozen times, but he already knew the answer. Grady would probably never sit up in bed again, let alone ride a horse and manage the Double Star.

Travis' heart had gone out to him, even though he was convinced that an act of fate had settled the man in a comfortable home and not on the streets.

Travis had found Grady at the home of an older woman just hours after arriving in town. The woman turned out to be a distant cousin of Grady's, and although she seemed almost as frail as her patient, he could see that Grady was in good hands. Grady had been gored by a bull, not once but several times. The foreman had lost consciousness, but witnesses had told him that he'd been tossed like a rag doll for several seconds. It was nothing short of a miracle he was alive.

Equally amazing was the fact that he had had every dime of Andrew's money in his pocket, and it had not been stolen. When Travis arrived, Grady asked his cousin to fetch the full amount from the bank, and he paid Travis every cent. Travis had left, but his conscience had bothered him. Andrew had given no such order, but Travis felt a need to help the older man. He'd gone back the next day to give Grady an amount he thought the owner of the Double Star would think fair. It was as he left the two-story home for the second time that he'd come face-to-face with Turlock's gun.

There had been no struggle. Convinced the sheriff had the wrong man, Travis lifted his hands and allowed Turlock to take the gun from his hip. He was concerned about the money in his coat pocket, but as soon as they arrived at the jailhouse, he watched the man with the badge put everything into the safe. Then the nightmare had begun. There was no reasoning with him. Travis had tried every argument he could think of to get Turlock to believe him, but to no avail. Turlock had immediately written to the sheriff whose name was on the poster and eventually gone to see Grady, but Travis remained behind bars.

The meal that night was tasty and plentiful, but Travis ate with little interest. Andrew Wagner had trusted him. And Rebecca. Would her heart forget him before he returned? The plate was still half full when he set it by the bars and stretched out on the bunk. His boots hung a laughable distance over the end, but he didn't feel like laughing. Once again he had the feeling that no one was up there. At times it seemed that God was real and working on the earth, but not now. Travis felt as he never had before that he was on his own.

❧

"There isn't going to be anything left of you if you keep on this way," Andrew commented during dinner, but Rebecca only shrugged and tried to smile. She knew she was horrid company these days.

"He'll come back, Reba," Andrew told her with more conviction than he felt. "You wait and see. He'll be back."

Rebecca looked at the worry in his eyes. She nodded and tried to perk up for his sake.

"Lavena's taking me to town with her tomorrow."

"Good! Buy yourself something pretty."

"Well, she's just going for supplies and such."

"That doesn't mean you can't shop. I'll get Lucky to go in with you, and you can spend the day."

"Shouldn't you ask Lavena?"

"Shouldn't you ask Lavena what?" The woman who'd heard her name spoke from the edge of the room, hands on her hips.

"I want Rebecca to make a day of it tomorrow. You stay in town until she's done."

"I'm an old woman, Andrew Wagner! I'm too tired to be running around Boulder on a winter day." With that she stormed out.

Andrew winked at Rebecca. "She says you can take all the time you need."

Rebecca laughed for the first time in days. Andrew hated to spoil the mood, but he had to have some answers.

"I heard from your aunt today."

"Did you?" Rebecca's look was open as she speared a potato with her fork. "Has she forgiven me yet?"

Andrew smiled. "You still haven't written her, have you?"

"No." Rebecca's voice grew soft. "I don't know if I can. One of these days, I'd like to explain."

Andrew pulled the letter from his pocket and watched as she read. Her face was sad and regretful, but not guilty. He knew it wouldn't be, but the whole thing was more curious than ever.

"I know you're sad about Travis, Reba, and I don't want to add to that, but I'd like us to talk tonight."

She nodded. "All right, Papa. Shall I bring some coffee to the living room?"

Andrew smiled. That was definitely an eastern custom. "Yes, I'll wait for you in there."

She wasn't long in joining him, but long after they had their coffee, Rebecca sat mute. Rebecca felt a headache coming on. How should she begin?

"A few years ago Hannah stopped leaving the house. I mean, we went to church, but she would stay home most of the time. She wanted me home too, but whenever I would question her, she would change her mind and let me go, almost as if she were afraid I would grow angry. It was strange because we never quarreled. And the reason she stayed home wasn't to clean or anything; in fact, the house just fell into worse repair as the months went on." Rebecca shook her head for a moment.

"Well, anyway, this one day was very odd because I was home alone. I couldn't remember being home alone in at least two years, but there I was on my own when the bell rang at the door. I went, and there was the mailman; we had letter service in our neighborhood," she explained, "but anyway, he said he'd missed a letter for me. Well, it was from you, the last one you had sent. I opened it right away and knew something was wrong.

"Hannah was just next door at Mrs. Wood's, but it never occurred to me to go get her. I read your letter, and suddenly everything became clear. It was your handwriting, and yet it wasn't. And the things you said, the things about wanting to see me. I was amazed."

Andrew's mind raced with where she could be headed, but he remained quiet and hoped that she would explain.

"I felt cold," Rebecca told him, her mind far away, her eyes on the fire. "I'll never forget how cold I felt, but then I looked at the stairs and for some reason I thought of Aunt Hannah's room. I was never allowed in there. She didn't share a room with Uncle Franklin. It wasn't at all unusual for Uncle Franklin to send me to find something in his room, but Hannah never wanted me in hers.

"I didn't stop to think; I just walked. I walked up the stairs to her room, and I began to look around. It wasn't long before I found them." Rebecca looked at her father. "Every letter you'd ever written me, Papa. The box was huge. She had been taking all of your letters and opening them. She always handed the letter to me already open, not because she read them, she said, but because she had a silver letter opener and it made the slit so neat.

"It was all a lie," she whispered, her face a mask of pain. "She had taken every one of your letters, read them, and then rewrote them in your handwriting before giving them to me. I took the box to my room and hid it just before she came home. That night I sat up until morning and read everything you'd ever said to me. You can't believe the way she lied. Your letters to me, through her, said so many things. She wrote that you had met a wonderful woman and that even though you and this woman both wanted me to join you, it was taking her some time to get used to having a child."

Andrew's eyes slid shut, and he couldn't stop the hand that went to his chest.

"It's all right now." Rebecca jumped up and ran to his side, spilling coffee and not even noticing. His face was ashen, and Rebecca hated herself for not holding back the truth. If her father died on the spot, she would never forgive herself.

"I understand now, Papa," she told him desperately. "I know she was lying," she tried to tell him, but he looked stricken.

"Lavena," Rebecca called. "Lavena," she tried one more time. "Please come."

Rebecca gasped with relief when the other woman appeared, took one look at Andrew and quickly exited. Rebecca helped her father lie back in the chair and loosened his tie.

"My precious girl," he gasped. "You thought I didn't want you. Oh, my Reba."

"No, Papa," Rebecca tried to comfort him. "I know better now, Papa, and that's all that matters."

Lavena appeared at her side, and Rebecca watched as Andrew drank the milky liquid she offered. His eyes were closed and his breathing labored, but his color was returning. When his eyes finally opened, Rebecca made herself speak calmly.

"It's all in the past, Papa. Please don't be upset. You're all I've got; please don't be upset and leave me now, not when I finally have you."

Her gentle voice and pleading eyes got through to him. He thought that if his sister were in the room right now he could easily shoot her, but he mustn't have such thoughts. They caused a pain in his heart, and as Rebecca stated, he was all she had.

Andrew nodded and tried to sit up. Rebecca pushed him back down and smiled.

"Just rest," she told him. He managed to smile in return. She began to tell him about her cookie-baking fiasco from the week before. It wasn't long before he was chuckling and even asked to have his coffee warmed up. He still didn't have all the answers he needed, but he'd had all he could handle for the moment. It was all in the past, as Rebecca had said. If he could only remember that, it would be okay.

Again, his sister's face came into view, causing his breath to catch. He pushed it away. *You had her for 11 years, Hannah; you'll not separate us again.*

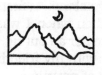

6

"I need to speak with you, Reba."

Andrew was at Rebecca's door early the next morning. He'd done little but think about their conversation the night before. Rebecca was dressed, readying to leave for town with Lavena, but he caught her while she was still brushing her hair. She looked into his face and saw that he looked good, but still she bit her lip in indecision.

"Are you certain, Papa? I can't stand to see you hurt."

He put his hand up. "I know, honey, but there are some things that don't add up, and they're going to be more upsetting to me if I don't know."

Rebecca hesitated, but then nodded and went to the bed. She sank down on the edge and waited for her father to take the rocking chair by the window. He did look fine this morning, but the memory of the night before made the young woman understandably tense.

"Rebecca," he began, "if my letters said something about a woman, why did you never question me when you wrote back?" To his amazement Rebecca blushed and dropped her gaze. She spoke with her eyes on the small rug at the side of her bed.

"Aunt Hannah was not all to blame, Papa. She would tell me things, and I would believe them because I *wanted* to believe them." She finally looked him in the eye. "I lived in a dream world. When Hannah would advise me not to think about something you said or even address it in my next letter to you, I would gladly go along. At first I would feel hurt about what you wrote. But then when I was young, Aunt Hannah would offer me a new toy or an outing. When I got older it was a new dress or a party with my friends. I pushed you further and further to the back of my mind.

"Later, when I learned the truth, I also realized that if she could rewrite your letters, she could do the same thing to mine. Even if I had written something that would have made no sense to you, she would have changed it."

Andrew stared at her. "Were you ever in love with the boy named Marcus?"

Rebecca shook her head. "We were just friends."

Andrew lifted his gaze to the ceiling. The gesture seemed impatient, but his face was calm. "The letters sounded like you were nearly engaged."

"Oh, Papa."

He tried to smile. "That hurt me the way the 'other woman' hurt you. She wanted us both to believe that we were making a life for ourselves and that we didn't need each other. Did your Uncle Franklin know about this?"

"I'm not certain, although I don't know how he couldn't. He would get the oddest looks on his face, but he never went against Hannah. It was almost as if he were afraid to. If I did ask him, he would just say, 'If your aunt says it's so, then it's so.' It got to be less convincing as time went on, and I think that's why I went to her bedroom that day."

"Tell me about the day you left."

"I was too tired the morning after I'd read all night, but just 24 hours later I was out of the house before sunrise. I usually slept rather late, so I knew I wouldn't be missed. I left a note for Hannah, telling her I knew about the letters and that I was going to live with you." Rebecca smiled a little. "I was pretty dramatic, telling her not to even think of sending someone after me because she would never find me."

"And the trip? You made light of it that first day, but I've never asked you further about it."

Rebecca shrugged. "It was pretty amazing. I had the money I took from my secret drawer, as well as some of Hannah's I found in the letter box, and I was able to buy train tickets and everything else I needed. I won't tell you I wasn't afraid, but I was so angry that for the first 200 miles no one even dared talk to me. I was carried along on the anger for a long time."

"I think I'd like you to see the letters I received, Reba. I want to know if you wrote them."

Rebecca got an odd look on her face, but she didn't do anything until Andrew stood. Then she came off the bed in a single move and walked to stand before him. She put out her hand.

"Hello, my name is Rebecca Rose Wagner. I'm pleased to meet you."

Andrew looked down at her hand and then into her eyes. "You can really put it behind you, Reba?"

"Yes. I'm through living in a dream world, but I can't stand the thought of drumming it all back up. If you want to know if something is true, ask me, and I'll do the same for you."

Andrew ignored the hand and pulled her into his embrace. They hugged one another for a long time before Andrew held her at arm's length.

"Go to town now and have a good time. We won't think about this or anything else that makes us sad today."

Although his name was not mentioned, they were both thinking of Travis. Rebecca nodded and hugged him one more time. She went back to her hair when he left, and not until she was ready to go downstairs did she see the money he'd laid on the dresser. For the oddest reason it made her think of Travis. Did he have enough money? Was he even alive?

Rebecca made herself push the thought away. *He's not the man you thought he was.* Taking a deep breath against the pain she felt, and against the tiny voice inside her that refused to see Travis in that light, she reached for the door handle and walked downstairs.

<hr />

"And you'll drive slow," Lavena was telling Lucky in no uncertain terms.

"Yes, ma'am," he said with a grin, but charmed as she was, Lavena ignored it.

"And you'll not wait for us in the saloon. You'll stay with the wagon and horses."

"But, Lavena." The grin was still in place. "I'll freeze."

"It'll do you good," she snapped, but she had already lost him. Rebecca was coming from the house, and he suddenly straightened to full height.

"Rebecca." He breathed the word only to have Lavena hiss at him.

"That's Miss Rebecca to you!"

He only glanced at the older woman before he grabbed the hat from his head.

"I'm ready, Lavena. Do we need anything from the house?"

"No. Now get in; we have things to do."

"Hello, Miss Rebecca," Lucky spoke as Rebecca looked up into his eyes. She smiled kindly at him, and he felt the air leave his body.

"Hello, Mr. Harwell. How are you?"

"You can call me Lucky," he told her, not having even heard her question.

Lavena snorted, but Lucky didn't hear her as he dashed around the wagon to help Rebecca over the wheel. She smiled her thanks but was too busy adjusting the heavy blankets around her legs to notice his look of adoration.

Lavena had been forced to help herself aboard, where she sat next to Lucky on the front seat. Andrew had a comfortable buggy, but it seated only two, so they had had to take the large wagon, which sported two seats. Andrew came out just as Lucky picked up the reins.

"It doesn't look like snow, but keep an eye on things, Lucky."

"As if I don't have sense enough to know when to come home!" Lavena shot at him, but Andrew only looked to his daughter, who was leaning over to talk to him. She looked into his eyes and kept her voice low.

"Are you sure you're all right?"

"Yes."

"Promise me you won't think about it, Papa."

"I promise." His voice grew a little gruff. "I've work to do anyway."

Rebecca smiled and sat up. "Bye."

"Good-bye," Andrew told her, and with that the wagon moved toward town.

The ride was uneventful. Lavena muttered over her list, and Rebecca was only too happy to enjoy the mountains and valleys, now barren of the summer's lush plant life, as they waited for the snow to fall. Lucky was simply delighted to be so close to Rebecca. He hadn't been able to find a single excuse to talk with her since Travis had left and nearly did a jig in the bunkhouse when the boss approached him about taking the women to town. A day out of the saddle was always welcome, but a day spent in the company of Rebecca Wagner was a gift from heaven.

"I want to start in the general store," Lavena was saying.

"That's fine," Rebecca replied. "I want to get a newspaper and check the mail before I shop."

"What are you shopping for?"

"Oh, nothing in particular, but Papa gave me money."

Lavena snorted. "I suppose you'll be wanting to eat lunch at the hotel."

Rebecca smiled from the backseat. In truth, she hadn't even thought of it. She agreed with a voice so sweet that even Lucky had to hide his smile.

Fifteen minutes later they stopped before the general store. It was a large building with a single door. Inside were seven well-stocked aisles, as well as floor-to-ceiling merchandise on nearly every square inch of wall. As she and Rebecca stepped down from the wagon, Lavena again told Lucky to stay with the team, but he followed them inside. He wasn't bold enough to actually follow Rebecca around the store, but his eyes never left her as she began to peruse the goods.

Rebecca didn't notice. Forgetting that she wanted the mail first, she started in the first aisle and looked over flatirons and stovepipes. She didn't linger long over the bridles and saddle blankets, but the teapot, even with its small chip, and the silverware held her attention for quite some time. Handkerchiefs and thread for tatting were her next interest, before she moved to the dishes. Rebecca fingered a cut-glass berry dish for quite a while before returning it to the shelf.

At that point she simply realized that she wasn't truly in the mood to shop. Her father hadn't talked of him, and she'd done everything in her power to forget, but everywhere she looked she was reminded of Travis. It hadn't helped to turn her eyes away from the black cowboy hats; she still saw his and the way it sat on his head, making him look taller than ever. Even Lucky was a painful reminder because he was one of the few men in town who came close to Travis' height. It wasn't long before she gave up and found Lavena.

"I'm going to the post office now."

"I thought you were going to shop."

"I didn't find anything."

For once Lavena's sharp gaze softened. The older woman believed with all her heart that Travis would return, but she couldn't tell Rebecca that.

"You be careful on the street now, do you hear? There's a reading room across the way. You could check there for books if you want."

"Reading room? I didn't know Boulder had a reading room."

"Well, it does, but if anyone so much as looks at you sideways, you get yourself back in here to me."

Rebecca couldn't help but smile. Lavena came only to her chin, but it was clear that she would take on the world if asked to. The older woman turned back to her list, and Rebecca felt free to leave. She couldn't help but think of her aunt as she looked around the simple shop. It was fairly clean, if not rough in places, but Aunt Hannah would have swooned to see Rebecca shopping so casually in such a place.

Unbidden, bitterness rose inside of her. Her father was not well. Who knew how long he would live? But Aunt Hannah had kept them apart. She was a sick woman in Rebecca's opinion, and just like her father, Rebecca would have been tempted to violence if Hannah had been present.

"Did you need something, Miss Rebecca?"

Rebecca started abruptly at the sound of Lucky's voice, her hand going to her throat.

"Oh, Mr. Harwell, yes. I'm going to the post office."

"Let me get the door for you."

"Thank you," Rebecca said absently, but then noticed he stayed by her side. Her look must have questioned him because he swiftly said, "The streets can be a little rough. I thought I should walk with you."

"Oh," Rebecca said. She couldn't think of any reason for his not walking with her, so she continued on her way. When the boardwalk ended at the alley and started again on the other side, Lucky took her arm. He felt her stiffen, however, and dropped his hand even before they had crossed the alley.

He held the door at the post office but waited for her outside. There was a letter for her father, a package for Lavena, and another letter, this one addressed to Ray Sugars, but nothing for her. She slipped everything into her satchel and moved back to the door. Again Lucky's presence startled her, but she didn't show it. She looked at his face. He was certainly handsome, but for some reason his looks made no impression on her.

Rebecca would have been surprised to know that Lucky was more than aware of this. His experience with women told him that they always loved the one they were with, but this was not turning out to be the case. However, one never knew what the future might bring. Travis could show up with a wife and kids and make Rebecca so angry that she would turn to him in an instant.

"Mr. Harwell." She pleased him by stopping and speaking his name. He loved her voice. "Lavena told me that Boulder has a reading room. Do you know where it is?"

She didn't expect him to know, but she had to start somewhere. To her surprise, Lucky pointed behind her.

Rebecca turned to look across the street and then back to Lucky, her eyes huge.

"Thank you."

The surprise in her voice was almost insulting, but Lucky Harwell was not easily put off. As the petite beauty turned away from him he grinned and followed her across the dirt street.

"I've read this one too, but I didn't enjoy it as much."

Again Rebecca stared at Lucky. They'd been in the reading room for only 20 minutes, and he'd managed to surprise her repeatedly. Lucky was only thankful that he was living up to his name. A year ago he'd dated a girl from the saloon who loved to read. In order to gain ground with her, he'd read in his every spare moment, and even some after she'd moved on. Seeing a new appreciation in Rebecca Wagner's eyes as she looked at him, Lucky knew with a certainty that all that time and energy was going to pay off again.

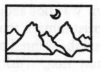

7

Travis Buchanan spent Christmas behind bars, and even when 1870 gave way to 1871, he remained in prison. In Sheriff Turlock's mind, he still had a murderer on his hands. Travis, not easily angered, grew more frustrated by the day. It was past the middle of the month before Turlock opened a letter from a lawman in Texas whose words made it possible for Travis to go free.

"They hung him."

Travis heard the man but didn't answer. Half the time he didn't want to hear what the sheriff had to say anyhow.

"They've hung Hank Randall."

This brought Travis off his bunk. He moved to the bars and looked through. Turlock glanced up at him.

"Says it right here." He held the letter aloft. " 'Bout six months back they captured and hung Hank Randall. The marshall says he was too busy to contact us sooner."

Travis had still not uttered a word. He stood motionless as Turlock rose from the desk, went for the keys that hung on the far wall, and approached the cell. The door swung open for the first time in nearly two months.

"You're free to go."

That was it. No apology or regret for the mistake. Just, "You're free to go." It wasn't flowery, but Travis would take it. He walked from the cell and stood by the desk. The sheriff, whom Travis found a bit dim at times, came alive. It wasn't ten minutes before Travis was back in possession of his hat, coat, gun, and all the contents from his pockets, including Andrew Wagner's money. Travis was not about to thank the man; indeed, he didn't even trust himself to speak, but just before he turned away, he grabbed the wanted poster from the desk.

"Hey! You can't have that," Turlock protested. "I have to have that for my files."

But Travis was already folding the poster to put in his pocket. He turned to the man, his eyes clearly showing his rage.

"There were people counting on my return." His voice was low and menacing, and the other man knew an instant of fear.

"I'm going to take this," Travis held up the folded handbill, "and with it I'm going to explain where I've been. Now, where's my horse?"

The question came out calmly, but it took an effort. Travis wanted to lift the smaller man by the shirt front and tell him that if Diamond had so much as a scratch, he'd be back to beat the life out of him.

Turlock swallowed hard but managed, "He's stabled out back, but you won't get far today. It's supposed to snow."

Travis ignored him. He slipped the paper into his breast pocket and moved to the door. He exited the sheriff's office and Denver itself without a backward glance.

Boulder

"It's amazing, isn't it?" Rebecca asked, her eyes drifting out the living room window.

"What's that?" Lucky questioned her with his usual attentiveness.

"The snow. It doesn't snow for weeks, not even for Christmas, and now at the beginning of February the ground is covered."

Lucky finally transferred his attention to the window. "I think we'll get more before nightfall too."

Rebecca turned to smile at him. He had become such good company. Every Sunday afternoon since that day in town, he had come with a different book and stayed to visit as well. It didn't erase all the hurt Travis had left behind, but it was a start. Rebecca knew by the way Lucky talked that he had broken a thousand hearts in his lifetime, and she determined never to be one of them, but his companionship was a great help.

Lucky now held his cup out for more coffee. Rebecca smiled and obliged him. He wasn't anywhere near as far as he'd planned to be where Rebecca was concerned, but he was a patient man. Along with that he was the envy of the whole bunkhouse, and that had its points as well.

When the knock sounded at the front door, Lavena was in the kitchen. Both Lucky and Rebecca heard it, but Rebecca also heard her father leave his study to answer it. Andrew stared up at the tall, snow-covered figure until something hit his chest. He looked down.

"It's your money." Travis' voice was rusty from lack of use. "I have an explanation if you want to hear it, but I wanted you to have the money first."

"Come in, Travis." Andrew finally recovered enough to recall his manners.

The nearly frozen man stepped inside and just stood. It was by sheer force of will that he kept his teeth from chattering. Andrew had glanced down at the money again, but he was now looking in surprise at Travis, his eyes showing his shock.

"You found Grady."

"Yes, but he won't be back."

Andrew nodded, and then shook his head to clear it. "Come in. Come to the study, and I'll give you a drink."

Andrew went ahead of him, and Travis was turning to follow when he looked up and saw her. Her dress was pale blue with long sleeves and high neck, and her hair sat atop her head in a golden crown, but all Travis could see were her eyes as they looked at him with longing.

"Reba," he said the word softly and even took a step toward her before he heard the voice. The other man was out of sight in the room behind her, but Travis knew the owner of that voice.

"Who is it, Rebecca? Should I come?"

Rebecca watched a shuttered expression come over Travis' face. The light in his eyes dimmed so swiftly that she almost gasped. A second later he turned, walked into the study, and shut the door.

"The resemblance is incredible," Andrew commented nearly an hour later as he continued to study the poster, "but it says right here that he was 5'8". What was the sheriff thinking?"

"I don't know, but he had the key and there wasn't a thing I could do."

Andrew eyed him sharply. "You could have sent word."

"No, I couldn't," Travis returned flatly. "Turlock had it in his head that I might be sending for my gang."

For the first time Andrew smiled and then chuckled. Travis wanted to join him, but he was still too stiff to find much amusing.

"I'm glad you paid Grady; it sounds like he needed it," Andrew told him when he turned serious. "The foreman's job is yours if you'll have it, Travis."

Travis stared at him without really focusing. Could he keep working here while Rebecca was seeing another man? The anger he felt over her betrayal was enough to drive the chill away, but he still remembered the harshness of his ride from Denver. It was too cold to be looking for work. He'd stay the rest of the winter, but with no promises beyond that.

"I'll take the job."

"Great. You can move upstairs. Lavena has Grady's room all clean and ready. I'll send his gear to him this week."

"I appreciate the offer of the room, but I'll decline until I can get a bath and some clean clothes."

"Lavena can do that," Andrew insisted and stood. "Your gear is stowed in the bunkhouse. Lucky is visiting with Rebecca, so I'll have him bring your stuff in, and I'll order you a bath."

Andrew had gone to the door and missed the look on Travis' face, or he would have questioned him. When he gained the entryway once again, both Rebecca and Lucky were standing there. Travis heard Andrew speaking to Lucky, but he kept his eyes averted.

"Go on up, Travis," he told his new foreman when he had finished with the hand. "Go ahead to your room. Turn right at the top of the stairs. It's the second door on the right."

Travis was able to mount the stairs without looking at Rebecca. Her eyes, however, followed him to the very top.

~

"I knew you'd be back," Lavena muttered, pouring hot water over his back. Travis had told her to get out, but she hadn't listened. "I didn't say anything, but I knew you would. I thought that little girl was going to waste away to nothing."

"Get out, Lavena," Travis said, and this time she heard the tone.

"You don't think she's fallen for Lucky, do you?" Lavena was well and truly outraged, but then so was the cowboy in the tub.

"Get out, Lavena, and I mean now."

The older woman drew herself up to her full diminutive height, her chin thrust at an aggressive angle. "Go ahead," she challenged him. "Think what you like. But if you don't claim that girl's heart this day, you're a fool, Travis Buchanan."

She did leave then, but Travis didn't continue to wash. Indeed, it was some time before he noticed the water turning cold. He dried slowly and knew suddenly that he'd made a mistake. How could he stay and watch Rebecca with Lucky Harwell, or any other man?

His eyes suddenly roamed the room he'd been given. It was spacious and comfortable, the bed wide and the floor covered with a thick carpet. Lavena had already put his things in the fine wood dresser, and his few shirts now hung in the built-in closet. On the wall by the door hung a mirror. Travis walked to it. He fingered his jaw as he realized he'd lost weight while in that Denver jail. Since he'd had so little activity, he was surprised. He'd felt it in his clothes, but he'd been so driven to return he'd given little notice. He was still studying his reflection when someone knocked on the door.

"Who is it?"

"Rebecca," came the voice from without. "Lavena said she's putting dinner on."

Travis stood, his hands clenched at his side. Just the sound of her voice was like a knife in his side. He had wondered what he would do if she had forgotten him, but not until he'd heard Lucky's voice did he admit to himself he never really believed he could lose her.

"Travis?"

"I'll be down," he told her curtly, and stood still when he heard her move back down the hall. He knew then that he would stay. Not because he wanted to, but because he couldn't walk away from her just yet. In the weeks to come he'd see her with Lucky, and it would work like a purge. He would be more than ready to leave when spring finally arrived.

❧

"Happy birthday," Lavena said with a measure of pride, placing the frosted cake on the table. Travis, who had been back a week, turned wide eyes to her when he realized she was talking to him.

"What day is this?"

"February 9," Andrew told him. "Happy birthday."

Travis' mouth opened and shut, and then he turned to Lavena. "How did you know?"

"Grady had some records on you. Biscuit keeps track of the men, so I keep track of the foreman."

With that little bit of news she turned and left them. Travis watched as Rebecca reached for the cake and knife. He thanked her when she passed him the first piece, as always, a picture of gentle politeness. Indeed, Travis was so civil that it chilled her to the bone.

Andrew began to talk business again as soon as he had his cake. Rebecca sat quietly and listened. Her father knew that things had changed between his daughter and the now-permanent foreman. He had already talked with her about it and informed her that it was all *her* fault. He hadn't been cruel or unreasonably harsh, but he never did countenance her having Harwell in on Sundays. It had crushed Rebecca when he'd taken Travis' side. That conversation took place the day after Travis returned, and the wound in her heart was still raw. However, she had not given up on the angry foreman. They finished their cake just a few minutes later, and Rebecca did something she hadn't tried before.

"Travis, would you like to join us in the living room for coffee?"

Travis looked at her, his face expressionless. She'd asked before—she'd asked every night—but never in front of her father. And indeed, her plan worked.

"Oh, certainly, Travis," Andrew declared. "Join us. I just have to get some papers from my desk, and I'll be in."

Travis was as tense as a cat. He walked into the living room ahead of Rebecca but did not take a seat. He was moving around the room, nearly stalking it, when he realized Rebecca stood inside the door watching him.

"Aren't you worried that Lucky might come in and find me here?" The polite mask had fallen away.

Rebecca shook her head. "Lucky came only on Sundays, and anyway, I told him I thought I'd be busy from now on."

"Oh, really," Travis sounded bored. "What will you be doing?" His voice told her he didn't care.

Rebecca shrugged, her eyes miserable. It was almost more than Travis could take, but he kept the wall shored up around his heart.

"I just thought I might be busy." She said the words so softly that Travis almost missed them. He had to turn away from the pain in her eyes. Why had she been seeing Lucky at all if she felt that way? Both of them felt relieved when Lavena came in with the coffee. Not long after, Andrew joined them. Rebecca stayed for an hour but then retired while the men discussed the ranch.

8

"Travis." Rebecca called his name early Saturday morning, and she could tell she had surprised him. His eyes narrowed as they looked at her, not with anger but in defense.

They were in the upstairs hallway, and Travis knew very well that Andrew had already gone downstairs. Did she know how she looked to him? She was dressed, but there was a morning softness about her, and her hair lay loose on her shoulders.

"What do you want, Rebecca?"

"I just want to talk to you."

"I have work to do."

She sighed. "It's not the way you think," she began, but cut off when he shook his head.

The night before, he'd actually spoken kindly to her. It had been a moment of weakness on his part, but the way he had spoken to her on his birthday had bothered him. He'd been ready to ask her for a walk when someone knocked on the front door. The shutters had gone back into place when Rebecca opened the door and Lucky stood there asking to see her. Travis hadn't stayed around to see what the two of them did, but he did resolve not to be caught out again.

"I won't fight Harwell for you, Rebecca," he said suddenly.

"I don't want you to."

"Then what do you want from me?"

To have things the way they were. To have you take my hand and look into my eyes. But she didn't say any of this outloud. Travis was still angry, and she didn't know how to handle his anger. Hannah and Franklin had never been angry with her, and even when her father scolded her, he did so in a kind voice. Travis' biting tone and angry eyes were more than she could take.

"Can't answer me?" Travis went on, more furious than before.

Rebecca's hand came up in supplication. "What do you want from *me,* Travis?"

"I'll show you," he bit out, and before she could guess what he might do, he pulled her into his arms. The kiss he gave her was not nice. His lips crushed Rebecca's tender mouth; his arms locked her against him with bruising strength. Rebecca couldn't cry out, and she couldn't breathe. It was awful. She felt more frightened than she'd ever been in her life, and just as black spots began to dance before her eyes, he loosened his hold. Travis' anger had deserted him.

The hands that now put her away from him were not angry hands. They were gentle, but it didn't register with the small, frightened woman who stood trembling and feeling very cold.

Travis looked down at his handiwork. Rebecca's hair was a snarled mess, her mouth was already swelling, and huge tears filled her eyes. He wanted to be sick to his stomach. How could he have treated her that way? He wanted to tell her he was sorry, but the words wouldn't come.

He reached to brush the hair from her cheek, but stopped when she flinched. His hand dropped to his side.

"Put a cold cloth on your mouth, Rebecca. Or better yet, some snow. It'll help the swelling."

Rebecca's hand went to her lips as he said this, and it hurt her to touch them. Travis stared at her with regretful eyes before turning to go on his way. He would work the day out, but come dinner he'd tell Andrew that he had to resign. His boss had trusted him, and he'd betrayed that trust.

Travis' plans were honorable, but no one, least of all Travis, could have predicted what the next few hours would bring.

~~~~~

The doctor came from the sick room on Sunday afternoon. Andrew had suffered another spell the night before. He was flat on his back and desperate. Travis and Rebecca stood in the hall, not talking or touching. The doctor had also come Saturday when Travis had ridden into town for him, but now he came out to tell Travis that Andrew was asking for him.

"And Rebecca?" Travis asked, not looking at the woman beside him.

"He wants to see her afterward."

Travis looked down at Rebecca. She seemed to have put the kiss out of her mind. She looked up at him and said in a soft voice, "Go ahead, Travis. I'll wait here."

Travis nodded and went in. "You don't have to do this," he heard Lavena quietly saying to the ranch owner as he opened the door, but the older woman's mouth shut with a snap as soon as she saw him. She moved from the room. After he shut the door, Travis approached the huge bed. Andrew's eyes were open, his face ashen.

"How are you, sir?" Travis whispered.

"Foolish," came the equally soft reply. "I thought I could bargain with God."

Travis stood still. What could he say to this?

"I want you to marry Reba."

Travis blinked stupidly at the man.

"You heard me," Andrew said softly, his eyes on Travis' face. "I want you to marry Reba. I thought I would be around forever. I've been so happy with her here, but my heart is failing me. I have to know she's going to be taken care of. Men like Lucky . . ." He had to pause for breath. "She's too innocent. She doesn't understand that they only want one thing."

"Mr. Wagner," Travis cut in gently, "you don't know what you're asking."

"You don't care for her?"

"I do care," he assured him honestly. "More than I can say, but we haven't been close lately. She would never agree."

"But if she did, would you marry her, Travis? Would you take care of my girl? Would you make her your wife?"

"She'll never—"

"Would you?" Andrew cut him off, and Travis' heart slammed with alarm to see the man's face flush.

"Yes," he told him swiftly, feeling breathless himself and wondering if he really meant it. "But I can tell you she'll never agree."

Andrew's sigh was huge. It was as if he hadn't heard a word. "She'll agree," he said very softly. "She's a good girl, and she knows I'm taking care of her. I still plan to beat this, but just in case I don't, she'll have you. You understand ranching—even more than Grady did. You'll run things, and she'll be safe from Hannah."

He saw the question in Travis' eyes but said only, "Reba will tell you about Hannah someday. You'll have lots of time to get to know each other." With that, Andrew appeared to go to sleep. Travis stood for a moment in indecision, but as he was softly crossing the carpet, his employer said, "Send Reba in, Travis. I need to see her now."

Travis did as he was told and looked down at Rebecca as she went into the room. The eyes she turned to him were wide with appeal, and Travis realized that she had forgiven him his reprehensible behavior the morning before.

As soon as the door closed on Rebecca, Travis moved to his room. Once inside, he shut the door and leaned against it. Reba. Reba as his wife. It was almost more than he could take in. Before Denver he wouldn't have even argued with Andrew;

he'd have dragged Rebecca to the alter in the blink of an eye. But they had become distant. He knew some of it was his fault. She had wanted to talk to him, but he would have none of it.

And the marriage would save Andrew—Travis was certain of it. His heart could rest and find peace that his daughter was well taken care of. Travis pushed away from the door and moved to one of the windows.

Who are you kidding, Buchanan? You're not marrying that girl to save her father. You're marrying that girl because you can't live without her. In that instant Travis heard himself. He was talking like it was a done deal, because in his mind it was. He turned from the window and stepped back out into the hall. The doctor stood there alone. Travis found his heart talking to the owner of the Double Star Ranch.

You've got to make her see, sir. I'll take care of her, rest assured of that. Make her see that I'm worthy of another chance because I'll cherish her forever.

❧

Rebecca sat very still and watched her father's chest as it rhythmically lifted the sheet. She couldn't have moved if she wanted to. How in the world had he talked her into such a thing? What girl doesn't dream of being courted, told she's loved, and then asked that wonderful question? Rebecca had been no different, but her father said this way was best. Indeed, he looked as if he were going to expire on the spot when she didn't agree fast enough.

And now she was to be married. It was the very reason she was sitting in her father's bedroom long after he'd fallen asleep. If she left the room she might run into Travis, and right now she'd rather die. Her father had bought a husband for her. Rebecca felt sick and must have made a sound. She looked over to see her father's eyes on her.

"What is it, Reba? What has you upset?"

"How can you ask me that?" Tears filled her eyes. "My father buys me a husband and wonders why I'm upset."

Andrew's head moved on the pillow. "It's you he wants, Reba. Trust me. He never even mentioned the ranch."

"How can you be sure?"

"Because I've known a lot of men, and Travis Buchanan is a cut above the rest. He's not without his faults, Reba, but he's special. Get to know him. I can see great things for the two of you, and I plan to be here to watch. But just in case, married to him I know you'll be all right."

Slipping back into her dream world, Rebecca was comforted—but only momentarily. The bubble had burst when Travis started for her in the entryway and Lucky spoke from the living room. Then there had been his awful coldness and punishing kiss. Now her father said they would make a life together. The side of Rebecca that wanted to walk through life in a dream wanted desperately to believe him, but the other half of her was terrified. Her father was about to make it worse.

"I've talked with Lavena. She's setting it all up. You'll be married this week."

"This week?" Rebecca whispered, telling herself not to faint.

"Look at me, Rebecca." He sounded almost stern. "I have to see the job done. I have to rest in peace."

Rebecca's hands came to her face. How in the world would she make it?

"Trust me, Rebecca. I promise to do right by you."

She tried to nod, but her head hurt so badly. She didn't hear the door, but suddenly Lavena was there. She helped the young woman to her feet and down the hall. Rebecca didn't remember much about being helped into bed, but the night passed swiftly, as did the first half of the week. Before she knew it it was Wednesday, and the preacher was coming from town at 5:00.

Travis smoothed down the hair at the back of his neck and wished he had taken time to get it cut. He slipped into his only dress jacket and adjusted the string tie at his throat. The only pants he had were jeans, but they were clean and well pressed—Lavena had seen to that. With palms that were slightly damp, he went to the door of his bedroom. Lavena was down the hall, outside of Andrew's room. She actually smiled when she saw him. Travis tried to return the gesture, but his face felt stiff.

"They're waiting for you," she told him when he stopped before her.

Travis nodded, and she opened the door. He stepped into Andrew Wagner's bedroom and barely noticed as the preacher's head tipped back to look at him. He had eyes for only one person, and her face was so pale that Travis wanted to sweep her into his arms and promise her anything to calm the fear he saw in her eyes. He forced himself to look at his employer, who was propped up with pillows in a chair by the bed.

"Well," Andrew spoke with deep contentment, "let's begin."

"Fine, fine," Pastor Craig jumped in. "It's Travis, is it?"

"Yes."

"Fine, fine. You stand here next to Rebecca. Fine, fine. That way Mr. Wagner won't miss a thing. That's right, fine, fine."

Travis tuned the man out as he began to position Lavena. He looked down at Rebecca, but she was staring straight ahead.

"It's all right, Rebecca," he said for her ears alone, and watched as she looked at him. He bent slightly to give them privacy, and ran a single finger down her soft cheek. His heart knew peace when her eyes softened as they looked into his. A moment later he straightened.

"Now then." The pastor was ready to start. "Do you, Travis Buchanan, take Rebecca Wagner to be your lawfully wedded wife?"

"Yes, I do."

"And do you, Rebecca Wagner, take Travis Buchanan to be your lawfully wedded husband?"

"I do."

He beamed at them for just an instant. "Before God and this small gathering, I now pronounce you man and wife. You may kiss the bride."

Travis hadn't even been ordered to take Rebecca's hand, but he watched her stiffen beside him. However, she need not have worried. The kiss he brushed across her lips was so light she might have imagined it. And Lavena was approaching now to give her a hug. Had it really happened? Had she really married Travis while wearing a dress she'd had for two years? If the smile on her father's face was any indication, she had done just that.

"Come downstairs now," Lavena was saying. "I've made some supper."

"I can't stay," Rebecca heard the pastor say. "The little woman is expecting me, but it all went fine, fine. I hope to see you all in church. We take an offering every week."

With that he was gone, and Travis was relieved. The man had shaken his hand and muttered some religious drivel that Travis immediately put out of his mind. Travis was only too glad to see the back of him. He turned to see Rebecca bending over her father. He was touching her face, and whatever he said made her smile. Travis' heart lifted at the sight of it.

"Go down now, you two. Have something to eat."

"Why don't we bring our plates up here?" Travis offered.

"That's a wonderful idea," Rebecca agreed. "We'll come back up and bring you something."

But Andrew would not hear of it. He said he was too tired from the ceremony, and they could not persuade him. Lavena halted the discussion when she appeared with a special tray for him.

Travis and Rebecca walked silently down the stairs to the dining room. Lavena had prepared a feast. They sat across the table from each other and began serving themselves. Rebecca didn't know how she was going to eat a bite, but she filled her plate. Travis watched her.

"I wouldn't have said you would be that hungry."

Rebecca's startled eyes flew to his, but there was nothing challenging in his manner. Her shoulders slumped a little.

"I'm not hungry at all, but I didn't want you to know that."

Travis nodded, appreciating her honesty. "It's going to take a little getting used to."

"Yes."

They looked at each other for just a moment. There didn't seem to be anything else to say. Travis had not taken much food himself, but even so, he was not able to finish. They didn't retire to the living room for coffee but shared it at the table while trying to do justice to the cake Lavena had baked. Neither one could manage it. The magnitude of what they'd done was pressing in upon them.

It wasn't long before Rebecca bid Travis good night and went upstairs. Travis watched her go, his mind running down a thousand different paths. He realized his head was pounding. Finally, moving to the kitchen, he thanked Lavena for her work and then headed to the stairs as well.

9

Rebecca stared at her father in horror. She hadn't even made it past his bedroom to go to her own room. His door had been wide open, and although back in bed, he had been waiting for her.

"You can't mean it," she barely managed.

"I do mean it. I never meant for you to have a marriage of convenience."

Rebecca couldn't breathe. Hadn't he already asked enough? Hadn't she already married a near stranger so his heart would stay calm? And now he expected this. Rebecca took a deep breath and tried to collect herself. She tried to explain.

"I think that given time, Travis and I might—"

"No, Rebecca." Andrew's voice was soft, but she heard the determination. "Tonight. It can't wait."

"Papa," she began, but stopped when his face began to flush. For an instant her eyes slid shut as she tried to gain strength to do this. *Do what?* she asked herself. *Fight my father or go down the hall to my husband's room?* When she opened her eyes, Andrew was looking at her, and she knew there would be no reprieve. Seeing his heaving chest, she swiftly made her decision, wishing for the first time that she'd remained in Philadelphia.

Rebecca turned to the door but stopped. She looked back at him for an instant longer and then shut the portal firmly. Not until she stood in the hallway did she realize how violently she was trembling. She looked down the hall to Travis' door; hers was to the right, and his room was exactly opposite the long hallway on the left.

Maybe he would send her away. *Yes,* she reasoned to herself. *He won't want this either.* Feeling somewhat calmer, Rebecca moved to his door.

Travis heard the footsteps just before the soft knock. He had hung his coat up, pulled his shirt free of his waistband, and removed his tie, but that was as far as he'd progressed. Wondering what Lavena could want, he opened the door. He stared down for a long moment at his wife, his expressionless face masking the rage of emotions within. When Rebecca didn't speak or move, but stood looking at him with uncertain eyes, he stepped back, opening the door wide. To his amazement she slowly entered, and Travis, without thinking, shut the door.

Rebecca heard the click of the latch and turned to look at him, her eyes now showing her fear. Travis found himself mentally asking Andrew Wagner what in the world he'd said to this girl. However, he also saw this for the opportunity it was. How many men had a chance to redeem themselves this swiftly? At least part of Rebecca's mind must see him as a monster. Tonight he could show her otherwise.

"Does your mouth still hurt?" His voice was deep and gentle, but Rebecca, who had gone into something of a trance, started.

"I don't know," she admitted and shrugged. "I don't know."

"Shall we find out?" he asked, and quickly saw that she looked ready to bolt.

With movements slow and measured, his eyes never leaving hers, Travis took the four steps that put him in front of Rebecca. She watched him in near terror as his head lowered, but her fear turned to confusion when he pressed a kiss only to her brow.

"You look beautiful in that dress," he whispered, his breath falling on her temple.

"Thank you," she whispered automatically.

"Is it new?"

"No, there wasn't time."

"I'm glad you wore it."

Her eyes slid shut when his mouth brushed down her cheek. The next place he kissed was her chin, and Rebecca's fear was fast beginning to fade. By the time he did kiss her mouth she wanted him to. Her mouth was still a bit tender, but his touch was so light that she knew nothing but pleasure. She didn't remember his taking her hand or leading her to the bedside, but he was seated on the edge now, and she stood in front of him, lessening the differences in their heights. The arms that held her were warm and strong, but she was not crushed.

I'm a wife now, she naively thought some time later. *I hadn't really understood what that would mean, but I'm a wife now. Travis' wife.*

However, when Travis suddenly moved away from her and turned the lantern high, Rebecca, still feeling shy around him, tugged the covers over her shoulders.

"You're mine now, Reba, and I'm yours," he said as he raised up on one elbow above her and stared down into her eyes. "There's no one else for me, and there's no one else for you."

"There never was anyone else, Travis," she told him, and he saw the truth in her eyes.

He kissed her gently.

"You're not sorry I came in here?" she asked quietly.

Travis couldn't keep himself from smiling.

"No," he told her, laughter filling his voice. "I'm not sorry." He kissed her and held her again, and it wasn't long before the events of the day began to exhaust her. She wondered if she was supposed to move back to her own room, but the bed was so soft, and her husband's shoulder was so warm. Sleep came to claim her before she could decide. When she woke the next morning, Travis was already gone.

❧

Rebecca took a sip of her coffee, her eyes on the snow-covered hills. She'd just spent some time with her father, but now she was alone in the kitchen, trying to sort through the events of the last 24 hours. Rebecca sighed and took another drink. She wanted more than anything to tell Travis that she loved him, but something was stopping her. Was it normal for husbands and wives to share that sentiment, or was she to continue keeping her feelings to herself?

Maybe if I told Travis I loved him, he would say it to me. But the moment the thought formed, she dashed it away. She had to say it because she felt it with all her heart, not because she wanted him to say the words back to her. The longer she thought on it, the more convinced she was to keep still. She believed she loved Travis, but they both needed more time. Rebecca picked up her coffee again, her heart already feeling lighter. She couldn't expect to know exactly how to act at this stage, and neither could Travis. *I do love Travis,* Rebecca decided with sudden conviction.

"The coffee still hot?" Lavena asked as she came into the room.

"Yes. You make it nice and strong, Lavena. Just the way I like it."

"How did your aunt make it?"

"She didn't. We always had tea."

Lavena snorted. "And I suppose it was having tea in the parlor that always has me carrying a heavy tray of coffee all the way to the living room."

Rebecca smiled. "Your life is so hard, Lavena."

The old woman's mouth swung open as she stared at Rebecca, who was still smiling. "I never said that. What foolishness!"

Rebecca had to laugh. It seemed as if Lavena didn't even listen to herself. No wonder her father hadn't been hurting for company over the years. The sudden thought of him sobered her very swiftly.

I've been a good daughter, she told God. *I've obeyed my Papa. Please let him live. Please let him be all right.* Rebecca prayed on with only a small measure of guilt. She rarely had time for God when things were going well. *But He's God,* she thought with a touch of anger. *He's supposed to heal and comfort.* The thought calmed as swiftly as it had flared, but she continued to pray for some minutes. She'd have been very surprised to learn that her father was awake upstairs trying to have conversation in the same way.

✑

I know why this happened. I promised You I'd go to church if You brought Reba to me and I haven't gone, but this time I mean it. Just let me get out of this bed and back on my feet and I'll go. I'll put a new roof on the building or whatever they need, if You let me get up again. I'll even read the Bible. I don't know where mine is right now, but I'll find it. And I'll see that Travis and Reba go to church too. Lavena too, if You want her. We'll all go, God—just let me make it this time.

In a matter of sentences Andrew managed to exhaust himself. He wanted to sob like a baby. His eyes were closed, but a single tear slipped out the corner of his eye. A few minutes later he was once again asleep. When Rebecca checked on him some 30 minutes later, the tear had dried and she took no notice.

✑

That night Travis and Rebecca ate dinner in Andrew's room. His color was good and his face was animated as he questioned Travis about the stock and hands.

"Biscuit impaled his hand," Travis told him at one point, careful to omit the details.

"Lavena mentioned it. Was he able to cook tonight?"

"I think he was, but he still talked Woody into helping out."

"Woody? Can Woody cook?"

Travis grinned. "He can but says he hates it."

"You could ask Lavena to help out," Andrew said with a small smile.

"Shall I also tell her it was your idea?"

Andrew's smile turned into a full-blown grin. "If you wait until I'm out of the territory."

"Oh, come now," Rebecca put in. "She'd help if you asked her."

"True," her husband told her, "but none of us would ever hear the end of it."

When Lavena had cleared the dishes away and they had their coffee, Rebecca and Travis sat on the small settee so that Andrew could ask more questions.

Rebecca knew that Travis, who seemed to love ranching, was interested in sharing his day, but more than one time she felt his eyes on her. At one point she looked up and smiled at him, and her heart melted a little when he reached for her hand. The coffee perked her up for a time, but she had spent the day dealing with her emotions, and it wasn't long before she told the men good night.

Andrew had additional questions for Travis, who was more than happy to answer, but he also had news for Travis.

"Paul West was out here today."

"Do I know him?"

"Probably not. He's a lawyer. Got a small practice in town. I'd say he and the wife are nearly starving on what he takes in, but I had business for him today."

Travis waited.

"I've changed my will."

Travis shook his head. "You're not going to die. In fact, I think you'll be out of that bed this week."

"Well, I plan to be, but just in case . . ."

Travis shook his head. "Don't talk like that."

"I have to, and I want you to listen!"

It was the last thing Travis wanted to do, but Andrew looked agitated, so he made himself sit quietly.

"I've left it all to you, Travis," he said softly. "To you and Reba. This marriage may not seem like a match from heaven, but I know you'll take care of my girl."

Travis frowned. He would take care of Rebecca, no matter what, but he didn't care for people thinking he'd used his wife to get the ranch.

"I don't care what people think," Andrew went on as if he'd read his thoughts. "Rebecca needs you, and that's all there is to it. I have your word, don't I, Travis? Before God, you will take care of her, won't you?"

"Yes, sir, I will. I'm confident that you'll be here to see it all happen, but no matter what, Rebecca is my wife and I'll take care of her."

Andrew nodded, his head falling back on the pillow.

"Can I do something for you, sir?"

"No, no. Lavena will be up to settle me. I just want to sit here awhile."

"All right. I'll see you tomorrow, sir."

"Good night, Travis."

"Good night, sir."

Travis walked calmly from the older man's room, but his step livened perceptibly when he hit the hall. He smiled in anticipation as he opened his door, but his face fell when he found the room empty. His disappointment that Rebecca was not waiting for him knew no bounds. He sat on the edge of the bed and took his boots off, all the while contemplating his next move. It didn't take long to decide. Although he'd already washed for dinner, he again removed his shirt, scrubbed his face, neck, and arms over the washbowl, dried off, and put on a clean cotton shirt. Leaving his boots in his room, he exited and started toward his wife's door.

Rebecca had been pulling her hair back with a ribbon before going to bed for as many years as she could remember. Tonight was no different. When the knock sounded on the door, she was already in bed, sitting up against the headboard, hair in a blue ribbon, a lace-trimmed nightgown on her frame, and a book in her hand. When she heard the knock, she assumed it to be Lavena as Travis had the night before.

"Come in," she called, not raising her eyes from the page. It took a moment for her to realize it wasn't the housekeeper. She wasn't startled or upset, just curious. However, Travis spoke before she could ask a single question.

"I was pretty disappointed not to find you waiting in my room."

Rebecca's brow lowered. "Why? Was I supposed to come to your room?"

Travis should not have been surprised by the question. Rebecca had learned the previous night that he was capable of great tenderness, but she had not learned about passion. He came to the bed and sat down, his back against the footboard.

"I won't stay if you don't want me to, Reba."

She loved it when he called her that and said softly, "You can stay if you want to, Travis. I don't mind."

Travis smiled at her. His hand waved toward her high neckline. "I think I like this outfit even better than the dress you had on yesterday."

Rebecca's hand went self-consciously to the lace, but she smiled with pleasure. Travis leaned forward very slowly and took the book from her lap. Rebecca made no protest. He set it on the nightstand and then moved to kiss her. It crossed Travis' mind that their relationship was unlike anything he'd ever known. Rebecca was still trying to figure out why she should have come to his room, until she lost herself in his kiss and thought to herself that she'd married the most handsome man in the territory.

⌒～

The next morning Andrew shocked everyone in the household by coming down to the breakfast table. They all stared at him, but he looked wonderful.

"A fool," Lavena said. "That's what you are, a fool." She served him anyway and hovered around him until he sent her away.

"I'm going to ride for a time today, Travis," he told his foreman. "I won't go far, but I need to get out."

"Can't that wait, Papa? It's still so cold," Rebecca put in softly, but Andrew ignored her. Her eyes went to her husband's, but a small shake of his head told her he'd keep an eye on things.

Andrew was so anxious to be off that he left half of his meal in the process. This gave Travis and Rebecca a few minutes alone. Travis went to her side of the table and pulled her out of her chair. He captured her jaw in his hand and kissed her.

"I'll see you tonight," he promised, his face still close. The new bride's eyes turned dreamy.

"Shall I come to your room?"

Travis' smile was loving and intimate. "No. Just climb into that lacy gown again, and I'll come to you."

He gave her a quick kiss and reluctantly let her go. Following him all the way to the door, Rebecca watched his long, jean-clad legs carry him to the barn. She had known a moment's worry that her father had purchased a husband for her, but it wasn't true. Rebecca knew Travis loved her, even though he never said so. And the wave he turned to give her before disappearing inside the huge stable stayed with her the rest of the day.

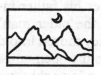

10

There wasn't a hand on the Double Star Ranch who didn't know that Travis Buchanan had married the owner's daughter on Wednesday of that week. And to a man, while they envied him his bride and position as the owner's son-in-law, they secretly wished him well, though no one offered a word of congratulation. Lucky had been rather quiet on the job the day before, but not angry. Travis had been watchful, but today he could tell it would be more difficult for his own heart than for Lucky. All he wanted to do was think of Rebecca.

Now as the men mounted up to head out for the day, he had to force himself to the task at hand, making sure his father-in-law did not collapse off his horse. The older man was in high spirits, laughing with the hands, but Travis could still picture Andrew's pale face on the pillow just days before.

They moved out as a group and rode together for some time. When they split off to ride the range and check the herds, Andrew, Travis, Lucky, and Race Paulson were together. Normally Travis and Andrew would have split up, but today Travis wouldn't have left his boss even if he'd been ordered to.

The day was warmer than earlier in the week, but by midday, when they stopped to build a fire and warm up, the steaming coffee was very welcome. Talk around the fire was all business, but when Travis saw Andrew surreptitiously rubbing the middle of his chest, he sent Lucky and Race off on their own. Andrew and Travis rode over several more acres, but Travis managed to steer his father-in-law back to the ranch house while salvaging the older man's dignity. Andrew was still in high spirits as they moved into the house, and since the ride back was as cold as the open range, Lavena's fresh coffee, better than Lucky's by a long shot, was more than welcome. Rebecca had cookies waiting for them as well, and her father felt so good that he teased her.

"These are better than the last ones, Reba. You're improving." She smiled at him, but Travis looked confused.

"She can't cook, you know." His voice was jovial. "I didn't want you to know that ahead of the vows, but Reba can't cook." Andrew laughed at his own joke.

Travis' brows shot into the air as he looked at his wife, but he laughed too, especially when he saw her red face. However, the lightness of the moment didn't last long. Andrew was saying something else, but Travis did not attend. In so many ways he'd married a stranger. It didn't matter to him what she could do, but the reminder of how little they knew about each other was sobering.

Rebecca read his look all wrong. The change in Travis' expression crushed her. After a time, Lavena and Andrew went their separate ways, leaving husband and wife alone in the kitchen. Try as she might, Rebecca was not able to keep the hurt from her voice. Travis didn't notice at first.

"It's cold out there today, but it could be worse," he offered.

"Oh, really?" Her back was to him and had been since the others left.

"I look forward to spring."

"Yes."

It was on that word that Travis noticed her stiff posture. He moved up behind her and spoke.

"Is something wrong?"

Rebecca turned hurt eyes to him. "I never meant to keep my lack of cooking skills from you. It just didn't come up."

Travis blinked. "I don't care whether you can cook or not, Reba," he told her sincerely.

"That's not true," Rebecca argued with him. "I saw your face."

Travis shook his head. "My mind was a thousand miles away. The cooking doesn't matter to me."

Rebecca searched his face, and then her small hands rose to pull on the front of his dark leather vest. Travis began to lower his head but hesitated.

"I smell like a horse."

"I don't care," his wife whispered, and Travis gladly kissed her. They heard Lavena's steps returning so they broke apart, but it was the start of a wonderful evening—first eating dinner and laughing the evening away with her father, and then turning in together. She hadn't felt so warm and loved for a long time.

~

Travis wanted to grab Lavena and shake her. She was standing in the kitchen, her face pale, and telling him that Andrew Wagner was dead. Travis knew it couldn't be true. Why would Lavena say such a cruel thing? It simply couldn't be true.

"He's not." Travis' voice was flat.

Lavena's eyes fixed on a distant spot out the window. "I only went to check on him." There was a note of amazement in her voice. "He's still in bed. It must have happened in the night."

Travis' hands fisted at his side. *No,* his mind screamed at God, *You can't do this. He was fine yesterday, and last night, better than ever. How could You?*

The thoughts halted when he remembered his wife. How in the world would he tell her? He'd left her sleeping like a child, and now he must wake her and destroy her world. If that wasn't enough to make Travis writhe in pain, the next thought made his heart clench in agony. He cared for his wife beyond all description, but . . .

Everyone will think I married Rebecca for the ranch.

"No one had better say that around me." Lavena spat the words, and Travis stared at her. He hadn't meant to speak outloud.

"It's not true," Lavena went on, her bony chest heaving with indignation. "It doesn't matter what people say. Rebecca knows otherwise, and that's all that matters."

"Does she?" Travis suddenly doubted. "Does she know?"

Lavena shook her head. "That's your grief talking, Travis. You know she knows it."

"Lavena!"

The housekeeper's name was screamed from above them. Travis bolted for the stairs. He wouldn't have to tell Rebecca the news; she'd clearly found out on her own.

Feeling cold and alone, Rebecca sat in her bedroom later that day. Travis had been the one to go to town and make arrangements for the burial, but in his own grief his manner had been curt. She wanted to cry in his arms, but she felt so frozen that she could not reach out to him. Her father was gone. It was too impossible to be true, but she'd seen the evidence with her own eyes. Andrew Wagner was dead. She hadn't even been home six months, and her father was now gone from her forever. He had warned her that this was the reason she should marry Travis, but Rebecca had believed that the very act alone would keep him alive.

In the next few seconds grief overtook Rebecca's good sense. What if Travis didn't take care of her? What if Travis decided to send her away and keep the ranch for himself? Rebecca had spent the previous evening in a happy cloud, sure that nothing could touch her secure world, but now she was alone—more so than when she had been halfway between

Pennsylvania and Colorado Territory with no choice but to push on. Panic clawed at her throat, but it didn't last. Moments later, she was angry. Hannah Ellenbolt had done this. Hannah had kept her from her father, and now he was dead.

With movements that were almost vicious, Rebecca found paper and quill. The day was cloudy, so she lit a lantern, set it on her writing table, and began with a vengeance.

My eyes were so blinded, Hannah, but no longer. I can see now what you really are. The lies I believed about my father now make me sick to my stomach. He's gone, and you're to blame! I'll never forgive you. I married a stranger! I was forced to marry my father's foreman, and all because you're a selfish, sick old woman! It's all your fault that I'm alone.

She went on for paragraphs, not meaning half of it, the words scathing and mean, but the end was near. Rebecca's mind moved to the love she always saw in her father's eyes, and with that she broke down. She crumpled the paper and threw it aside, sobbing into her folded arms.

Travis stood like a statue at the graveside of Andrew Wagner, not feeling the cold or seeing the blinding sunlight. The service had been over for an hour and still he stood, seeing his mother's grave as clearly as the one before him. Lavena had said that Rebecca's lips were turning blue and had taken her back to the house, but Travis could not make himself move. He had a beautiful wife, and he now owned a ranch, but Andrew Wagner was dead and Travis found no joy in his position. It niggled at the back of his mind that Rebecca needed him; they all needed him. He was the owner of the Double Star and they needed his stability, but right now he felt worthless.

How could You do this? he asked God for what must have been the hundredth time, but no answer came. He was going to have to go on by himself. He was going to have to be strong for everyone else, even if he was dying inside.

Another hour passed before he began the walk back. Lavena had some food ready, but he wasn't hungry. He didn't ask after Rebecca, assuming she'd gone to her room. With measured tread he moved toward Andrew's study. Like no other in the house, this room was the man himself. His presence pervaded every nook and cranny. Travis wandered the floor, not touching anything, but looking and letting his eyes caress the huge desk, fine leather chair, and simple furnishings. Another hour passed before he sat very carefully in the desk chair. His eyes slid shut with pain, and fatigue overcame him.

His wife's pain at the moment was no less than his own, but added to the hurt was fear—fear that she would be sent away and left all alone in the world. It did nothing but cause more hurt and fear when she came down an hour later and found Travis asleep in her father's chair.

❧

Lavena thought she would scream if she had to go another day with the silence in the house. Travis and Rebecca went through the day-to-day motions, but it was as if they'd died with Andrew. Her own grief knew no bounds, but she forced herself to keep on. Three days. Could it be only three days since they'd laid him in the ground? It was amazing that they'd been able to dig the frozen earth. It looked like spring would come early, but no one took notice.

It also crossed Lavena's mind that Travis and Rebecca had been married for one week. But as they were in such obvious pain, it gave her no joy. She knew deep in her heart that they could make a go of it. The love she'd seen in their eyes for each other had given that secret away. And even though the circumstances surrounding their marriage had been unusual, Lavena knew their hearts were involved.

And indeed, Lavena was right. Travis and Rebecca did care deeply for each other. In fact, they were both to the point of needing to reach out to the other. Travis came off the range early to find Rebecca and talk to her, but Biscuit, who was now Travis' responsibility, had a gripe. The crotchety old man was waiting for him in the barn.

"I'm not gonna put up with it," he spat.

Travis sighed but kept his expression open. "What's the problem, Biscuit?"

The old man spat again. "There ain't no respect 'round here. No one tells me anything. I cook for six, but only four show up. Why, I—" and on he went.

Travis wanted to tell him he sounded like a fussy old woman but refrained. What did it matter how much food he fixed, especially in winter when things would keep? Biscuit often served the leftovers the next night anyhow, and the men never raised much of a fuss.

"I can see you won't be any help. You just care about the money."

He had Travis' full attention now.

"What is that supposed to mean?" His voice was cold.

"You know very well."

Travis saw a bitterness in the man's eyes that he had never noticed before.

"At least she's pretty," Biscuit added contemptuously, "which makes it a little easier, I'd say."

Travis was angry enough to plow his fist into the man's face but only gritted out, "I think you'd better shut your mouth, Biscuit."

"Can't stand to hear the truth, boy? Is that your problem?"

Travis didn't answer him but turned and walked out, never once seeing his wife in the shadows of a stall. She had so needed to be near him that she'd come to the barn to await his arrival. Not wanting to talk to the cook, she had remained hidden. Now she wished she had run away and not heard a thing.

Rebecca made her way slowly back to the house, but didn't search out her husband or Lavena. She came to the supper table, but Travis did not. He did not seek his own meal for many hours, so busy was he in the office, making plans for the ranch, in order to prove Biscuit wrong and make Rebecca the proudest woman in the Colorado Territory.

Had he made an appearance, Rebecca might have reconsidered, but by the time she crawled into bed and lay looking at the ceiling for most of the night, her mind was made up.

11

Lavena paced the floor like a caged animal waiting for Travis to come home. Her mouth was dry, as it had been all afternoon, and she thought that if he didn't hurry she'd be tempted to mount a horse and go find him. Her stomach churned.

After her husband drank himself to death eight years ago, she had walked out to the Double Star Ranch and told Andrew Wagner that he needed her. He had been ready to send her packing, but she had come prepared.

From seemingly nowhere, she had produced a pie. It had been in her bag, and the sight of the confection alone had halted Andrew in midsentence. It had taken her all afternoon to get to the ranch, and if he'd turned her away she was going to sneak into the barn and sleep before returning to town. But suddenly she was invited in. He never did tell her that she had the job, but while he devoured over half the pie, she started on the mound of dirty dishes in the kitchen. There had never been any talk of her leaving. She was now as much a part of the Double Star as the earth itself.

However, she was too old for this. She was too old for the heartache of seeing people in pain. She wasn't even 60, but days like this, days when her stomach churned and she had no answers, she felt like 100. All day she had paced between the living room windows, which gave her a view of the road, and the window in the kitchen, which gave her eyes a clear shot of the

99

barn. She was in the living room when she heard Travis come in the back. With a hand to her heart she went to him. One look at her pale features and he knew something was wrong.

"What is it?"

"Rebecca went to town right after you left this morning. She said she wanted to be on her own for a while and hasn't returned."

Evening was falling, but that didn't stop Travis. He immediately pushed his hat back on and went out the door. Lavena watched from the door as his long legs ate up the distance to the barn. It wasn't five minutes before he rode Diamond from the stable yard. He wasn't beating the horse into the ground, but Lavena knew without a doubt that his mind must be going ten times faster than his mount.

Rebecca stood behind a tree, sagged against it, and begged God or whoever was in charge not to let her be sick again. It had started on the stage. At first she was certain it had been the rocking, but she'd been off the stage for two hours and still her stomach rolled.

Why did I leave? Why did I run like this?

Rebecca laid her head back against the tree and told herself she was not going to cry. What a time to get sick. All she could think to do was to get away, away from Travis and away from the memory of her father. Lavena had wanted to go to town with her, but Rebecca had lied and said she wanted to be alone. She could never have left with Lavena there, and now she wished she had allowed her to come. Much like when she left her aunt's, her anger had carried her for miles, all the way through the first day and part of the second, but now on the third day she just wanted to throw herself at her husband's chest and cry her eyes out. Right now she didn't care why he'd married her; she just wanted to be home and safe in her own bed.

"Is someone there?" A husky feminine voice spoke out of the gathering darkness. Rebecca started. She tried to shrink back against the bark, but the woman was headed her way. She stopped less than a dozen feet off.

"Come away from the tree, please."

Rebecca held very still, but the voice called again, and this time it sounded amused.

"If you're going to hide in my backyard, the least you could do is tell me your name."

Rebecca let out a sigh. What was the use?

"Rebecca," she spoke quietly. "Rebecca Wag—" Again the sigh. "Buchanan."

"Well, come here, honey. I'm not going to hurt you."

Rebecca hesitated but then stepped toward the woman. Evening was gathering swiftly, but she could still make out a tall-looking figure in rather fancy evening clothes.

"I'm Angel," the sultry voice said when Rebecca stopped some six feet in front of her. "You passing through Pine Grove or here for a time?"

"I'm not certain."

"Which means you're out of money," she said knowingly, her tone matter-of-fact. "Will you be looking for work?"

"Yes, I suppose I will."

Angel stared at her for a moment. "Come on in," she finally said and moved, assuming Rebecca would follow. Rebecca hesitated only a moment before covering the distance to a small house and climbing the stairs into a small kitchen. It was very dark and dim in the house, and since her host had disappeared, and Rebecca froze. A match flared from beyond the kitchen door, and Rebecca saw a rising glow.

"Come on in," Angel repeated. Rebecca shut the door and moved with quiet steps toward the light, which grew much brighter as she neared. This short walk brought her to a rather large sitting room, fully illumined by the lantern. Through a wide archway, she could see what looked like a dining room table and chairs. Again she found herself under Angel's inspection. The other woman's eyes, very knowing and shrewd, took in every aspect of Rebecca's grubby appearance.

"There's only one thing in the world that can make a woman look like you do," Angel said without preamble. "A man. I don't expect you to tell me about it if you don't want to, but just know that I know."

Rebecca dropped her eyes. The last thing she wanted to do was talk about Travis.

"You're just into town?"

"Yes." Rebecca looked up. "On the stage."

Angel nodded. "How old are you?"

"Nineteen."

Again the look came, the woman's eyes narrowing slightly. Rebecca looked back. Angel was beautiful, but there was a hard worldliness about her.

"Can you cook and clean? I hate to cook and clean."

Wanting to lie, Rebecca blinked but just said, "A little."

The next instant Angel's front door burst open. Rebecca started violently. She stared wide-eyed at a tall man, also dressed for an evening out. He was coatless, but his tie, shirt, and pants were spotless and without wrinkle or crease.

"Preston is looking for you, Angel. You'd better put a move on it."

Angel didn't even look at him.

"Angel?"

"I heard you, Dan. You can tell Preston to keep his shirt on."

The man did not look the least bit offended, but his eyes suddenly landed on Rebecca. He made no effort to disguise his interest.

"New girl?"

Angel cocked her head to one side, still taking in Rebecca's huge eyes and exhausted expression.

"I don't think so," she said slowly, finally turning to the man. "Tell Preston I'll be right along."

Dan's eyes swept Rebecca's features one last time, his gaze lingering on her eyes before he slipped away. Angel looked back to her guest.

"If you want to cook and clean house for me, you're hired."

Rebecca hesitated.

"Or you can come down to the Silver Bell, and Preston can find work for you there."

"The Silver Bell?"

"Yes. Pine Grove's post prestigious dining establishment. The owner is always looking for girls to serve drinks and meals, or to dance and sing on the stage."

Rebecca was speechless. Serve drinks? Dance on the stage? She had the vague thought that there must be more of Aunt Hannah in her than she realized.

"Or," Angel drew the word out, "you can cook and clean for me."

It never once occurred to Rebecca to refuse both. She was tired, three days' stage ride from home, and completely out of money.

"I'll cook and clean for you, but I'm not the best."

"Anything has got to be better than cooking for myself. I'll warn you though, I work nights, sometimes staying late when we're extra busy. I like to sleep into the morning."

"So you'll need quiet."

"No, I can sleep through a hurricane, but you'll be on your own much of the time."

Rebecca nodded, suddenly so tired she could hardly stand.

"Go on upstairs. My bedroom is the first. You can take the other one. Don't worry if you hear me come in late. And don't worry about doing anything tomorrow. Get rested up, and we'll talk about your duties sometime after noon."

All at once Rebecca wanted to cry. A shrewd judge of faces, Angel felt a deep stirring of compassion. It was an unusual emotion for her—she'd learned early that a woman couldn't let her heart get involved.

"The stairs are behind you," she said quietly as she pressed the lantern into Rebecca's hand. "Have you got a bag or anything?"

"I left it by the tree out back," Rebecca answered in a wobbly voice.

"I'll put it in the kitchen on my way out. Go on now. Go upstairs and just crawl into bed. We'll talk tomorrow."

Rebecca couldn't answer. Travis' face loomed in her mind, and then her father's. She turned and found the stairway, telling herself to take one step at a time. Angel had said she would put Rebecca's bag in the kitchen, but a few minutes later the other woman, carrying the small satchel, came to the door of her room.

"Here, let me get those buttons."

Tears were pouring down Rebecca's face, but she stood obediently with her back to Angel and allowed her to undo the back of her dress. When she continued just to stand and cry, even after the buttons were free, Angel pulled Rebecca's dress from her shoulders and then pushed her toward the bed. She actually managed to divest Rebecca of dress and shoes before ordering her to lie down. Rebecca did so out of misery and confusion, suddenly not able to tell where she was. It didn't last, however. The younger woman was asleep before Angel had time to blow out the lantern.

～

Preston Carwell, the owner of the Silver Bell, enjoyed a fair amount of respect in Pine Grove. For the most part he was a fair man, one who had gone after everything he wanted and eventually gotten it. The only exception was Angel Flanagan. Not that she knew his feelings. He'd been very careful over the years. He'd never once hinted that she was a woman he couldn't live without, because in his business a man didn't show his heart. However, when Angel arrived very late, her brow creased in what appeared to be anger, he approached.

"Problems, Angel?" His voice was typically casual.

"Nothing I can't handle."

Preston's brow rose in question.

"I found a kitten on my back doorstep," she explained. "She was more helpless than I first believed."

"I could send Dan to get rid of her."

Angel suddenly remembered the look in Dan's eyes and shook her head.

"Trust me when I tell you that's the worst thing you could do. This one is dangerous."

Preston smiled cynically. "Are you telling me I might lose my heart?"

Angel's smile was of the same variety. "Not you, Preston, and not me. But then, we're not quite human."

Preston's eyes hardened and so did Angel's, but their thoughts were self-condemning and not directed toward each other. Preston watched as Angel plastered a beaming smile on her face and went to greet the evening's first diners.

Rebecca woke slowly and stared at the lace curtain on the window. Not only was the curtain all wrong, the window itself was in the wrong place. She shifted her head against the pillow to find the door and in doing so caught the slightest hint of perfume. The night before flooded in on her.

Because she felt achy and a little sick to her stomach, Rebecca rose slowly and padded to the door. The floor felt gritty under her feet, and she remembered Angel's words about hating to clean.

Her steps still quiet, Rebecca moved down the hall. The light from her own bedroom window illumined the hall as did the light from the bedroom she was approaching. Rebecca didn't cross the threshold, but from the doorway she looked at her hostess, or rather what she could see of her.

Angel's face was hidden, but a wealth of pale blonde hair lay fanned over the pillows. There was no sound and there was no movement, and Rebecca also remembered that Angel said she was a sound sleeper. She went back to her bedroom and had a swift look around. She felt little emotion at the moment and realized that she was simply too tired to care. Her head swung in the direction of Angel's room as though she could see through walls. The other woman had made it sound as if she would sleep half the day away.

A noise came from outside, wagon wheels or a cart, and then a dog barked. Rebecca knew they would never disturb her as she climbed back into bed in broad daylight, something she had never done in her life. She was asleep in less than five minutes.

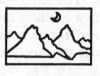

12

Four days. Travis' hand balled into a fist as he stood at the window of his bedroom. His wife had been gone for four days. He had ridden to find her, that night and again in the morning. He had nearly driven his horse into the ground as he searched the closest towns, but no one had seen her. He had been forced to come home last night; he'd left in such a hurry that he was out of provisions and money. A part of him had also wished to come home and find her there, with a simple explanation of their misunderstanding. But things between them were not simple, not in the least. Now he waited for the sun to rise in the sky so he could start again. He had to find her. He had to know where she was.

The livery had been no help that first night. She had left the horse and buggy with them but only talked to a stable hand who had remembered next to nothing about the whole incident. The agent at the stage office had been even less help.

Travis' eyes left his own reflection in the glass and glanced around his bedroom. He knew he should turn the lantern out in order to see the first streaks of light in the sky, but his gaze landed on the bed. He was tired enough to lie down and sleep for a week, but he resisted. Instead he picked up the lantern and moved down the hall. He forced himself not to look at the closed portal to Andrew's room as he moved toward his wife's door. What he hoped to see there was not clear to him, but maybe, just maybe, she'd dropped some sort of clue.

With the light held high in front of him, he pushed the door open and stepped inside. The room was just as tidy as he'd remembered, but there was a coldness inside that had nothing to do with the temperature. Travis set the lantern on the small writing table near the door and stood still, letting his eyes roam at will. He spotted the sleeve of a garment hanging from the ornately carved wardrobe in the corner and approached.

Here, all was not as neat. Inside it looked as if Rebecca had grabbed things in a hurry. The possible implications of the jumbled mess made his heart clench. He thought, however, that most of her things were there. The remaining dresses, ones that he loved seeing on her, were knocked askew or lay in a fallen heap in the bottom. He closed the door softly and turned slowly back to the room. Nothing leapt out at him until he moved to the lantern again. He lifted it and caught a glimpse of something in the wastebasket. It was only a small ball of paper, but Travis felt compelled to pick it up.

He unfolded the wad slowly and recognized his wife's handwriting. He saw right away that it was a letter to her Aunt Hannah, but he read it anyway. The words were like a lash.

I was forced to marry my father's foreman, and all because you're a selfish, sick old woman!

Travis' hand shook, but he made himself read it all and then read it again. She had been forced—Travis had known that. It hadn't been a violent, tempestuous act with tears and shouting, but neither had it been a gentle courtship over a reasonable period of time, one that ended with a declaration of love and much-anticipated vows at the altar. Even with his understanding of all that had happened, this lashing out, this anger and disgust in the letter, was a surprise to him. He knew she'd written it in grief and pain, but still . . .

Travis made himself calmly fold the paper and put it back on the writing table, the edge tucked under the heavy crystal inkwell. He could no longer stand the sight of the room and the remembrance of their time there together. He blew the lantern out and stood helplessly in the dark. It didn't take more than a few seconds for his eyes to note that the sky was growing light. He knew he could ride now, but should he? Should he go after a woman who obviously wanted nothing to do with him?

Pine Grove

Rebecca looked across the kitchen table at Angel and marveled just a little. Even right out of bed she was beautiful. She had been sipping hot coffee for 20 minutes and not spoken, but that was all right with Rebecca; she wanted only to stare at her clear skin, high forehead, delicate nose, sapphire blue eyes, and light blonde hair.

"I didn't get in until late." Angel's morning voice was husky. "But you seemed to be sleeping soundly."

"Yes. I slept well."

Angel's gaze came off her coffee cup, and Rebecca felt a little nervous under her steady regard. Angel managed to give her the impression that she could read her mind. Rebecca would have liked to ask if the offer from the night before still stood but felt that would be presumptuous.

"I'll tell you what I had in mind," Angel spoke as she rose, convincing Rebecca that she *could* read her thoughts. The younger woman watched as she reached toward the shelf for a frying pan and a bowl of eggs. "I can pay you 50 cents a week, plus room and board, if you'll keep the whole house clean, do my laundry, and have a meal on the table for me when I get up each day."

Angel glanced over her shoulder. "You're welcome to make this your home, but if your friends start tearing up the place, they'll have to go." She took in Rebecca's wide eyes and continued calmly. "Like I said last night, I work nights, but I like to get up and relax in the afternoons before I have to be at the Bell. If you are going to have friends in, I'd rather it be in the morning before I get up or in the evening after I leave for work. I'm off on Monday nights, and I'd rather you didn't have any company at all then."

109

Rebecca nodded, but was confused. What friends? A little shiver ran over her. The last person she thought was a friend had turned out to be anything but. He had married her for the ranch. It must be a relief to have gotten rid of her so easily.

Oh, Travis, her heart cried, *for a few days I thought we really had something. I thought it was going to last. Didn't you know how much I needed you? Didn't you understand how I hurt over Papa's death? Why didn't you punch Biscuit in the face and tell him it was me you wanted?*

Awash with misery, Rebecca looked up to find Angel's eyes on her. She averted her own gaze, and Angel didn't comment. Nothing was said by either of them until Angel passed Rebecca some food and she thanked her in a small voice.

Rebecca looked at the burned food in the pot and bit her lower lip. Angel would be up in less than an hour, and she had nothing for her to eat. Lavena had made it look so easy, but the potatoes in the pot were so stuck to the bottom that Rebecca wondered if she would have to throw the pot away. And she felt dreadful. When she'd gone to the cupboards to see what Angel had on hand to eat, she'd come across a plate of spoiled food that had caused her to gag and nearly be sick. She had held a dishcloth over her mouth and nose in order to dispose of it, but the thought still turned her stomach. Now the potatoes. What in the world was she going to do?

The thought had no more formed when there was a knock on the back door. It opened before Rebecca could move or speak. A man, the one who had put his head in the front door two nights before, now walked calmly into the kitchen.

"Good morning," he said pleasantly as he smiled in Rebecca's direction.

"Hello," she said warily, wondering if the sound-sleeping Angel would even hear her if she cried out.

"We weren't properly introduced the other night, but I'm Dan."

"Hello," Rebecca said again, but only stood warily.

Dan, who was quite accustomed to female attention, was more intrigued than ever. He forced himself to gaze around the room before looking back at her. In an effort to reopen the conversation, he gestured toward the pot with his hand.

"Smells like it burned a little."

Rebecca hated herself for the tears she felt gathering, but blinked them away.

"I don't know what I did wrong."

Dan's jaded heart broke. He took a step closer and looked down at the black mess.

"It looks as if you let the water boil dry."

"Water?"

"Yes." He wanted to laugh but didn't. "Didn't you add any?"

She only shook her head miserably and averted her eyes. Dan came to the rescue, gently taking the pan from her grasp, his voice matter-of-fact.

"Well, let's start over. Does Angel have more spuds?"

"Yes."

"Why don't you grab some, and I'll find another pot."

"Is the pot ruined?"

"Well, not quite," he stated tactfully, "but it'll take less time if we just use another one."

Rebecca moved silently to the small pantry and came back with four more potatoes. She set to peeling them without comment, but when Dan returned from the pump, he saw that she was cutting away most of the potato.

"Here," he stepped in, his voice too kind to be intrusive. "Let me show you."

Rebecca watched for a moment and then tried again when he handed the knife back to her. She was not as fast or smooth as he was, but there was more potato left the second time.

It was the start of a very enlightening half hour. As though they'd been friends for years, Dan spoke casually and showed her how to cook the potatoes, toast the bread, fry the little strips of bacon he'd unearthed, and perk a pot of coffee. It was all unbelievably complicated to her, but she knew if she didn't learn swiftly she would lose her job.

"Here," Dan poured a cup of the freshly brewed liquid and passed it to her. "You deserve this."

Rebecca took it but said, "I didn't do anything."

"Sure you did. You catch on quickly, and this is just the start. You'll do better tomorrow, Miss—"

Rebecca's eyes widened in surprise. Had she really not told him her name? Miss—? All at once her eyes became shuttered.

"My name is Rebecca."

"I'm Dan."

Rebecca nodded. "I remember seeing you before."

Dan was pleased but managed to keep it hidden. "I take it you'll be living here with Angel?"

"Yes," Rebecca said with a sigh. "If I can do the job."

"What did she hire you to do?"

"Cook and clean."

Dan smiled; he couldn't help himself. He glanced around the wreckage from the meal they had just prepared. He was on the verge of commenting, but Angel walked in.

"The parlor looks great, Rebecca. Oh, hello, Dan. What brings you—" Angel stopped when she caught sight of the room.

"Rebecca had a little trouble with the meal," Dan said smoothly. "But she's okay now."

Angel looked toward the younger woman. Her look was not accusing but questioning. Rebecca dropped her eyes and admitted, "I can't cook. There wouldn't be a meal at all if Dan hadn't come." She forced herself to look up. "If you want to throw me out, I'll go quietly, Angel."

Angel looked to Dan, but he was staring at Rebecca. Rebecca's eyes shifted to the man as well. He spoke when she looked at him.

"If Angel says you have to go, Rebecca, you can live with me."

The color drained from Rebecca's face, and her mouth and eyes opened wide in astonishment.

Dan's laugh was soft. "Don't panic, kitten. I was only kidding." With that he reached for the hat he'd set on the shelf by the door, his nonchalant movements helping Rebecca to breathe again.

"I'll see you at the Bell, Angel."

"We have plenty of food, Dan," Angel offered sincerely. "Why don't you stay?"

"Another time, Angel, but thanks." Before Rebecca could even guess his intentions, he dropped a kiss on her cheek. "See you later, kitten."

The silence in the small kitchen was heavy, but Angel moved very casually to get the plates. Rebecca took her cue and put the flatware and bowls of food on the table. The women were halfway through their meal before Angel said kindly, "You'll get the hang of it, Rebecca. Don't worry about your job."

"Dan was a big help," she admitted.

"He's a nice guy."

"Yes. I appreciated his stopping."

"But not enough to go and live with him."

Rebecca's eyes flew to Angel's. "He said he was only kidding."

Angel smiled. "Of course; so was I."

Angel watched the younger woman go back to her food and wondered at herself. She was a plainspoken woman and brutally honest. She wondered what it was about Rebecca's eyes that had kept her from telling the truth about Dan's interest.

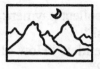

13

Rebecca was still bent over a washtub full of clothes when Dan arrived the next day. He walked in much as he'd done the day before, only this time he sat down at the table as if he lived there. In good spirits, he remarked, "Somehow I thought you would be burning potatoes by now."

Rebecca, who had greeted him absently, now looked full into his handsome face.

"What time is it?"

"Almost 4:00."

"Oh no!" she wailed. "I had no idea." She tore at the damp apron she was wearing and only managed to put the tie in a knot. Dan watched her calmly and wondered at his feelings. Never, not in 32 years of living as he pleased, had a person gotten under his skin so quickly. He was completely captivated by this woman.

"Here," he finally spoke, rising. "Let me help you."

He worked at the knot, gently easing it free, but as he'd done once before, he drew Rebecca close without warning and pressed a kiss to her brow, his head lowering still more, this time toward her mouth. Her eyes wide, Rebecca sprang back, hitting her seat on the stove.

"I can't pay you for helping me cook," she gasped.

"I'm not looking for payment," Dan told her, his hands still holding her waist.

"Yes you are. I can't pay you money, and I can't pay you with kisses."

"I'm not trying to collect payment, Rebecca."

"Then why the kiss?"

Dan's smile was tender. "How else does a man show a woman he's interested?"

"Interested in what?"

Dan blinked. Could she really be so naive?

"Why, in a relationship," he said calmly.

"But I'm not."

"Not interested in a relationship?"

"That's right."

Dan looked at her, forcing the hands that wanted to caress her waist to remain still.

"You haven't even given me a chance, Rebecca. You may find that you're very interested."

Rebecca shook her head in mute appeal. "I can't," she whispered. "I can't, and that's all there is to it."

Dan read the near panic in her eyes and knew he was going to have to back off. Tonight was his night off. He'd planned to come back when Angel went to work and get to know Rebecca more intimately, but he had never forced himself on a woman and certainly didn't plan to start now. He finally dropped his hands.

"Well, we'd better get started on supper."

"You're staying?" Rebecca asked in wonder.

"Of course. I think you still need a little help with this kitchen work."

"And you're willing to do that?"

"Certainly. That's what friends are for."

Rebecca could only stare at him. Dan caught the look.

"Unless you'd rather we weren't even friends, Rebecca. If so, I'll leave."

"No," Rebecca whispered. "I didn't know you'd be willing to be friends."

116

Dan knew very well that feeling as he did about her, friendship would never work, but he couldn't stand the thought of not seeing her again. If he walked out that door, he knew in his heart she would never call him back. Maybe this way he had a chance. He thought it might be a comfort to her to know that he did not have marriage in mind, but for some reason he kept this thought to himself.

"Now." His voice was all at once businesslike. "Potatoes again tonight?"

"Yes, and there are some apples."

"Okay, you can start to peel the spuds, and I'll do the apples."

Rebecca complied without comment, but a thought niggled at the back of her mind. Could a man who wanted to kiss you really be just a friend? She hadn't had any experience with such things, but the idea seemed odd. However, the next few minutes spent working with Dan seemed to mock Rebecca's very thoughts. He was as friendly and unassuming as he could be. Angel was down to eat by the time they put the meal on, and Dan even joined them. He helped with the cleanup and kissed Rebecca's cheek much as he had the night before. His smile was kind as he left, and Angel followed an hour later. Rebecca spent the rest of the evening on the laundry.

⌒

"Oh, Angel," Rebecca said with surprise the very next day. The older woman had risen several hours ahead of schedule. "Did I wake you?"

"No, I planned to get up early. We're out of food, and I think we should shop together."

"Oh." Rebecca felt awful. "I'm sorry I can't just do all of this on my own."

Angel smiled understandingly, but again she had surprised herself. Her mind told her that her new housekeeper was more trouble than she was worth, but Angel couldn't bring

117

herself to tell her to leave. Angel never had tender thoughts toward anyone, but the idea of Rebecca taking a job at the Bell,
or somewhere less respectable where she might be prey to
men, made Angel feel anxious. She knew that Dan was interested in Rebecca but also that he was a decent guy.

Less than half an hour later they were in Pine Grove's general store. It was nothing like the one in Boulder, but Rebecca
pushed the comparisons away. She liked the mingled aromas
of leather and fresh goods, but the store was cold unless you
were quite near the potbellied stove that sat in the middle of
the room. The stove was surrounded by a selection of mismatched chairs, some occupied, some empty.

"Pick out some potatoes, Rebecca, and then look at those
onions."

Rebecca wasn't certain exactly what she was looking for,
but she picked out the ones that seemed to be freshest.

Angel did some wandering on her own and found pickles,
tins of peaches, and some laundry soap. She scanned Rebecca's basket, and then they shopped together for a time before heading to the counter with enough food to last them
several days if not a week. Angel had been kind enough to introduce her to the store owner, and Angel was still explaining
things to Rebecca as they started toward the door.

"Hello, Angel," a deep voice spoke just as they left the
building. "Working tonight?"

"Yes, I am, Cradwell. Not that it's any of your business."

Cradwell's smile was mocking. "Everything having to do
with the competition is my business." His gaze shifted to
Rebecca. Stark interest lit his eyes.

"I hadn't heard that the Bell had a new girl."

"It doesn't," Angel informed him baldly. "This is Rebecca
Buchanan. You may call her *Miss* Buchanan, Cradwell, and
don't get any ideas."

"My, my," Cradwell now mocked her in earnest. "This
must be a little sister or a cousin to hear you talk like that.
Why, you'd think she was a real lady the way you protect her."

"She is a real lady, but then you wouldn't know." Angel's voice was frigid. "You wouldn't know a real lady if she dropped a scented handkerchief on your filthy boots."

In fine humor, Angel was incredible; angry, she was magnificent. Head held high, she turned and swept down the boardwalk as if she owned the boards herself. Rebecca had no choice but to follow in her wake. It should have been a comfort to her that Angel was ready and willing to protect and stand up for her, but it wasn't. Why did everyone treat her like a child, or some delicate little flower to cosset and protect? Aunt Hannah had been obsessed. Even Lavena and her father had tried to keep her world small and protected. Her thoughts made Rebecca boil. By the time they reached the house, she was in a fine fury.

"Why did you say all of those things?" She let Angel have it as soon as the door closed.

"All what things?" Angel was surprised but didn't show it.

"About my being a lady! You don't know anything about me, Angel. For all you know I've—" She cut off when Angel stepped forward and reached for one of her hands. Rebecca didn't resist but watched as the older woman turned it palm up, examined it, and let it go.

"I may not know *you*, Rebecca, but I know what my eyes tell me." Her voice was soft and resolute. "Your hands are covered with blisters. You've never done a day's housework in your life. And your dress. It may have a stain and a small tear on the cuff, but you won't find any fabric in Pine Grove to equal it. I know a lady when I see one, Rebecca—even if she doesn't have a scented hankie."

Rebecca couldn't say a word. She might indeed be a lady, but she was tired of being protected.

"What is really bothering you, Rebecca?" Angel asked. She had watched the emotions chase across the younger woman's face but not found any answers.

"I think I can take care of myself."

"Is that why you ran?"

"No." Rebecca didn't pretend ignorance. "It's not why I ran, but now that I'm away, I think I can fend for myself."

"Can you, Rebecca? Are you sure about that?"

"I don't know what you mean."

"I mean, if you had met Cradwell on your own—if I hadn't been there—how would you have handled him?"

Rebecca shrugged. "I don't want to get involved with any man, Angel. Surely I have a right to that decision. I'd have just walked right on by."

Angel shook her head very slowly. "He's married to the sheriff's sister, Rebecca. He's been accused of attacking women on several occasions but never even arrested."

"Attacking women?" The words were nearly choked out.

"Yes, Rebecca. The eyes Cradwell turned on you were not trying to gauge the cut of your dress. They were trying to imagine you without the dress."

All color drained from Rebecca's face. Her eyes were huge as she stared at Angel. Dan chose that moment to walk in. He found the women facing one another in the kitchen. Confrontation was nothing new to him, so he did not shy away from it, but he never expected to find it here.

Without taking her eyes from Rebecca's face, Angel spoke to him.

"Dan, please take Rebecca into the parlor. I'll work on supper tonight."

Rebecca made no protest when Dan took her arm. He led her to the settee and then sat down beside her.

"Do you want to tell me what happened?"

Rebecca looked at him and then away. It was beyond humiliation. She could never tell him what Angel had said about Cradwell's intentions.

"I think you'll feel better," Dan coaxed.

Rebecca looked down at the hands in her lap. "We met this man on the street, and Angel didn't think I could have taken care of myself if I'd been alone."

"Well, depending on the man, she was probably right."

Rebecca turned to look at him. "Meaning?"

"Only that you're new in town. The Bell is a respectable place, so Angel is well liked and has quite a network of friends. A man would think twice before pushing his attention onto her, but with you there would be no one to stop him."

"But I didn't do anything to encourage him, Dan. I didn't even speak to him."

Dan shook his head. "With some men it wouldn't matter."

Rebecca looked utterly defeated. She didn't want to live in fear of going to the store. It hadn't been like that in Boulder, but then her father had been well known and respected there. In Pine Grove she was a nobody. Angel had taken her in when she was lost and alone, but outside of Dan, Angel, and now the owner of the general store, she didn't know a soul.

Dan silently watched the emotions pass across her face and grew more captivated by the second. He ate supper with them again and waited while Angel changed so they could walk to work together. It didn't occur to Rebecca until after Angel left that she'd been in a cloud for days. She didn't even know what Dan did at the Silver Bell.

Rebecca attacked the supper pots and pans with unusual vigor, ignoring her fatigue and the pain in the small of her back. It was time she made a place for herself in this town. Marriage or no, there was nothing in her past to draw her back to Boulder. Travis had not really wanted her anyway. Yes, it would be easier to live on the ranch and be waited on, but what had that gained her so far? Nothing. From now on, she was on her own.

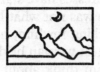

14

The days began to meld one into another for Angel and Rebecca, and it was surprising how comfortable they became with each other after Rebecca's blow-up. Their conversations had never ranged too far into the personal, but Rebecca now allowed herself to be protected by Angel. At the same time she ventured out in ways she had never done before. She even started her own business. It was quite by accident, but it was prompted by a comment Dan made about his laundry.

"It's not my favorite job, but that's probably because I'm so picky."

"Well," Rebecca said kindly. "In your job you have to look well pressed." She had finally learned that he worked as an assistant to Preston and also served drinks and changed large bills. She had never been in the Sliver Bell, but from both Dan's and Angel's clothing, she could tell it was one of Colorado's finer restaurants.

"That's true, but I get sick of washing my shirts."

"Surely there's someone you could hire to take care of it, Dan. Maybe the woman you board from."

Dan shook his head. "No, she's not all that neat herself. I wouldn't trust her with my good shirts."

"I could do it." What had prompted Rebecca to say such a thing she didn't know, but the words were out.

Dan began to shake his head, but warming to the idea, Rebecca kept on.

"I could, Dan. I've been working for Angel three weeks now, and she says her dresses have started to look very good."

Dan eyed her. This was not what he had in mind. He did not want Rebecca working for him, he wanted her living for him. She was the sweetest woman he'd ever met, the only one who had ever made him think about settling down, but she truly wanted friendship and nothing more from him. There had been times when they'd had physical contact, an occasional bump or brush of the hand, but she now felt so at ease with him that she only smiled and moved away. His own heart had pounded, and several times he had broken out in sweat, but his nearness did not have the same effect on her.

Dan still didn't know how she'd coaxed him into taking his laundry. It must have been the appeal in those chocolate-drop eyes, but one minute he was saying no and the next minute he was agreeing. And that had been only the beginning. The night Dan had dropped off his first load of shirts, Angel had been on hand. She surveyed the situation with shrewd eyes but didn't say anything until after Dan left.

"You're doing his laundry, Becky?" she asked, using the name she had come to calling her.

"Oh, Angel." Rebecca's hand flew to her mouth. "I never thought to ask you."

"That's not it, Becky," Angel said honestly. "I just don't want you to work yourself into an early grave or cheat yourself. Is it just for Dan?"

"Right now, yes, but he told me he could spread the word."

Angel eyed her. "Are you certain you're charging enough?"

"I think so." She named an amount that made Angel's brows shoot in the air. The older woman didn't say anything, but two nights later when Dan showed up with the two waiters who worked at the Silver Bell, Rebecca told them they would have to pay extra for ironing. They didn't so much as blink an eye when they agreed and handed her their shirts. She told Dan when they were alone that his would be the original price since he was a friend, and Dan had looked very amused as he kissed her on the cheek and gone on his way.

Now two more weeks had passed, and it was finally their night off. Angel didn't work on Monday night, and Rebecca had started taking the day off as well. She had become quite proficient in the kitchen, but on Mondays she fixed a light meal and took it easy. With few dishes to occupy her this evening, Angel was teaching her to play cards.

"You've never played any card games?"

"No. I was raised by my aunt, and she didn't allow them."

"Where was this?"

"Philadelphia."

"Philadelphia? I was born there!"

"Angel! Were you really?"

"Yes. We were only passing through, but that's where the big event happened."

"Your family was traveling?"

"Yes. We had come up from the South and were headed to my aunt's home in New York, but my mother went into labor and we never made it. We ended up settling in Pennsylvania for a time, but my father took off when he couldn't find work and never returned."

"What happened to all of you?"

"We drifted apart after that, one by one. I was raised by my older sister, who did whatever she had to do for money. We ended up traveling a lot."

Rebecca bit her lip. She had never known anyone with such an awful upbringing. Angel did not seem overly upset by it. Her voice was neutral, bored even, but Rebecca could imagine the pain.

"Do you have regrets, Angel? Do you wish it could have been different?"

"Just with my mother," she admitted. "She died an awful death. I'll never forget it."

Rebecca did not press her. Angel's voice had changed with the mention of her mother; there was no disguising the hurt.

"Why don't I see if the coffee is still hot?"

"Oh, that sounds good. Have we got any of that cake left?"

"Yes," Rebecca told her and rose. "We've only had one piece each. Dan might have had two."

"Well, you wouldn't know it by you, Becky," Angel said with a good-natured laugh. "For all the hard work you do, you're starting to look like you ate the whole cake. It's all right in your stomach." Angel felt herself go cold as soon as the words were out of her mouth.

"I *am* putting on weight," Rebecca said with exasperation, her back to Angel. "It must be the potatoes. I've never worked so hard in my life, but my dresses are all getting tight. It doesn't seem fair."

Rebecca moved to the table bearing two steaming mugs. She put them both down before she looked into Angel's pale face.

"What's the matter?"

"Becky," she began softly. "When you ran—" She had to clear her throat and start again. "When you ran and came here, were you running from a man?"

Rebecca's face showed confusion and a little hurt. She opened her mouth and shut it again.

"Becky," Angel went on, her voice still quiet. "All the weight you're gaining is in your waist. Is there any chance—"

Angel cut off when Rebecca began to grope for the chair. She watched as she sat down hard, her face a mask of shock. She kept shaking her head and opening her mouth, but no words came out. The reality hit Angel like a blow. Fury exploded inside her that a man would play games with this innocent girl. She stood like an enraged warrior.

"They're all the same!" she spat. "Men can be disgusting, I tell you. Enlighten me, Becky." Her voice was now dripping with sarcasm. "Tell me about this wonderful specimen of manhood who came into your world, got you with child, and then left—or did he throw you out?"

She began to pace now. "If he were here right now, I'd have it out with him. Of all the low down, sick actions! I am disgusted by men who leave a trail of fatherless children and wounded mothers."

"Angel."

"I mean it, Becky, if he were here I'd be tempted to shoot him on the spot. Here you are working yourself to death, and he's probably off having the time of his miserable life!"

"Angel." Rebecca spoke the second time and finally got through. Angel turned and immediately looked contrite. Rebecca had never seen her so out of control, but now Angel's eyes were filled with compassion.

"Listen to me carry on. I'm sorry, Becky. I was just so surprised. No wonder you left. Actually," she reasoned, "he probably sent you away."

"No, I left," Rebecca told her quietly, and Angel finally stopped talking all together. "I was the one to go, and he did marry me, but I ran anyway."

Angel Flanagan, who had seen all and heard all, was utterly speechless. Rebecca was married. Her sweet, innocent housekeeper was a wife. It just couldn't be. She remembered the way Rebecca stumbled over her name the night they'd met, but until now she'd given it no thought. She was not a woman to pry, but her speechlessness was deserting her fast. She had to have answers.

"I want to ask you some questions, Becky, but I don't want to intrude."

Rebecca felt a numbness settling over her. "It doesn't matter."

She sounded so lifeless that Angel became alarmed. She knew she would have to keep her emotion out of it.

"When was all this, Becky?" Her voice became businesslike.

"In February. My father was dying. He wanted me taken care of, so he insisted I marry his foreman."

Angel licked her lips. "And did you live as husband and wife?"

127

"Well, yes, I mean, I think so."

"Did you share a bed?"

Rebecca nodded. "For three nights."

"Did he hurt you?"

"No," Rebecca whispered, the memory surfacing swiftly. "He was wonderful, but then my father died."

Angel's eyes closed in pain, but for just an instant. "I think I can guess why you ran, but I'm not exactly sure."

"It was the ranch," Rebecca told her. "I found out that the ranch was the only reason he married me."

Angel nodded, but this was not what she thought at all. A man who had treated her tenderly, but married her only for the ranch? It didn't really make much sense. And the baby. It had all been such a short time ago. *Did the father know there was a child?* Impossible, Angel decided. Becky had only just realized herself. *But would the man care? Had he looked for Becky or just let her go?* These and many other questions swarmed through Angel's mind, but before long her thoughts zeroed in on one thing: the child.

"Becky, when was all this, I mean, the exact date?"

"I was married on February 15." The numbness was still there, and she felt chilled, but she answered automatically.

"And you spent your wedding night together?"

"Yes."

"Is there a chance you were pregnant before this?"

Rebecca shook her head, the soft waves of her hair bouncing against her cheeks and shoulders.

"This is only April 3," Angel contemplated aloud. "You're awfully big for just six weeks."

"Maybe I'm not really—"

She cut off when Angel shook her head.

"Look at yourself, Becky," the older woman returned gently. "It can't be anything else. Your arms and shoulders are thinner, but your breasts and waistline are fuller. Haven't you missed your monthly time?"

"I have, but I didn't give any thought to it. What am I going to do?"

"What are you going to do?" Angel repeated in surprise. "You're going to have a baby, that's what you're going to do."

Rebecca didn't cry, but she looked utterly defeated. She could feel Angel's eyes on her but didn't look up. How long would it be before her pregnancy would be obvious to everyone? What pride she had been guilty of. She was going to show this town what she was made of, but now she was only going to look like an unwed mother. And Travis. He hadn't wanted to share the ranch with her, but what about their baby? Did he have the right to know? What was she to do about him?

Suddenly she was overwhelmingly tired. She felt drugged, or as though she hadn't slept in days. In a small voice she said, "I don't really care to play cards tonight, Angel. I'm awfully tired all of a sudden."

"All right. Why don't you go on to bed. We can talk again tomorrow."

Rebecca nodded and rose.

"I'm going to go for a walk, Becky. I'll check on you when I come in."

Rebecca didn't comment, but Angel knew she had heard. She sat alone at the table for some minutes, waiting for the quiet upstairs that would tell her Rebecca was in bed. At that point she went to get a light wrap and blew out the lantern. The door opened soundlessly as she let herself outside.

~

"Well now," Preston spoke easily when Angel came quietly into his office. "Angel Flanagan visiting the Silver Bell on her night off. I think this might be a first."

Angel's smile was distracted, but knowing she was welcome she stepped in and took a chair across the desk. Preston put the papers he'd been reading aside and simply stared at her for a moment. Finally he said, "What can I do for you, Angel?"

She sighed. "I hate to ask it, Preston, but is there any chance I could have a raise?"

"I think it's possible. Can you tell me what's on your mind?"

Angel hesitated. She knew that Preston would stay quiet, but what did it matter? The way Rebecca's shape was changing, her pregnancy wouldn't be a secret for long.

"Rebecca is expecting."

"I see."

"No, you don't," Angel said patiently, "but I'll explain. She's married but didn't realize her condition until just tonight. I want to be able to give her a little more money. That's the reason for the raise."

"Why doesn't she just go back to her husband?"

"She doesn't want to right now, and I for one would never force her. She's doing Dan's laundry and some shirts for a few of the boys here, but I don't want her to take on any more than that. I'm not sure what babies cost, but I think we'd better start putting something aside now."

The use of the word "we" and the tender look in her eyes were not lost on Preston. He stared at the woman across from him for a full 30 seconds, his heart finally admitting that he was in love with Angel Flanagan. But he would have been foolish to try to reckon with his feelings at the time. He forced his mind back to Rebecca.

"What is it about this girl, Angel? Both you and Dan seem so attracted."

Angel shrugged, her face more open and vulnerable than Preston had ever seen.

"I don't know, Preston. She's like the kid sister I never had. She's so sweet and unassuming, and so innocent I'm afraid to let her out of my sight. Now I find out that she's expecting."

"Are you sure she's not having one on you, Angel?"

"I'm sure. I was the one to point out to her that she must be pregnant. I thought she might faint. I can assure you, there was no pretense."

They were quiet for several seconds before the man spoke.

"Well, plan on your raise this week." He smiled just slightly. "I'll have to come by sometime and meet this woman I'm supporting."

"Why don't you come to dinner?" Angel asked kindly. Again, Preston was amazed at the change in her.

"Rebecca always has supper ready for me before I go to work. You could eat with us before we have to come here."

"All right." Preston knew that his voice sounded different as well. "What night?"

"Thursday. Come Thursday about 4:00."

Preston nodded.

"I'll ask Dan too. He comes often anyway."

Angel had stood now and was at the door when Preston spoke again.

"Does he know about Rebecca's baby?"

"No. He's got to be told, but it's really her affair. I know she doesn't see his feelings for her."

Angel said the words but heard them as if someone else had spoken. She looked into Preston's eyes, and for a moment she couldn't move or speak. It was some seconds before she nearly whispered, "I'll see you here tomorrow night."

"All right, Angel," Preston's voice, equally soft, sounded like a caress. "And I'll plan on Thursday."

Angel didn't say anything else before she left, but her eyes told Preston that she was pleased about his coming; surprised by the fact, but very pleased indeed.

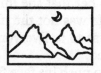

15

Rebecca woke slowly, her mind full of the night before. In the last few weeks she had become adept at retreating into her own little dream world, but now it was time to face the truth. She was having Travis' baby. She had run away from the man but now carried his child.

Not able to sleep after she heard Angel leave, Rebecca had lit the lamp again and slipped the nightgown back over her head. With the curtains drawn against the night, she stood before the mirror and made herself face the facts. There was no getting over the bulge in her abdomen or the thickness of her waist. She was going to have a baby. Not even 20 years old, and only three nights with her husband, but she was going to have a child.

At that point she couldn't do any more. She had climbed back into bed and fallen instantly asleep. She hadn't even heard Angel come in or check on her, but now, with the morning light peeking around the curtain, it was time to rise and make plans.

She decided almost instantly not to contact Travis. She was not afraid of him, but neither did she want him involved. It never occurred to her how she would feel if Travis kept a child of theirs away from her. She knew only that she didn't trust him right now. She *had* trusted him, but now she felt used. She asked herself how she would feel if she were to learn that she'd been all wrong about the situation. How would she respond if she learned that Travis loved *her* and not the ranch? The idea was so inconceivable to her that she immediately dismissed it. He'd had his chance. He was not the man her father thought, and that was all there was to it. Everyone made errors in judgment, her father included.

Rebecca struggled to push his face from her mind—not the Travis of the last few days, hurting and distant, but the Travis who had met her at the stage office and had taken her on walks and held her hand, treating her like she was a rare bloom.

But that didn't last for long, did it? Her anger sparked unaccountably and without warning. *He certainly didn't want to stop at holding my hand, and now I'll have a baby to show for it!*

That Rebecca was not thinking logically was not entirely clear to her. Her emotions were too close to the surface. It was true that she had been coerced into marrying Travis, but for some reason her father's role failed to surface in her memory. Travis Buchanan had not forced her into anything, but before she rose for the day she was convinced that the only thing her husband had *ever* wanted was to own the Double Star and to get her into bed for a few nights.

It was unfortunate for Dan that he came in just after Rebecca had decided all men were dogs. She seemed glad to see him, and even told herself that this man was different, but her heart was a bit wary. Dan had no idea about the storm that had brewed in her mind a few hours earlier.

"Can I talk you into joining me for a picnic lunch?" he asked with a kind smile.

"Is it that warm out?" she asked him.

"You'll need a sweater, but I know a place that's protected by some rocks. We'll never feel the wind."

Rebecca smiled, feeling pleased all of a sudden, and Dan took that as a yes.

"Who knows," he went on innocently, his voice light and teasing. "Maybe I'll even be lucky and steal a kiss."

The eyes that Rebecca turned to him were so cold that Dan blinked.

"I thought we were just friends," she told him stonily.

"We are," Dan said gently, thinking he understood but sorry he had opened his mouth.

"Then why would you even think about kissing me?"

Dan's heart melted. Still not understanding the situation, he approached. His hands went to the arms that Rebecca held stiffly at her side. He rubbed ever so gently, his voice tender.

"Rebecca, I was not threatening you, but I'm not made of wood either. A man would have to be dead not to be affected by your sweetness." Dan's hand pushed a stray curl from her cheek. "Not to mention the fact that you're a very lovely and desirable woman."

Rebecca's eyes shot sparks. "Friends?"

Dan stared at her outraged face and calmly said, "Yes, Rebecca. Friends."

"Be *friendly* to Rebecca," she went on coldly. "And what will that get me? Probably *another* baby!"

Dan's mouth literally swung open. He had never heard her talk like that. Indeed, he hadn't thought her capable of such thoughts. She had voiced her thoughts so loudly that Angel had awakened. Dan caught her at the edge of his vision as she joined them just inside the kitchen, but he kept his gaze on Rebecca.

Not having fully taken in what she had just said, Dan tried to make amends.

"Rebecca, what is wrong? What did I say?"

"You know very well what you said." With that she burst into tears, brushed past both Dan and Angel, and bolted from the room. They both stood still long after her bedroom door slammed shut upstairs. Some minutes passed before Dan looked at Angel. She was still in the doorway, a robe thrown carelessly over her frame.

"I just asked her for a picnic," Dan said, "and teased her about stealing a kiss. She got upset when I told her she was desirable. What woman doesn't want to hear that, Angel? And what is this talk about a baby?"

Angel thought that if her heart got any softer she would melt, but Dan's words were almost too much for her. She told him to sit down and checked the coffeepot. It was fairly warm, and before joining him, she poured them both a cup of stale coffee.

"She's pregnant," Angel told him straight out. "She realized it only last night. And what's more, Dan, she's married. I didn't know that until last night either."

Angel watched as the color drained away from Dan's face. She knew he had it bad, but not until she'd looked into his stricken eyes did she realize how bad.

"Who is this man?" he finally strangled out.

"I don't know. She hasn't wanted to share much, and I haven't pressed her. It doesn't really matter, at least not to me. I went to Preston last night about a raise. That way Rebecca won't need to take on any more laundry than she already has."

"She's not going to do *any* laundry in her condition!" Dan thundered, but Angel shook her head.

"We can't do that do her, Dan. I want her to take it easy, but I think that, baby or not, she's discovering who she is for the first time. As for the man, if he could let a woman like Rebecca get away, he doesn't deserve her."

Dan sat for barely a moment and then spoke fervently. "Nothing has changed for me, Angel. I don't care about the other man or the baby or anything. I care about Rebecca. I've got to make her see that."

"Well, don't start by telling her you don't care about the baby."

"No, of course not, I just meant—"

"I know, Dan, but that was my clumsy way of saying you're going to have to go easy."

Dan nodded, his eyes moving to the ceiling as though he could see through the boards. "I'm not leaving here until I talk to her."

Angel, not knowing whether that was wise or not, felt it best to keep her mouth shut.

"Look at yourself," Rebecca, now dry-eyed, hissed at her own reflection. "You've enjoyed his attention, and now you know what he wants. He wants what all men want! When are you going to grow up and face facts?"

With a move that was almost vicious, Rebecca grabbed her thick blonde hair and scraped it back away from her face. The style was too severe—it hardened her eyes and made her face look thin—but she found a piece of string and ruthlessly tied the hair back. She glared at her own reflection, vowing not to cry again.

How stupid to react the way she had. What did she care if Dan desired her? Well, let him. No man was going to use her ever again. Not Dan, Travis, or anyone. Ever! Dan's knock cut into her angry musings, but Rebecca remained stubbornly silent.

"Rebecca." The knock sounded again. "Are you in there?"

Still she stood mute.

"I want to talk to you."

"Well, I *don't* want to talk to you," she told him when she couldn't hold the words in any longer.

"That's too bad," Dan spoke sternly. "If you're not dressed, you better get behind the screen, because I'm coming in."

The door opened before Rebecca could move or protest. She was across the room from Dan but showed her disapproval by moving to the window and looking down at the backyard. The door did not close, but Rebecca knew Dan stood looking at her.

"You could have just told me about your husband and the baby." His voice was soft.

"It's none of your business." Her retort was deliberately brutal.

"Well, I'm making it my business."

"You have no right," Rebecca told him, spinning from the glass. "It's none of your concern."

"Everything about you concerns me, Rebecca, and this is no different."

His tone and the look in his eyes completely disarmed her. For a moment she stared at him. Dan stared right back.

"I want you to take it easy," he finally said.

"You're not going to tell me what to do, Dan."

"As long as you take it easy, I won't, but I meant what I said. You're going to take it slow."

"And I meant what I said, you're not—"

"I'll tell everyone the baby's mine and that we're getting married if you don't do as I tell you."

Rebecca was thunderstruck. Her mouth opened but then closed again. He could do it. She knew he could do exactly as he said, and everyone would believe him. She didn't want that. She had been prepared to stand up to him, but she was helpless against this. The fire left her in a hurry. Watching her shoulders slump, Dan thought he'd gone too far, but when he went to her side she did not push away.

"I'm thinking of you, and I'm thinking of the baby, Rebecca." His voice was no longer stern. "I don't want you to take on any more than you are right now."

Thinking logically for the first time in hours, Rebecca saw the wisdom of his words. After all, she still had extra laundry to do as well as Angel's jobs. At last she nodded silently and let her eyes stray to the window again. Dan wanted above all else to take her into his arms, but he restrained himself. Maybe in time he could still find a way. Maybe in time he could show her how he felt.

To cover his emotions, he cleared his throat and said, "What did you do to your hair, anyway?"

Rebecca's chin rose in the air, a gesture Dan had never seen before.

"I pulled it back. Do you like it?"

"No, I don't," he said honestly but kindly.

"Then I'll leave it up," she snapped. Dan had to work at not smiling. Something told him he was headed into a new phase with Rebecca, one that might not be all that fun. However, nothing short of a broken neck would cause him to miss it.

~

"You don't have any color in your face at all," Angel commented on Thursday afternoon. "Why not let me use a little tint from my jars upstairs?"

"It doesn't matter," Rebecca told her succinctly. "I'm not a hostess at the Silver Bell."

"Meaning?" Angel pressed her, and Rebecca turned to look at her across the dining room.

"Angel." She sounded as though she were addressing a child. "What does it matter what I look like for dinner with friends? In your job you have to look good. I don't."

"But you have to care, Becky. I mean, your hair and everything—it's like you no longer care at all."

Rebecca put her hands on her hips. "Shall we talk about what my vanity got me, Angel? Pregnant, that's what! And Dan wanting to kiss me besides. Now, I'm not conceited enough to think that Preston is going to drop at my feet, but neither am I going to doll myself up because he's coming over."

"But Dan's coming too, and I—"

"Dan sees me every day, Angel." Rebecca was bent over the table and not really attending Angel, "and knows what I look like. Beyond that, I don't care. In fact, I may take pains to look even worse."

"What do you mean?"

"Bruno seems to think I need company too."

"Bruno? Bruno who works at the Silver Bell?"

"That's the one. He winked at me when he picked his shirts up this morning." Rebecca turned to look at Angel. "And that was with my hair pulled back!"

Rebecca spun back to the table, and Angel covered the smile that spread over her mouth. What a changed girl Rebecca was from even the beginning of the week! Monday night she realized she was in a family way, and by Thursday she was telling both Dan and Angel what she would and would not do. She did laundry all day Wednesday, cleaned the house Thursday, *and* prepared a gorgeous supper for four.

It concerned Angel that Rebecca had begun to look at men as the enemy, but wasn't she like that herself? She and Dan had been friends for a long time, and Preston had always dealt honestly with her, but there weren't many men she trusted.

With Preston coming to mind, Rebecca and her situation momentarily faded from Angel's thoughts. Had she really seen something different in Preston's face on Monday night? It was so hard to know. Nothing seemed to have altered between them as she worked all week, but he had been so ready to accept her dinner invitation that night. They had never socialized before, not in five years' time, but now, with little or no warning, he'd been more than willing to come to dinner. Angel mentally shrugged. She was getting fanciful. He was probably just starved for a home-cooked meal.

16

Preston was a man who liked to have a cigar after a good meal, but this afternoon he refrained. Angel wouldn't have batted an eyelash, and Dan might have joined him, but Rebecca did indeed look like a woman who needed tender care. He thought she would be much more attractive with her hair down, but as it was, she was very lovely and brought out feelings in him that he hadn't known existed.

What had Angel said? Something about the kid sister she never had. Preston now knew what she meant. He hadn't expected to share Angel's feelings, but in some ways it was a relief to have Rebecca distract him. Otherwise he would have been gawking at his hostess. Because he and Angel had never socialized, he had never seen her like she looked this afternoon.

There had never been a time when she didn't seem alluring, but this afternoon, dressed in a simple cotton dress, her hair pulled back at the sides but not piled atop her head, she was so approachable that Preston nearly embraced her. He could almost feel how wonderful it would be to pull her close and bury his hands in the thick fall of her hair.

He realized suddenly that he had been staring at her a little too long. He forced his gaze around the room and again felt surprise. Having Angel greet him in a cotton gown with her hair around her shoulders was hard enough to take in, but her house was another story all together. It was remarkably homey. Preston

141

thought he could have laid money on the fact that it would be elegant like the Silver Bell, but nothing could be further from the truth. There were simple lace curtains on the windows, and the little endtables had doilies on them like ones he might have found at his grandma's house. There were pillows on the chairs and sofa, ruffled edges and all.

"Coffee, Preston?" Angel stood at his elbow and asked. He pulled his eyes from the room to focus on the woman who occupied much of his thoughts.

"Thank you." He knew he sounded stiff, but years of covering his feelings did not dissolve in a week.

"Sugar?" Angel asked, and he looked on in amazement when she blushed.

Angel gave a nervous glance. "I guess I don't know if you like anything in your coffee or not."

"Just black, thank you." This time he managed to sound a little less formal.

Watching them from across the room, Rebecca wondered at the interchange. Just as Rebecca had become more bold in the past week, Angel had become more tender. However, Rebecca never thought to see her flustered or blushing. She glanced at Dan, who warned her with his eyes to stay quiet.

"I'd better get changed for work," Angel said suddenly, fully expecting Preston to say he was going on ahead of her. He surprised her.

"I'll wait for you, Angel. You go ahead, Dan, and if anyone is looking for me, tell them I'll be right along."

"All right, Preston. Thank you for supper, Rebecca. You've learned a lot in a few weeks."

Rebecca smiled at him. "I think all the credit can be given to my instructor."

Dan smiled as well, kissed her cheek, and a few seconds later went on his way. Rebecca turned. She was alone with Preston. She took a seat across from him, thinking comfortably how easy it was for a woman when she didn't care whether or not she attracted a man.

"I forgot to ask you, Preston," she began. "Do you own the Silver Bell or just manage it?"

"I own it," he told her kindly. "I didn't start it, but I own it."

"How did you come to own it?"

"In a poker game," he said easily, and Rebecca felt her jaw drop.

Preston laughed. "I think I've surprised you."

"You have," she admitted. "I didn't think that kind of thing really happened; I mean, you hear about it, but it seems too fabulous to be real."

Preston was still smiling. "It's not quite as glamorous as it sounds. The Bell was little more than a soup kitchen when I won it. It was called the Silver Spur, but I thought the name Silver Bell had more class. I added the bar and stage."

Rebecca shook her head. "I know so little about business. Are some times of the year busier than others?"

"Absolutely. When it's cold, and no one wants to search in the snow for gold or silver, things are much busier."

Rebecca had the impression that this was a subject he loved, and she would have elaborated, but both of them heard Angel coming down the stairs. Preston stood. Angel stopped for an instant and looked at him, then ducked her head. She was at her most glamorous. Her hair was piled high, bright purple feathers sprouted from the fat curls atop her head, and her face was made up to perfection. Her dress was gold satin, elegant in its simplicity, and a perfect foil for the gold highlights of her hair. For the first time Rebecca wondered how old Angel might be. She was one of those women who looked good right out of bed, and even without the makeup. Rebecca could only guess at her age.

"Well, Becky," the older woman turned, seeming relieved for a place to look. "I guess we're off. Thank you for supper."

"You're welcome. Have a good evening, and I'll see you tomorrow."

"Thank you, Rebecca," Preston added. "I'll have to have you over to the Bell sometime and show you a little of my own hospitality."

143

"I'll plan on that, Preston. Thank you." Even as she said this, Rebecca thought that it wouldn't be long before her shape prevented her from going anywhere at all. She tried not to let it depress her.

As always, thoughts of her shape brought on thoughts of the baby. It was becoming clear to her that she hadn't truly accepted the reality of her pregnancy. When it would sink in, she didn't know, but it was the last thing she wanted to dwell on at present.

Boulder

Travis looked at the calendar on the desk, his eyes staring at the date until they burned. His wife was 20 years old today. He had no idea where she was. He had no clue as to whether or not she was even alive, but this was May 15, Rebecca's birthday.

How many towns had he searched? How many people had he asked? He had even gone so far as to put a personal ad in the *Denver Daily News*. It read simply:

Please come home, Reba.
—T.

He knew there was little hope, but the disappointment he felt when he heard nothing told him he had wanted to hear something.

A deep sigh left him feeling tired and without expectations. With both Rebecca and Andrew gone, Travis grew restless in the study. It was a beautiful room, but the date on the calendar seemed to haunt him. He moved out the door to pace in the living room until he grew hungry, but the sight of the food Lavena set before him made him feel sick.

An hour later he still sat alone at the dinner table. He had made Lucky Harwell his foreman. Lucky still bunked with the men, but he ate inside. However, the younger man had a date tonight. Travis couldn't remember the girl's name, but Lucky had been more serious with her than any of the others.

144

Lavena chose that moment to bustle into the room. She caught him staring across the table at nothing.

"There isn't going to be anything left of you! You pick at breakfast, and you pick at lunch! Now eat, Travis!" With that she stormed from the room, but Travis still did not reach for his fork.

Where is my wife? I think I would know if she were dead. She can't stay away forever, but it already feels like an eternity. Where is my wife? Despair threatened to overwhelm him, and for the first time in many months Travis tried to pray.

Pine Grove

It had taken Dan a good deal of time to believe that Rebecca was expecting, but there was no doubting the evidence now. Summer and fall had come and gone. With the calendar turning to November, it was obvious that Rebecca was well and truly in a family way. The doctor had talked like it might be twins. Angel did not believe it. Rebecca, Angel reasoned, was a small woman, and she didn't hesitate in telling Dan her opinion.

"And," she went on to him. "Rebecca told me her husband is a large man."

"Angel," Dan replied patiently, "he'd have to be a giant to have a baby that large."

Angel shook her head as if he hadn't spoken. "Becky's frame is very tiny. Look at her wrists."

"How many women have you known who had babies?"

"Not many, but—" Angel began quietly, but Dan cut her off.

"The doctor even thinks it might be twins."

"It's *not* twins," she replied adamantly.

"But what if it is, Angel?" Dan tried to reason with her.

"It won't be."

Dan fell silent. Why did Angel have such a problem with twins? He wanted to pursue the matter further, but Preston came in and found them talking in his office.

"Well, now, you called a meeting in my office but didn't bother to tell me."

Neither Dan nor Angel commented. Preston wasn't upset; he was even smiling a little.

"We're discussing Rebecca," Dan told him.

"She's due any time, isn't she?"

"Yes. The doctor told Dan it might be twins, but it's not."

Both men stared at Angel until she became irritated. Knowing his presence would only make things worse, Dan excused himself to head back to the dining room. Angel had still not said anything, but she turned for the door as well. Preston beat her to it, and by the time she tried the knob, he'd come up and put his hand against the top. Angel turned to lean against it, her eyes angry and defensive. Preston was as calm as usual.

"Strip off the veneer, Angel," he said quietly. "What's really going on?"

"I don't know what you're talking about. She's not having twins, and that's all there is to it."

"Do you hear yourself?" he asked her, his voice still soft. Their relationship was on more personal terms than ever, but there were still walls between them. "She could be having twins, Angel. You can deny it forever, but it won't change the facts."

She couldn't look at him. He was standing very close; she could feel the warmth from his body. It was tempting to lay her head on his chest and sob, but Angel reminded herself she didn't have those types of needs. Why that was hard to believe right now, she didn't examine too closely.

"Angel." Preston's voice came again, and this time she looked at him. "Talk to me."

She looked into his eyes, and as he'd commanded, the surface paint fell away. Her gaze shifted from him once again, and her voice grew flat and hopeless.

"My mother died having twins. She was enormous with them. My father had left us, so it was just my sister and me.

My mother tried to deliver for days and finally gave up and bled to death. The babies died inside her."

Preston closed his eyes. He had not known. He never even suspected. He thought Angel must have come from a background as rocky as his own, but it had never been his place to ask. Angel looked exhausted, as if the weight of the world had fallen on her shoulders. Gazing intently at her profile, Preston spoke to her kindly, but with conviction.

"How old were you?"

"I think I was eight." She still did not look at him.

"I can see how that would scar you for life, Angel, but it doesn't mean that what happened to your mother will happen to Rebecca. There is no reason for you to think that history is going to repeat itself. Rebecca will not be alone as your mother was. She'll probably be fine."

"Probably," Angel repeated dully.

Preston caught her jaw and forced her to look at him. He spoke when she met his eyes.

"I'd be a fool if I tried to promise you anything else, Angel, but for Rebecca's sake you've got to put your fears away."

Nothing he could have said would have carried more weight. Rebecca had not asked for this. Angel had made Rebecca her responsibility. Even if she was terrified inside, she must put on a brave front for the expectant mother. In truth, she'd known all along that the doctor was right. Rebecca would have twins; she felt it in her bones. She wasn't happy about it, but she would have to rise to the occasion as she had done all her life.

It took her a second to realize that Preston still held her jaw. Up to this point, physical contact between them had been nonexistent. Before she could stop herself, she stiffened. Preston noticed immediately and dropped his hand. Angel wanted to cry out when the shutters dropped back over his eyes and he stepped away.

"I guess you'd better get back out front," Preston said as he moved to his desk.

"Yes, I'll do that. Are you coming?"

"Not right now." He was already seated at the desk and didn't even look up. "Tell Dan to make sure the show starts on time."

Angel left, but she felt as if she'd just let something infinitely precious slip through her hands and shatter on the floor.

17

Rebecca very kindly timed her first contraction for the next Monday the women had off. It was early in the day, and because the pain startled her, Rebecca sat down as soon as she could get to a chair. Dan had told her the day before that he had plans and would not be around, and Angel was still asleep. Rebecca sat and wondered how long she would be alone. Not that she was afraid. She had become quite independent of late, and as uncomfortable as she'd become in the last few weeks, she was rather pragmatic about the whole thing.

There was, she knew, a certain amount of detachment involved. She didn't really know the little people inside of her, and only once had she let herself dwell on the fact that they might be boys who would look just like their father. The thought brought on tears that lasted far into the night and gave her a raging headache that lingered into the next morning. From that point forward she became more disinterested than ever. Now that the birth was seemingly upon her, she had only pain on her mind.

Angel came down at her usual time, and even before she reached the first floor she knew something was amiss. Typically she could smell the coffee brewing and the start of lunch. The small house was also too quiet. Since the stairway emptied into the living room, she got no further than the last step before she found Rebecca on the sofa.

"Has it started?" Angel asked with more calm than she felt. She approached swiftly.

"I think so. I only just lay down, but the pains have been coming since early this morning."

Angel felt sweat break out on her entire body. She forced herself to sound calm.

"Will you be all right while I run upstairs and get dressed?"

Rebecca smiled. "I've been alone so far, Angel." She looked up to see the strain in the older woman's eyes.

"I'll be fine," she said kindly, and was glad the next pain didn't hit until Angel had rushed from the room. It was obvious to her that Angel had never been involved in a birth before. She almost laughed at herself: *She* had never been involved either.

As the hours progressed, the clock slowed to a snail's pace. Angel thought she would go mad. It was close to midnight before Rebecca felt the need to push, and it was a good thing Dr. Creamer was on hand, because Angel was nearly catatonic by then. She couldn't have assisted if she had wanted to. She sat on a chair in the hall and listened to Rebecca pant, thinking she could scream for her. She refrained from such an act, but still felt unable to move or help in any way. It seemed like years passed, and even after the first tiny little wail broke the air, it took several seconds before she could respond.

"A boy," she heard the doctor tell Rebecca. Angel finally stood and moved into the room like a woman in a trance.

"There's another one there all right," the doctor was saying, "Just hold on, Rebecca. Fresh pains will start soon enough. Here, Angel." He turned to her. "Take this little one so my hands are free. I should have brought my nurse," he mumbled softly, placing the newly wrapped infant in Angel's hands.

She looked down at the baby and then glanced up to see Rebecca watching her with half-closed eyes. Angel had never seen the younger girl's face like that. As apathetic as she had become in the last weeks, Rebecca now looked beyond caring. Angel's mother had been like that too. Angel went to her side.

"Look at him, Becky. Your little boy."

"I'm so tired, Angel," she said softly, her eyes not focusing on anything. "I don't want any more pains, Angel. I'm too tired for more pain."

"It'll be okay, Becky." She forced herself into false heartiness. "Just a little more pushing, and you'll have another baby. I'll help you with everything. Maybe it will be a girl this time, or a brother for this little guy."

Rebecca tried to focus on her friend, and Angel talked on in a soft voice until the next pain hit. It wasn't more than three minutes, and only five more after that before another wail hit the air.

"Two boys!" Dr. Creamer's voice was jovial. "Twin boys, Rebecca. You're going to have your hands full!"

Rebecca managed a smile as her second son was passed into her arms. She had been so tired, but a jolt of excitement passed through her as she held him. Suddenly she felt like she could take on the world. Angel placed her first son in the crook of her arm.

"They're so tiny," Rebecca said with half a sob. "I can't believe how small they are."

Both babies had been crying, but now one, the second to be born, stopped abruptly.

"It's all right," Rebecca crooned to the first baby, everyone else in the room forgotten. She noticed that her quiet son was staring at her.

"Hello there," she whispered, and laughed breathlessly. "You're here," she said in wonder. "You're finally here." Again she gave a soft, incredulous laugh, and the first baby stopped crying as well.

"Do you feel better?" Rebecca asked softly, her head turned into his face. His tiny brow was creased in evident concentration, and Rebecca laughed in delight. She startled both babies in the process, and after a few minutes they began to howl again. Angel laughed as well and Rebecca turned, only just realizing she'd been there all along.

"I did it," she told the older woman, a smile stretching the corners of her mouth. Angel felt something clench around her heart. She hadn't seen such a look of joy and hope on Rebecca's face in many weeks.

"You did it," she agreed softly, clearing her throat. She wanted to say more, but her emotions were too close to the surface. These babies were so tiny, so vulnerable. It was easy to see how the cemetery could be filled with little graves. How did ones so small and helpless make it to adulthood?

Dr. Creamer interrupted her thoughts, and Angel's attention came back to the moment. Both babies were now crying in full voice, but Angel listened carefully as he explained to Rebecca how to care for them in the hours and days to come.

"They're both hungry, Rebecca. Nursing won't be comfortable at first, but the sooner you start to feed them the better. Come for me, Angel, if there's any problem."

With that he was gone, and Rebecca, still flat on her back, was left to Angel's care. Angel propped her up immediately, jostling the wailing infants in the process, and then helped Rebecca start nursing. It was a long process. Angel, bent over the bed, thought she would never be able to straighten her back again before the babies settled in and began to suck, but it was infinitely satisfying to have everything go quiet and to watch their little mouths work.

"Does it hurt?" Angel asked quietly. Her mother had never gotten this far.

Rebecca looked up, her face still alight with wonder. "Not really, but it feels strange." *Travis should be here.* The unbidden thought invaded her mind and wouldn't leave. *I've had his babies. I've had Travis' babies. I never dreamed how that would feel. Will I see his face when I look at them? Will they grow up and ask me where he is? Will they shoot up and tower over me with tall strength as he did?*

"Rebecca, are you all right?"

Rebecca's eyes flew to her friend. "I think so. Why did you ask?"

"Your face," Angel told her. "You looked as if you were in pain."

"I was thinking of their father," she admitted with a deep throb of agony. "I wonder what he would think."

Angel's eyes grew hard. "He should have given consideration to that before he married a woman for her property and slept with her without giving a thought to the consequences."

But I ran from him, Rebecca's heart reminded her. She didn't know what she was feeling. It was all too much to take in. She had given birth to Travis' twin boys. What if she'd been all wrong about him? She could be robbing the boys of a wonderful life with their father. Thanks to Aunt Hannah's and her father's choices, she had been forced to live most of her life without her own father. Could she really do the same thing to her sons? *You're a father, Travis,* her heart cried before she shook her head slightly to dispel the image of his face; it was all too painful right now.

One of the babies had stopped nursing and lay asleep in the curve of her arm. A large wooden cradle had been set up in the corner of the room, but when she asked Angel to take the baby, Angel kept him in her arms. Another ten minutes passed before the other baby joined his brother in sleep, and after Rebecca was made more comfortable, the women, each with a baby in her arms, sat and looked at the wonders before them.

"What are you going to call these little ones?" Angel asked after a quiet few minutes. "I don't think Sarah and Emily are going to work."

Rebecca laughed. Those had been the only names she could put to her babies for the last few days. She looked down into their faces, both sound asleep, her eyes thoughtful.

"Tell me again who was born first," Rebecca asked after a moment.

Angel shifted the baby in her arms. "This one. He was born first, and I put him in your right arm. This guy," Angel now touched the downy soft head of the baby in Rebecca's left arm, "came about eight minutes later."

Rebecca nodded, her look content.

"You've decided," Angel said, smiling.

"Yes. You're holding Garrett, and this," Rebecca shifted her bundle, "will be Wyatt."

"Garrett and Wyatt Buchanan." Angel smiled as she said the names.

"Garrett Wagner Buchanan, and Wyatt Andrew Buchanan," Rebecca corrected her, and Angel's grin widened.

"Why Wagner?"

"It's my maiden name."

"And Andrew?"

"My father's name."

Angel nodded. "He would have been proud of you, Becky."

Angel's words brought tears to Rebecca's eyes, and seeing them, Angel knew her own were very close to the surface. She didn't want to cry. She stood, Garrett cradled close against her.

"I think maybe I'll put this one to bed."

Rebecca watched as she moved to the cradle, placing Garrett gently within. She did not protest when Angel came back for Wyatt. The young mother was suddenly very tired. Angel kept these kinds of hours on a regular basis, but Rebecca was often in bed asleep by 9:00.

"Sleep now." Angel, back at her side, easily read the fatigue in her eyes.

"All right. Thanks, Angel."

"Sure, Becky. If you need something, pound on the wall. If not, I'll see you in the morning."

Rebecca thanked her again and watched as she turned the lantern low and left the room. Feeling tired herself, Angel walked down the hall, looking forward to a good night's sleep. She had always called herself the world's hardest sleeper, but the babies cried three more times in the night, and Angel woke every time in order to assist Rebecca. It was the longest night of the women's lives.

Boulder

"You don't look like you've slept at all!" Lavena accused Travis the next morning.

He didn't answer her or even look up, but tucked into his breakfast without comment. While it was true that he hadn't slept all night, he didn't care to talk about it. He'd just about given up looking for Rebecca. He'd ridden to other towns and run another ad, but to no avail. But after last night, he thought he might search again. He had not been able to get her from his mind. So tortured was he that sleep had been miles away. Maybe she died last night. Maybe she'd been hurt. He didn't know, but that his heart told him something profound had happened.

Lucky Harwell chose that moment to join him at the breakfast table. Both men were silent as Lavena put a plate in front of the Double Star foreman. Lucky had little to say this morning, and that suited Travis fine. He was in no mood for small talk. They ate, reached for their hats, and walked to the barn, all without need for speech. In Travis' mind, the days stretched on without purpose or hope, but Lucky's mind was in a different place all together.

Travis gave little thought to this as the day progressed, but when evening came and they sat again at Lavena's perfectly prepared table and evening meal, Lucky spoke.

"Margo is pregnant. Her father says we have to get married."

Travis looked at the younger man.

"You're certain it's yours?"

Lucky's face flushed with anger. "Margo's not like that. She doesn't see anyone else and never has."

Although Travis felt angry much of the time now, he was sorry he'd said anything. He had no reason to think that

Margo's baby might be some other man's, but he was spoiling for a fight and spoke the first words that came to mind. He knew it wasn't fair to take out his own feelings on Lucky.

"How serious is her father?"

"Freeman Roderick? You know what his temper is like. He's threatened me twice."

"Well, do you love the girl or not?"

"Yeah, I do."

"Then what's the problem?"

Lucky wouldn't speak or even look at his boss. It wasn't hard for Travis to figure out. He even managed a note of kindness when he said, "No man wants to be forced, Lucky, but if you love her, you'll put your pride away. I would guess from the little I've seen of Margo that she loves you too. Don't let that slip away, Lucky. You may never find it again."

Lucky looked at his employer with surprised eyes. He'd never heard Travis open up like that. Indeed, since Andrew Wagner had died and Rebecca had left, he was one of the most closed-mouthed men Lucky had ever known.

"I would probably be living in town," Lucky said seriously.

"That's fine. You'll still have your job. I may even see my way clear to give you a raise."

They fell silent again now, each busy with his own thoughts—Lucky thinking how much he did love Margo, and Travis trying to picture Rebecca with a child. In some ways she had been little more than a child herself, so for him the image was impossible. Considering how short a time they'd lived as husband and wife, it was also improbable. By the time Lavena brought dessert, he'd dismissed the possibility from his mind.

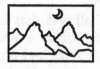

18

Dan held Wyatt in his lap and smiled at the intent way the boy watched the red ribbon in Dan's large hand. No matter where he moved the satin strip, the baby's eyes followed. He was captivated with the red object. Dan had been holding three-month-old Wyatt for nearly an hour, and the little guy hadn't made a sound. He'd been so quiet that he'd given his mother a chance to fall asleep while nursing Garrett.

Dan looked across the room at her. Rebecca was in the rocking chair, a quilt over the baby and herself. From the lack of movement under the blanket, Dan guessed that Garrett had fallen asleep as well. It seemed to Dan that that was all Rebecca and the babies did lately. The house was not as clean as it had been, and Rebecca was taking even less notice of her clothing and looks. Dan shook his head.

He'd never had an interest in any woman who wasn't a picture of loveliness, style, and grace. Well, Rebecca was lovely and she was graceful, but Dan thought that a hound dog would probably have more interest in the latest fashions. But what was even more remarkable were his feelings. He loved this woman. He loved her as he'd never loved anyone in his life.

He'd been completely flabbergasted when she'd had the babies while he was away. The boys had been nearly 24 hours old by the time he'd seen them. And a part of him had been very hurt. There was nothing Rebecca could have done to stem the tide of their delivery, but Dan had dreamed of being there for months, thinking as always that his presence was the way to show her his heart.

The hardest part of all was that it still wasn't working. He'd told himself that with time he would win her, but it had been nearly a year. His feelings had not lessened in any way, but he was starting to lose hope. He knew she cared for him and appreciated his help and friendship, but she wanted nothing more personal. From time to time Dan had tried in subtle ways to court her and show his love, but she always saw through it. In her sweetest voice she would tell him to find a better woman, one who could give him her whole heart. He never said it aloud, but in truth he would have taken whatever portion of her heart she could give. The fact that she was a married woman didn't bother him in the least.

He knew she'd come from Boulder, and the times he had been tempted to ride there and find Travis Buchanan were legion. One thing stopped him: What if Travis had never wanted her to leave? What if the faceless Mr. Buchanan wanted Mrs. Buchanan back? Dan knew that such a thing could happen and happen easily. After all *he* wanted her with every fiber of his being. What man wouldn't? No, Dan was no fool. He was not about to take the risk of bringing on a reunion by doing something so foolish as confronting Rebecca's husband. Curious as he was, he would remain in Pine Grove and try to claim Rebecca's heart, futile though his efforts seemed.

Boulder

"What have you done!" Travis thundered at Lavena in a way he'd never done before, but the tiny scrap of woman stood her ground.

"It's for your own good," she snapped. "This is your home and your ranch. It's time you started living like it."

"I don't need you—"

"Do you think I don't have eyes? It's been a year. You're 24 years old tomorrow, and next week is your first wedding anniversary, and the week after that it will be a year since she left! Well, I don't know if she's ever coming back, but the way you live is wrong!"

Travis was speechless with pain and anger. He had been pushing the events of the past from his mind for so long he'd become cold. Now Lavena had spelled out his whole miserable life for him and expected him to be pleased. And that wasn't the worst of it. She had actually moved his belongings into Andrew's room. Travis was horrified. It was the largest, most beautiful bedroom in the house, but it wasn't his. He allowed her to boss him most of the time, but this time she'd gone too far. He turned to her now, his eyes so cold with fury that not even Lavena dared to speak.

"I want it changed back, and I mean *now*. I'm going into town to get drunk, and when I return, you had better have my room put back together."

He didn't say a word as he turned and left her, but he should have known it was a waste of breath. Lavena didn't speak either, but her chin jutted upward as she watched his back. It would be a hot day in January before she'd move his clothing back down the hall.

❧

Travis' intentions were honest. He had come off the range early, cold and hungry, to find his room bare—bed stripped, dresser and closet empty. When he'd gone in search of his housekeeper and some answers, he'd found her arranging his things in the walk-in closet in Andrew's room. His hairbrush and shaving gear were on top of the dresser, and the quilt that had been on his bed now adorned Andrew's huge oak bed with the ornate footboard and headboard.

159

It was more than he could take. There was some liquor in the house, but Lavena would have hidden it. He wanted to run from all the pain, and getting drunk was the fastest method he could think of. But he hadn't counted on the way neat whiskey would feel on an empty stomach. Without bothering to taste, he tossed back four shot glasses before he realized he was going to be sick. Not normally a drinking man, Travis' system simply couldn't take it. He told himself not to vomit as he moved to the door, not even paying for the bottle he'd left on the table.

Once outside, the first thing he spotted was the hotel. The thought of food made him ill, but he knew he'd never make it home unless he ate. With darkness just beginning to fall, he lurched across the street, thanking his lucky stars when he found the opposite boardwalk without mishap.

"Easy there," a masculine voice spoke calmly, and Travis found himself looking straight into another man's eyes. He must have run right into him. His equal height was something of a surprise, and Travis could only manage to stare.

"Are you all right?" the cultured voice asked.

"I need food," he managed.

"Well." Again the voice was affable. "I'm headed to the hotel dining room myself. Why don't you join me?"

Five minutes later he found himself across a small table from the man. He didn't even have the strength to protest when the stranger ordered for both of them.

"And hot coffee," the man said to the woman beside their table, just before he looked back into Travis' eyes.

"I'm Robert Langley."

"Travis," the other man began. "Travis Buchanan."

"It's good to meet you, Travis. I hope you like pork."

Travis was saved from answering when the waitress reappeared with two steaming mugs.

"Just keep them coming," Robert told her. He took a long pull while Travis carefully raised his cup.

Coffee did arrive regularly after that, but the men were halfway through their meal before Travis felt he could speak coherently. Robert had not forced him to converse, and this greatly impressed the half-intoxicated man.

"Thanks for getting me in here," he said at last.

"You're welcome. Are you feeling better?"

"Yes. I just needed some food."

Neither man mentioned the obvious drinking that had taken place to put him in such a state.

"Are you new in town?" Travis asked. "Or have I just not seen you?"

"I am new in town," Robert told him. "I'm originally from the East, but I'm here in Boulder to start a business."

"Some make it and some don't," Travis replied conversationally, feeling more like himself by the moment.

"True, but I think everyone would agree that Boulder needs a bank."

Travis' brows rose. He again felt impressed. There was a quiet confidence to Robert Langley that he liked very much.

"Is it still in the planning stages?"

"Until next week. The building should be started on Monday or Tuesday."

Travis nodded. He liked a man who accomplished what he set out to do.

"What do you do for a living, Travis?" Robert took a moment to ask, his expression kind and open.

"I own the Double Star Ranch," he told Robert without thinking, the words coming naturally to his tongue.

"The cattle ranch," Robert nodded. "I've heard of it. It's a good-sized spread, isn't it?"

"Fifteen hundred head," Travis said with quiet pride, his mind still not registering the change in him.

"Do you have many hands?"

"Five regulars, more during roundups and cattle drives."

"You must market in Denver."

161

"Yes." Travis was surprised that he knew. Robert's pristine suit did not indicate he would know anything of ranching. "We also drive into Cheyenne, but Denver is usually more profitable."

"I've read about that. I think this area is only going to grow for ranchers. I wouldn't be surprised if the competition comes right to your door in the next few years."

"Is that why you chose to settle in Boulder?"

"Yes. I realize it's not New York City, but I think it's a town with great location and potential. The mountains and wildflowers alone will be a great draw. It's just the right distance from Denver, which is growing by leaps and bounds and getting a little too big for some. The railroad is swiftly heading this way, and I for one like the challenge of a new town. I know many other people who feel the same."

Travis nodded. It had obviously not been a spur-of-the-moment decision.

"Where are you living?" Travis asked.

Robert smiled as his eyes went to the stairway that led to the rooms above them.

"The Hotel Boulder. Room 24."

Travis smiled as well.

"The bank will have two apartments above it. I'll take one and rent the other."

"You sound like you've done this before."

"Yes. My family has been in banking for three generations. I never lived in an apartment above a bank because my father was established before I was born, but it's the way my grandfather started out."

It was on the tip of Travis' tongue to ask Robert what his wife thought of this move, but Robert might decide to return the question, and the answer was not something Travis was willing to discuss. Still, such thoughts took his mind back to the ranch and home. He reached into his front pocket and put a coin on the table.

"Thanks again," Travis said as he pushed his chair back. Robert made to rise as well.

"My pleasure. Maybe I'll see you around."

Travis liked the idea. He wouldn't have initiated it but now suggested, "You'll have to come out and see my spread sometime. And have one of Lavena's home-cooked meals."

"Your wife?"

"No, my housekeeper." Travis was amazed at how normal he sounded, but now he wanted to get home more than ever. "Good night, Robert."

"Good night, Travis."

They parted on that note. Robert had stood but did not leave. Taking his seat again, he drank another cup of coffee and sat alone for more than an hour. His room upstairs would have been quieter, but as intently as he was praying, it wouldn't have mattered. Robert Langley was begging God to bring Travis Buchanan into his life again.

It wasn't that Travis had forgotten his conversation with Lavena, but by the time he reached the ranch house, he had resigned himself. Indeed, he didn't even turn right at the top of the stairs toward his old bedroom, but went to the left and stood in the doorway of Andrew's. Lavena had lit a lantern, and Travis moved over the threshold to see that everything was just as it had been before he'd left in a towering rage.

The lantern still low, he let his eyes roam the room. The double doors that led to a private balcony over the front porch were shut, but Travis now walked to those doors. He opened them wide and stepped out. The crisp night air hit him as he stood and looked at the moonlight bouncing off the snow-covered mountains. A moment later he turned back to the room that held dozens of memories.

A man had died in that bed, but with sudden clarity of thought, Travis realized that death was part of life. *I own the*

Double Star Ranch. His own words to Robert Langley leapt back into his mind so swiftly that he felt his breath quicken. He had been given this ranch and had made a promise to care for it, as well as the woman who went with it. Travis realized for the first time why this had been no strain. He loved this place, every square inch of it. He'd never in his life felt so at home, not even in the house in Texas. Not to mention the fact that he'd planned to cherish Rebecca for the rest of his life.

But Rebecca had not wanted to stay. Travis didn't know exactly why, but he now saw that she was the reason he had kept on here. If she ever came back, he and the ranch would be ready. This was their home now, and he would do his best to preserve it for her no matter how long that took. However, Lavena was right. He'd been only half living. He never went anywhere near Andrew's or Rebecca's rooms, but why not? This was his home.

For just an instant he entertained the idea of having Lucky and Margo live with him, but he pushed the thought swiftly away. The only woman he wanted in the house was Rebecca. Lavena didn't count in the same way. He couldn't take the risk that Rebecca would come back someday and think that Margo had taken her place.

It felt good to have his mind made up. With sure steps he moved to the lantern, turned it high, and reached for the buttons on his shirt. He swiftly readied for bed, telling himself that if it wasn't comfortable, Lavena, with her interfering ways, would see that it was adjusted. He need not have worried. Travis slid beneath the cool sheets and lay his head on one of the pillows. He was instantly comfortable, but as good as he had felt a few minutes before, he now braced himself against the torturous thoughts that were sure to assail him. After all, he was in Andrew's bed. Strangely, no such thoughts materialized. His mind moved back to his dinner companion. There was a peace about Robert that Travis had never known. It must have come from knowing what he wanted and having the means to go after it. Travis fell asleep before he could decide whether there might be more to it than that.

19

Three months later, on February 17, Lucky Harwell and Margo Roderick were married at the small, high-steepled church in Boulder. The ranch foreman, who usually had a joke for everything, was pale with emotion, but the eyes he turned to his young bride were kind and tender. Margo's simple blue dress was straining a little at the waistline, and the sight of it reminded Travis that he'd promised Lucky a raise when he got married.

The bride's parents were both in attendance. Margo's mother, Yvonne, was teary, but her father looked stern. Two or three of Margo's friends were also in the church, along with the other Double Star ranch hands. Woody, who had taken over as camp cook when Biscuit finally quit, was sitting with Lavena. It was not a long ceremony, but because it was performed by the same man who had married Travis and Rebecca, Travis was more than happy to be finished and going outside. Rumor had it that Pastor Craig was moving out of the area, but it obviously hadn't happened yet. Travis had yet to darken the door of the church on a Sunday morning, and had no immediate plans to do so, but he knew that if he ever did decide to attend church, it would be after Pastor Craig was gone.

When the couple was pronounced husband and wife, the group assembled outside of the church, and the men, who all genuinely liked Lucky, stepped forward to shake his hand. Lavena went to greet the couple and pressed a small gift into their hands, but Travis knew that she was put out because there was no talk of a reception. The bride and groom would be living with Margo's parents for the time being, and something told Travis this was not an ideal situation.

In some ways Travis was relieved by the lack of festivities; however, before he left he shook Lucky's hand, told him he would see him in a few days, and gave Margo a hug. It had been a spur-of-the-moment decision to do more than shake her hand, but the young, grateful eyes she turned to him gave him a tremendous sense of satisfaction. As a man, he'd speculated only on Lucky's feelings, but now he asked himself what Margo might be feeling this day. She was clearly in love with Lucky, but her father's angry visage must have cast a pall over her wedding day.

Lavena and the others had come to town in the big wagon, but Travis, not in the mood for their idle chatter, had ridden Diamond and come on his own. He wasn't intending to remain in town, but once he'd mounted his horse, the sound of hammering and general construction drew him further down the street.

It was a cold day, and snow lay in drifts along the buildings, but work on the bank had commenced. Travis hadn't planned to do anything more than have a look and ride back out of town, but he spotted Robert Langley at the edge of the street and swung off his horse. After tying Diamond's reins to a nearby post, he approached. Robert turned when he was just five feet away.

"Well, Travis," he said with obvious pleasure. "What brings you to town?"

"My foreman was married today."

"He certainly picked a cold day for it," Robert commented. His smile was in place, but his red cheeks told tales about how long he'd been standing in the wind.

"How long have you been out here?" Travis asked.

"Too long. I can't really do anything, so I just stand around and grow steadily colder."

Travis could not get over how drawn he was to this man. It was odd since this was the first time he'd even seen him in broad daylight, but Travis' forthcoming offer was made in genuine kindness and interest.

"Come on over to the hotel, and I'll buy you a hot cup of coffee. You look like you could use a little warmth."

"I think you're right," Robert agreed with a laugh. "Give me just a minute."

Robert turned back and spoke to one of the workers before joining Travis. They were both bundled warmly against temperatures below freezing, but both also knew that prolonged periods outdoors were not comfortable or safe.

"It helps to have the sun shining," Robert told Travis when they were seated at the table, "but the men are about to give up for the day."

"It'll be slow going in this cold weather. You may not open when you'd planned."

"You're probably right. There will be quite a bit of stonework on the front, so we may get held up waiting for deliveries on materials as well."

"The unfinished front won't stop you from opening for business, will it?"

"It might. I can't very well let people come through the front door if rocks are going to fall on them. Bad for business."

The men talked on for more than an hour. They each had work to do, but they both found so much to say to each other. Robert was very heartened that Travis had sought him out, and Travis seemed in no hurry to be off. They even agreed to meet again, this time for dinner sometime the following week. It was to be the start of a fascinating friendship.

Pine Grove

"I swear, Becky, I don't think I can remember the last time you looked so rested."

Rebecca smiled at Angel and answered in a hushed tone, "It helps to have the babies sleeping through the night."

"Can you believe they're six months old?"

The young mother's face grew thoughtful. "In so many ways the time has passed in a fog. For so long I was too tired to even think straight."

"Speaking of tired, why are you up so late?"

"I just woke up and came down to get something to eat. I had no idea it was late enough for you to come in."

"Actually, it's a little early."

Something in Angel's voice snagged Rebecca's attention. "Did something happen at the Bell?"

"I'm not sure," Angel replied cryptically.

Rebecca stared at her. The older woman was still in a satin dress, her hair piled high, but Rebecca wore a gown and old robe. It was stained—Wyatt and Garrett had seen to that—still, it was comfortable and warm. The women sat across the kitchen table from each other, Rebecca with some bread and jam, Angel with only water.

"What happened?" Rebecca finally asked.

Angel sighed. "It's Preston. His behavior has been odd lately."

"You've said that before."

"I know, but it's worse now."

"Is it, Angel?"

The hostess looked at her. "What does that mean?"

"Only that I think he's been changing toward you for a long time, and maybe you don't *want* to see it."

Angel frowned at her. At one time that would have set Rebecca on the verge of tears, but no more.

"Are we about to have an argument?"

"Of course not," Angel answered, but she sounded testy. "I don't know what you're getting at."

"Don't you?"

"Stop saying that!" Angel snapped, standing up.

"Why should I?" Rebecca countered, her voice still calm. "You never fail to tell me that Dan's in love with me, and that if

I had any sense I'd move in with him. Well, Preston's building a house even bigger than the one Dan just moved into. When are you going to pack *your* bags?"

"You don't understand, Becky," Angel began, but she could see that her housemate wasn't listening.

"Why do you fight this, Angel? You've made up your mind that you and Preston are no longer capable of these kinds of feelings. Well, someone should tell that to Preston, because the looks he gives you have nothing to do with his being your boss."

Angel stared at her in outrage for a moment and then turned away. She didn't look defeated, but neither did she look ready to agree. "I'm going to bed," she finally announced, but Rebecca stayed where she was.

There was a little bit of banging around upstairs while Angel readied herself for sleep, and Rebecca, still sitting in the kitchen, thought that if Angel woke the babies there really would be an argument.

Boulder

"Sure, I'd love to come out to the ranch."

"Great. How's Sunday morning?"

"Fine. I'll come right after church."

A shuttered look came into Travis' eyes that Robert had never seen before. Months had passed, nearly a year's worth, but the men had not seen much of each other. They had met several times in the spring to talk business, but Travis had been gone on roundup and on a cattle drive most of the summer and into the fall. In October, Robert had headed east on a business trip and to see his family. By the time he returned to Boulder, winter had set in and Travis had not come to town often. Christmas and New Year's had come and gone, and with the quiet of January, Travis found Robert on his mind. The cowboy sought him out in Robert's private office in the bank.

"Is there a problem, Travis?"

"No," he said, but the warmth in his eyes was gone and Robert was not convinced. He had swiftly figured out what the problem was and knew that the only way to deal with it was head on.

"If my going to church bothers you, Travis, I need to tell you that my beliefs are not new. And if you recall, I've never tried to cram my views down your throat in the past."

Travis felt like a fool. He didn't know why it put him off to think of Robert in church, except that Travis wanted nothing to do with church. Having an area they could not share was difficult. The time around Christmas had been long and lonely. Lucky and Margo had been out to the ranch with their baby girl, Sarah Beth, but Travis had spent much time alone. Why it hadn't occurred to him to seek out Robert before, he couldn't say. Now, to learn that he was a religious man took some of the pleasure out of the meeting.

"If you want to withdraw your offer, Travis, I'll understand." Robert's voice was kind, but also very quiet, his own disappointment evident. Both Robert's words and tone drew Travis' attention. He was being ridiculous. Of course it didn't matter if Robert went to church. What did he care what the man did on Sundays?

"Of course not, Robert. Please come. Make it for dinner if you can."

"Okay. I'll be as close to noon as possible. How do I find you?"

Travis told him which road to take, and then Robert walked him to the door. The men shook hands and shared their anticipation of the weekend. Travis felt much better. As he rode out of town, he told himself this was what he had needed all along. Lavena enjoyed reminding him that he had withdrawn into himself, and now he thought she must be right.

Robert returned to his office to think and pray. Things had been on a good footing by the time they parted, but Robert could see that there might be many walls to scale before he really knew Travis. Indeed, each man was looking forward to Sunday, but for very different reasons.

"I thought the view in town was spectacular, but out here it's all so fresh and unspoiled."

Travis nodded with satisfaction. The men were standing on the balcony of his bedroom, taking in the snow-covered mountains. It meant a lot to Travis to have Robert share his view on the beauty of this land, and as they turned and walked from the room, Robert went on.

"And this house! It's huge, Travis. Really beautiful."

Travis smiled, something he'd been doing for the last 20 minutes. "I rather like large places."

Robert now smiled in return. His office at the bank was very spacious, and Travis had only just commented on that during their last meeting.

"I hope to build a house soon," Robert told his host as they came down the stairs. "I think I've convinced Dale Wright and his wife to sell me their extra land."

"Dale Wright? His place is right on the road to the Double Star."

"Yes, we'd practically be neighbors," Robert exaggerated good-naturedly.

"I never dreamed you'd want to live so far from the bank."

"Well, in actuality, the land I'm looking at is across the road from Wright's. I wouldn't really be that far out."

"But you're tired of your apartment."

Robert shrugged slightly and said quietly, "In truth, I'm very comfortable above the bank, Travis, but I've met some-one rather special, and I'm thinking it might be time to build."

The men had been walking around the downstairs, continuing their tour, but Travis now led them to the warmth of the living room. The fire blazed, and both men took chairs and made themselves comfortable.

"I know a few of the women in town," Travis went on, curiosity riding his heart, "but they're all married."

"Eddie's not from Boulder," Robert explained easily. "I met her on my trip east last fall." There was no disguising the elation in Robert's eyes. Whoever this girl was, she had well and truly captured the banker's heart.

"Eddie," Travis repeated the name thoughtfully. "Must be a nickname."

"Yes, but there's nothing masculine about her. Edwina Fontaine is her full name, and she's the oldest of five girls. I haven't met her family, but she's written about them in her letters."

"How did you meet?"

"Well, if I believed in accidents, then that's what I'd call it, but I simply had the wrong address."

"Why don't you believe in accidents?"

"Because I believe God is sovereign. I believe He is in control of everything, even things that seem to be inconsequential, like getting the wrong address. But then I met the woman I've been waiting for my whole life."

"Could just be good luck."

"I don't think so," Robert disagreed kindly. "Luck means things are left to chance, and I can't go along with that. There are too many verses in the Bible that say otherwise."

"Now you sound like Pastor Craig." Travis had not completely closed up, but his expression altered.

Robert frowned. "You didn't get to know Pastor Craig very well if you think we sound alike."

Travis shrugged. "You're right. I've had little contact with the man, but I wasn't impressed."

"I wasn't either." Robert paused and thought about what he'd just said. "Let me clarify that for you, Travis. I didn't agree with all Pastor Craig's views, but I still attended church."

Travis didn't have a comment for that, but then there wasn't really a need. He recognized the fact that he wasn't comfortable with religion. Travis saw Robert as a religious man, but he liked him as a person. His expression became open again, just as Lavena came to the door and told them dinner was on the table. The subjects of God and His Word were not mentioned for the rest of the day. Over their meal the conversation turned to cattle and banking, but never ranged back to the personal.

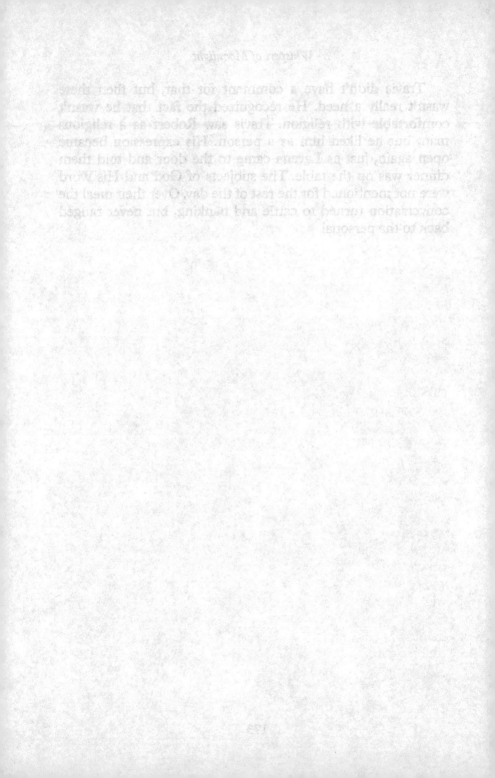

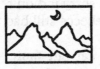

20

Rebecca opened the front door quietly but could immediately tell there was no need for silence; both of her sons were howling loudly from the bedroom they shared with their mother. Rebecca laid her things aside and moved for the stairs. She was met in her bedroom by Angel, who looked five years older than when Rebecca had left her.

"I don't need to ask how it's gone," Rebecca remarked as she joined Angel on the edge of the bed. The 15-month-old twins swarmed all over their mother. Their cries had ceased, but they clung to her as if she'd been gone for days instead of minutes.

"I was certain they were asleep when you left, but the moment the door closed downstairs, they called for you and then the tears began."

Angel, who had only grown more compassionate as the weeks had passed, now sounded a bit testy. She wasn't lacking sleep—the hour was early for her—but Rebecca caught the first note of frustration. She couldn't blame her. The boys wanted only their mother. Dan was feeling some irritation as well and hadn't been coming to see them very often. Rebecca's friends adored the two little boys and would have enjoyed helping her, but unless the twins could see their mother or be touching her, they were not happy.

Rebecca eyed her friend.

"It was a good idea for me to get out, Angel, and I do appreciate your offer. I'm sorry it didn't work."

Angel shrugged. Rebecca still had the impression that she was angry.

"You still need to get out more, Becky. When the boys were little you could just let them cry, but they were out of their beds before I could even get down the hall. Had the door been open, they'd have chased you."

Rebecca looked down at her sons. One was as dark as the other was light. They both had their thumbs in their mouths, and both looked sleepy. Rebecca knew, however, that if she tried to put them in their own bed, they would cry and carry on.

"I guess they're just too young," Rebecca offered lamely. Angel, not really knowing better, agreed with her.

"Well, I'm going to go put on a pot of coffee. Come on down when you can."

"All right. Thanks, Angel."

Angel stood, bent over, and kissed the boys' foreheads in turn. Secure in their mother's arms, they both smiled around their thumbs, but made no move to embrace Angel. She left without further word, but Rebecca's heart was still troubled.

Boulder

"What do you do with things like the flood?"

"As in Genesis, with Noah and the ark?"

"Yes." Travis' voice was calm, but as usual when these weekly sessions with Robert turned to spiritual matters, he was tense. "Am I really supposed to believe that this man and his sons built a boat so large that it held two of each animal in the world?"

Robert sighed to himself. Travis was fighting so hard. His question was more than reasonable, but as usual they were diverted from the main issue, which was Jesus Christ and His work on the earth. Robert had this thought so often that he finally decided to voice it.

"Is that really what's bothering you, Travis?"

"What do you mean?"

"Only that I'm not sure you really care one way or the other about the ark. I don't think you want to believe anything God has to say."

Such a statement would normally have made Travis angry, but not this time. "Maybe you're right," he admitted, "but I'm not certain I want to get into that right now."

"I can appreciate that," Robert told him, and carefully shifted the topic off God and Bible-related issues.

Some time later, Robert saw Travis to the door of his small apartment. They parted on friendly terms, but Robert felt a vague sense of dissatisfaction. The Lord was swift to remind him that Travis hadn't been meeting with him for very many weeks; things would take place in His perfect time and not before. For the rest of the evening, Robert worked at committing Travis to the Lord.

⌒

Travis rode straight home from Robert's, but as he moved down the main street of town, he couldn't help but hear the sound of feminine laughter as it floated from one of the saloons. His mind had been on the evening's conversation with Robert, but suddenly all he could see was Rebecca. It wasn't as easy to envision her face these days, but the sound of her laughter lingered in his mind. And always the questions began. Where was she and why did she leave?

If he consulted Robert, that man would say that all things were ordered by God. But Travis wasn't buying it. What kind of God would let Rebecca leave him? What kind of God would order that type of pain? He'd been given no choice but to give up looking for her; it was obviously fruitless and caused too much pain, but his heart still thought of the possibilities. She could be dead for all he knew, or maybe she needed him but had no way to get home. Travis had to push the painful thoughts from his mind.

As the horse's hooves moved Travis farther out of town, he slowly shook his head. Robert also wanted him to believe the Bible, which taught things too fantastic to be real, such as God coming to earth as a man in order to save a sin-sick world— one that didn't want Him in the first place. Travis' doubts were so strong that he wouldn't even consider the possibility.

The stable, yard, and house were quiet as he made his way inside. There was a light under Lavena's door off the kitchen, but all else was black. The house had become a near extension of himself, and he needed no lantern to find his way to his room. As he often did, he hesitated on the threshold and let his eyes stray down the hall. At times he would visit Rebecca's room, but tonight he wasn't up to it. He didn't feel up to anything but sleep at the moment. With an effort he pushed both Robert and his wife from his mind and took himself off to bed.

~

The letter began "Dear Robert," as it usually did, and although letters from Eddie were always wonderful, it only took a few sentences for Robert to see that something was very different.

"I have some incredible news for you," she began. "We're moving to Colorado. I can hardly believe it. My Uncle Mitch was just in touch with my father for the first time in many years, and he asked my father to join him in business. I nearly fainted when Father told me the business was in Georgetown, Colorado Territory."

Robert wanted to keep reading, but his hand was shaking too much. She was coming! Eddie was coming. She would not be on the East Coast, but right here in his area, accessible and hopefully wanting to see him as much as he wanted to see her.

Robert's eyes slid shut with a prayer of thanksgiving before he eagerly read on.

"Father wrote Mitch that we'd be with him this summer. Mother has already begun making lists and informing friends and neighbors. Father has talked to a man about buying our house. We've lived many places, but never that far west. We're all very excited, but a little nervous too."

Again Robert had to stop. It was too wonderful to be true. He was in his office at the bank and would have sat for hours just dreaming about the possibilities when a knock sounded at the door. He called a carefree welcome from his desk, but his jubilant mood was quickly snuffed out when he saw Travis' pale features.

"What is it, Travis?" Robert rose and asked immediately. "What's happened?"

"My new man, Morgan, is dead," he told him, his voice low. "He must have been drinking, fell off his horse, and landed against a rock when he tried to come in last night. The boys found him this morning."

Robert opened his mouth to speak, but Travis cut him off, his voice low with fury.

"Is this the way your God does things, Robert?"

Robert said nothing, but even if he had, Travis was in such a cold rage he would never have heard.

"He was only 18. What's the point of a young man like that dying? He left his family in the East to come here and make a life for himself. He planned to send for his mother and sister when he was settled, and now they'll never see him again."

Robert's eyes flicked to the clock. It was just past 1:00, and he wasn't done until 3:00. He was certain, however, that his teller would be able to handle the afternoon customers.

"Why don't we head up to my apartment, Travis? We can be more private there."

"No," Travis replied coldly. "I don't want to hear anything you have to say. You'll only offer excuses that I'm not foolish enough to buy."

179

Robert stood very still as Travis walked back out the door. He could chase after him and try to reason with him, but the timing was all wrong. Travis wasn't ready to listen. Robert was beginning to think he never would be. A customer's request called him out of the office not five minutes later. He was forced to put Travis into the back of his mind. He determined, however, that whenever Morgan's services were held, he would be there. Maybe that would be a better time to try to talk with his friend.

Pine Grove

Preston Carwell was a patient man; there was no denying that. He had not given Angel the rush act but still made it very clear that he was interested. It had taken months for her to see that it was true, and he could tell by her face that she was still in the process of figuring out what she was going to do about it.

Many of the men he worked with took physical love where they could find it, but it had never been that way with him, or Angel for that matter. Over the years many young dancehall girls had made it more than clear they would welcome his interest, and Angel's looks always drew male attention, but neither of them ever fell into casual affairs.

The night he'd been asked to have dinner with Angel and Rebecca had been the first of many, but it wasn't the first step to further intimacy he had hoped. Indeed, for a time he felt he had to be more careful than ever. One day he decided to lay his cards on the table. He hinted that Angel should visit his newly built house sometime, but she never came. He now took the plunge and asked her outright, not only to see the house but also to join him for dinner. He stood absolutely still when she said yes and walked away. He might have stood still all night if Dan hadn't asked him a question. The younger man looked at him oddly for a minute but didn't press by asking Preston what was wrong. Preston was relieved to finally make his way back to his office where he wouldn't have to hold his detached expression in place. There he could give way to his emotions: too excited not to let it show on his face, but also too afraid to hope.

Boulder

Pastor Henley, a man Robert admired tremendously, held the graveside service for Morgan Sears. Robert knew it couldn't have been easy because the pastor didn't know the young cowboy, but he did a fine job. Robert recognized the hands that turned out from the Double Star, along with Lavena and Lucky's wife, Margo. They were all visibly shaken. Lucky's face was pale, his eyes somber, but Robert noticed that most of the other hands headed for the saloon as soon as they could get away. Only Lucky hung back, seeing his wife and Lavena to a waiting wagon.

Travis held back as well, standing quietly by the grave. Robert watched as Pastor Henley went forward and spoke for several minutes to Morgan's boss. When the pastor moved off Robert approached, watching for signs that he might be intruding. Travis turned when he came close, yesterday's anger gone from his eyes.

"Hello, Travis," Robert said softly.

"Thank you for coming, Robert."

"Certainly. I only wish I'd known Morgan. I'm sorry for your loss."

"I'll be writing to his mother. She'll be glad a few were here."

Robert nodded, and both men looked down at the box waiting to be lowered into the ground.

"Andrew Wagner died," Travis said quietly to the ground. "I was his foreman. He left me the Double Star." Travis' eyes finally came to Robert's face. "I don't have more than a handful of things to send to Mrs. Sears."

"She'll appreciate the gesture nevertheless," Robert said, feeling the words were inadequate.

"Pastor Henley talked to me."

"I noticed that."

"He invited me to church."

"Did he?"

"Yes. You never have."

"No, I haven't," Robert admitted. "I'm sorry. It was foolish of me to assume that after our conversations you wouldn't want to come."

Travis' eyes went back to the grave. *I wouldn't have believed two pastors could be so different. Pastor Henley and Pastor Craig. Pastor Craig turned my stomach, but Pastor Henley is like Robert, a man who doesn't put on a show but believes what he preaches.*

Travis' mind ran riot for several minutes as he tried to come to grips with the pain in his heart. He didn't know why he accused Robert of never asking him to church; he wouldn't have gone anyway. As though he had no control over himself, Travis turned back to Robert. He heard himself asking when the service started on Sunday.

"Eleven o'clock," Robert told him simply. "Do you need to head home right now, Travis, or can we go for some coffee at the hotel, and maybe a bite to eat?"

Travis shook his head. "Thanks, but I do need to get back." Robert watched as the black hat went back on his head. "Maybe I'll see you Sunday."

Robert nodded and smiled. His hand came out, and Travis gripped it firmly. Their eyes met for just an instant, but it was enough. Church or not, Robert Langley would still be his friend.

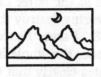

21

On Sunday morning, Travis' face was nearly as pale as it had been in the Boulder Cemetery. He came into the church just before the service began, spotted Robert, and slipped into the pew beside him. The banker's heart went out to him, but surprisingly enough, when the singing was over and the sermon began Travis seemed more relaxed. Robert wondered if he had had visions of being called on to sing a solo or stand and give his name. Again the older man's heart squeezed with sympathy. He was also sensitive when Pastor Henley asked the small group of worshipers to open their Bibles to the book of Job. Robert shifted his Bible so Travis could follow along.

"I'm going to read from all over the book today, but before I do that I'm going to remind you where we have been with Job. In the space of just minutes, Job lost his children, flocks and herds, and most of his servants as well. Later he lost his health and even his friends turned against him. Now keep all of that in mind as I read from various chapters.

"Chapter 1:20, 21, and 22 start us out. 'Then Job arose, and rent his mantle, and shaved his head, and fell down upon the ground, and worshipped, and said, "Naked came I out of my mother's womb, and naked shall I return. The Lord gave and the Lord hath taken away; blessed be the name of the Lord."' In chapter 2 he said this to his wife, 'Thou speakest as one of the foolish women speaketh. What? Shall we receive good at the hand of God, and shall we not receive evil?' Then

183

19:25 and following says, 'For I know that my redeemer liveth, and that he shall stand at the latter day upon the earth: And though after my skin worms destroy this body, yet in my flesh shall I see God.' And 28:24 says, 'For he looketh to the ends of the earth, and seeth under the whole heaven.' Now to chapter 33, verse 12, which states clearly that God is greater than any man. Verse 13 says God does not give account of any of His matters. In other words, He doesn't have to ask our permission for anything.

"And now some of Job's last words in the book, in chapter 42, 'Then Job answered the Lord, and said, I know that thou canst do everything, and that no thought can be withheld from thee. Who is he that hideth counsel without knowledge? Therefore have I uttered that which I understood not; things too wonderful for me, which I knew not.' "

At this point Pastor Henley took a moment to catch his breath, his eyes scanning the attentive faces in the pews. He went on with quiet conviction.

"Some say that Job was God's plaything. Some say that Job was one of the biggest fools alive. But I say Job was one of the wisest men to have ever lived. The loss of his family must have been painful beyond anything I have ever experienced, but Job recognized something of extreme importance. He recognized that were it not for God he would never have had anything to begin with. He understood that God alone had the right to claim everything as His.

"We can fight God, my friends, but it is pure foolishness. All we have is from God's hand alone. We must come to a point where we love and accept this. God allowed Satan to take things from Job, but God was still in control. Not Job, but God. Job was able to grasp this, and even though he had heartache over his loss, he knew that his life had great purpose."

Pastor Henley continued, but he had lost Travis. Travis still didn't know why he'd come into town. All the way to the barn, and then while he saddled Diamond, swung into the saddle, and started for town, he had told himself he was a fool, but still he kept on. It had taken the first notes of music to propel him inside the building. He had been standing and looking at the outside of the church, never once understanding what it was all about.

I'm fighting God, Travis now thought to himself. *Why did I never see it that way before? I'm fighting God with all my strength.* The thought so stunned him that he couldn't even think.

Robert sensed something had happened and turned to look at him, but Travis was in a world of his own. His face was pale again, his eyes focused on the man up front without really seeing him.

Travis stood when it was time for the last song and prayer, and Robert watched as he solemnly shook the pastor's hand on their way out. In a quiet voice, Travis agreed to Robert's offer of going to the hotel for lunch, and Robert was thankful when they had taken their seats and he could finally question him.

"Are you all right?"

Travis really looked at him for the first time. "I don't know. I discovered something about myself this morning, and I'm still thinking about it."

"Can you tell me?"

"Yes. I'm fighting God." There was wonder in his voice. "I don't know why I never saw it before, but that's what I'm doing."

Robert nodded. "I've done that at different times in my life," he admitted.

Travis was so taken with the admission that he unconsciously leaned forward across the table. "What did you do about it?"

"Well, it usually involved my not wanting to give something up or accept some new aspect of my life. I'm a very logical person, Travis, and at times like those it comes in handy. I think I'm going to be utterly miserable if I give in to God, but then I take stock of my present situation and learn that I'm already

185

about as miserable as a man can get. It usually doesn't take too much longer after that to surrender my will to God's. And I'll tell you something, Travis. Nothing in the world can compare to the peace of God."

Travis licked his lips. It was on the tip of his tongue to tell Robert that God would want nothing to do with him if He knew what a hatred he had felt for his father over the years or what a mess he'd made of his marriage, but very swiftly Travis knew how foolish such thoughts were. God was God. He knew it all anyway. Why was that so suddenly clear to him?

At the same time Travis realized Robert was right. He couldn't get much more miserable than he was right now. However, he wasn't certain of the next step. Should he read the Bible? If he suddenly agreed with God that everything bad happens for a purpose, would that give him peace? And what about Rebecca? If he began to pray and read the Bible, would God tell him if she was all right?

"You look like you have a lot on your mind."

Robert's comment broke into his thoughts, but Travis could only nod. Robert could see that he didn't want to talk, so he let it pass. Their food arrived before the silence grew too long, and when the meal was over Travis rode out of town without ever having told Robert what was on his mind.

Pine Grove

Preston lay back in bed and watched Angel brush her hair before the tall mirror in his bedroom. He had been a fool. He told himself if he could just claim her as his woman, it would be enough, but it wasn't, not even close. Every time she spent the night, he wanted her to stay for the rest of the day. Every time he saw her in his kitchen, he wanted her there forever, across the table from him or working side by side on a meal.

He wanted her clothing hanging in the closet beside his, and her hairbrush on the dresser by his own. For weeks now they had been intimately involved, but it wasn't enough.

The first night he'd asked her to come to dinner and she'd accepted without a moment's hesitation came rushing back to his mind. He'd known such regret that she had been so swift to agree he wished he'd asked sooner. He wasn't going to wait and think about this for weeks; he would ask her just as soon . . .

His thoughts cut off when he realized she was staring at him in the mirror. Their eyes locked and held, but Preston didn't speak until Angel turned and continued to look at him.

"Move in with me," he commanded her softly and watched as her eyes grew tender.

"I wondered what was on your mind."

"You are. And I want you here all the time."

He watched her sigh.

"What are you thinking about?"

"Becky. Dan has been seeing someone pretty regularly, and I'm here all the time." She paused. "I can't just leave her and the boys."

"I don't know why not. You told me the two boys drive you crazy."

Again she sighed. "It's funny really; it's the first love-hate relationship I've ever been in. I love it when they let me hold them or when they stand still while I talk to them, but when they wrestle on my bed and get into my clothes and makeup, I could kill them."

Preston was quiet for a few minutes, his eyes still on her as he weighed his next words. Finally he ventured, "Have you ever thought that it might be a relief for Rebecca if you were gone."

Angel's brows rose.

"I mean," he went on easily, "the boys could have your room, and she wouldn't have to worry about them disturbing your things."

He could see that he'd made her think, but her face quickly clouded.

"She couldn't afford it, Preston. She does all the domestic work around the house, but she isn't even doing outside laundry right now, so mine is the only income."

"Well, give her some warning. She could have a small business going by the time you leave."

"She's tired enough right now with just the boys and the house."

"Well, if she doesn't like the idea of supporting herself, she could go home to her husband."

Angel flinched. He sounded so cold, but part of her was complimented. He wanted her to move in badly enough that he was willing to dump Rebecca in the street.

"Tell me something, Angel." His voice was now soft and beguiling.

"What?"

"If Rebecca wasn't in the picture, what would your answer be?"

"Yes," she answered instantly and noticed that he did nothing to hide his pleasure. She was feeling pretty pleased herself and joked, "Should I be afraid that you're going to have my friend and her sons disappear?"

"No." Preston's mouth was stretched into a grin. "But if Rebecca and the boys are the only thing holding you back, then just leave it to me."

Angel's face suddenly grew serious, but she wanted this as much as he did.

"You'll be gentle, won't you, Preston?"

"Indeed I will, almost as gentle as I am with you."

Angel's eyes turned tender with love. She had learned many things about Preston in the last few weeks, and at the top of the list was that when he cared for someone it was with his whole heart. Angel found herself hoping that Rebecca would take the news well, because in her mind she was already half-packed.

Boulder

"I wish you had come to me, Travis, and told me what was on your mind. I could tell you were searching, but I wasn't sure what the questions were."

"It was pride," Travis replied, his voice telling of his peace. "I thought I had to do this on my own. I see now that it was only pride."

"Tell me about it."

"Well, do you remember about five weeks back when I first came to church?"

"Of course."

"You knew I was fighting God. I was tormented all the way home, and when I got there I went for a Bible that has been in an office drawer for years. I picked it up and began to read. At first I was taken aback by how swiftly violence entered the world, but then I remembered what you said about God's purpose for sending His Son. If people hadn't sinned there would have been no need.

"I still have questions," Travis now added, "but I also know, just like Job, that my Redeemer lives and that I'll see Him some day."

Robert's smile was huge. "I've prayed, Travis. I've prayed with all my heart that you would understand and believe. What was it, Travis? What was the turning point for you?"

"I think a combination of things, like the reading I was doing. I read through the book of Genesis but then went to the New Testament. Matthew is a great book, and I saw for myself that Christ was more than just a man: He was God's Son. Also, you said something when we met on Wednesday. You said that your grandfather told you God was very patient, but also that no man knows when he is going to die. I thought about Morgan. Did he take care of things between himself and God before it was too late? It's impossible for me to know, but I would say probably not since he never planned to die.

"I went home that night and thought of nothing else for the next 48 hours. Then it was so late last night when I finally knew I wanted to believe that I waited until this morning to come."

Robert's chest rose on a deep breath. The men were sitting in the banker's office, and he was pleased they hadn't been disturbed.

"There are no words to tell you what I'm feeling right now, Travis."

"I think I understand. I do have questions, though. Is there a time we can get together?"

"Sure. Today after work or tomorrow after church. Either one is fine, and I'll tell you all I can."

"Let's do it tomorrow. Today I'm headed to the reading room to see if there are any books over there."

"That's fine, Travis, but I will warn you of one thing." Robert reached out and tapped Travis' Bible. "This must be your final authority. God's Word alone must be believed and obeyed."

Travis looked a little uncertain about Robert's remark, and Robert prayed for him. Travis was a child when it came to a saving knowledge of Christ, and Robert recognized it might take time for his friend to understand that there are no half measures with God, that God wants to be everything to His children. Indeed, Robert knew He would settle for nothing less.

22

Rebecca stood very still. Preston had been gone for some time, but it felt as if time stood still. She didn't want to cry, and she wasn't angry. She only felt numb. Did Preston know that just that morning Dan had come to tell her he was marrying his girlfriend? Dahlia was pregnant, and Dan had found that he really did care for her. Rebecca was pleased—she didn't want him pining over her—but she suddenly felt all alone in the world. Dan was getting married, and Angel was moving in with Preston.

Two weeks. Preston said that he and Angel had decided two weeks ago that this was what they wanted, and he'd been working since then to make it possible for all of them.

"Every single worker at the Bell complains about not having their laundry done right," he'd told her. "It could be a huge business for you."

"But where am I going to do this, Preston? It's hard enough to boil water now without fear of the boys being scalded."

"The dining room," he had answered immediately. "I've got a plan to convert the dining room for you, a plan that includes a partition; well, a gate actually. You can look out, but the boys won't be able to get in."

And that had been just the beginning. For every question Rebecca raised, Preston was ready with an answer. She had thought he'd come to see Angel, who was still asleep upstairs, but he'd come to tell her the news.

A noise came from upstairs, and Rebecca's head turned toward it. The boys would be tumbling down anytime now. She could never get them to bed on time, but at least they slept late in the morning. And then there was Angel. Once the boys came down, she would soon follow. In the past she had been able to sleep through anything, but now the boys were too boisterous.

Rebecca didn't have to ask if that was part of the reason Angel was going; she knew her housemate had no patience with her overactive sons. But did Angel know that Preston was going to talk to her today? Because she felt like they had plotted against her, the question raced around the small blonde's mind. There seemed to be no answers.

Rebecca turned now and looked toward the dining room. The table and chairs were made of a lovely wood, but no one ever used them. Everyone always ate in the kitchen. Rebecca hadn't mentioned this to Preston, but she now thought about how tired she was with just the boys and housework. How would she ever make it through days and days of laundry? Of course, Preston had said that Angel would rent the house to her for as long as she lived in Pine Grove. If that was the case she wouldn't have to clean it at all.

On that thought her chin rose in the air. The boys were laughing their way down the stairs right now, and Rebecca went to kiss them good morning. She still felt like her world was caving in, but no one—not Angel, Dan, or Preston—was ever going to know that.

❧

"What in the world do you have on?" Angel exclaimed as she found Rebecca in the living room. Rebecca smiled before she turned in a circle to model the sacklike dress she wore. It gave her no shape, and the color was dreadful.

"Don't you like it?" Rebecca faced her and asked.

"No, it's hideous," Angel told her bluntly, which only widened Rebecca's smile.

"Good! Maybe my male customers will get the hint."

"Becky." Angel's voice took on a patient tone, but Rebecca stopped her with a hand in the air.

"You are the *last* person who can give me advice about men, Angel. You knew Preston for four years before you would even get near the man."

"But Becky, I still dated, at least a little. You don't have anyone."

"That's the way I want it," she said firmly. "I'm just surprised that it's taken me this many months to figure out what I should do about it. I do not want to attract attention. I'm not into casual flings, and the men who bring me their laundry are not looking to settle down with a ready-made family."

As if she'd mentioned the family by name, the boys suddenly came bursting into the room.

"Angel!" they shrieked, and the older of the two women steeled herself against their onslaught. They flew at her as usual, each bumping and shoving the other for position to hug her. Angel ended up with one in the front and one in the back. She was smiling down at them until someone mashed her toe.

"Boys!" Rebecca warned when she saw Angel's face. "Stop it! Garrett! Wyatt! That's enough!" But in typical fashion they ignored her. It was some minutes before Rebecca made herself heard, but the boys left Angel's tangled skirts only because they heard a dog barking out front. Angel sighed, straightened her skirt, and then sent Rebecca a telling look.

"You might find a man who wants a ready-made family if you would discipline those boys once in a while, Becky."

"I know, Angel," she said tiredly. "I try, but I just can't seem to punish them."

Angel only looked at her. "I've got to go."

"All right. Don't forget the boys' birthday is Friday. We're having cake at 7:00."

"Preston and I will be here," Angel assured her, parting on those words. What she didn't tell Rebecca was that she would plan on wearing one of her older gowns. The twins, with the excitement of their second birthday, would certainly be more out of control than usual.

Boulder

"Well, friend, this is your last Christmas as a single man."

Robert's eyes twinkled. "It's a tough job, but someone has to do it."

Travis chuckled and reached again for the turkey platter before passing it to his guest. Robert declined, but had some more potatoes and gravy. Both men were more than satisfied when they set their napkins by their plates.

"Well, that was the meal to end all meals," Robert told his host as he rocked onto the back legs of his chair.

"Lavena is a real find, I assure you, Robert. If your Eddie needs any help with the house or cooking, just pop out here to the ranch for a few tips."

Robert chuckled, thinking of the scones and tea Eddie had prepared when he visited in September. He shook his head at Travis. "I think my Eddie will do just fine, but thanks for the offer."

"Speaking of Eddie," Travis continued, "what were her plans for the day?"

"She's with her family, including Uncle Mitch, and I think Clay Taggart and his family had been invited to join them."

"You've mentioned Clay Taggart several times," Travis commented.

"Yes. I was very impressed. He lives in Georgetown. He's a mine surveyor, but he's not caught up in that world of trying to get rich quick. Eddie tells me that his dream is to teach school."

"Well, we can certainly do with some well-qualified men and women for that profession," Travis said fervently. "If the rumors in town can be trusted, Boulder's new schoolteacher is not what they hoped she would be."

"Yes, I'd heard that as well. It's a large class, and I don't think she's assertive enough."

Lavena chose that moment to scurry into the room.

"That was a feast, Lavena," Robert told her.

She managed to look pleased without smiling. "Did you save room for pie?" she demanded.

"Not at the moment," he admitted, hands in the air.

Lavena speared Travis with her eyes. "You see that he stays around long enough to enjoy some of my pie, Travis Buchanan." With that she was gone.

The two men shared a smile.

"Lavena has spoken," Travis said with a false shudder.

Robert laughed. They rose from the table and made their way to the living room. A fire crackled in the huge stone fireplace, and they both sank into comfortable chairs near the blaze.

"Tell me the date again."

"March 14," Robert answered without hesitation. "Eddie and her mother set that date because her father wanted her to be 18 1/2 before we married."

"That's about 3 1/2 months from now," Travis said thoughtfully. "And what day do you want us to leave for Georgetown?"

"I think we better go March 5. Is that going to work for you?" Robert asked his best man.

"What if I said no?" Travis teased.

Robert smiled. "I think I'd get up and go tell Lavena that she has to run the ranch for you in March whether she likes it or not."

"You can't do that," Travis warned him. "She'd probably do a better job and never let me have it back."

The men fell silent for a time. It was a comfortable silence that lasted until they were almost drowsy, but then Robert asked Travis if this Christmas were different for him.

"You mean because I've come to Christ?"

"Yes."

Travis stared at the fire for a moment. "It is different because there's an awareness now that there's more than just me. Now there's a God in heaven whose Son came to earth. For so long I never thought of anyone but myself. Maybe I'm still too selfish."

"What do you mean?"

"I don't know if you realized it, but Tuesday was my anniversary. I believed in Christ seven months ago that day. And because of that, it's like Christmas is not as set apart. It feels as though I've celebrated Christmas every month from that day."

Robert thought that was one of the most special things he'd ever heard. He thanked Travis.

"For what?"

"For reminding me. I need to celebrate Christ's birth all year long, and I don't."

Travis smiled and nodded. He knew that Robert was often the teacher and he the student, but Robert never failed to thank him if something he said was a rebuke or a reminder. All of this turned Travis' thoughts to Eddie Fontaine. Travis had yet to meet her. He hoped and prayed she would be as special as the man she was marrying.

Georgetown

"We're going to stay with Uncle Mitch," Robert told Travis. The younger man couldn't hold his laughter.

"What did I say?" Robert demanded.

"Oh, nothing." Travis was still smiling. "You've only reminded me four times that we're staying with Uncle Mitch whose apartment is above the store."

Robert had to laugh at himself. "Come on, Travis, we've got to drop our gear at the store so you can come with me and meet Eddie." He would have walked on, but Travis spoke.

"I think I should stay at Uncle Mitch's and you should go on your own to the Fontaines."

Robert turned to look at him in complete confusion, but Travis only stared back.

"That's a good idea," Robert finally said softly, wondering why he hadn't thought of it himself. The men went to the store and met both Mitch and Morgan Fontaine, but Robert was so preoccupied that Mitch took pity on him and swiftly sent him on his way. Partway to Eddie's he remembered Travis and wondered how he would find his way to the Fontaines later. Then he remembered Travis saying that he would come with Morgan. All of the arrangements cluttered Robert's thoughts until the front door opened and he looked down at the woman he loved. For the moment, he dismissed his best man from his mind.

Travis had never experienced anything like the Fontaine family. They were warm and loving, and they made him feel like a special guest. The church family in Boulder was also warm, but he hadn't really become close to anyone except Robert. The Fontaines naturally included him in their meal, laughter, and close fellowship. It was a wonderful evening with Robert, Eddie, and her whole family, but Travis was a man accustomed to his solitude, so in some ways it was nice to have it come to an end.

It was dark when the men made their way back across town to Uncle Mitch's. They had to move through the shadowy store to the stairway where there was a door. Uncle Mitch's apartment was beyond that door. The main part of the living area was down a hallway where the apartment split into several smaller rooms, all on one side. One room was a kitchen and dining area, and one was Mitch's sitting room. The rest were bedrooms. Some of the rooms connected, and others stood alone. The original builder and owner had probably intended to rent the rooms out, but Mitch kept them for himself.

Now the two guests moved as silently as possible in order not to disturb their host. Once in their room, which sported two small beds, they found he had left a lantern burning.

"Well, what did you think?" Robert whispered as both men sat on their own beds to undress.

"I think you're marrying the kindest woman God put on the earth."

Robert smiled, his chest filling with a huge sigh of contentment. "She's wonderful. That big house," Robert said, referring to his newly built home in Boulder, "has been just plain lonely without her."

"It won't be long now."

"No."

The men were silent as they continued to ready for bed. Robert ducked under the covers first and said, "It's too bad Jackie's not a little bit older." Jackie was the sister two years younger than Eddie.

"It wouldn't matter, Robert; she would still seem too young. Even Eddie seems young."

Robert raised up on one elbow and stared across the room.

"I don't know what you mean, Travis. You're younger than I am by three years."

"It's not a measurement in years, Robert. Eddie is very mature, and she's going to make you a wonderful wife."

Travis fell silent, and Robert gave him a moment.

"I haven't shared a lot with you, Robert, but my life before Christ was pretty worldly. I look into the eyes of those sweet sisters, and I know they haven't seen anything of what this sinful world has to offer."

This Robert could understand. A man wanted a wife who would understand him, and even have an understanding of what he was thinking before he said it. Eddie had done that on countless occasions in her letters; she could read between the lines and guess Robert's thoughts even before he voiced them. Travis was not saying he wanted a worldly wife, just one who would understand where he'd been.

"I'm glad you told me, Travis."

"Yeah, me too. Good night, Robert."

"Good night, Travis."

Travis blew out the lantern and listened as Robert got comfortable. Travis, on the other hand, lay flat on his back and stared into the darkness, his mind going back earlier in the evening to his swift exchange with Addy Fontaine.

Should I be worried that you're going to elope with one of my daughters, Mr. Buchanan?

As lovely as they are, Mrs. Fontaine, I'm not in the market for a wife.

Travis asked himself if it had been a sin not to tell Robert about Rebecca. Robert was very sensitive about not invading his privacy, and Travis thought that might be one of the reasons he was so comfortable with him, but it seemed that tonight would have been a perfect time. On the other hand, this was a time of great joy for Robert, and Travis didn't want to do anything to dampen it.

Travis lay quiet and thought long and hard about what he'd said to Robert. Had he been misleading? After all, he had married a woman who was as sweet and naive as the Fontaine girls.

Travis took time then and there to pray about his situation. He could not logically find a reason to tell Robert. He still thought of Rebecca—he thought of her off and on all day long, every day of every year—but for some reason he saw no need to talk about her to anyone but the Lord. Travis fell asleep asking God to help him know what to do if the question of his marital status were ever asked of him directly.

23

Travis couldn't help but think of his own wedding day as he watched Eddie come down the aisle to stand at Robert's side. The bride's face was flushed with happiness, her eyes on the man she loved. Rebecca's face had been so pale, her eyes so solemn, as they had become man and wife. Where was she? It was the question he always asked, but since trusting God, he asked it without anger. He would have been made of stone not to wonder, but the rage was gone. He felt his mind beginning to linger on Rebecca and, with a mental shake of his head, pushed her from his mind. This was a special day for Robert and Eddie, and he did not want to miss a thing.

The wedding, and indeed that whole day, was unlike anything he had ever known. He'd never been with such a large group of people who were able to have fun and laugh without using alcohol. The women had fixed a veritable feast for the reception, and close friends and family stayed with the bride and groom as they opened gifts. Something caught at Travis' heart as he readied the team and saw the happy couple on their way to the hotel. His own wedding night came to mind, and suddenly he wanted to be alone. Uncle Mitch had not stayed for the gift opening, and once Robert and Eddie left Travis was relieved to be able to make his excuses and head back to the apartment above the store.

Uncle Mitch had turned in, so all was quiet. Travis was only too glad to seek his own rest, but when he was finally settled in bed, he lay wide awake, his mind going back over the day. Jackie was in love with Clayton Taggart. Travis wondered if either one of them realized it. Sammy had stared at him the whole day, and he had worked at being kind to her without giving her a reason to hope. He knew she was little more than a child, but he had no desire to play with her heart.

Finally realizing that he was not going to sleep, Travis relit the lamp. He read in his Bible for a time—his favorite, the book of Job—and then blew out the lantern and sat by the window. It was a dark night, the moon only a sliver, but Travis stared at it. Suddenly he wanted to be home. He wanted to be in his own house and his own bed. He wanted Lavena's scolding and cooking. It had been great to come and an honor to be a part of the wedding. He was even enjoying the prospect of going to church in the morning, but boarding the stage and returning to Boulder with Robert and Eddie on Monday couldn't come fast enough for him.

Boulder

"We want you to spend Christmas with us."

Travis shook his head. "You and Eddie will want to be alone, Robert."

"No, we won't. The Henleys have already agreed to join us and so have Raymond, Lena, and Carl." Lena worked for Robert and Eddie. "We're also planning to ask the Danz family."

Travis was so surprised that for a moment he couldn't speak. Certain he was going to be alone on Christmas Day, he had already been preparing his heart.

"What did I say, Travis, that has caused that look?"

"I don't know. I just assumed that you and Eddie wanted to be alone."

Robert only shook his head and stared at his friend.

"I'd love to come," Travis finally said. "Will Eddie's family try to be here?"

"No, but we just received a letter from Addy. They're all doing well but staying in Georgetown for Christmas." Robert's eyes went to the ceiling as he tried to recall the contents of the letter. "They miss Uncle Mitch—this will be the first Christmas without him—but everyone, even Morgan, is adjusting to his death. The girls are doing well at school. The Taggarts have moved to Denver. I think you knew that, but Clayton is writing regularly to Jackie, so she's delirious. Sammy still asks about you, and Addy thinks Morgan still works too much. There was more, of course, but right now I can't recall it."

Travis nodded. The Fontaines were not the perfect family, but Travis was still fascinated with them. Maybe it was because he'd never had siblings of his own or a happy home, but so many people in one family tumbling around that huge house just seemed like fun to him.

"Have I lost you?"

Travis grinned. "Just for a moment. What time on Christmas Day, and what can I bring?"

"I know we're eating at 1:00, but I'm not exactly sure what Eddie has planned for us to eat. Would you happen to know where we could get some nice beef roasts?" The question was asked so innocently that Travis roared. Robert felt free to laugh at his own joke, but then Travis accused him of only wanting his company that day for the meat. Robert admitted sadly that it was all too true, and it was all the more humorous since Travis saw it for the lie it really was.

Pine Grove

"Merry Christmas," Rebecca said softly as the boys came down the stairs. They were still half asleep, but the sight of the tree, gifts spilling out from underneath, was enough to wake them in a hurry.

"Look!" Garrett shouted and began to run, but Rebecca caught him.

"Not so fast. We're going to do this quietly."

She soon found that it wasn't that simple. Wyatt shot around both her and his brother, went right to the tree and began to open a gift.

"Wyatt," Rebecca scolded him. "Put that down!"

But now both boys were digging under the tree as if mining for gold.

"Mine!" Garrett proclaimed.

"Boys," their mother tried again.

"No, mine!" Wyatt argued.

"Give it!"

A fight broke out, and if Rebecca hadn't been on hand, they'd have knocked the tree over. She ended up grabbing each son by the arm and literally dragging both of them, kicking and screaming, into the kitchen. They were completely out of control, howling in rage, by the time she tried to put them in their chairs. Only by blocking the door with her body and shouting to be heard did she manage to get through. When they stopped and looked at her, she went on more quietly, saying the words again.

"You're not going to get any toys if you don't stop."

It amazed her that it worked. The threat of spankings never did because she didn't follow through, but this was not something she'd tried before.

"Now, we're going in by the tree, but you will *not* touch the gifts or tree, do you understand?"

They nodded very solemnly—anything to get back in the living room.

"Sit on the davenport," she instructed as she stepped aside and they shot in the door. They made a beeline for the tree, but stopped when she said their names sternly. They didn't sit on the sofa, but stood looking at the tree. It wasn't exactly what she wanted, but Rebecca thought she had their attention at last. She knelt down in front of them and spoke gently.

"Christmas is not just a time for getting; it's a time for giving. Won't it be special when you can shop for Mama?"

"When are presents?" Garrett whined at her.

"I want mine," Wyatt whined as well.

"You'll get them, but first I—"

"Now?" Wyatt pleaded.

"Yes, now!" Garrett was more demanding. A moment later they'd scooted around her to attack the gifts. Rebecca moved to the sofa, defeated. The boys had eyes only for the gifts. A sadness stole over her, but as she watched their antics, even their fights, she laughed a little, reminding herself that they were only three. In the minutes that followed, she convinced herself that she couldn't expect too much.

It was a little harder when she tried to tell herself that she was happy living alone with her boys and working 12 hours a day, but she managed. After all, she'd been able to buy them the toys of their dreams. Indeed, right now they were playing and laughing to their hearts' content.

Eighteen seventy-six was a week away. Rebecca couldn't help but ask herself what it would bring. For the first time in months, she let herself think of Travis. Had he settled very nicely without her? Did he ever think of her? It played in her mind that she could at least write to him and see how he was doing, but she dismissed the thought almost immediately.

A moment later, Rebecca stood, her chin going in the air as it did every time she felt determined. Eighteen seventy-five had seemed to fly by in an instant. Eighteen seventy-six would be the same way. So would 1877 and 1878, she told her heart. She hadn't needed Travis Buchanan this year, and she wouldn't need him in the future. Her mind thoroughly made up, and amid the sound of her sons' noisy play, Rebecca went to the kitchen to fix the boys some breakfast.

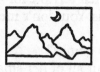

24

"Do you realize how much you've grown, Travis? Do you see the changes God has made in your life?"

Travis nodded, but he was feeling discouraged. It must have shown on his face because Robert tracked him down right after church. The men stood by the Langley coach. There was snow on the ground, but the sun was shining.

"God may have made changes, Robert, but nothing I've ever said to Lavena or my men has ever had an effect on them. I've taken your advice and tried to live my beliefs before them, but they're a worldly group. Lucky and I are close, and he's a fine foreman, but all he sees is the here-and-now. I was just like him, Robert. I never thought of eternity. But just like you with me, I want more for my men than they even want for themselves."

Robert nodded; he remembered feeling that same way. He was about to comment, when Travis cut in.

"What kind of a friend am I, Robert?"

"What do you mean?"

"I mean, you've got your sister-in-law so heavy on your mind, and I'm dumping on you when we're barely out the door of the church."

Travis was referring to Jackie Fontaine's accident the year before, which had caused her to go completely blind. The Fontaine family was not having an easy time of it in Georgetown, and Robert and Eddie were making plans for Jackie to come live with them. Travis knew it was taking a great deal of thought and time, and felt terrible for being an added burden.

"It's all right, Travis. You don't mean any less to me than Jackie."

"How are the plans going?"

"Well. Eddie has put all of her small breakables away and anything that doesn't need to be on the floor, like plant stands and such. There are no loose rugs waiting to trip Jackie, and her bedroom is set up in such a way that she'll be able to move around very easily. I'm sure she won't be happy about any of it, but we'll make it work."

"You'll be taking on a lot."

"Yes, but Addy is not going to hold up if we don't step in. Morgan has tried to help, as have the three younger girls, but they need a break. Now," Robert spoke encouragingly, "back to you, Travis."

Travis shook his head. "I'm just being tempted to doubt God. I want to see immediate results, and when I don't, I think God has stepped out of heaven and deserted me."

"How many years has it been, Travis?"

"Since I came to Christ?"

"Yes."

"It'll be three years next month, May 23."

Robert smiled, a smile of pure pleasure. "Again, Travis, I have to remind you of the changes. You are a completely different man. You've forgotten how cold you were toward any and all discussions about the Lord. It's the same way for Lavena and your men. You can't look at their hard hearts and write them off. I don't know Lucky and the others as I know you, but I remember an angry, unsaved Travis Buchanan. There were times when I thought I was going to get myself punched in the mouth, but I had something you wanted. Given time, Travis—God's time, not yours—your workers at the ranch are going to feel the same way."

"I need to keep trusting and believing."

"Yes. It's like you said, when the results are not immediate it's easy to doubt, but you must fight this."

The sermon that morning had been on prayer, and Travis could see where he'd fallen down on the job. Lately it had been easier to worry than pray, and he was anxious all the time. The ranch was doing well—come summer they would be headed out on roundup for a few weeks—but Travis had forgotten to be thankful for all he had.

"Am I interrupting?" Eddie's soft voice cut into their conversation, and the men immediately turned to her.

"Not at all." Travis spoke so Robert would know he was doing all right.

"How are you, Travis?"

"I'm doing all right. How about yourself?"

"I'm fine. Why don't you join us for Sunday dinner, Travis?"

"Yes," Robert put in. "Do come, and we can continue our conversation."

"All right," Travis accepted. "I usually let Lavena know, but it won't hurt to let it go this time."

"Good," Eddie proclaimed with a smile. "Come right now, and I'll have it on just as soon as I can."

It was an offer Travis could not pass up. The three of them went directly to the Langleys where they talked and ate and then talked some more. When the meal was over, and they were comfortably settled in the living room with coffee, Travis asked Eddie how she was doing. Tears threatened, but she still shared.

"I simply find it impossible to believe that Jackie can't see. It's not that I haven't accepted it; it's just that I can't picture her blind. So much is communicated through the eyes, and as sisters so close in age we did a lot of that. I can't imagine it otherwise."

"And you said that Jackie hasn't tried to write to you or anything?"

"No, nothing. According to Mother she won't do anything unless she's forced. I think we told you that Mrs. Munroe is helping out, but Jackie fights her every attempt to help. The family is exhausted. I know we might be taking on more than we bargained for, but in some ways I can't wait to get Jackie to myself."

"She's never been to Boulder, has she?"

"No," Robert put in.

Travis shook his head. "I can't imagine not ever seeing the mountains here or the flowers in the spring."

Tears did fill Eddie's eyes this time, and Travis' heart clenched in regret. "I'm sorry, Eddie."

"It's all right, Travis," she spoke softly. "I've learned a lot since we got the news, and one of the things is that this blindness is like a death in the family. I'm in mourning for my sister's eyes. For a time I tried to squelch the grief, but it was making me ill. It feels as though I've cried more in the last seven months than I have in a lifetime, but I know God understands."

"I think He does too," Travis encouraged her. "I was just reading about the way Jesus welcomed the children into His presence. I think He must have such a tender heart, especially when His children are hurting."

"I was just reading at the end of Matthew 23 about the way Jesus lamented over Jerusalem, mourned for them actually," Robert added. "He certainly understands grief."

The discussion went along on that topic for a time, but it wasn't long afterward that Travis realized how much of the day had slipped away.

"When do you leave?" he asked Robert when he was led to the door.

"This week, if the weather holds."

"Is there anything I can do?"

"Lena will be in a few times, but if you'll just keep an eye on the place, that would be a help."

Travis shook Robert's hand and told him he and Eddie would be in his prayers. He didn't see either one of them that week, but when the next Sunday rolled around and they were not in church, Travis knew they'd gone to Georgetown.

~

"I don't want you to be such a stranger," Robert told Travis. He and Eddie had been home with Jackie for several weeks, but the young rancher had seen what a stress it was for Eddie's sister when they were at church and only shook his head.

"I can't do that to Jackie right now, Robert. I can see how hard it is for her, and my presence is only going to make things worse. I can tell that she thinks everyone is staring at her."

"Well, many of them do," Robert admitted, "but it's not in the pitying or negative way she imagines. She and Eddie came into town to shop today. We went to lunch. I could tell she was terrified, but Eddie plans to take her every week until she's more comfortable.

"She should enjoy that once she gets used to it."

"I hope so, but now we're off the subject. Why don't you come for dinner tonight?"

Travis began to shake his head, but Robert put a hand up, his voice at its most persuasive.

"It's already after 4:30, so there's no need for you to go all the way home, and you don't have to stay long after we've eaten. I know Eddie would like to see you."

"All right, I'll come. When are you going to head home?"

"Around 5:00, but don't wait for me. Go on to the house and keep Jackie company. She needs to get out of herself."

"All right."

The men stood. "By the way, how are things going with Lucky and the ranch?"

"I'm not any farther along with Lucky, but things at the ranch are running well. Maybe I'll have a chance to tell you about it tonight."

"All right. I'll see you at the house."

⟨⟩

"I can't remember what color your eyes are," Jackie admitted shyly.

"Blue. Light blue."

"Do you wear a hat, Travis?"

"Yes. A black cowboy hat."

"Felt?"

"Yes. Here," he lifted it off the seat beside him. "Feel it."

He pressed the hat into Jackie's hands and watched as she studied it through her fingertips.

"What color is the band?"

"Black. Black on black. Not very exciting." His voice was kind.

"It's so soft."

"Here now." Travis rose and came to her. "Try it on. You live in Boulder now, and you have to look the part."

A small smile pulled at the corners of Jackie's mouth, and when he put the hat on her head, she asked, "How's that?"

"You look fine," Travis told her, but a small spark of pain hit his chest. A seeing person would have moved it back as it nearly covered her eyes.

"Robert just came in," Eddie announced from the doorway. "Why don't you come into the dining room and sit down?"

"Okay. May I offer you my arm, Jackie?"

"Sure." She stood and waited for him to remove the hat. Moving carefully, Travis put the hat back on the chair and then took her hand to draw it through his arm. He was just as careful as he led the way to the dining room, but he couldn't miss the strain on her face. He wondered what she was thinking. Travis' thoughts ran in all directions, and he was so concerned that his eyes sought Eddie's as soon as they entered the room. She only smiled kindly at him. Jackie reached for the table, and Travis forced himself to let her go. He watched anxiously as she felt her way around, but Eddie and Robert, who had now come into the room, took it in stride.

Jackie did not volunteer many words during the evening, but she did need help with certain things. Travis saw for the first time what a great job the Langleys were doing. They were patient and kind, never once showing Jackie any pity. The meal was wonderful and conversation was satisfying, but Travis left with a special appreciation for all that the banker and his wife were doing. They hadn't had time to talk about the ranch, but that was all right with Travis. He spent the rest of the evening praying for everyone under Robert Langley's roof.

25

"No, no, I won't get in!" Garrett kept up his crying for many minutes, but Angel persevered. He had managed to soak the entire kitchen and Angel in the process, but she finally had him in the tub. He repeatedly told her he would not get in the tub even after she had him in place, but at least the job was getting done.

"If you get soap in your eyes, don't blame me," Angel now gritted out. For a moment the howling four-year-old settled.

"I don't want a bath. Where's Wyatt?"

"I've got him locked in the closet," Angel told him without a hint of mercy as she scrubbed at his ears, and even with the cloth plugging one ear he could hear his brother's cries of outrage and his booted feet as they kicked the inside of the pantry door.

"I want my mama," Garrett began to cry.

"That makes two of us," Angel said, her voice still hard. "Now," she spoke with Garrett's head held in her hands, "you get into your pajamas and sit on the bed and wait for me. If you don't, I won't give you any supper."

Looking into Angel's outraged face, Garrett nodded obediently, but only because he knew she meant it. He and Wyatt had gone without supper just the night before.

"It's too bad you're not old enough to go to school," Angel muttered as she wrapped a piece of toweling around his small dripping frame.

"I'm almost five," the dark-haired twin told her defensively, his chin jutting forward at an aggressive angle.

"Not until November, and that's nearly two months away. Now get upstairs and do as I told you." Angel glared at him until he was out the door and then went to wrestle an insulted Wyatt from the closet. She was twice as wet when she was finished with the second boy, but both were subdued during dinner and at bedtime.

"It's still light out," Wyatt complained as Angel finally ushered them into the bed they shared, the bed that had been hers for so many years. "We don't go to sleep till it's dark."

"You will tonight," Angel told them, but she said it without heat.

"When will we see Mama?" Garrett asked. Angel finished adjusting the covers and sat down against the footboard. The boys sat in front of their pillows, not identical in looks, but clearly brothers. One was as light as the other was dark. Had Angel but known it, Garrett had his father's dark hair and light blue eyes, while Wyatt was blond and brown-eyed like his mother.

"I don't know yet," she told them honestly, without giving any details. "Preston is going to come in a little while and stay with you, and then I'll go and visit your mother at Dr. Creamer's."

"Why can't Gary and I go too?" Wyatt asked.

"Because your mother is still too sick. She can't hold you or take care of you, and you might catch what she has and get sick too. I'll tell you what," Angel said as she stood. "If you'll go right to sleep, I'll tell you first thing in the morning how she's doing."

They were clearly not happy with this, but both lay back on the pillows. She leaned over them, pulling the covers high, and kissed both their foreheads.

"Go to sleep now and dream nice things."

"Is Preston bringing his stick?" Garrett's voice wobbled as he asked.

"Yes, but he won't need it if you stay in bed."

Both boys nodded and watched as she pulled the shade on the room's single window. The room darkened slightly, but not so much that Angel couldn't see their faces. They looked like they could worry themselves ill, but sleep was rushing in too fast. Angel left with a small shake of her head. Never had she known anyone like them.

❧

"I've never known anyone like her," Dr. Creamer commented as he and Angel left Rebecca's sickroom. "As if two boys weren't enough, she takes on laundry for half the town. Did you see her arm? Skin stretched over bone."

"I know." Angel's voice sounded resigned. "She's bound and determined that those boys won't go without a thing."

"The only thing those boys need is a crack to the backside," the doctor said grimly.

"Well, Preston has seen to that a few times, and they're doing fairly well. But they're too much for Becky."

"Only because she won't discipline them. How are you holding up?"

"I'm all right. Getting tired. It's no wonder that she got sick, and I'm only taking care of the boys. I don't know how she does it all."

"Clearly, she doesn't," the doctor spoke bluntly. "Although I think she's out of the worst of it. For a time I thought we might lose her."

Even having heard this before, Angel was visibly shaken at the thought of Rebecca's death.

"Why don't you head back, Angel." His tone was compassionate. "It will be some time before she's up and around. Go on now; Preston will be looking for you."

Angel did as he bade. She was holding up well as she went back down the street but nearly crying when Preston met her at the door.

"She's not—" he said in fear.

"No," Angel told him huskily. "I'm just upset at the idea of it. Doc says the worst is over, but she'll not be on her feet anytime soon."

"Come on," Preston urged her, and they sat close on the davenport.

Angel's eyes went to the stairs. "Any noise from up there?"

"No, I've checked on them twice. They're both out cold."

"Good," she said softly and let Preston pull her close. She lay against him with her head on his shoulder. The feel and scent of his clean shirt relaxed her in a moment.

"How was she exactly?" he asked at last.

"Resting comfortably, but so thin and pale, Preston. It hurt to look at her."

Angel fell silent for a time. Preston was only too glad to hold her, although he knew he needed to get back to the Bell. His eyes roamed the room and came to rest on the small, round table that stood at the side of the davenport. With two fingers he lifted a pair of thin spectacles and brought them out for Angel's inspection. She sat up with a disgusted snort.

"Aren't those the most ridiculous things you've ever seen!"

"Weren't they yours?"

"Yes, but I don't know where I got them; they have only regular glass in them. Becky latched onto them when she was at the house a few weeks ago. As if it isn't enough to scrape her hair back like a peeled grape and wear ugly, shapeless clothes, she now adds those dreadful spectacles to her ensemble."

"I still don't understand, Angel. What's the point?"

"She can't stand to be attractive, Preston. It terrifies her. Everytime one of her customers shows the least bit of interest, she does something else to make herself repulsive."

"It doesn't work, you know. I haven't seen her with the glasses, but even with her hair pulled back and wearing that shapeless, mud-brown dress I always see her in, her face is still lovely."

"That must be why she went to the glasses," Angel guessed. "I wish I could talk some sense into her. I've lost track of how many times I've tried."

"Have you thought about what we would have done, Angel?" Preston now asked, his voice very soft.

"About what?"

"About the boys if Rebecca died. What in the world would we have done with them?"

Angel looked at him with something akin to horror. She'd been terrified for Rebecca's life but never once thought about the boys being orphaned. Without saying anything to Preston, Angel knew that she would have had to take them home with her; what choice did she have? However, a few days of obedience from the boys did not set the pattern for the next several weeks. By the time Rebecca was back on her feet some three weeks later, Angel knew she could never do it.

❧

"Well, now," Rebecca said in surprise when Angel knocked rather late one evening and came through the front door. "Not working tonight?"

"I'll be going in late," Angel told her and made herself comfortable in the living room. "One of the small perks of knowing the boss?" Rebecca asked with a cheeky grin.

"He's in love," Angel said with a smile.

"So are you," Rebecca told her, earning another smile.

Rebecca took a chair across from Angel. This was her time to get things done, as the boys were both asleep, but she was glad to be off her feet for a moment.

"Your color is good," Angel commented after taking a long look at Rebecca.

"I feel like it never happened."

"I think you've even put on weight."

"I do have my appetite back, and of course Preston got rid of some of my work." Rebecca's voice turned dry at this point, and Angel was glad to see she wasn't angry over Preston's interference.

"He told me he talked to you."

"Yes. I wanted to argue, but it feels so good to be back on my feet that I kept my mouth shut."

Angel continued to look at her friend, trying to ignore the appalling glasses perched on the bridge of her nose. Rebecca certainly seemed to be in a good mood. Angel hoped so, because what she had to say next was going to hurt.

"You do realize, Becky, just how sick you were," Angel commented on a serious note.

Rebecca pulled a face. "You're not going to turn religious on me, are you, Angel? Dr. Creamer's wife tried to tell me about God and heaven when she was taking care of me."

"No, I've come about something much more practical, but you're still not going to appreciate it."

Rebecca only stared at her, so Angel decided to plunge directly in.

"I've done a lot of thinking about what I would have done if you had died, Becky, and I've come to some sobering conclusions. To put it plainly, I wouldn't take the boys. I couldn't. I already told you that Preston had to take a stick to them several times, and that put them in line for a while, but I won't raise those boys, Becky."

Rebecca nearly laughed at her friend's dire tone. "I don't think it was that serious, Angel."

"Then you really don't realize how sick you were." The older woman leaned forward from her chair. "I *saw* you, Becky. I watched as your lungs fought for air. You nearly died. I learned in a hurry that there are no guarantees on this earth, Becky. We nearly lost you."

Rebecca no longer felt like laughing. She was quiet for some time, her face not showing the rush of emotions inside.

"So what's your point, Angel?" she asked at last.

Angel took a deep breath and said softly, "If you die, those boys will be out on the street. I won't take them in, Becky, and that's a promise. Dan would probably want them, but with the way Dahlia has always been jealous of you, I doubt if she would stand for it. I might try to contact their father, but if he didn't show up, I'd drop them at the nearest orphanage."

The room grew utterly still. The clock on the wall had not been wound, so there was nothing to break the awful silence.

"I can imagine that you must hate me now, Becky, but I had to tell you the truth."

Rebecca couldn't believe that she could feel compassion for someone who had just spoken so cruelly to her, but there were tears in Angel's eyes and Rebecca's heart was moved.

"You're not going to believe this, Angel, but I don't hate you. I can't imagine how you could cast them off, but you're right—they're not your responsibility."

"What will you do?"

"I don't know if I need to *do* anything." Rebecca's voice turned just a bit testy. "Yes, I'll agree with you that I might have died, but I didn't. I'm here, and I'll take care of my sons."

Angel nodded and stood. "I know I must have hurt you just now, Becky, but I am glad you made it."

"Of course you are." Rebecca's voice was now cold. "Otherwise you'd be stuck trying to find some way to dispose of my sons."

Angel looked at the floor. "I deserved that, Becky; I know I did, but I thought you should know how I feel." She moved to the door, and Rebecca came to her feet. She couldn't stand to have it end this way.

"Thanks, Angel," she said softly. The tall blonde turned.

"I'm sorry, Becky. I wish it could be different. I'll see you."

"All right. Don't be a stranger."

"I won't. Good night."

With that she was gone. Rebecca stood still for just an instant and then took the stairs on swift, quiet feet. She lit a lantern and stood over her boys, both sound asleep. Garrett's face was turned away from her, but Wyatt's baby-soft cheek was toward the light, his pale hair shining in the glow. Their foreheads were nearly touching, and against the pillow between them the fair hair mingled with the dark.

Rebecca felt her throat close. They were so precious. They never did a thing she told them, and they slapped at her, shouted, and threw horrid tantrums when they didn't get their way, but Rebecca loved them to distraction. Most of the time they were more than she could handle, and she found it easier to give in than fight them. But no one else saw the way they came to her when they were hurt or frightened, or how cuddly they were when they were sleepy.

Rebecca tried not to picture them alone and helpless, but it was impossible. She saw them in the street after dark, terrified and cold. She had to rush from the room so her tears would not awaken them. She closed the door of her bedroom and sank down onto the floor, her heart tearing in agony as sobs racked her body.

It was the start of a sleepless night and several sleepless nights to follow. Rebecca knew she couldn't go on as she was or she'd be sick again. Finally, on the fourth day, she faced what she must do.

26

What a time it's been, Travis thought as he headed toward town. The date was October 28, and he was going to Clayton Taggart's house. That summer Clayton had been hired as the new schoolteacher in Boulder, not knowing that Jackie Fontaine now lived with her sister or that she had gone blind. Theirs had been a tempestuous meeting, but Christ's love, which never gives up, as well as Clayton's own devotion, finally broke through. Now Clayton and Jackie were getting married. Travis had offered to take Clayton to the church, but he hadn't bargained on how nervous the groom would be. When Travis arrived, the younger man was beside himself.

"I can't stop shaking," he admitted.

"Second thoughts?"

"No," he smiled, laughing a little. "None of that, just . . . I don't know."

Travis smiled compassionately and decided that now was not the time to tell him his hair was on standing end. Once they got to the church, he would hand him a comb.

"What if she's having second thoughts?" Clayton suddenly asked Travis.

"I don't think she is," he said calmly. "I think she was ready to marry you weeks ago."

This arrested Clayton's attention as nothing else could.

"Why do you say that?"

"It's just something I've observed, Tag," Travis replied, calling him by his nickname. "I'm no expert on women, but when a lady blushes every time she's in your presence, there's something going on."

"But she doesn't do that."

"Not now, but a few weeks back, before she really got comfortable with you, she was beside herself to say the right thing every time."

Clayton nodded. He had seen some of this, but not the way Travis would have observed. Things always looked different when one's own heart was involved. Clayton told himself to ask the older man what else he had noticed, as Travis was a very observant man. The conversation would have helped Clayton's nerves, but instead he started to pace again. There was less than an hour to go, and it felt like an eternity.

It was not a large wedding. The church family had been invited to a reception in a week's time, but today's gathering was small. The short guest list included the Langleys, Pastor Henley and his wife, Beryl, Raymond and Lena, and, of course, Travis. Everyone was already inside the church when Robert stopped the wagon that carried the bride and Travis came out to lend a hand.

"Is Clayton here?" she wished to know.

"No," Travis teased her. "He jumped on the stage and ran for it."

"Oh, Travis, you have to stop" she told him and giggled, her face already red.

The rancher hustled her inside where Eddie and Lena were ready to make adjustments to her dress and to hand her over to Clayton. She had not wanted to walk up the aisle and have to grope about to find Clayton, so he was going to walk her up himself.

It took a few minutes, but Travis watched from the front where he stood next to Robert as Clayton turned with Jackie and started up the aisle. Jackie had not wanted music, and she'd asked everyone to stand for the ceremony. It was all rather unusual, but Travis found it very special. The bride and groom stood opposite Pastor Henley, and the rest of the party stood to the sides of them, forming a half circle around the clergyman.

It was not a long service, but serious and unique. Clayton and Jackie turned to each other and said the things that were on their minds. They wanted these special friends and family to witness their vows and hold them accountable. Eddie bawled her way through the proceedings, and even Robert was overcome a few times. As it had with Robert and Eddie in Georgetown, Travis' mind went back to his own wedding. Thankfully he wasn't given much time to ponder over it. Soon there was much laughter and talking as everyone filed from the church to head to the Langleys' for a special dinner.

Out at the wagons, they watched as Clayton helped his bride get comfortable in the buggy. Robert was going to ride with Travis in order to give Jackie and Clayton some time alone. Eddie went ahead with Lena and Raymond. Pastor and Mrs. Henley were on their way as well.

The two men had just come to Travis' wagon when two girls, looking to be around 14 years old, passed by. That they found the big rancher good-looking was more than obvious, and as they climbed aboard the seat, they shared a smile.

"You get stared at by a lot of women, Travis," Robert suddenly commented.

"Do I?"

"Yes. I just never realized it before now. Maybe it's time you get married," Robert teased.

Travis, who had raised the reins, went very still. He forced himself to turn and look at Robert, who looked right back.

"I'm already married, Robert. I'm sorry I never told you before."

Stunned, the banker stared at him. "You're married?"

"Yes."

Robert was silent for a full 30 seconds.

"Where is your wife?"

"I don't know," Travis replied painfully. Robert only nodded. "Maybe someday I can tell you about it."

"Sure." Robert's voice was kind. "Whenever you want to or don't want to, Travis."

Travis thanked him and slapped the reins. Robert was a good friend, and he felt relief at finally having told him. Maybe someday it could all come out, but not now. Now he needed to go and help Clayton and Jackie celebrate and get off to a good start. His prayers were that their marriage would be far different than his own.

$\sim$

"The first thing I need to do, Robert," Travis began, "is tell you that I'm not sorry."

Robert looked at his friend in confusion but stayed silent.

"I know that must sound odd, but a long time back I asked the Lord to help me know the right time to tell you. Then yesterday when it came out, I apologized. It does feel good to have you finally know about Rebecca, but I never felt the time was right before."

"Of course, Travis," Robert assured him. "I certainly don't hold any hard feelings toward you. I've never wanted to pry, so I've never pressed you about your private life. I can't say that I haven't been curious, but there was no point in digging into your past if you didn't want to talk about it."

"I appreciate that, Robert."

The men were doing what they often did—talking by the wagons after church. Other people were grouped off as well. Eddie was with Beryl Henley, and Travis hoped he could gain a few more minutes of privacy.

"Did you say her name was Rebecca?" Robert now felt free to ask.

"Yes, and her father was the owner of the Double Star. It's hard for me to believe it, but we were practically strangers. Andrew Wagner asked me to marry his daughter because his health was failing and he wanted her protected and cared for. He died just days after we were wed. It was a strain, but I thought we were going to make it work. I came in off the range a week after we said our vows, and she was gone. I haven't seen her since."

"How long ago was this?"

"Over five-and-a-half years, six years in February."

Robert looked thunderstruck. "I'm so sorry, Travis."

"Yeah, I'm sorry too," the tall rancher agreed. "It's taken a long time to accept that she's not coming back."

"Did you ever look for her?"

"I only stopped looking for her last year. I even put ads in the *Denver Daily News.* I've ridden from town to town, sometimes for miles. And when we take cattle into Denver, I can always feel myself looking. I've searched, Robert, even when it became clear she wasn't coming back."

"And she left you no note, no word of any kind?"

"No. Lavena was beside herself by the time I came in, but when I got into town here, she was gone."

Robert was still in shock but said quietly, "It must have caused you such pain to see Eddie and me married, and then Clayton and Jackie yesterday."

"Yes and no, Robert. I did think of my own marriage, but I couldn't have been happier for the four of you, and that's the truth."

Robert glanced up to see Eddie coming toward them, so he spoke softly to Travis. "Just so you know, I haven't told Eddie anything. I didn't want to do that without talking to you first."

"I have no problem with your telling Eddie; I know she'll be discreet. If Rebecca were here, it would make sense for people to know, but as it is—" Travis ended the sentence with a shrug, and Robert's hand went to his shoulder.

Eddie joined them just seconds later, and although he could see that their offer was genuine, Travis declined to join them for lunch. He rode home to Lavena's cooking, Rebecca very heavy on his mind. As always happened when he couldn't get her off his mind, he ended up in the study. He didn't know why he came to this room; it had been Andrew's room, not Rebecca's. Maybe it helped remind him as to why he stayed on at the ranch.

In the blink of an eye he had become a wealthy land owner in Colorado Territory, now the state of Colorado, but that had never been important to him. Keeping this place active and profitable, spending long days in the saddle, hiring or firing men, making it through days when he thought his hands would freeze to the reins, losing cattle, and having costs run higher than he figured—all of this for that moment when he might face Rebecca again. At times it had been all that pushed him on. But now, suddenly, he knew it wasn't going to happen. He still didn't think her dead, but neither did he think he would ever know what had happened to her.

Lavena told him that his meal was on the table. He followed her to the dining room, watched her pour his coffee, thanked her, and bowed his head over the plate to thank God for all He had provided. Travis realized that there were no holes in his life, no gaps—God had filled them all. Travis ate with the pleasure and warm serenity of God's grace, and even though he still prayed for her every day, for a time he put his wife from his mind.

Travis stood with the letter in his hand, too stunned to move. It wasn't possible. Not 24 hours before, he'd been convinced he would never hear from Rebecca again, but the letter in his hand now mocked that assurance.

Usually working the range, Travis had stayed in the barn today seeing to some repairs. He'd come in midmorning to get a cup of hot coffee. Lavena had parked the buggy by the back door when she'd returned from town. She had brought the mail with her. Hannah Ellenbolt had never mastered Rebecca's handwriting, but it was close enough so Lavena recognized the letter. When she handed it to Travis, she came right out and said, "This is from your wife."

Travis looked at the postmark for Pine Grove and wanted to argue with her—he'd searched there—but something told him Lavena was right.

"What did she say?" Lavena suddenly appeared again but stopped when she saw he hadn't moved. "You haven't opened it." For once she didn't sound bossy, just resigned. "I can't think that it will be easy, Travis, but you should just get it over with."

Travis' head turned as he watched her walk away. The sound of her steps had barely died away when his hand went to the corner of the envelope. He had not taken off his coat or moved from the entryway, but stood and read.

> Travis,
>
> I know it's been a long time, but I thought I should write and see where we stand. It is my assumption that you've made a new life for yourself, and along with those thoughts, I wonder if we are still married. I live in Pine Grove and am known by my married name. I would appreciate hearing from you about this matter.
>
> Rebecca

Travis thought it sounded more like someone addressing a letter to a catalog company than correspondence between an estranged husband and wife. Travis read the short missive again. She was all business, no emotion, but he couldn't say the same. His heart pounded in his chest, and he felt his face flush. Reba. Reba was alive and wanting to know if they were still married. Having given up or not, Travis had always known what he would do if she ever got in touch. With a swift decision to go by horseback and not on the train, he turned toward the kitchen.

"Pack me three days' provisions, Lavena. I leave in less than an hour." With that he hurried upstairs to prepare. He didn't even hear Lavena mumble to herself that the job was already half done.

~

"That's amazing, Travis," Robert told him. "Why just yesterday you'd resigned yourself. I told Eddie about it last night and we prayed, but I never . . ." The banker's words trailed off in wonder.

"I've put Lucky in charge and I'm headed out now, but I would appreciate your keeping this quiet. I'm trying not to have expectations. My only hope is that we can open some line of communication so I can know if she's all right."

"I'll pray, Travis; in fact, let's take a moment right now." Travis bowed his head and prayed along silently with his friend.

"What a blessing it is, Father, to know that You know what lies ahead. We thank You for Rebecca, Lord, and pray Your blessing upon her. Guide Travis' steps as he rides, and keep him safe on the trail. Help him to be loving and kind when he sees his wife. The unknown can be so hard, Lord, but You will go before Him. And if it be Your will, Father, let Travis' wife be restored to him. In Your name I pray, Amen."

"Thank you, Robert," Travis said, knowing he'd been a little too stunned through the recent events to say some of those things to the Lord.

The men shook hands, and Travis left Robert's office. The banker's prayer prodded Travis' mind, and as he covered the miles on the way to Denver and beyond, he poured his heart out to the Lord. It didn't make the trail smoother or the saddle more comfortable, but Travis knew that God was going before him.

27

Travis remembered Pine Grove but also saw that changes had been made. There were signs of new housing and several new storefronts. Travis remembered checking with a man on the street concerning a small, blonde woman, but the man hadn't seen her. His next stop had been to inquire at the Cradwell Tavern and Dance Hall, but he had also come up empty there. It wasn't what he would have called an exhaustive search, but he hadn't had the impression she would go so far out of Denver. Obviously, he'd been mistaken.

Travis stayed on his mount as he rode through town, his eyes scanning the houses and streets. He spotted the post office but decided to leave that possible resource until he'd had a look around. He didn't know what compelled him to turn, but a block past the stage office he turned down another street. The houses were simple, almost all two stories, some kept up and others left in disrepair. Nothing stood out to him. In fact, while on this street Travis realized that Rebecca might not live in a house at all. It was more likely she lived in a boardinghouse somewhere in town. Just then he heard the voice.

"No! Now stop that. Stop that this instant!"

Travis' head whipped around, and he craned his neck to see through the backyards in time to see a blonde woman go into a two-story white house. His eyes did not catch the two little boys that took off the other way because he was too busy moving Diamond in the opposite direction. He rode back to the main street, counting houses by the backyards, and then counted front yards as he moved down that street. It was the only white house on the street, and the paint looked new. It was remarkably easy to find. Travis tried to think calmly and slow the furious pounding of his heart. What if it hadn't been her? He heard his pulse in his ears as he tethered Diamond to a bush and went up the front porch to the door.

He knocked softly, and when there was no response, knocked louder. A voice called to come in, and Travis did so. He was more convinced than ever that Rebecca lived there, and that gave him boldness to open the door.

Rebecca was not in the mood for company. The boys had just run off, and because they'd been naughty, dumping wash on the floor as they wrestled, Rebecca had two extra loads of washing to boil before nightfall. She was tired and hungry and ready to scream. However, she remembered that someone had come in.

"Just put your bag on the floor and tell me your name," she called from the laundry area that had once been the dining room. From where she was standing, she did not have a view of the front door.

Travis stood very still, letting the sound of her voice wash over him. He didn't answer her but let his eyes take in the front room until they went to the gated-off archway that led to the laundry room. While he watched, Rebecca swiftly stuck her head around the partition and froze. Their eyes locked. At least Travis thought they might have locked. He was having a hard time seeing her eyes behind the glare of her glasses.

As he stared, she put her hand on the gate and pushed it wide open. She walked through, clearly not able to believe he was here. Travis felt a little uncertain of that fact himself. She didn't look the same, but it was Rebecca. His Rebecca.

"I can't believe you're here," she finally said softly, and again Travis felt pleasure at hearing her voice.

"I got your letter." His voice was rusty with emotion.

"I wasn't sure if you would. I mean, I didn't even know if you were still in Boulder."

"I'm still there, and we're still married," he said evenly, working hard to keep his voice steady.

Rebecca nodded, still looking bewildered. Travis was there, in her living room. And he looked absolutely wonderful. His eyes were clear, and he was as tall and handsome as ever. For the first time since she ran, Rebecca regretted the way she kept herself. It was with effort that she didn't pluck at her ugly dress and try to offer some sort of explanation. However, the sound of childish voices and the back door slamming put all such thoughts from her mind. She looked over in time to see Wyatt fly into the room.

"Mama, I'm not playing with him anymore. I hate Gary! I—" Wyatt cut off when he saw the very tall man at the front door.

"Just go out and make the best of it," Rebecca said swiftly to her son when she saw Travis' stunned look.

"Who's that?" Wyatt asked, but Rebecca had a hand to his back.

"Go now, Wyatt. Do as I tell you." Rebecca breathed a sigh of relief when he looked around her only one more time and went out the kitchen door. Rebecca turned back to the room to find Travis' eyes pinned to her.

"You have a son?"

Rebecca swallowed. She had sent the letter, so certain he would no longer be at the ranch, or just as certain that he would reply and tell her to stay out of his life. But here he was in her living room. *Deal with this, Rebecca. You deal with everything else; now deal with this!*

Her chin came in the air. "Yes."

Travis' mind had run in many different directions, but never to this. How old had the child been? He couldn't tell; he didn't know that many children. But that wasn't the difficult part—obviously Rebecca had found someone else with whom to share her life. No wonder she wanted to know if they were still married.

"Well," Travis said inanely, but nothing else would come. He stood wishing he could turn back the hands of time and just write Rebecca the answers to her questions. Travis had never known such pain. He'd told Robert he was going without expectations, but clearly that had not been true. He had never thought Rebecca would turn to someone else. Travis had no idea how long he'd been standing mute when another child came in, another boy, this one with dark hair.

"Mama," he bellowed loudly, "Wyatt says there's a stranger. I want to see him."

"No, Garrett, now run and play."

Garrett didn't argue as he usually did, but he stood and looked at Travis for a few seconds before turning and going out the door.

Travis felt worse than ever, but he wouldn't have let Rebecca know this for the world. He forced himself to sound normal and interested.

"How many children do you have?"

"Two," Rebecca said softly. "Twin boys."

The word "twin" made something like a bell ring in Travis' head. His mind was asking questions he could barely fathom, so his voice was low and soft when he said, "Twin boys?"

"Yes." Rebecca's was equally low.

"How old are they, Rebecca?"

His heart sank when her eyes went to the floor.

"They'll be five next week."

Travis thought for a moment, and then his eyes slid shut. He felt as if someone had just slugged the air right out of him.

"I have twin sons?" He forced the words past a throat that was closing fast, and Rebecca nodded miserably, suddenly ashamed at the way she'd kept them apart.

Travis turned away from Rebecca for a moment, his hand going to his face. *I have sons. I have two boys. Did you hear that, Lord? Twins. What will I do?* The question had no more formed in his mind than Travis knew the answer. He turned back to Rebecca and moved toward her so swiftly that she backed up. He stopped just a yard in front of her.

"Come home with me, Rebecca. I want you and the boys to come home with me. I want them to see the Double Star."

Rebecca was so stunned that she couldn't move or talk, but she wasn't given time.

"What are their names, Rebecca?"

"The boys?" she asked stupidly.

"Yes. What did you name them?"

"Garrett Wagner and Wyatt Andrew."

Travis held his breath. "Buchanan," he managed. "Do they go by Buchanan, Rebecca?"

"Yes. Garrett and Wyatt Buchanan."

Travis nodded. "They're fine names. Almost five, is that what you said, they're almost five?"

"Yes, on Tuesday."

Travis nodded, his heart swiftly growing possessive. His next words came out as more of a command than he intended, and he found out in a hurry that he no longer knew his wife at all.

"You're coming back with me, Rebecca—you and the boys. It's not right that you're not with me. We'll start packing you today." Travis began to glance around the room as if looking for crates to do the job, but Rebecca's voice came coldly to his ears.

"I don't think so, Travis."

He slowly turned back to her. Her face was as frigid as her tone.

"You're not really in a position to be telling me what to do. The boys and I will be staying right here in Pine Grove."

Travis' mind backpedaled swiftly, but he was far from through. His voice was kind, but he now wanted answers.

"Why don't you want to come back?"

"That is none of your business."

"I disagree with you. You are my wife, and those boys are my sons. Everything about you is my business."

"Get out, Travis." Her voice was still cold. "You're not wanted here. When you're gone, I'll file for a divorce settlement myself."

Her words shook him to the core, but still he asked her, "Why did you leave, Rebecca?"

"I don't care to discuss that with you, Travis. Now leave."

Travis thought fast. "I will go, Rebecca, if you give me a reason for why you left me."

Her eyes glared at him from behind the glasses, and again her chin went in the air. She was very angry now, and he steeled himself.

"I'll tell you why I left," she nearly hissed. "I left because I found out the real reason you married me! I was in the barn that day Biscuit accused you of marrying me for the ranch. I waited and waited for you to deny it, but you just walked away. I was a nightly diversion for you, as well as your ticket to owning your own ranch. You never loved or wanted *me!*"

Travis wasn't surprised at her thoughts, so he did nothing to deny them. It wasn't true, but she would have to learn that for herself.

"Well, I asked, and you told me."

Rebecca nearly blinked at his calm tone.

Travis' eyes went around the room and then beyond her shoulder to the kitchen before he heard the door slam. He spoke almost conversationally.

"It's funny I didn't find you the first time I searched for you."

Rebecca did blink then. "You searched for me?"

"Yes."

"In Pine Grove?"

"Yes, but no one had seen you."

Rebecca took some time to drink this in. Why would he go so far out of the way, unless . . .

"Where else did you look?"

"Name a town."

Now it was Rebecca's turn to feel like the air had been punched from her.

"Good-bye, Rebecca," Travis said calmly. He put his hat on his head and left without another word.

Rebecca's entire frame shook with the magnitude of her feelings. He'd searched for her, and she had sent him away. Wyatt and Garrett were both calling her to the kitchen because they were fighting over a cookie, but Rebecca walked out the front door after her husband. She could see where his horse's hooves had been, but he was gone. Were it not for those marks, she might have wondered if she had dreamed Travis' visit.

Whenever Rebecca found herself on her own, her chin would rise in the air and she would stoutly convince herself that she needed no one. But it wasn't working this time. She wanted to cry Travis' name and chase him down the street. Eventually turning back, Rebecca found the boys destroying the kitchen. She didn't scold them or say a word about the incident, not then or at any point that evening. She was too busy trying to decide if she'd been a fool to write the letter in the first place—or a fool to let Travis leave.

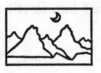

28

Travis walked into his room at the Pine Grove Hotel and immediately lowered himself into the room's one chair. He didn't know how he had managed to walk out of that house, but the look of stunned surprise on his wife's face told him he'd done the right thing.

"My wife, Lord, I've found my wife," Travis' joyful heart whispered to God. "I'm not leaving here without her or the boys. I don't think You would want me to do that. Maybe You want me here—obviously she has a business she's running—but we have to be together. The ranch waits for us. Please give me the words to help her see."

He felt physically drained but knew he would have to rouse himself for the bath he'd ordered. He remembered the time when Jesus had fallen asleep in the bottom of a boat that probably had water standing in it. He'd been so tired that He would have slept through the storm if His disciples hadn't wakened Him.

Travis prayed on for some minutes and then finished by saying, "You know all about fatigue, Lord. Just give me the strength to go on. I know now what I'm supposed to do; just keep me going until I can get the job done."

The water was delivered by two of the hotel staff, and when he was alone Travis sank gratefully into the steaming tub. He was as hungry as he was dirty, but he knew he needed sleep more than anything. A young boy had come back to check on him just as he was finishing. Travis slipped a coin into his hand and asked him to tell the cook that he would need to eat early.

∽

Rebecca's heart nearly stopped in her chest. It was the next morning when she heard the boys shrieking with laughter, a sure sign that they were up to no good. Hurrying to the front porch, she arrived in time to see Travis giving them a ride in a wagon. She could not make herself move as he pulled away from the front of the house and moved down the street, but just as she was getting ready to shout, he turned the team around.

Rebecca watched as Travis halted the team in front of the yard and then stepped down from the porch to have her say. However, her sons' eyes were glued to their father, and Rebecca stood on the fringe of their conversation for a few minutes.

"What's your name?" Wyatt wanted to know.

"Travis Buchanan."

"Our name is Buchanan," Garrett told him.

"Your mother told me. Now, who's Garrett and who's Wyatt?"

"I'm Garrett, but Wyatt calls me Gary."

"What do you like to be called?"

The dark-haired twin shrugged. "Garrett or Gary."

"You must be Wyatt." Travis turned to the blond, who nodded. "Do you like to be called Wyatt?"

"Yeah. Mama called me another name when I was a baby. I don't like it now."

"How do you know our mama?" Garrett now asked.

"I'm married to her," Travis said with quiet conviction. He forced himself not to look at Rebecca.

The boys stared at him with new eyes. He could tell that he'd shocked them, but that he was also something of a fascination.

240

"Mama," Wyatt spoke when he saw her. "Are you—"

"Go play," Rebecca cut him off. Something in her voice got their attention. "Both of you, go play." Surprisingly, the boys scrambled down from the back of the wagon and moved off. Rebecca waited until they had gained the front porch before opening her mouth to let Travis have it.

"Did you file for divorce?" The question was put so calmly that some of Rebecca's fire left her.

"What?"

"Did you file for divorce?"

"No."

They stared at each other.

"I thought you were leaving," she said at last.

"I did leave. I left your house."

"I thought you were leaving Pine Grove."

"Not without my wife and sons."

Rebecca looked away in frustration.

"You're not wanted here, Travis."

"Then why did you write to me?"

Rebecca didn't answer him. Her attention seemed to focus on the wagon.

"You didn't come here in a wagon, did you?"

"No, I bought it this morning. The wagon and the team."

"Why?"

"How else are we going to get your things back to the Double Star?"

Rebecca's face took on a longsuffering look. "You just don't get it, do you, Travis?"

"Of course," Travis went on as if she hadn't spoken, "I could wire Lucky and tell him to run things for the winter, since I'll be living here with you." His head went back to study the sky as if he had all the time in the world. "In fact, we might just be stuck here if we don't leave soon. I think it could snow anytime." Travis' head dropped back down, and he stared at her.

241

Rebecca felt panic claw at her throat. What in the world would she do in this small house with this huge man? And there were only two bedrooms!

She tried a new tactic. "You had no right to tell the boys we're married."

"Why did you write me?"

Rebecca shook her head in frustration. "You wouldn't believe me if I told you."

"Try me."

Rebecca's eyes closed, but she admitted softly, "I got sick and nearly died. When that happened I found out that no one would take the boys if anything happened to me. I was afraid for them. All you ever wanted was the ranch, but I was afraid for my sons, so like a fool I wrote to you."

Travis was off the wagon seat in a flash. Before she even saw him coming he was standing in front of Rebecca, her upper arms in his hands.

"Don't you see, Rebecca? We need to be together. It's not right that you're not with me, and the boys need their father. What if something should happen to *me*? The Double Star is theirs, but they wouldn't be there to claim it."

Rebecca felt almost faint as all of her beliefs, beliefs she'd clung to for five years, crumbled to her feet. But it wasn't that easy. They couldn't just pick up where they had left off. It would never work.

"We can still try," Travis told her when she offered him the argument.

"And you're willing? You're willing to take us home with you on my terms?"

"As long as you don't ask me to go along with something I think is wrong."

"Such as?"

"Rebecca, we don't know each other any more. We never really did," he said reasonably. "I don't know what situations will arise, but whatever tomorrow brings I would hope we could talk things through."

Travis bent his face lower to hers and transferred one hand to her jaw.

"Come home to me, Rebecca. I won't leave here without you."

The clothing and hair don't mean a thing to him. Not even the glasses. He still looks at me with desire. I've managed to put off every one of my male customers, but in just a few minutes Travis has stripped it all away.

That was still the last thing Rebecca wanted. She took a step backward, and Travis immediately dropped both hands.

"I don't want that kind of relationship, Travis. Let's be perfectly clear about that. I don't need a man. The boys need their father—I'll go along with that—but I don't need a husband."

She was so hard. He had watched her eyes soften for just an instant, but now the wall was back up.

"None of that changes the way I feel, Rebecca. I still want you and the boys to pack your things today."

She hadn't known what he would say, but this was a surprise. He was completely serious about them packing up that minute. He watched her vacillate.

"Say, yes."

"I don't know if I can do that."

"That's all right," he said, startling her again. "I'll head to the telegraph office and send word to Lucky about the ranch and to Lavena so she can send my things down."

Again Rebecca felt panic. She thought of the huge space at the ranch—the ranch home with more bedrooms than they needed and acres for the boys to run in and explore.

"We'll go with you." Rebecca's rush of words halted Travis in his stride. He had not been bluffing, so he was truly surprised that she'd changed her mind.

"That's great," he told her sincerely. "The boys will love the ranch."

Rebecca took a huge breath. "I was thinking the same thing." *I also know I'm going to love having a house big enough to keep you at a distance.*

"Good. I think it's time we told them more about who I am."

"Now?" Rebecca's voice squeaked a little.

"Yes. I don't expect them to throw themselves at me, but they're already curious and I won't live a lie."

Again Rebecca sighed. She didn't like the idea, but neither did she have a good reason for saying no. It was with a heavy tread that she turned back to the house, Travis behind her, to call the boys and get the job done.

∽

"He's our papa, and we're moving?" Garrett asked again, his eyes going back and forth between the adults.

"Yes. Travis . . ." she hesitated and tried again. "Your papa and I own a ranch, and he wants us to come and live with him."

"Why don't we live with him now?" Wyatt questioned.

"Because I wanted to live here for a while."

"But you want to live at the ranch now?"

"We're going to." Rebecca evaded the question and Travis' eyes.

"Are there horses?"

"Yes." All questions were still directed toward Rebecca.

"And cows?"

"Yes, many of them."

"Is there a school?"

"In Boulder there is, but the ranch is out of town a little way."

The boys were silent then, and Travis looked at their faces. It was a lot to pile on them at one time, but he still felt it was best. They had a few more questions for their mother, and sent many looks his way, but when Rebecca told them to go play for the fourth time, they finally did as they were asked.

"I really do want us to move swiftly, Rebecca, because of the weather. I think it's milder here than in Boulder, and I don't want to get halfway there and get caught in a blizzard."

Rebecca nodded. Suddenly she felt very tired, but not so with Travis. He was on his feet and talking. "We'll figure out just what you need for now. We can always come back and get the rest in the spring or have someone send it."

It was all too much, but Rebecca felt powerless to stop his relentless energy. She listened to Travis for a moment and then made an excuse to leave the room. He let her go. Rebecca moved through the kitchen and out the back door. Wyatt was standing at the back of the house, and she moved to kneel down in front of him.

"Wyatt, I want you to go get Angel. She was probably up late and will still be sleeping, but tell her Becky needs her."

"Can Gary come with me?"

"No, last time you guys broke her vase and she was mad for a week. Just go and tell her I need her to come here."

Wyatt ran off, and Rebecca made herself return to the house. Travis was waiting for her in the kitchen.

"I need to apologize to you, Rebecca. You obviously have a business here, and I haven't asked if you can leave it."

"I do laundry, and I won't have any trouble leaving it. I'm nearly caught up with what I have now, so I'll just finish what's here and return it tonight."

"And the house?"

"It belongs to a friend. I rent from her, but there's no obligation."

Travis had expected a battle, but Rebecca seemed resigned. Travis simply didn't know of another way to handle the situation. Had it been just Rebecca, he might have left and written letters to her, but seeing her raising his sons on her own had galvanized him into action.

"Why don't I go upstairs and try to figure out how many bags we'll need? The ranch house is so complete that I'm mostly concerned with collecting your personal effects."

Barely aware of his leaving, Rebecca sank down at the kitchen table and nearly jumped from her skin when Angel shot in the back door.

"I'll kill Wyatt," she said loudly when she spotted Rebecca. "He made it sound as if you were dying. I was sound asleep and—"

"Oh." Travis came back into the room and stopped dead when he saw his wife's guest. "I didn't realize you had company."

"Travis," Rebecca said softly, "this is my friend, Angel Flanagan. Angel, this is Travis Buchanan."

"It's nice to meet you," Travis told her, but Angel only stared at him.

"I'm going to run down to the general store, Rebecca, and see if they sell trunks or luggage. I'll be back as soon as I can." With a long look at her, he was gone.

"Your husband?" Angel whispered.

"My husband."

"Get those glasses off! We'll pull your hair back from your face and let it hang down your back. I've got that nice blue dress that hangs just a little off the shoulder. Have you got any figure left under all the material?"

"Stop it, Angel."

"No. You stop it. You are *not* going to let that man get away. Now give me those glasses, or I'll wrestle them off of you."

"I'm leaving." Rebecca stopped Angel's tirade with two words.

"When?"

"Today or tomorrow. He's packing us up right now."

"You and the boys?"

"Yes."

Angel sat down across the table from Rebecca. "Tell me what's happened."

"I wrote to him. When you said you didn't want the boys, I got scared. I wrote to him, and he must have come as soon as he got the letter."

Angel was silent for a full minute before saying, "That doesn't sound like a man who married you for your ranch."

Rebecca sighed. "No, it doesn't, does it?"

"Was he always that gorgeous?" Angel couldn't resist asking, and a small smile turned up the edges of Rebecca's mouth for the first time since Travis had arrived.

"Yes, he was."

Angel grinned at her. "You might as well take the glasses off, Becky."

"Why?"

"Because I can tell by the way he looks at you that they're not working."

Rebecca's hand went unconsciously to the neckline of her dress, but Angel only laughed, making the prodigal wife more determined than ever to be repulsive to her mate.

29

The hours that followed were like something out of a dream for Rebecca. She found herself packing and sorting alongside her husband. Angel had gone home, cleaned up, and then come back to help. This did more for Rebecca's state of mind than anything else, since seeing Angel reminded her that if something had ever happened, the boys would be on their own.

"We'll need all the quilts off your beds. It feels colder today than it was yesterday, and we'll need them all to stay warm."

Rebecca had only nodded. It was laughable really. She had been her own woman for so many years, and now she was acting like a mute and doing everything Travis instructed. On top of that, Angel was right. The Silver Bell hostess looked good in a gunnysack, and when she'd come back in a simple dress to assist them, she looked lovely. But Travis had eyes for Rebecca alone. Mrs. Travis Buchanan had made it clear that she didn't need a husband, but she hadn't come right out and said hands off.

At one point during the packing she faltered on the stairs, and his hands had been there, catching her around the waist to steady her. Another time he stopped to tell her something and reached without thought to brush a few loose strands of hair from her forehead. Rebecca's mind was in a complete muddle.

There was, however, light in the midst of this darkness: She had never seen the boys so well behaved. Travis would give them jobs, and they would run to obey. He would ask them questions, and they would answer without two dozen of their own. At one point they began to quarrel, and Travis quietly said, "Break it, boys." Rebecca had watched in amazement as her sons stepped apart.

At any rate, the time to leave was upon her before she was ready. All Rebecca had done for years was work, so there were few friends to say good-bye to her. There was no sign of Dan, Dahlia, and their little Joey, but that evening Preston came with Angel to give them a basket of food and a short send-off. Rebecca was glad they didn't prolong it, but Angel's final words to her were much too unsettling.

"I'll miss you; you know that," Angel said sincerely. "We'll keep an eye on your things, and we won't rent the house. If you don't come back in the spring for your stuff, we'll send it on. And who knows, maybe Preston and I will visit."

"I would like that. The ranch house has plenty of room."

Angel looked her in the eye. "Don't reject a man who clearly wants to lay the world at your feet."

"I don't know how you can know that."

Angel shook her head. "You're not able to view this objectively. Believe me, he would come running if you only bent your finger—not to mention how good he is with the boys."

"He is good with them. I've appreciated that."

Angel wanted to ask her how she could have left this man in the first place but refrained. She knew full well that it took two. When they hugged, however, she whispered, "Take down the wall, Becky. Let Travis love you."

She and Preston left on that note, but Rebecca couldn't get the words from her mind.

⌀

"No, Travis, no," Rebecca protested, but he lifted her gently. She had fallen asleep beside him on the wagon seat and was still not fully awake.

"It's all right. I'm putting you here beside the boys."

Rebecca had no idea what he was talking about—she only wanted to get away—but then she felt the softness of the quilts and the warmth of her sons' bodies and no longer cared who had her.

They were only an hour outside of Boulder. It had been a long, cold journey, and Travis could not stand to see her droop in the seat any longer. The boys had spent their birthday huddled under the blankets. They had run into flurries along the way, but no heavy snow. With home just up the trail, Travis knew the only thing that would keep him from finishing the trip this evening was a whiteout. He asked God to hold the snow, and hold it He did. Home had never looked so fine. Travis pulled the wagon up to the kitchen door and startled Lavena when he stepped inside.

"I've been looking for you for two days," she grumbled. "I gave up because it was giving me a sideache."

"It took a whole day to pack up their stuff."

This gave her pause. "Their stuff? Who have you got with you?"

Travis stared at her. "Rebecca and I have twin boys."

It was the first time Travis had ever seen Lavena speechless.

"Rebecca wants her own room, and I want the boys across from her."

Lavena only stood there.

"Get on it, Lavena. Make sure things are ready."

His voice had been mild, but Lavena lit out of the kitchen as though her skirt was on fire. Travis went back out the door. The sky was darkening fast, but Travis could see movement under the blankets. He lifted both boys at the same time and carried them to the kitchen swathed in blankets. Garrett was still sleeping when Travis put them side by side in Lavena's rocking chair, but Wyatt was looking at him.

"Just sit tight, buddy," Travis said close to his face. "We're home now."

Travis went immediately for Rebecca, who woke when the blanket lifted and she felt a rush of cold air.

251

"The boys!" She looked anxiously into Travis' face.

"Already inside," he told her, and continued carrying her to the door.

He set her on her feet and steadied her with hands to her arms.

"Mama?" Wyatt called to her softly. Rebecca went to the chair.

"I'm right here, Wyatt. Are you cold?"

"I don't think so."

"Do you want them to eat or just head to bed?" Travis came close to ask.

"I'm sleepy," Wyatt said now. His voice held a distinct wobble.

"Okay, honey, we'll get you into a nice warm bed."

Travis did not wait to be asked, but moved Rebecca gently out of the way and lifted his sons again. He moved confidently through the house, his boots making a deep, thudding sound whenever they left carpets and hit the hardwood floors. As Rebecca trailed him, she was reminded how much a stranger she was here. Things were familiar, certainly, but she had left this home. Not until this very moment did she think about how it would feel to walk through it again. She knew it would be especially hard when she passed her father's bedroom. She had not even given herself time to mourn him before she ran.

At the top of the stairs Travis had gone to the left. She followed him past her father's room, without looking in, to the end of the hall. If Travis had gone left again they'd have been in her room, but he turned right to the room across the hall from hers. Here they found Lavena, who had pulled the covers back just enough to use a bed warmer. Travis laid the boys on the bed. Garrett roused enough to use the bedpan, but Wyatt was asleep again when his father laid him down.

Travis might not know anything about raising children, but that didn't stop his next action. When the boys were down to their underdrawers, Travis's hand gently checked their limbs. All hands, feet, fingers and toes were warm to the touch. His large, work-roughened hands went to their ears and cheeks as well. Rebecca looked on, her throat growing tight as she watched his tenderness.

Travis stood back when Rebecca bent to kiss them and then followed her from the room. He began to shut the door, but Rebecca asked him to leave it open. He followed her into her own room. Lavena had disappeared down the hall, but they found she had left a lantern lit.

"I might just sleep in there." Rebecca swiftly turned before her eyes could take in much of the room. "I want to hear them if they cry in the night."

Travis nodded. "I can understand that, but you can rest easy, Rebecca. I'm a light sleeper. If you do sleep through, I'll hear them if they cry."

"I still might sleep in there, Travis, since you're all the way down at the other end of the hall."

"I'm in the master bedroom now."

Rebecca turned away from him, but not before he saw the flash of anger in her face. With a hand to her arm, Travis brought her right back. She did nothing to disguise the fact that she believed her husband to be completely out of line. Travis bent and spoke quietly into her face.

"You and your father have been gone for almost six years, Rebecca. How long was I supposed to wait to make this my home?"

It was all said without heat. His face was open, his eyes searching hers. Rebecca's anger drained away just that swiftly. "I'm sorry, Travis. You're right. There's no reason for me to criticize you."

"It's a bigger room, Rebecca. If you'd rather be in there, I'll move."

Don't reject a man who clearly wants to lay the world at your feet.

"No," Rebecca spoke as she pushed Angel's words away. "But thank you anyway, Travis."

253

Travis continued to look down into her eyes, his voice even softer. "Will you be all right?"

"Yes," she told him, but they both knew she'd answered automatically.

Travis stood studying her for a few moments longer before saying, "I'll leave you to your rest then. Oh," Travis turned back. "It's not very late. Did you want something to eat?"

"I think I just need sleep."

"All right. Good night, Rebecca."

"Good night."

Not until Travis moved out the door, leaving it open on his way, did Rebecca have the courage to look at the room. Her eyes swept over the familiar layout. Nothing had been moved, nothing had been changed, and suddenly Rebecca didn't want to see it. She didn't want to think about her life when she lived in this room or be reminded that she had been taken from Pine Grove, and her independence, to a place where she was not in charge. The lantern was on the desk, and Rebecca moved swiftly toward it, intent on turning it low when something caught her eye. At the edge of her crystal ink well was a folded sheet of paper. Rebecca recognized the stationery immediately and reached for one corner edge. It had obviously been crushed, but someone had made it as smooth as possible before folding it.

Rebecca unfolded it and painful, harsh memories assailed her. It was her letter to Aunt Hannah, the one accusing the older woman of everything. Rebecca read it over twice, one sentence in particular leaping out at her: *I was forced to marry my father's foreman and all because you're a selfish, sick old woman.*

Rebecca had not remembered until that moment how upset she had been. Her father was dead; she'd only had him for such a short time; and she had no idea how to reach out to her new husband or help him reach out to her. Her frame shook with the magnitude of her emotions. For so long she had pushed such thoughts aside, but now they were moving in with an intensity that rocked her.

Without bothering to remove her dress, Rebecca picked up the lantern and turned to the boys' room. She felt dirty and hungry, but her weariness and disappointment were greater. The boys were sleeping as usual, nearly lying on top of each other, so there was plenty of room to climb in beside them. Rebecca knew she wouldn't sleep. She was back in Boulder in her father's house, but her husband slept down the hall. Maybe this was why it felt good to be so near her sons. Not restful, but comforting. She put her glasses on the nightstand, blew the lantern out, and lay looking into the darkness, sleep feeling miles away. It was certain to be a long night.

Travis had removed his boots, so moving quietly back down the hall was not a problem. He wanted to check on Rebecca but knew that such an action would not be welcome. He could not think of a reason, however, that she might object to his checking on the boys. His lantern was turned low, and he moved with quiet precision into the room. He stopped in his tracks when he recognized Rebecca's form under the quilt. There was no movement, so Travis softly approached. She was sleeping as soundly as the boys. Travis had come with the intention of checking his sons, but minutes passed before he looked at them.

It didn't even look as if Rebecca had removed her dress. Her hair was still up, and she'd put only her glasses on the bedside table. Travis looked down at her, and his heart clenched in agony. How did a man fall in love with a woman whom he hadn't been near in over five-and-a-half years? Travis knew that it had to be Christ and the way He had worked in his heart. There was no other explanation. All he knew was that when Rebecca came out from her laundry area, her eyes locking with his, he'd never been so in love. He hadn't loved her when they first met or married. There had been desire and deep caring, but not love.

She doesn't know, Lord, Travis prayed in his heart. *She doesn't know that I would give her anything: my time, my attention, the run of the house and ranch. Anything she wants. I know she doesn't know You, but that doesn't change the way I feel. She's my wife. It doesn't make sense that I would feel this way—we only lived together for a week—but I do.*

Travis' eyes went to the boys now, and he prayed for them. One of Garrett's little feet had pushed out from under the covers. Travis wanted to push it back in for warmth, but he feared disturbing the threesome. However, the sight of that little foot proved to be too much for him. He turned from the room and moved as swiftly as he dared back to his own. By the time he sat down on the edge of the bed, tears were coming down his face.

I have children, Lord, his heart cried. *I have two boys. I can hardly take it in, Father. Sons. I have sons.* Travis gave up at that point. The last week crowded in upon him, and all he could do was cry. He mourned not having been there when they were born, but he also praised God that his family had been restored to him.

I don't take this for granted, he finally managed to pray before he fell asleep. *I don't think Rebecca will be settled here at all, but Lord, please don't take them away from me again. Please work in her heart. Robert prayed that my wife would be restored to me, but I can tell she's here only in body. Please don't let them leave me again.*

By the time Travis managed these final thoughts he was too spent to think anymore. He slipped beneath the covers of his bed and slept instantly.

30

Travis began the next morning with more prayer, but this time he started by confessing. *I panicked last night, Father, and told You what to do, but I can see now that I need to trust You. You've brought Rebecca and the boys back into my life for a reason, and no matter how brief the time, I am thankful.*

Travis also took a long time to read in his Bible. It was the first time he'd had a chance in many days, and his eye continually caught references to fathers and children: God the Father and His children, and children and obedience. Finally he turned to Job. He thought about what it would be like to lose ten children in an instant. Travis had only two, and he'd only known about them for a week, but the thought of losing them was not an easy one. Already he was very emotionally involved where those little boys were concerned.

If I'm not careful, Lord, my mind will run wild, and I'll be fearful over things that may never happen. If You take my boys for any reason, I know You'll give me the strength to carry on. You've proved Yourself to me over and over. Help me not to doubt now.

With a sudden, terrible intensity, Travis wanted to see Robert. It was early yet and he hadn't heard anyone else rise, but maybe this was the best time. Dressing swiftly and quietly, he went out through the kitchen. Lavena was just beginning to stir, and he told her he'd be back soon. It had snowed some in the night, but Diamond, after trailing a wagon all the way home from Pine Grove, was ready for a run. It wasn't long before he was tying the beautiful buckskin in front of Robert and Eddie's. He knocked softly on the door, knowing Robert would be readying for work but not wishing to disturb Eddie if she did not rise with him. It took a moment before the door opened.

"Travis!" Robert cried with delighted pleasure.

"Am I too early?"

"Get in here," Robert said with mock severity and put an arm around his friend once he was inside.

"You're back!"

"Yes, just last night."

"Come in," he urged him forward. "I have coffee on."

The men moved toward the back of the house and into the kitchen, and it wasn't long before they were sitting across the small table from each other, steaming cups of coffee in their hands.

"How are you?" Robert asked sincerely.

"I'm all right."

"Did you find Rebecca?"

"Yes, she's at the house."

"She came back with you?" Robert was surprised and pleased at the same time.

Travis nodded. "I didn't think it was going to work out. I had to convince her to come, but she's here."

"Do you think she'll stay?" Robert asked with his usual insight.

"I don't know, but Robert, there's more." Travis hesitated, and his friend watched him. Travis struggled with the words.

"I have sons," he whispered. "I have twin boys."

"Travis," Robert just breathed the word. "I had no idea."

"That makes two of us," Travis told him, and they both laughed a little.

They were silent for a moment, both busy with their thoughts.

"What are their names?"

"Wyatt and Garrett. They're five."

Robert shook his head, a smile now stretching his mouth. "What do they look like?"

"Wyatt is fair like Rebecca, and Garrett favors me. I think they might be a handful, but they did well on the trip."

"But you're not certain Rebecca will stay?"

Pain crossed Travis' features. "I decided we needed to be together, especially after I saw the boys. Rebecca wrote to me only because she got sick and almost died. When she recovered, she found out that no one would take the boys if anything happened to her. I made a decision to stay and live with her in Pine Grove if she wouldn't come back with me, and when I told her that, she agreed to come. I don't know what the next days and weeks will bring."

"How does she seem?"

Travis could only shrug. "I don't know her anymore. She's lived in a different world than I have. I think she worked all the time. I wasn't in a position to ask too many questions, but her closest female friend lives with the man she's seeing." Travis' voice sounded regretful. "Rebecca didn't seem to have any problem with it." He paused before going on.

"When I think of the way we were married; I mean, she did everything her father told her to do without question. I was never in the habit of ordering her around, but when I made a few demands in Pine Grove, I found out in a hurry that she's changed."

"But so have you, Travis," Robert reminded him. "I think if she stays around at all, that will become very clear to her."

Travis could only nod. It was amazing. They had ridden all the way from Pine Grove in the same wagon, but conversation had not been warm and open. Rebecca didn't know him at all. Indeed, if his actions in Pine Grove were all she had to go by, she probably found him as commanding as her father had been.

Travis had a sudden thought. What was it like for her to come back to the house her father died in? It had taken ages to piece all the parts together, but Travis now realized that

Rebecca had barely begun to know her father when he came into her life, and then Andrew had died so soon after the wedding.

"I'd better get back," Travis said suddenly, and Robert, already feeling like he'd lost him, didn't argue.

"I'll walk you to the door."

Eddie was just coming down the stairs and gave Travis a quick hug as he left. The men agreed to meet later.

"His wife actually came back with him?" Eddie questioned her husband when he explained. "That's wonderful! We'll have them to dinner right away."

Robert slipped his arms around Eddie and laid his cheek on the top of her head.

"I think that's a good idea, but let's put it off a few weeks. I would guess that they need some time to settle in."

Robert went on to tell Eddie about the twins, and he watched as she put a hand to her own expanding waistline.

"Don't even think about it, Eddie," he told her sternly, but couldn't keep the laughter from his eyes. Eddie only smiled up at him and got herself kissed again.

～

Rebecca stood on the threshold of her father's room, her heart beating almost painfully in her chest. It didn't look exactly the same, but the changes were minor. The quilt was different, and there was a pair of boots in the corner that would have been too large for her father. The sight of them made her wonder what they'd done with Andrew Wagner's things. It was no longer her place, but Rebecca walked to the closet. Inside were Travis' belongings. He wasn't a clotheshorse or anything quite so dramatic, but it still rankled her a little that he was so completely ensconced in the room.

Her anger didn't last. She remembered his question from the night before. It had been a long time. What had she expected him to do? She had certainly gone and made a life for herself with little or no thought of her husband. Her *husband*. Somehow it was hard to take in. She had lived so long doing as she pleased, that the idea of having a husband was now a little hard to comprehend.

"Did you change your mind?"

Travis' voice so startled Rebecca that she spun in surprise, her hand going to her chest. She stared at him, and he repeated the question.

"Changed my mind about what?"

"About moving in here. I can take my things back down the hall."

Rebecca shook her head and turned away from him. "I was just looking around."

Travis studied her profile. It was so hard to guess what she might be thinking. Her face was often a mask of cold composure.

"Did you hurt your eyes, Rebecca?"

She finally turned to him, her brows drawn in puzzlement.

"I mean, you didn't wear glasses before, did you?"

Rebecca's fingers went to the frame. Most of the time she forgot she had them on. Now she felt a fool.

"I just feel more comfortable with them on," she told him stiffly.

"Good," Travis told her sincerely. "I have a friend who fell and lost her sight a few years ago. I'm just thankful you didn't hurt yourself."

Rebecca wanted to run. She wanted to dash from the room and run as far and as fast as she could from this kind man. *Don't you understand, Travis, I don't want you. I don't want your care, and I don't want your kindness.* Rebecca's mind screamed these words, but nothing showed on her face.

"I think I'll check on the boys," she murmured softly, not wanting to be near him any longer.

"Lavena is fixing some breakfast. Come down when you're ready."

Rebecca nodded but didn't answer, and Travis felt he had no choice but to leave her alone.

∽

"Are they coming to eat?"

"I think so," Travis told Lavena while accepting the coffee she offered him. He took a seat at the kitchen table. "Rebecca was going to check on the boys, so I expect they'll be down in a while."

"How old are they?"

Travis shot her a look. "If you're asking if they're mine, Lavena, you're out of line."

"I wasn't asking any such thing!" she snapped at him in honesty, but still Travis ignored the question.

"Their birthday was Tuesday."

"Tuesday? When you were still traveling?"

"Yes. We didn't have a chance to do anything."

"I'll make a cake."

"I would appreciate that."

They both fell silent, but the silence didn't last. Rebecca and the boys could be heard coming through the house just five minutes later.

∽

Travis walked to the barn and thought about how well breakfast had gone. The boys had been very wide-eyed and silent as they took everything in, and Travis had enjoyed watching their response. Rebecca was quiet, but that was to be expected.

Normally when he returned from a trip, he was out the door early to meet with Lucky and check on the stock and barn, but this morning he took his time, eating slowly even though he knew it was way past time to get to work.

"I'll be in the barn for a time if you need me," he said to Rebecca, but she had only glanced at him and nodded.

Now Travis had turned and was headed back to the house. He wasn't leaving to ride the range for at least an hour. Why couldn't the boys come with him to the barn? He went back through the kitchen door and entered just in time to hear Garrett yelling in outrage.

"But I *want* to go out there. Why can't I?"

"Me too," Wyatt fussed beside him.

"Not now," Rebecca replied reasonably, but Travis watched Garret's face turn into a thundercloud.

"*No, no, no,*" he screamed at his mother, punctuating each shout with a slap at her legs or whatever he could reach.

"We want to! We want to!" Wyatt howled in the background as his brother got further out of control. Garrett kicked at and hit his mother, landing blows now and then, but she only spoke calmly and tried to fend him off.

"Stop that, Garrett." Travis had seen enough. He'd come up behind the little boy and taken his arm, but Garrett lashed out blindly.

"Let me go! I'm going to the barn. Let me go!"

Travis' free hand connected very hard with the seat of Garrett's jeans. The little boy was so stunned that he froze. He stared up at the big man, too shocked to cry or move.

"Do not hit your mother," Travis told him calmly, but his deep voice held an unmistakable note of authority.

As soon as Travis loosened his hold, Garrett dove for his mother, clinging to her leg as if he'd been beaten. Wyatt, who had only watched, now clung to her other leg, both looking with fear at their father.

"I came back in to take you to the barn," Travis spoke to his sons, "but I can see you're not ready."

"We'll be good, we'll be good." Wyatt let go of Rebecca and begged Travis.

Travis shook his head. "I can't have you two throwing tantrums and scaring the horses."

"We won't." This came from Garrett, who had also abandoned his mother's leg.

"Some other time," Travis said and turned to leave. The kitchen was long and narrow, and Travis was already back to the door when Rebecca's furious voice stopped him.

"You had no right."

Travis turned to find she had followed right behind him. He was amazed at the anger he saw in her eyes.

"No right?" Travis questioned her in quiet incredulity.

"No. They're not accustomed to spankings. You scared them. Garrett didn't mean any harm. He was just having a tantrum."

Travis bent until his face was closer, his eyes holding hers. "Don't ask me to stand by while my son attacks my wife, Rebecca, because I won't do it."

There was something in the possessive way he referred to her as his wife that warmed Rebecca, but she pushed the warmth down.

"We didn't ask to be brought here, Travis." She said the first thing that came to mind. "If you don't like the way I do things, maybe the boys and I should return to Pine Grove."

Travis stood to his full height and looked at her. She hadn't even been there 24 hours, and already he was hearing this.

"Is this what I can expect every time we disagree, Rebecca?"

Feeling stung by the rebuke, her chin went further into the air.

"You clearly need help with those boys," he went on calmly. "I hope your pride won't stand in the way of getting it."

It was true, but Rebecca didn't let her shoulders slump until after he'd gone out the door.

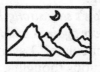

31

He was doing it again. Rebecca had been fighting it all day, telling herself that Travis was out of line and that she was angry with him, but there he was, back from his day outside, cleaned up for supper, and treating her like a queen.

"Are you warm enough, Rebecca?" he asked as he held her chair at the dining room table and pushed it in.

"Yes, thank you," she managed, but all she could feel was his hand on her shoulder.

"Here, Garrett." Travis took a seat and began to accommodate his wife immediately after he prayed, something else that was new to her. "Please pass these rolls to your mother."

The whole meal continued this way. Rebecca ate her supper but didn't taste it. She had had a speech all planned. She had been ready to tell him that it would never work for them to live together. She had steeled herself for a huge scene, but he'd not come home angry. She had been upset all day, but Travis walked in as if nothing had happened. And the boys were no better. They ran for their father, the man who had scared them just that morning, and nearly climbed all over him in order to ask about seeing the barn and horses, and how many cows he'd roped and branded that day.

Travis hunkered down to their level as if he had all the time in the world, and Rebecca felt so betrayed that she could have wept. It hadn't helped when he'd scooped them up and taken them to his bedroom to talk to him while he washed up for supper. Now at the table, he was so accommodating that she felt herself softening.

It won't work. If I don't stay strong I'm going to end up being everyone's floormat all over again. I will not live like that again!

"I hope you like chocolate," Lavena announced, breaking into Rebecca's tempestuous thoughts.

"A cake!" Wyatt shouted, jumping up from the table.

"Sit down," Travis ordered calmly just as Rebecca was opening her mouth. She wanted to be angry when her son obeyed without question but knew that Wyatt wouldn't have listened to her anyway.

"How did you know it was our birthday?" Garrett wanted to know.

"Why, your father told me, of course. We can't celebrate a birthday in the back of a wagon!" With that she went on her way, and Travis felt Rebecca's eyes on him.

"You need to thank your father, boys," Rebecca told them, but they only stared at him.

"It's not our birthday, is it, Mama?"

"No. Your birthday was Tuesday, but you wouldn't have a cake if your father hadn't told Lavena."

"That's a funny name." Wyatt was sidetracked.

"Say thank you to your father," Rebecca repeated, but the boys only cast mutinous looks at her. This had been one of Angel's biggest complaints. "It's common courtesy, Becky," she would say when the boys refused to thank her. Rebecca agreed with the complaint, but the boys were very stubborn about it.

"Actually," Travis spoke up when he saw their faces, "I think we should thank Lavena. I'll call her back in, and you can thank her. Okay, boys?"

There was complete silence at the table. Rebecca, knowing how bullheaded the boys could be, was silently begging Travis not to make an issue of this, but she could see that he expected better.

"Well." His voice was still calm. "Either way, I'm going to call Lavena back in. You can thank her, or she can take the cake back into the kitchen. Little boys who can't be thankful when they're given something do not deserve to have it."

Travis watched the boys exchange a glance and look back at him.

"Lavena," he raised his voice just enough. "Will you please come back for a moment?"

The older woman appeared, her brow knit with confusion. "Are you ready for coffee in the living room already?"

"No, but the boys have something to say to you."

Lavena glanced crossly at Travis, but he leveled her with a look. He turned to his silent children.

"Thank you for the cake," Travis prompted them.

"Thank you for the cake," Wyatt said, but Garrett sat quietly, his eyes going from his father to Lavena and back again.

"Now, Garrett," Travis said softly.

Wyatt's face was tense as he stared at his brother, but Travis was done waiting. He picked up the top dessert plate.

"We'll only need three of these tonight, Lavena. Thank you."

The plate was in the housekeeper's hand, and she was headed away from the table when the little boy blurted out a desperate thank you. Lavena turned to tell him he was welcome, returned the plate to Travis, and then slowly moved from the room.

"Good job, Garrett and Wyatt," their father told them. "I knew you could do it."

Rebecca had to work at keeping her mouth closed. She had never seen such looks of pride on her sons' faces. Why, they nearly beamed at their father. Rebecca ate the cake mechanically, but as with the rest of the meal, she barely tasted it.

"That was good," Wyatt said, the chocolate frosting and cake on his mouth attesting to that fact.

"Go tell Lavena you liked it."

"All right. Come on, Gary."

The boys shot off, and before Rebecca could guess his intentions, Travis moved to the seat beside her. He leaned close, his arm on the back of her chair.

"If I help you put the boys to bed, will you join me for coffee in the living room?"

Rebecca looked into his warm eyes and wanted to melt. She was so tired of doing everything on her own, and Travis was clearly waiting to catch her if ever she fell. *But he's taking over,* Rebecca reminded herself. *And if you don't resist him, there will be nothing left of you.*

"All right," she spoke outloud and then sat up very straight. "Actually, I have some things to say to you."

"Great." Travis smiled and touched her arm before he rose. He went after the boys and a moment later walked back through the dining room, one son flung over each shoulder. Listening to their high-pitched giggles, Rebecca rose slowly and began to follow them from the room. However, she stopped and looked at the mess on the table. Travis had taken a few dishes with him when he'd gone out, but most of them were still there. Right now Rebecca couldn't find a reason to go upstairs. The boys were delighted to be taken off by their father, and Rebecca, with no reason for her poor mood, was feeling put out about the whole thing. She turned to the table and gathered some dishes into her hands. From there she went to aid Lavena in the kitchen.

"And it's a true story?" Wyatt asked.

"Yes. That was a story from the Bible, so we know it's true."

"How big was the man?" Garrett asked again.

Travis smiled. They had missed his main point, but he was still delighted with them. They were more awed by the size of Goliath than by David's actions with God on his side.

"He was very big."

"Bigger than you?"

"Much bigger," Travis assured them, and watched their eyes widen.

"I think it's time you slept now."

"Where's Mama?" they wanted to know.

"I'll get her. You sit tight," Travis told them, but they made to follow him when he rose. He turned and looked at them, and without so much as a sound they scrambled back into bed. It was becoming more and more clear to Travis that his sons never obeyed, not even the simplest commands. Rebecca was so hard and angry with him, but with the boys she was so soft it was ridiculous. They were bright children. It wouldn't take them long to figure out who the pushover was. As he walked back down the stairs, he prayed a prayer of thanks that they had asked for her. The last thing he wanted to do was to replace Rebecca, but the boys were only going to have contempt for her if she didn't make them mind.

"The boys tried to tell me some story about a giant man," Rebecca spoke as soon as she entered the living room.

"Right," Travis said calmly, although he was feeling anything but calm. "I told them about David and Goliath."

Rebecca blinked. "From the Bible?"

"Yes."

Rebecca would have stood staring at him, but Travis was offering her a large mug of coffee. Rebecca welcomed the warmth and the distraction as she took the cup from his hand and sank down into the other chair in front of the fire. The flames danced and crackled, and for a time she kept her eyes on the logs.

Travis kept his eyes on Rebecca. With the reflection of the flames in her spectacles, he couldn't see her eyes, but her mouth looked sad. What was all of this doing to her? Was she miserable or confused or both? And how did a man go about telling his stranger-wife that he had come to a saving knowledge of Christ? Travis simply didn't know. He did know, though, that if they didn't learn to talk, their relationship was never going to work.

269

"Are you still upset about this morning, Rebecca?"

She looked at him. "No, I think I understand why you did what you did. The boys can be rambunctious."

Travis wanted to tell her to face facts, but he refrained. The boys were not rambunctious, they were . . . Travis' mind hesitated. What were his sons? He wanted to call them brats or monsters, but in truth they were sinners. Self-seeking sinners, as all people are.

Please, Lord, let me show them You. Help my attitude and care of them to be such that they will see a difference. Travis would have prayed on for his family, but he suddenly noticed Rebecca's scrutiny of him.

"Will you miss Pine Grove, Rebecca?" He asked the first question that came to mind. "Or should I not assume you're staying?"

Rebecca's eyes went back to the flames. "I don't know what to tell you. I can't say as I'm sorry we married, Travis, because I have the boys and I can't imagine life without them. But you have to admit, ours was not the best of beginnings."

Travis nodded. "Do you believe in second chances, Rebecca?"

He heard her sigh. "I don't know. I don't know you anymore, Travis." She now looked at him. "I'm certain you would say the same about me."

"Can I ask you some things?"

"Sure."

"I don't really want answers from you right now, but I want you to think about some of this."

"Okay."

"You grew up without your mother, is that right?"

"Right."

"And your father moved away when you were, what?"

"Eight."

Travis nodded. "I think I understand your reason for leaving, Rebecca, and I won't try to convince you that I didn't marry you for this ranch. I think you'll have to find that out on your own. But I hope you'll give us another chance. You basically grew up without your parents, and for different reasons, I did the same. I want better for our sons." He could see that he had her attention. "I'm not saying I don't care about you and me, because I care more than I can say, but if you need a reason to stay, Rebecca, please stay for the boys."

Rebecca's lower lip went between her teeth. This was the last thing she'd expected. She was glad he didn't want answers right then, because she couldn't have come up with any.

"We've both changed," Travis continued. "We're not the same people we were a few years ago, but we *are* husband and wife. I'd like us to try again." He wanted to tell her that he had no choice. He wanted to say that before God they were husband and wife and not to work on their marriage was not an option, but he feared putting too much pressure on her. Instead he left it as it was and waited for her to comment. When she didn't, he asked about what she'd said earlier.

"Did you say you had some things to talk to me about?"

"Oh." Rebecca seemed to come back to him from a faraway place. "I, yes, I wanted to tell you that—" but the words had left her. What had she wanted to say? *Don't correct our sons, Travis, because I'm jealous of the fact that they obey you rather than me?* It sounded as ridiculous in Rebecca's mind as it was sure to sound if she voiced it outloud.

"I guess I don't have anything to say. I was a little concerned about your treatment of the boys, but they seem to be all right."

"Are you satisfied with their manners and obedience, Rebecca?"

She hesitated. No one had ever asked her that. They had called her children brats and threatened them if they stepped out of line, but no one had ever asked her if she was happy with the job she'd done as a mother.

"I don't know, Travis," she told him honestly. "After all, they're only five, and I want them to be happy."

Travis could have told her she was going about it the wrong way, but something stopped him.

"I want them to be happy as well," he said, "and I think the best way to accomplish that is to let them know their boundaries and do whatever I have to do to keep them there."

Rebecca could hardly argue with that because it had worked so far, but the day had been long for her because she'd been afraid to let the boys outside.

"I could tell they felt very cooped up in the house today," she mentioned almost absently.

"Why didn't they go out?"

Rebecca's brow creased in sudden anger. "Because no matter what you said this morning, Travis, they would have gone to the barn. Also, I don't know what else is off limits for five-year-olds on a working cattle ranch. For all I know, there's some big hole out there that they could fall into!"

"It must have been a long day for you."

But Rebecca didn't want his understanding; she was suddenly in the mood to argue.

"Yes, it was," she said tersely.

Travis let silence fall between them for a time. Rebecca was looking bitterly into the flames, and Travis was watching her.

"I'll take the boys out in the morning and show them what's allowed. I'll also tell you what they can get into, so there will be no argument. If my orders are not followed, they won't be given a second chance. It's too dangerous for that."

Rebecca looked thunderstruck. "But Travis, they'll never make it. They'll be inside for the rest for their lives."

Travis stared at her. "You expect them to disobey, Rebecca, do you realize that? I give them a command, and I expect them to carry it out to the letter. Here on the ranch, that could mean their lives."

She looked so defeated by his words that Travis stood. He moved to the front of her chair and, taking her by the hand, lifted her from her seat. He was very close as he looked down at her.

"I've overwhelmed you after a long day. I'm sorry."

Rebecca didn't reply. She did feel overwhelmed, but over his presence, not his treatment of the boys. She didn't mention any of this to her husband. Still holding her hand, Travis reached with his free hand to draw a finger down her cheek.

"Your skin is still so soft."

Rebecca's heart sighed, but then Travis lowered his head and she stiffened. There was no need. Travis pressed only a soft kiss to her forehead.

"Why don't you go get some rest?" he asked softly, his voice full of caring. "I'll stay in long enough in the morning to talk with the boys. Do they have warm enough clothes to wear to play outside?"

"Yes." The word was barely audible, but his question was enough to snap her back to reality. With a soft good-night she left the room, her head in a muddle. Dan had waited for years to get as close as Travis had just been. Why hadn't she wanted his attention? And why did she still feel warm all over from Travis' simple kiss to her brow?

32

Travis lay on his bed for what felt like hours. He had been so tense in the living room. Rebecca hadn't sensed this, but he'd been so nervous about what she might say and how he might respond. At any moment he was certain she was going to walk out of his life again. He wished there were a way to know what the next few months would bring. He had said so much to her, given her so much to think about. If Rebecca came to him and calmly asked to be taken home to Pine Grove, could he do it? And what was Rebecca hiding in her heart? Did she hate all of this or him? Was she repulsed by him? He couldn't read her face anymore. Too often the glasses hid her eyes, and even when he could see them, he couldn't tell what she was thinking. And the boys—right now they were in awe of him, but what about the days to come?

Travis suddenly heard his own heart. *I'm in a panic, Lord. To hear me, You would think I'm the one in charge, and that I've got to figure all of this out in one night. Please help me to trust. You've already brought us so far. I know You'll finish the job.*

Travis knew that confessing his anxiety was right, but he also knew he had to get his mind off his wife and the days to come. He wasn't worried about the next day and showing the boys around the barn, but Saturday made his gut clench in dread. Saturday was the day he had to tell Rebecca that he went to church on Sunday, but that wasn't all—he wanted the boys with him. He wasn't going to tell Rebecca she had to go, but the boys would be going to church with him no matter what.

Years ago Mitchell Fontaine had told him about a little trick he practiced whenever he was worried or couldn't sleep. Travis now put it into effect. He arranged himself as comfortably as he could in bed and closed his eyes. He then began to list the attributes of God and any verses he could remember that pertained to the attribute. He fell asleep somewhere between "righteous" and "omniscient."

Just down the hall, Rebecca could have used such a system. The boys had been sprawled all over the bed, so she had had little choice but to tough it out in her own room. This room had been a haven of comfort and warmth when she arrived from Philadelphia, but now it held only painful memories.

Rebecca turned yet again, but felt no comfort. The quilts were warm and the mattress soft, but she felt sore all over. She continued like this for nearly an hour before giving up. She threw the covers back, wrapped a blanket around her shoulders, and moved to the hallway. A quick peek at the boys told her they were sound asleep, so she padded barefooted to the stairs. Travis' door was open, but she didn't hesitate or look toward the room. The downstairs was dark, but Rebecca remembered where everything was and made her way to the kitchen. Lavena had left a lantern on the table. Rebecca lit it and put the kettle on to warm. The heat from the huge woodburning stove and oven felt good, and she stood close to it in the semidark room. It took awhile for the water to heat, and in that time Rebecca let her mind wander.

I can't believe I'm here. I'm in Boulder. It's barely been 24 hours. I walked away from Pine Grove in a day's time. I didn't love it so much that I'll ache for it, but will I ever see Angel and Preston again? Do I want to see Angel and Preston again? Rebecca shuddered a little at the thought of going back on her own. How had she left it all those years ago? With the boys it now seemed impossible. She suddenly felt trapped, as if in prison. Travis was the jailer, and she was in the cell. Rebecca shook her head free of the image. It wasn't strictly true. He had acted nothing like a jailer. He wanted to give her whatever she wanted. The problem was, she didn't know what that was.

"Travis, is that you?"

Rebecca started violently at the sound of Lavena's voice. The older woman's bedroom was off the kitchen.

"Oh," Lavena said when she came fully into the room, "Rebecca. Can't sleep?"

"No."

"You want something to eat?"

"No, I'm just going to make some tea."

Lavena snorted. "Don't know if I have any tea. Let me look." She sounded as grouchy as ever, but Rebecca took little notice. Indeed, she was content just to stand with her hands over the stovetop. As the kettle was heating, she heard Lavena mumble, "Well, that's better anyhow."

Rebecca glanced at her. "What's that?"

"Your hair. You don't look like a skinned rabbit."

Rebecca's hand went to the hair hanging down on her shoulders, but she didn't comment.

"Where are your glasses?" Lavena now asked, but again, Rebecca didn't answer.

Rebecca picked up the kettle. Lavena had unearthed some tea, and Rebecca now prepared herself a cup.

"Do you want some?" she asked the older woman.

"No. I'm going back to bed. Turn that lantern off when you head up," Lavena warned her unnecessarily and went back to bed.

The tea was bitter to Rebecca—she hadn't had any in ages—but tonight she didn't mind. In some ways it went with her mood. All her life she had looked to other people to make her happy. First her aunt and uncle, and then her father. Her husband hadn't had much time to even try, but Rebecca was certain that she would expect it of him sooner or later. All that had changed when she met Angel. Angel had been a kind friend, giving her a home when she had none and putting up with the boys when they were tiny. Angel had been the first person Rebecca had known to be happy on her own. Even before she got involved with Preston, she had been a complete person in her own right.

Rebecca was truly glad that Angel and Preston had made their relationship work, but at times she had been lonely for the other woman's presence. Since her laundry business and the boys consumed her life, their times together were few, but there were moments when having another adult around would have been nice. Rebecca had known enough solitude to make her wonder what it would be like to have a real marriage with the man she now lived with.

In truth, Rebecca didn't know exactly what a real marriage looked like. Hannah and Franklin's marriage was not real. It was built on lies and pretense. She could hardly remember her mother, and so had no memory of her parents' marriage. She'd seen very little of Dan and Dahlia after they were married, so they were no help. The closest thing to a real marriage had been Angel and Preston's relationship. Rebecca thought back on all she had seen them do. They often looked at each other and smiled. Preston took every opportunity to touch Angel, and she touched him in return. Was that what love looked like? Rebecca simply didn't know.

Suddenly she was tired. Her cup was still half full of tea, but she was ready to sleep. She rose, put the kitchen to rights, and blew out the lantern as Lavena had instructed her. She moved through the kitchen, then the dining room and past the living room, her mind still dwelling on a dozen things. Then she saw Travis with the lantern. He had just arrived at the bottom of the stairs. Rebecca stopped when he spoke.

"Lavena?"

"No, it's Rebecca," she told him, but remained in the shadows.

"I heard noises. Are you all right?"

"Yes. I just couldn't sleep."

"Can I get you something?"

"No, I just had some tea."

"So you're headed back up?"

"Yes."

"I'll hold the lantern for you."

Rebecca hesitated but then moved forward. Travis was on the verge of stepping out of her way, but then she came fully into view. When he didn't immediately move, Rebecca looked up at him. She watched his eyes traverse her hair and face, and then back to her hair again.

"I'd forgotten—" he began softly, but cut off, his mouth compressing slightly.

Rebecca opened her mouth to ask what he was going to say but closed it again. Suddenly she didn't want to know.

"I'd better go up now."

Her voice seemed to snap Travis back to attention. He moved aside, and Rebecca made an effort not to look at his wide, bare chest as she passed. She told herself not to run, but the temptation to dash to her room and slam the door was great. Travis didn't even go all the way down the hall with her. He stopped when he saw that she'd gained her room. He returned to his own room and found that sleep was the last thing on his mind.

~

"You go to church?" Rebecca questioned him suspiciously for the second time, and Travis knew in that instant that this wasn't going to go well.

"Yes."

"Is that why you pray before meals now and tell the boys stories from the Bible?"

"No. I do those things, as well as go to church, because I have a different relationship with God than I did before."

Rebecca stared at him. It was Saturday, and they had just had lunch. The boys had run outside to play. Rebecca had planned to work on some mending, but Travis had stopped her before she could leave the dining room. At first her stance had been defensive; now she shrugged as if she didn't care.

"It doesn't really matter to me whether you go to church or not, Travis."

"I want you and the boys to come with me," he inserted gently. All of Rebecca's nonchalance fell away. She looked horrified, her eyes huge as she stared at him.

"I don't have anything to wear," she finally blurted, her whole body tense.

"Oh." Travis wasn't prepared for this but thought fast. "Well, I wouldn't want you to come if you felt uncomfortable about your clothes. Maybe you can get something out for the boys. I'd be glad to do it, but I thought you might have a better idea of what you want them to wear."

"They don't have any church clothes," she said a little too swiftly.

Travis shook his head, his face its usual calm. "There's nothing fancy about the church I go to, Rebecca. Jeans for the boys will be fine, just as long as they're warmly dressed. I want them to go with me."

This last sentence was said before Rebecca could open her mouth to gainsay him as she'd been about to do. Their eyes met and held. Travis was not going to rant and rave, but he would take the boys if he had to dress them himself. Rebecca finally looked away from him.

"I'll get them ready for you. What time do you leave?"

"About 10:15."

She nodded, her gaze still averted.

"If you change your mind, Rebecca, you're welcome to join us."

"Why do you want us to go with you, Travis?" She faced him directly.

This gave him pause, so he began slowly. "My relationship with Jesus Christ, God's Son, is a wonderful thing to me." His voice was soft, but she didn't miss his sincerity. "I've learned a lot in the last few years, and like I said, it's been very special. It's so special, in fact, that I want to share it with my family."

It was a very nonthreatening reply, and as Rebecca looked at him her expression was open. However, it became even more apparent to her than ever that she didn't know this man now and probably never had.

"Have I upset you?" Travis asked after watching her.

"No, but you have surprised me."

"If you had a dress you felt comfortable in, Rebecca, would you want to come?"

His face was a picture of vulnerability at that moment. His eyes watched her, and there was nothing demanding about him. Rebecca felt shaken just from the look in his eyes.

"This is important to you, isn't it, Travis?" Her voice was soft with her emotions.

Travis' eyes still drilled into her. "This marriage, Rebecca, actually this whole family—I want it to work. That can't happen if we each live in our own little world. I'm trying not to pressure you into things you don't want, but my life with the church here is very full. I want you and the boys to share in that. I want us to share everything. We haven't really talked more about things we discussed that first night, but this is part of what I was talking about. I want this to be a real home, and I think our attending church together could only help. I know I haven't given you much warning, but I hope in time you'll come with me and the boys."

"Maybe next week," she heard herself saying.

"Great," Travis said softly. "You still have some clothes in your room upstairs. Maybe this week you'll be able to find something you like."

Travis watched in amazement at the change that came over her. Her face became a mask, and her hand went to the high neckline on her dress.

"What did I say, Rebecca?"

"I don't need a husband," she told him coldly. Travis could only stare after her as she turned and walked from the room.

He shook his head to try and clear it. It was as if he'd imagined the woman from Thursday night, the one wrapped in a blanket, no glasses, and her hair around her shoulders and face. Rebecca did everything in her power to make herself look bad. Her clothing was nothing short of odd. At a time when fashions were fitted at the waist, Rebecca's dresses hung like a sack on her. The only tight part of her attire was the neck that sat so high on her own neck that it appeared to be choking her. And what had she said about the glasses? He had seen her wander around without them, but she told him they were comfortable to her. *I don't need a husband.* The light was beginning to dawn.

My sons will be with me in church tomorrow, Lord, Travis prayed as he headed out the door. *But I can see we all still have a long way to go.*

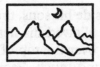

33

The boys' eyes were round and solemn as Travis ushered them into the pew the next morning. They had not been at all certain about getting in the wagon without their mother, but Travis had not left time for arguments. Usually so full of questions, Garrett sat very quietly. Wyatt, however, had been full of inquiries as the wagon took them closer to town.

"What're we gonna do there?"

"At church?"

"Yeah."

"We'll sing songs to start the service, and maybe have a few announcements. Then Pastor Henley will preach a sermon that will teach us about God and His Son, Jesus. We'll visit with people afterward and have a good time."

"Will we hear stories from the Bible, like you tell us?"

"Yes."

"Why didn't Mama come?"

"She wanted to find a different dress to wear before she came."

"Will we do it again?"

"Yes, I come every week."

"Is the church near the school?" This one question had come from Garrett.

"It's fairly close. Would you like to go look at the schoolhouse after church?"

"Yeah," he breathed the word softly and then was silent for the rest of the ride.

Now Travis sat beside his sons, their feet dangling over the edge of the pew, and allowed his heart to melt with love for them. They could see over the top of the pew, but as yet they were not looking around much. People milled around, some greeting Travis, but the boys sat as still as statues. Glancing down at them, Travis felt his heart squeeze in compassion. He reached over Wyatt's head to put his hand on Garrett's hair. Both boys looked at him.

"Are you all right?" he asked softly, but they only stared at him.

"Hello," a deep, kind voice spoke just then, followed by a feminine one.

"Hello, Travis, these must be your boys."

The three Buchanans looked up to find Robert and Eddie sitting in the pew in front of them.

"Hello, you two. Meet my boys." Travis smiled with pride. "This is Garrett, and this is Wyatt. Boys, this is Mr. and Mrs. Langley. Can you say hello?"

But the boys had no such plans. After a swift glance at the unfamiliar adults, their eyes dropped to their laps. Travis opened his mouth to remonstrate them but closed it again.

"I think I'll give them a little time," he said quietly to his friends.

"Certainly." Eddie's eyes were understanding even as they caressed the boys' small, bent heads. "We'll have lots of time to get to know each other."

The service began just a few minutes later, and Travis found himself glad that the boys were quiet. It was a lot to take in in one morning, and he wondered if a little awe of their surroundings might not be such a bad thing. It was not to last. The sermon wasn't five minutes old when they started to get squirmy. Travis cleared his throat, and they both sat still again, but it wasn't long before they were making faces at each other and moving again. Travis leaned over and told them to hold still, but that warning lasted only a few minutes before they began to giggle and wrestle in the pew.

Travis separated them, one on either side of him, but even that didn't take them very far into the sermon. Thinking he'd finally found a solution in their separation, Travis was amazed when Garrett reached across his lap to throw a punch at Wyatt, who tried to box him in return. Travis set his Bible aside and marched the boys out, his large hands holding theirs. He didn't bother with their coats, but swiftly shot out the door in order to keep the disturbance to a minimum.

"Is church over?" Wyatt wanted to know.

"Is it time to see the schoolhouse?" Garrett piped up.

"It's time to see a spanking if you don't sit still."

The boys' demeanor changed immediately. They stared at him with wide eyes, as if they had no idea what he could be talking about. At least Travis felt like he finally had their attention.

"Now," he said firmly, "church is not over, but wrestling and socking each other are. We're going to go back inside, and you're going to sit quietly, one of you on either side of me. You can do it with this warning, or you can have a spanking. The choice is yours."

"Is it lots longer?"

"Church? No, Garrett, but I expect you to sit still and try to listen no matter how long it lasts. Are you both ready?"

They were starting to shiver, so Travis was glad to see both heads nod yes. He took them back in, and other than a few wiggles, they sat quietly for the remainder of the sermon. Travis didn't think they got anything out of it, and for himself, he couldn't remember when he'd missed so much in a sermon.

"Well now," Robert stood after the final prayer and turned to his friend with a smile. "It sounds like you had an interesting time back here."

Travis had stood as well. He chuckled at his friend's words and spoke for Robert's ears alone. "They thought church was over when I took them out."

Robert shook his head. "I never giggled or wrestled in church, but that was only because my body forced me to sit absolutely still. I never remembered to take care of my personal needs before the sermon began, and my father had a hard-and-fast rule. He thought if we had to sit still and be uncomfortable for that time, we would never forget again. It didn't work with me."

Travis laughed, but Eddie, standing patiently nearby, didn't join in. Robert had forgotten again. In her condition she was constantly needing to be excused. Robert was blocking the path to one side and another family had clogged up the other escape. Not able to wait any longer, she said his name in a low voice.

"Oh, honey," he started, moving out of the way. "I'm sorry. Out you go."

She sent him a relieved smile and made for her coat and the door. Travis looked at him in confusion, and Robert was reminded that he'd missed all of this with his own family.

"The baby takes up all the room. Expectant women have to see to their needs more often."

"I didn't know that," Travis told him sincerely.

"I'm sure if you asked Rebecca, she could tell you. It must have been all the more trying with twins."

Travis' brows rose. It was sure to be true, but after he'd had some initial questions about Rebecca's pregnancy, he had forgotten all about it. How had it been for her? Travis turned to look at the boys who were now sitting side by side, their heads turned to watch some children across the church. Had they been big babies?

"Did I hear Travis' voice?" a soft voice came to his ears, and the tall cowboy moved to the end of the pew to greet Jackie.

"Good morning, Mrs. Taggart."

Jackie felt her way along the pew and stopped when she found Travis' hand out to shake hers. She smiled at him and spoke.

"Is she here, Travis? Is your wife here?" Her blind eyes stared straight ahead. "I want to meet her."

"No, but my sons are here. Garrett and Wyatt, will you say hello to Mrs. Taggart?"

The boys came forward, seemingly transfixed with Jackie's lovely features, but they didn't speak. Their gaze was locked on her face.

"Are they feeling shy?" Jackie asked softly.

"I think so," Travis told her, and was on the verge of turning back to the boys when Clayton arrived and slipped a possessive arm around his wife.

"Who do we have here?" he asked good-naturedly, and Travis introduced them. Their response was the same. Travis felt the need to elaborate.

"Mr. Taggart teaches school here in Boulder."

Garrett took a step closer. "You teach at the school?"

"Yes, I do," Clayton answered with obvious pleasure. "Are you going to be coming to school someday?"

Fascinated, Garrett could only nod in wonder.

"I am too," Wyatt added, his face coming over the top of his brother's shoulder.

"Well, that's fine. How old are you boys?"

"Five," they answered in unison.

"What are your names?"

"I'm Wyatt, and he's Gary."

"Garrett Buchanan," that boy finally managed. "I want to go to school."

"That's great," Clayton said. He had knelt down to their level, and Jackie stood beside him, a look of immense pride on her face. It was common knowledge that her husband had an extraordinary way with children.

"Have you seen the schoolhouse?"

"No, but we might go today. We want to. We asked about it. Our mama isn't here, but she likes school too. We didn't go to school in Pine Grove . . . it wasn't time yet. When does it start? What do we wear? Can we come now? Are there other

287

kids? Do we each have a desk? I have a pencil, and we found an old slate in the field."

Travis looked on in amazement. Their words and sentences tumbled all over each other. What one boy didn't ask, the other one did. Travis had never seen them so animated, and with a stranger! Clayton did his best to field all of their questions, and the boys eventually just stood staring at him.

"Is this your wife?" Wyatt said after a moment, his eyes now back on Jackie. He seemed quite taken with her.

"Yes, did you meet her?"

Wyatt nodded.

"Where do you live?" His eyes were still on Jackie's face.

"In a house by the school," Clayton answered with a smile. Wyatt's was the typical reaction of children his age; they were taken with Jackie's looks. Older children who understood her loss of sight would be watchful, but not openly stare. Clayton looked forward to telling Jackie later how she had caught Wyatt Buchanan's attention. Since her blindness her confidence was a bit bruised; it came with not seeing anyone's face or having eye contact. Knowing that the little boy had stared so sweetly at her would touch her heart.

"Are you boys ready to go?" Travis asked, and Garrett immediately reminded him about the schoolhouse.

"I think we can go if we keep it quick," Travis told him.

The boys tore for the door, ignoring their father's warning to return and say good-bye to the Taggarts and not to run in the church. The look and sigh he threw at Clayton and Jackie told them his boys would hear from him in the wagon.

❧

"They're sure taking their time," Lavena commented to Rebecca when she found her in the living room with a book. As had become a pattern, the younger girl did not answer unless she was so inclined.

"Why didn't you go?"

Rebecca's eyes had been on the window, but she now turned to the housekeeper.

"I don't have anything to wear."

Lavena snorted as Rebecca knew she would.

"What do you call that lot in the wardrobe upstairs? I wish I had dresses half that nice."

"I don't have a reason to doll up, Lavena." Rebecca sounded tired, but her mind was made up. Indeed, when she'd seen Lucky yesterday for the first time since she'd come back, it had been very satisfying to see the surprise on his face. She knew she looked a hag and was glad of it. However, Lavena was not through.

"That's ridiculous," the older woman nearly spat. "Every woman should try to look her best."

Rebecca's look was telling. "I don't see you dressing up to attract men, Lavena."

"Of course not! I don't have a husband, and I don't want one."

"Well, maybe I feel the same way."

It was such a bald-faced admission that some of the fire went out of Lavena.

"Rebecca, child, you've already got one."

Rebecca's gaze went back out the window. "I'm more aware of that than anyone, Lavena. Besides, I would think you of all people would understand."

"What do you mean?"

Rebecca looked at her. "My father never went into detail, but he led me to believe that your own marriage wasn't exactly a picnic."

Lavena suddenly sat down in the chair across from Rebecca. She lived with them, but she was normally not so familiar.

"You don't know what you're saying, Rebecca."

"I think I do," she said with calm assurance.

"No," Lavena was shaking her head. "There's no comparing Travis to my Frank. Frank was as cruel a man as ever to walk the earth. If I didn't do what I was told, he'd slap me around. He took pleasure in my pain. One time he hit me so hard I didn't wake up for several days." Lavena's face was a mask of pain as she remembered. "In the last few years it wasn't so bad because he was so drunk most of the time he could barely stand. But we had nothing, no food and barely a roof over our heads. Winters were long and cold. He didn't want me to work, and he couldn't. It was a relief to find him dead one morning."

Rebecca had never suspected. Her face was white with her emotions.

"I tell you, Rebecca," Lavena finished softly, "Travis Buchanan is no Frank Larson. You don't know how good you have it, having a man who loves you and provides for you."

Lavena left the room after that. The hand that Rebecca brought to her face shook with suppressed emotions. How could she have known? Lavena seemed so strong and self-sufficient, but clearly she'd been forced to be. In a way, she had been forced as well, but even at that, Rebecca reminded herself, she had left of her own volition. Her book was forgotten in her lap for many minutes.

"Why are we stopping? I don't see the school. Is it much farther? Can we go inside the school and see the desks? Are the horses tired? Wait until we tell Mama what we did."

The boys' comments and questions went on for a few minutes, and Travis let them rattle away as they sat on the seat beside him. He had deliberately stopped the wagon a block before the school could be seen. There was no one else around, and Travis felt he'd done the right thing to take them away from the church before he spoke.

"Boys." He spoke the word softly, but his tone was firm. His sons both stopped instantly and looked at him.

"I called to you when you ran from the church to come back and tell Mr. and Mrs. Taggart good-bye. I also called to you about running in the church. I don't want you to run in the church. And when you meet someone, it's polite to say good-bye to them. Do you understand?"

Garrett nodded, but Wyatt looked confused.

"What's the matter, Wyatt?"

"I like to run."

Travis smiled a little. "I do too, but we can't run inside the church or we could bump into someone and they might get hurt."

"I did that one time," Garrett volunteered. "I ran down the stairs and fell."

"So you know just what I'm talking about. We're going to go see the schoolhouse now, but I don't want you to forget that when I talk to you, you have to listen. If you hear my voice or your mother's, you stop and listen to what we have to say. Understand?"

Again the heads bobbed, and Travis felt he had said enough. How much could they take in at one time? There was so much to be covered. Although Travis tried to concentrate on how well they were doing, it struck him once again that they still had so far to go.

34

"We went inside. We saw the desks. We saw chalk. Mr. Tagged came too, just for a minute."

"Mr. Tagged?" Rebecca turned to Travis.

"Taggart," Travis corrected for them. Rebecca turned back to her ecstatic boys; indeed, they were nearly climbing on her. Travis was again amazed at their excitement. Their little faces were alight with pleasure as they tried to tell their mother everything in one breath. Travis waited until they had wound down some, and then did some explaining of his own.

"Wash up for dinner now, boys," he told his sons before turning to Rebecca. "They asked on the way to church if they could see the school. Then once we were there, they saw Clayton Taggart and they were more excited than ever. Have they always been this eager to go to school?"

"Yes. For as long as I can remember. Especially Garrett. I hate to see them go, but I guess it's time."

"I don't think—" Travis began, but the boys returned and cut him off. However, Rebecca caught it. She frowned in her husband's direction as they sat down to eat. Travis saw it and decided they would have to talk after lunch. The boys were not aware of this plan, though, and as soon as Travis prayed the subject of school came up again.

"Can we go, Mama? Can we go to school?"

"I think that's a good idea," Rebecca began, careful not to look at her husband.

"Did you hear that, Wyatt?" Garrett began, but Travis cut him off, his eyes sending a clear message to his wife.

"Your mother and I need to discuss this first, Garrett."

"Why?" the little boy turned to his mother and whined. "Wyatt and I want to go to school."

"You'll go to school when your mother and I decide it's time."

"I think they can go now," Travis was amazed to hear Rebecca say. He looked down the table to find her staring at him defiantly. Travis felt the first kindling of anger. He had tried to keep this low key in front of the boys, but Rebecca was bound to have it out now. Travis was just irritated enough to oblige her.

"They can't go now."

"Says who?" Rebecca's voice was belligerent.

"I'd rather we discuss this later," Travis told her, seeing that they were only going to argue.

"No. It concerns the boys; they can hear."

Travis could have throttled her. She was deliberately baiting him and the boys, whose futures were at stake, were taking in every word. He took some slow, deliberate bites of his food and then spoke to the boys.

"So you boys want to go to school?"

"Yeah," they said as one.

"Do you think you're ready?"

"We're ready. We want to."

Travis flicked a glance at Rebecca. "And you think they're ready?"

Rebecca shrugged, still irritated. "I don't know what you mean by ready. They can't read, but that's what you go to school to learn."

"But you think they're ready in other ways? Like doing what they're told? Respecting other people's property? Sitting still for a reasonable length of time in order to do their lessons and learn?"

Rebecca's face flushed with anger. "They're only five, Travis. They'll learn those things along the way."

"I don't agree with you, Rebecca. By the time we're five we're supposed to have those things down." Travis' voice rose as well. "They couldn't even make it through a church service that was an hour long. How do you expect them to sit all day in a schoolroom, no matter how interested they are?"

"What happened at church?" Rebecca was still angry, but Travis wasn't going to tell her himself. He turned to the boys, who had lost all excitement over school.

"Tell your mother, Wyatt and Garrett. Tell her how it went this morning."

The boys sat silent, their eyes on their plates. Travis let the silence hang for several seconds.

"This is what I'm talking about, Rebecca." Travis' voice was now calm. "If the boys won't do something as simple as talk when they're told to, how can we expect them to go up front and recite their lessons when the teacher asks them?"

Rebecca's face was a mask of frustration. "You must love being right, Travis. It must make you feel good to belittle me."

Travis could have howled in frustration—this was not about them—but instead he forced himself to remain calm.

"Pick up your plates, boys," he instructed them. "Now walk into the kitchen and finish eating in there. Tell Lavena that I sent you, and that if you eat all your food, you can be the first to have dessert."

The boys did this without question, and as soon as they were gone Travis speared his wife with his eyes, his voice low and intense.

"You've turned this into a competition between us, Rebecca, and it's not going to work. We're talking about the boys' future. We can't let our pride stand in the way. If you think I'm so wrong, then get another opinion. I didn't even talk to Clay about the boys attending. If you think they're ready, then take them to school tomorrow and ask him. He's the teacher."

The argument went out of Rebecca in a hurry. She felt utterly defeated. Travis watched her face and felt defeated himself. She thought he wanted only to belittle her, and that was the last thing on his mind. What he wanted to do was love her for the rest of their days, but he wisely kept that to himself. After a few quiet moments, Rebecca finally spoke, her voice sad.

"Everything you said is true, Travis, but because it's true, it also means that I'm a complete failure as a mother. I don't mind telling you that that doesn't sit very well with me."

"You're not a failure, Rebecca," he told her sincerely, hating the pain on her face. "I know the boys are a handful, but you and I have got to agree on what's right for them. I'm sorry this came up in front of them, but I was afraid you would promise to take them when I can see that it's too soon."

"They want to go so badly."

"Yes, they do, and we can give them hope. We can remind them that they can't go to school unless they learn to obey and respect us. That will give them a glimpse of what will be expected of them, as well as help in their training." Travis hesitated now but went on gently. "I've noticed that you have a hard time saying no to them. Maybe this will help. You can remind them that boys who go to school have to do what their elders tell them. Every time, not just when they feel like it."

Rebecca stared at him. "How did you learn about this, Travis? How did you learn about training little boys?"

She had stumped him. He had no idea where it came from. He knew only that he wanted better from his boys than he was getting. He said as much to Rebecca.

"I don't know what you mean."

"Well," Travis thought hard and tried to explain. "Some of the children I know from church seem pretty special. They're sweet and fun, but I don't have that much contact with them. In the past when I *have* been in contact with children who were disrespectful, I simply ignored them and went on my way. The last thing I want to do is ignore my sons. But when I walked into the kitchen that morning, Rebecca, and saw them screaming at you, I knew things had to change. I will not allow anyone to treat my wife like that, especially my own sons.

"There are going to be battles with the boys, but I'll do whatever I have to so they will grow up respecting authority and the rights of those around them. It would seem to me that they've been the ones in charge up to now, and it's time they learned otherwise."

Rebecca wanted to argue but could not. Her boys did run things where she was concerned. Angel had asked her who was in charge in their home any number of times. It all still rankled. No one enjoyed having her faults pointed out, and Rebecca simply didn't like Travis enough right now to see that he had been very gentle and was doing it all for her and the twins.

"You're angry," Travis said quietly. "I can see it in your face."

"It's just very arrogant on your part when you think about it, Travis."

"What is?"

Rebecca was sorry she'd spoken but now refused to back down. "We were getting along fine for five years, and now you come in and say everything has to change."

Travis stared at her. "Do you hear yourself, Rebecca?"

"Of course." Her chin went into the air to give her courage. "We were fine."

"*You* left me, Rebecca," he reminded her. "*You* wrote to me."

"I had my reason for leaving, Travis, and once gone I didn't ask to be brought back from Pine Grove and have my world turned upside down."

"So you want me to believe that if I'd left you there, you would have carried on as usual? No regrets, no need for someone else to share your life and help you with the boys?"

"That's right." Her chin went up even further.

Travis stood slowly and lifted his half-eaten plate of food. His voice was low, his eyes sad.

"Not only do you lie to me, Rebecca, you lie to yourself."

He left the room before Rebecca could say a word, but her fury knew no bounds. She went to her room for the better part of the afternoon and wouldn't speak or even look at Travis for the rest of the day.

"We saw her again on Sunday," Wyatt told his mother at bedtime. It had been over a week since she and Travis had quarreled. She hadn't said more than five words to him the whole time. They each took time in the evenings with the boys, but not together. Rebecca was no longer joining him for coffee in the living room. He had tried to talk to her, but she would have none of it. For the last two nights he had been gone, having taken the train to Denver on business. Rebecca told herself that she wished he would stay away forever, but it was getting harder to keep that in mind.

"Who did you see?" Rebecca asked absently.

"That pretty lady." Wyatt's voice was dreamy, and Rebecca stared at him. She had never seen Wyatt look like that, not even with Angel, and he'd been very taken with her. She licked her lips and forced her voice to sound calm.

"Someone in town?"

"At church."

"What's her name?"

"I think she has a boy's name."

This was not what Rebecca wanted to know.

"How did you meet her?"

"She always talks to Travis."

"Yeah," Garrett chimed in. "She smiles real pretty and holds his hand. Are you going to tell us a story, Mama?"

Rebecca said yes, but then her mind went blank. She ended up telling them about something silly she did as a child, and the boys ended up giggling and wrestling so fiercely that she threatened to spank them. She never had in the past, so the warning had no effect. Not until one of the boys got hurt and there were many tears did they calm down. Still telling herself that Travis was wrong about what the boys needed, Rebecca was only too glad to leave her sons for the night and find her own bed.

Travis slowly climbed the stairs, his bare feet making little sound on the wood. It was well after midnight. The train had been held up with track problems for hours. He was cold and tired, but the bath Lavena had prepared for him had been worth the effort of coming home tonight and not waiting an extra day. Knowing he could wake up in his own bed was the other attraction. Discarding his jeans, he fell into bed and was asleep within a minute.

The lateness of getting to bed didn't help his difficulty waking, but it was more than that. Travis struggled up from the haven of slumber and listened again to the odd noise. Not until he heard the boys cry out was he able to gather his wits in the darkness. But then it wasn't dark, at least not all the time. *Thunder and lightning in November?*

Rising to the accompaniment of another crash and flash of light, Travis moved swiftly down the hall. Another blaze told him the boys were cowering in terror at the head of their bed. Without words, Travis went to them, taking one in each arm and carrying his sons to his own bed.

"I don't like the noise." Wyatt's voice quivered.

"It's all right. God sends the thunder and the rain and the snow. He'll watch over us."

Travis' words were punctuated by another flash and bang, and his sons nearly choked him before they reached the bed. In an instant they scrambled under the covers. Travis edged them over and lay beside them.

"Come on up here on the pillow," he urged. "Come up here and try to go back to sleep."

"Where's Mama?"

"She's asleep just like you should be."

"She doesn't like storms. Do you think she's scared?"

"No," Travis assured them. "She's sleeping soundly."

There was a slight rustle and tussle, and Travis heard someone say, "I want to be by Travis." There was more rustling, and finally a little body lodged itself next to Travis and lay still.

"Are you settled?"

"Yes."

"Who's next to me?"

"Me. Wyatt."

"Are you all right, Garrett?"

"Yes."

They fell silent for a time. Travis prayed that they would all fall asleep; he was certainly ready to, but someone had a question.

"Where did you go, Travis?" It was Garrett.

"I had to be in Denver for a few days. I needed to see a man about buying some of our cattle."

"I haven't seen lots of cows," Wyatt told him, his voice starting to fade.

"You will. Come spring, you'll see plenty of them."

"Will we get to ride horses?"

"Go to sleep, boys. We can talk about it in the morning."

Travis made himself stay awake until he was certain they were sound asleep, and then he finally let his body relax. The storm had calmed some but was starting up again. The days of travel, however, were getting to him. He was just about asleep when he heard Rebecca's voice.

"Travis?" she said softly.

"Right here," he called just as quietly toward the doorway.

"Are the boys with you?"

"Yes. They were afraid of the storm."

The room lit momentarily, long enough for Travis to see that Rebecca wasn't comfortable with the storm either. Her arms were wrapped around her waistline, and she was hugging herself as though terrified. He thought the boys had just been talking when they said she was afraid of storms.

"Come on in," he urged her. "We have room. Go to the other side and crawl in beside Garrett."

He could feel her hesitation in the darkness and thought for certain she would decline, but a moment later he heard her feet on the floor. The bed moved ever so slightly as she slipped under the covers.

"Are you all right?"

"Yes," came her soft reply.

"Good night," Travis told her, and Rebecca returned his comment.

As tired as Travis was, he suddenly felt every nerve in his body. It was late and he was exhausted, but his wife was across the bed from him. It didn't help that his bed was a perfect fit for two but a little cramped with four. Assuming he would never sleep, the weary cowboy was completely surprised to open his eyes sometime later and see that it was morning.

35

Travis woke slowly. The room was just beginning to lighten, and he felt warm and comfortable. He was on his side, and Wyatt was still cuddled up against him. He felt better than he had the night before but thought he could still sleep more. However, it was a workday, and he knew Lavena would be preparing breakfast. He also needed to meet with Lucky to talk about what he'd learned in Denver. He peeked one eye open before both eyes opened wide. The person snuggled against him was his wife. Travis couldn't stop his smile. It had been too long since he'd held her to identify her in his sleep, but now with his eyes open he wondered how he couldn't have known. The boys were no longer between them. He didn't know why, nor did he care.

Not the least bit worried about waking her, Travis eased his arms around her and pulled her a bit closer to his chest. She was warm and soft and smelled like Rebecca, his Rebecca. Travis half hoped that she would wake up and see where she was, but it didn't happen. She slept on, completely unaware. Travis knew a strong sense of contentment and would have been more than willing to let the feeling linger, but he fell back to sleep a few minutes later.

Rebecca woke up feeling completely disoriented. She was warm and the storm was quiet, but she couldn't move. There was a small, warm body to her back and a large, warm presence to her front. Rebecca's eyes popped open all at once when she realized very suddenly where she was. However, she was awake by herself. Travis was holding her securely against him, but he was still sleeping. The boys were obviously asleep as well, or they would not have still been in bed.

She wanted to be outraged. She wanted to be furious, but a quick shift of her eyes told her that she was the one who had moved. Travis was still on his side of the bed, but the boys no longer separated them. She quickly realized that it was impossible for her to shift or move. If she rolled, she would land on her son; if she climbed out she'd have to go over Travis, not to mention the fact that his right arm was keeping her from even sitting up. Rebecca was still deciding what to do when she was pulled even closer. Her eyes flew upward to find Travis looking at her.

"Good morning." His voice had a morning growl to it, and Rebecca felt something inside her melt.

"Hi," she barely managed.

"Did you sleep well?"

"I think so. I seem to have moved."

Travis' smile, a little sleepy and very intimate, was devastating. Neither one spoke, but at the moment no words were needed. For the first time since her return, Rebecca didn't stiffen. For the first time, all defenses were down. She was warm and huggable, and Travis was going to enjoy what was offered. His head dipped, and his mouth touched hers ever so gently. He heard her sigh, and his own heart tumbled.

"Oh, Reba," he breathed before kissing her again.

Rebecca gave herself up to her husband's kiss, her brain barely functioning. It felt so right. He held her tenderly, and Rebecca decided that she never wanted to move.

"What are they doing?"

"Kissing. Haven't you seen kissing before, Gary? Remember Angel and Preston? They kissed all the time."

Travis and Rebecca both turned to watch the owners of this conversation. The boys sat side by side at their mother's back and stared at Travis, fascinated with the way he held Rebecca in the curve of his arm, his free hand tenderly cupping the curve of her cheek.

"How come you're kissing?" Wyatt wanted to know.

For Rebecca, the spell was broken.

"We're not," she told him, sitting up in one move, forcing Travis to drop his arms. "I think you boys should go get dressed. It feels quite late, and you haven't had breakfast."

The mention of food was enough to propel the boys forward. They scrambled off the bed. Rebecca began to follow them, scooting to the other side of the bed to leave, but Travis caught her before she was off the mattress. With her gently pinned against the other pillow, he asked, "What happened just now?"

"I don't know what you mean."

Travis looked at her closed face. "So everything is fine?"

"Yes."

"And when I turn in tonight, you'll be here, your things all moved into this room?"

"No." Her voice was cold.

"Then I'll ask you again—what happened just now?"

Rebecca turned her head away, but Travis brought it back with a gentle hand to her jaw.

"Rebecca," he said with soft urgency. "What is it? If it's too soon, then tell me, but don't shut me out."

Rebecca just stared at him, and Travis moved away in defeat. She lay there as he climbed from the bed and then stood on his side of the bed looking down at her.

"I don't know what to do next, Rebecca. One minute you're kind and warm, and the next you're like a porcupine. And this silence . . ." Travis shook his head, his hand going to the back of his neck. "I'm bone weary of living with a woman who won't talk to me."

Rebecca felt awful as he walked to the closet and disappeared from view, but she didn't know how to make things right. It had been wonderful to be held by Travis, but she didn't want to raise more children on her own. Her pride was already so great that she wouldn't even ask for help with the boys. If she and Travis became intimate again, she would have even more children to deal with. And if she were ever to tell Travis how she felt, he would remind her that she was the one who had left. Rebecca didn't know what to do, but soon there was a bump in the closet and she was reminded that Travis would be coming back out at any moment.

The frightened wife scrambled from the bed and headed toward the door. Her whole frame shook as she shut the door to her own bedroom and told herself to dress. She was determined to push Travis' kiss from her mind. She rushed into her clothing and ruthlessly brushed her hair back away from her face. Her spectacles were on the dresser. As she put them on, she looked at herself. The image in the mirror was just what she needed.

In the glasses and bun I not only look ugly, I feel ugly. Rebecca leaned close to inspect her eyes again. "You just remember that, Rebecca, when you're tempted to fall into that man's arms," she spoke outloud. "There can't be anything good come of it. You just remember."

"Who are you talking to?" Wyatt wanted to know as he burst in without knocking.

"Just myself," Rebecca said lightly.

"Oh. Lavena says breakfast is ready."

"All right."

She followed her son from the room without a backward glance. She would talk to Travis if he kept his distance, but she wasn't going to fall under his spell again.

"How do you romance your wife?" Travis addressed to the air as he rode toward Boulder, or more specifically the Langley home. "No," he said testily, "that isn't right. How do you romance your wife when she wants nothing to do with you?" Travis wanted to howl with frustration. He felt a headache coming on. It didn't matter how he said it, he couldn't bring himself to ask Robert Langley for help. He was desperate, nearly beside himself, but he had no idea what to do. Rebecca was speaking to him—she had been for almost a month—but only if he kept his distance.

He was at Robert's front door before he was ready to face him, and his friend greeted him kindly. Why Robert had suddenly decided that they needed to meet for Bible study he didn't know, but here he was on Tuesday morning as scheduled.

"Do you want some coffee?" Robert asked as soon as they'd gained the kitchen.

"Sure," Travis told him and accepted the cup gratefully. "How are you doing?"

"I'm all right. How about yourself?"

Travis shrugged. "I'm a little weary right now. It's hard riding the range in such cold weather."

"Do the boys go with you much?"

"Some. They sure love the horses, but I won't let them ride on their own. I can tell they feel torn. Other than the one time Lucky took one of them on his mount and I took the other, I can only take one at a time. They usually stick pretty close together, which means that even when it's Wyatt's turn to go, he spends the first 100 yards looking back at Garrett, who's in the yard with his mother."

Robert laughed. "They're doing well in church."

"Yes, they are," Travis agreed, the Lord reminding him in a hurry that he had that to be thankful for. "I'm very proud of them. They even asked me some questions about Sunday's sermon."

"That is good news. How about Rebecca? Any interest at all?"

Travis shook his head. There was no disguising the pain he felt. It was the same pain Robert had witnessed in Travis on Sunday when Pastor Henley had asked him about Rebecca. Robert had determined on the spot to meet with his friend on a regular basis. He knew that living with an unsaved spouse could be an emotional desert.

"Do you want to talk about it?"

Travis looked uncertain. "I don't know, Robert."

"You're discouraged because she won't go to church," he tried to guess.

"No, I'm discouraged because she keeps a wall up between us." Travis was utterly relieved to have it out, and it hadn't been all that painful. "I certainly want her at church, but I want her to give us a chance just as much."

"Have you tried talking to her?"

Travis hesitated again. He had tried to talk to Rebecca, but she always accused him of wanting her in bed and then shrank further behind her wall of glasses and high-neck dresses. How in the world did he explain that to Robert?

"Can't talk about it?"

"I don't know, Robert. She thinks I have hidden motives. She's made it clear that I can be a father to the boys and take care of all of them, but she doesn't want a husband."

Robert stared at his friend with compassion. What a hard position to be in. However, he believed there was hope.

"Have you shown her how much you care, Travis? Does she know that you love her?"

"I haven't told her I love her, if that's what you mean. I thought she would feel pressured if I shared my feelings. As for the other, I've done everything I can think of to show her I care."

Robert wasn't certain where the thought came from, but he suddenly said to Travis, "Show her your heart."

"My heart?"

"Yes. Don't be afraid to tell her all about yourself. Let her see the real man—who you were, who you are now."

Something came over Travis' face, and Robert knew that the words had hit a nerve, not understanding just yet that it all made such perfect sense to the searching cowboy.

"I think I've lost you."

"No, you haven't," Travis told his host, "but you have made me think. There is more I can do to get close to Rebecca. I'll just have to think of how to go about it."

Robert nodded but didn't question him. It was clear that Travis had enough on his mind. The men ended up talking over a few verses from James and spending the rest of the time in prayer. Travis was on his way back to the ranch just an hour later.

~

"The hotel? You want us to stay the night at the hotel?" Rebecca stared at her husband.

"No, just to go for dinner, the two of us."

Rebecca still stared, but Travis was not going to be put off.

"You never get out on your own, Rebecca; that is, without the boys. I thought it might be nice to get away for a while. The food won't be as good as Lavena's, but I think you need to get out."

This was the last thing Rebecca would have thought of, but the prospect of leaving the ranch was wonderful. She did feel completely cut off so far from town, but she had no idea that her husband was aware of her loneliness.

"Well—" Rebecca felt shy all of a sudden, and her gaze would not meet his. "I'd like that."

"Great," Travis said and had to tell himself not to shout and jump around. "I'll tell Lavena that she'll have the boys tonight."

"What time did you want to leave?"

"How's 6:00?"

"Fine," she said as she finally looked up.

"Be sure to dress warmly, Rebecca." His voice was kind. She could only nod and look at him.

"I'm sorry, Rebecca." His heart was in his eyes. "I'm sorry I didn't take you out before. You must be getting tired, and I wasn't sensitive to your needs at all."

"It's all right," she told him and meant it. "I'll be fine."

Travis smiled down at her. "I'd better get to work."

"Sure."

"I'll see you later."

"Stay warm today," Rebecca called after him, and he raised his hand in a wave. She had had a dozen things on her mind, but now it was wiped clean. Once again, Angel's words came back to her: *Don't reject a man who clearly wants to lay the world at your feet.*

36

You're in a panic over nothing, Rebecca told herself for the fifth time. *He's just taking you to dinner, that's all. You've been like a caged animal for days. Go and enjoy this.* But it still didn't work. Rebecca was so worked up by the time she was ready to go downstairs that she thought she was going to be sick. Rebecca waited for Travis in the living room and tried to calm her stomach. The boys were already in the kitchen with Lavena. Of their own volition, her thoughts went to Travis. He had not acted too boldly when he asked her to join him or when he'd come off the range, but there was a difference about him. She couldn't put her finger on the exact cause, but something was up.

She knew he had gone to see Robert Langley that morning but didn't think that could be the cause. He had also told her that the Langleys had invited them to share Christmas dinner with them. Travis said they would only go if she wanted to, but Rebecca had been unable to give an answer. Was Eddie Langley the pretty lady Wyatt had seen at church? Rebecca didn't know why she wanted to know, but their talk of Eddie had really bothered her. It was laughable really, considering she'd made it more than clear that she didn't want a husband. *You don't want him, but you can't stand the thought that someone else would have him. What kind of a child are you, Rebecca?* For some reason the thought was calming; the pretty lady and dinner with the Langleys went out of her head. By the time Travis sought her out in the living room, Rebecca had decided to make an effort and enjoy the evening.

The Travis Buchanans were rather quiet on their way into town—Rebecca with her new resolve but no idea where to start, and Travis thinking his wife was lovely. If he had been pushed into a corner, he would have chosen for her to remove her glasses, but he could still see her huge brown eyes and the soft shine of her hair. And she smelled good. He'd helped her with her coat and leaned as close as he dared to inhale the smell of her hair and skin.

"How were the boys today?" Travis asked as they entered the outskirts of town.

"They were okay."

"Good. I couldn't take either of them with me, and I didn't want them going into a mood and giving you a hard time. They were no trouble at all?"

"Well, just a little." Travis asked every day, and Rebecca had learned to be no less than completely honest. "They were sassy over lunch, but I was firm with them and they calmed down." Rebecca's voice took on a tone of wonder. "It surprised me a little because they don't do as well for me, but then Garrett said you had told him something."

"What was it?"

"Wyatt agreed with him. They both said they're supposed to take care of me when you're gone."

Travis nodded, but it was too dark to see. "Yes, I did tell them that."

"Why, Travis?" she asked without heat. "They're only five."

It was a good question, and good for Travis to have to think about.

"I guess I said it because my grandmother said it to me one time."

"You knew your grandmother?"

They were in front of the hotel now, and after securing the horses, Travis helped Rebecca from the wagon. It was quiet on this Tuesday night in December, so they were given a table right away. Travis knew they would be interrupted by the waitress, but he wanted to get back to their conversation as soon as they sat down.

"Where were we?" he asked, and to his surprise Rebecca knew instantly.

"You were saying you knew your grandmother."

"Oh, yes, until I was ten, when she died of consumption."

"Were you close to her?"

Travis shook his head. "No one in my family was what you could call close, but I did care for her."

"Whom did she tell you to take care of?" Rebecca seemed fascinated.

The waitress picked that moment to tell them what was on the evening's menu, but she was gone a few minutes later, leaving them with hot cups of coffee.

"She told me to take care of my mother," Travis went on. "My father had run off for a time; he did that often. But this time my mother was sick, and my grandmother had gone up the street to help a woman give birth. I was so little, probably five like the boys, or maybe even four, and her telling me to take care of my mother made me feel very proud."

Rebecca's eyes were thoughtful. "The boys felt pride, too. I didn't recognize it at the time, but I do now. They were very pleased to tell me what you had said."

The couple fell silent for a moment.

"Did your mother die at that time, Travis?"

"Not right then. In fact, she died just before I met you."

"Oh, Travis." There was real compassion in Rebecca's eyes. "You never said."

"No." His voice was quiet. "It was too new and painful at the time. I didn't grow up in a very happy home, and having my mother die just added to the sadness."

Again silence fell, and then Travis spoke thoughtfully. "My mother and I were alone much of the time. I worked on a cattle ranch from the time I was just a kid, always trying to bring enough home so we could eat, as well as keep ahead of the bills my father ran up at the saloon whenever he wandered back into town. I heard later that he died in a fire."

Travis' gaze had been on his hands, but he now looked at his wife. She looked upset, and he suddenly realized he had not planned to spend the evening on such a cheerless note. It was all true; he was the man he was today because of where he'd been, but tonight he wanted to center on Rebecca.

"So tell me," he said, his tone changing to one of interest, not introspection, a smile lighting his face. "Did the boys take care of you?"

"I guess they did," Rebecca answered with a smile of her own. "They played outside for most of the morning, and the two times I asked them to obey me, they did so very swiftly."

Travis nodded with satisfaction. "Good. It means that all our talking and even the spankings are getting somewhere."

Rebecca nodded, but her mind was elsewhere. She was sorry about his mother and the hard life he had lived, but her thoughts were on Travis' father and then her own. Why did men go away and leave their families? Rebecca started slightly when Travis touched her hand.

"Are you all right?"

"I think so. Why?"

"You looked so sad."

Rebecca looked down at the table. "I was thinking about the way my father left me in Philadelphia, and now I learn that your father left you too. Why do men do that, Travis? Why do men have children and then abandon them?"

Travis' brows rose. It was a good question. "I think men are tempted to wander no matter what, but the reasons must vary. With my father it was disillusionment, or so my grandmother used to say. At the time they were married, my mother was beautiful, but she was sick a lot after I was born. She lost her looks and her desire to roam around the country, so he roamed without her. By the time my mother died, I hadn't seen my father in a year."

314

Just then their food was placed in front of them. Travis said a brief prayer of thanks for the meal, and then asked a question for which he knew the answer but had no details. "So your father didn't stick around either, Rebecca?"

"No," she answered honestly, "but he didn't actually desert me. We were living in Philadelphia with my father's sister, Hannah, and her husband, Franklin Ellenbolt. Father came west to make a place and name for himself. He had every intention of coming back for me but circumstances arose that neither of us could have stopped."

Travis cocked his head to one side. "Can you tell me about it, or does it hurt too much?"

"It did for a long time, but it's so far in the past now." Rebecca took a breath. "I never saw the letters my father wrote to me, nor did he see mine. My Aunt Hannah was a sick woman. She intercepted all of our letters, copied our handwriting, and rewrote them so we would read what she wanted us to hear. She lied—not too outrageously, because we would have caught on—but enough so that both my father and I were under the impression that we were both happy with our lives the way they were. I didn't think he wanted me, and he felt the same about me. She even wrote me that my father was involved with a woman, and thinking that my father had said it, I naturally believed it."

Travis' face was a mask of shock, his brows raised in incredulous question.

"It's true," Rebecca assured him. "I discovered her deception very suddenly and left two days later, before she could stop me. I hated her for a long time." Her voice grew very soft. "But I've learned that people will do desperate things when they think they have a reason."

Suddenly they were no longer talking about Aunt Hannah; Travis knew it, and Rebecca knew it. Travis reached across the table just as he had before and touched his wife's hand very briefly.

"I know it hasn't been easy for you, Rebecca," he told her sincerely. "And your view of me hasn't been very positive, but I'm very glad you're home."

"Thank you, Travis. For the first time, I'm glad too."

Travis' heart filled with contentment until she went on.

"I didn't realize how much I needed help with the boys."

Disappointment knifed through Travis, but he was careful not to show it. He was again reminded that she wanted him only as a father to her boys. He forced his mind to other things.

"When I met you here in town that day, you had just come from Philadelphia?"

"Yes," Rebecca answered very softly but didn't elaborate. Travis was not to know that she was remembering for the first time how she felt when she saw him, his hat in his hand, his deep voice calling her "Miss Rebecca." She had lost her heart in that moment and wasn't sure even yet if she'd ever recovered it.

Suddenly she was back in Pine Grove, coming from her laundry area to find him standing in her living room, tall and gorgeous and looking ready to eat her alive. She relived the scene in the living room at the ranch when he'd pulled her to her feet and tenderly kissed her brow. And then in the master bedroom when he held her tightly in his arms. The kiss had been so wonderful and sweet.

Fish or cut bait. The voice came out of nowhere to Rebecca's mind. *Are you going to make a marriage of this or not, Rebecca? You can run but you can't hide. Travis clearly cares for you, or you wouldn't be in town tonight. Now, what are you going to do about it?*

"That's certainly a fierce look." Travis deliberately kept his voice light. "Am I in trouble?"

Rebecca gave a small laugh, her cheeks heating. "No, I am."

Travis opened his mouth to question her, but the look she gave him from behind the glasses did not invite inquiries. They ate for a time in silence. It was as Travis predicted: The meal was good but not comparable to Lavena's cooking. Dessert was a nice treat of fresh apple pie, full of cinnamon and sugar.

316

Travis finished Rebecca's when she said she was too full. She then toyed with her coffee cup and studied him.

"I want to say that you're different than before, Travis, but I didn't know you well enough to tell. Are you different?"

The question totally surprised him, but he answered calmly enough. "I think I am, Rebecca, and my close friends say I'm different. I believe it's because a few years ago something happened that changed me completely." Travis didn't go on, not because he was afraid, but because a look of cynicism had entered Rebecca's eyes. His own eyes dropped. He ended with, "I can tell you sometime if you want to hear."

"Not now?" Her tone was cynical too.

Travis looked her in the eye. "Do you *want* to hear right now?"

Shame washed over Rebecca, and for the first time she didn't fight it with anger.

"That was horrid of me, Travis. I ask and then cut you off. I do care, but I'm a little afraid of what you're going to say. Did you say you would be willing to tell me another time?"

"Yes, I did. Just ask me when you're ready."

"I'll do that. It, umm, I mean, it has to do with the church, doesn't it?"

"I wouldn't put it that way, but you could say it does."

"How would you put it?"

"I would say it was Jesus Christ. Church is an important part of my life to be sure, but so often when people talk about church, they're taking about religion. I'm talking about a real relationship with God through His Son, Jesus."

Her eyes didn't shutter or become cynical, but Travis stopped there. He felt a certain peace steal over him. He had planned for this to be a night to get to know Rebecca, but the Lord had also opened up an opportunity to talk about Him. Travis left the hotel with a strong feeling of contentment.

The conversation was light on the ride home. Rebecca went with Travis to the barn when he stabled the horses for the night. They continued to talk about the ranch and other topics. Once inside the kitchen, Travis took her coat and then brought up the subject of Christmas.

"I'm going to tell Robert and Eddie that we'll join them another year." Rebecca could only look at him, her lip tucked under her teeth. Travis went on. "I think you'll be more comfortable if we just stay here."

"You would do that for me?"

"Certainly. And I know we'll have a great time on our own."

"Thank you, Travis."

"My pleasure. You realize it's six days away?"

"It is, isn't it?" She was very serious. "I haven't even shopped."

"Well, you'd better get at it. I expect a huge gift from you."

Rebecca's eyes shot up to see he was laughing at her. "You can stop that teasing, Travis Buchanan," she now scolded him, "or there won't be a thing under the tree with your name on it."

"You could put yourself under the tree," he told her with merry eyes, his smile warm.

Rebecca pushed down the pleasure that spiraled inside of her and told herself not to laugh and encourage him. She opted to change the subject. "Speaking of trees, when are we going to get one?"

"This is Tuesday. How about Friday or Saturday?"

"Will we take the boys?"

"Certainly. We'll make an outing of it. Do you suppose Lavena will want to come?"

Travis had heard her come up behind him and enjoyed teasing her.

"That's all I need, to be dragging through the snow and cold in search of a Christmas tree!" Lavena almost snorted her disgust.

They both smiled at her tone but tried to cover it as they turned.

"How was your meal?" Her voice was a bit softer.

"Not as good as your cooking, but it was nice to get away," Travis told her honestly. "How were the boys?"

Both younger adults watched in amazement as a tender light came into Lavena's eyes. "They both did fine. They cried when you weren't here to kiss them good night, so I let them sleep in my bed."

"The boys are in your room?" Rebecca's voice was incredulous.

Travis was already moving that way, and the women followed.

"I'll move them upstairs," Travis said, his voice hushed.

"Oh, leave them, Travis, for mercy's sake! I'm fine in the living room, and I can hear them if they cry."

Travis and Rebecca exchanged looks but remained silent.

"Go on now before you wake them! It's after 9:00. You should all be in bed."

Travis and Rebecca allowed themselves to be bullied out of the room and toward the stairs. Rebecca started up, but Travis stayed below and bid her good night.

"Not coming up?"

"Not yet. I've some papers to see to in the office."

Rebecca hated for the evening to end. She had dreaded it but without grounds; the entire evening had been wonderful. She was glad, however, that her face was in the shadows, and Travis couldn't read this in her eyes.

"Good night, Travis. Thank you for the evening."

"You're welcome. We'll have to do it again."

Rebecca went on her way, and Travis went to the office, but it was a while before the small blonde actually readied for bed or until Travis moved to read his papers.

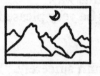

37

"You pray, don't you, Travis?"

Travis turned his head very slowly, and he looked at his foreman. The men were in the barn at the end of the day. The other hands had headed to the cookhouse, and the owner and foreman were alone.

"Yes, Lucky, I do," Travis told him softly. "Why do you ask?"

Travis noticed for the first time that Lucky's eyes were red-rimmed, and that Lucky was looking at him in a kind of desperation.

"Sarah Beth choked last night," Lucky told him, referring to his 4½-year-old daughter. "She got some meat lodged in her throat." Lucky shuddered slightly as he remembered. "I thought we were going to lose her."

"Is she all right?" Travis asked as alarm slammed through him. He didn't see Sarah Beth very often, but she and Margo were precious to him.

"Yeah," Lucky told him, his throat tight. "But I can't stop thinking about it. I mean, I really think God saved her, Travis, and I want to thank Him, but I don't have a clue as to how. None of us did a thing. We all froze while she got blue in the face, and then before any of us could get to her, she suddenly spit it up. I know it was God, Travis, but how do I—" Lucky raked a hand through his hair, and Travis worked at keeping his thoughts clear. Never in a decade would he have guessed that God would work this way.

"I think God must be very pleased that you want to thank Him, Lucky."

"You do?"

"Yes," Travis told him sincerely. "We can get too attached to this world, and when something reminds us that we wouldn't even be here without a Creator-God, well, I think that's good."

"I've never felt this way, Travis," Lucky admitted. "I know you go to church, and Margo's mother tries to pray, but I've never felt anything toward God, not really. And then last night I held Sarah Beth, you know, afterward. She cried and cried, and I wanted to cry myself. I wanted to thank God for letting her live. I don't know where the thought came from, but I still want to."

"I'd be happy to pray with you right now, Lucky. We can take time right this minute to thank God for sparing Sarah Beth."

Lucky gawked at him. "You don't have to be in church?"

"No. God is everywhere, and He delights to hear the voices of the people who have made Him their Lord."

The young cowboy's look sobered. "I haven't done that, Travis. I haven't ever prayed before."

"God already knows that, Lucky, and He takes it very seriously, but He loves you anyway. I can pray if you'd like."

"You can do it for me?"

"Well, I can't commit your life to Him—you would need to do that—but I can thank Him for sparing Sarah Beth."

Lucky nodded. "Should we get on our knees?"

"It's awfully cold, Lucky. The Lord will understand if we stay on our feet."

Again Lucky nodded, his heart pounding. At the last moment he remembered to remove his hat.

"Father in heaven," Travis began, his voice utterly normal, "I thank You that Lucky is my foreman. He works hard and is an asset to this ranch. I also thank You that You've given him Margo and Sarah Beth. You have blessed him greatly, Lord, and for the first time Lucky is seeing this. I thank You, Father, that You saved little Sarah's life. We could be praying near her grave right now, Lord, but You had other plans. I thank You that she is still with us and that Lucky understands Your hand moved or she would not be here. Please continue to show Lucky what You would have him know about You, and help him to listen. I pray these things in Christ's name, Amen."

Travis opened his eyes to find Lucky staring at him.

"You just talk to Him, Travis," he said, his voice amazed. "I didn't think it was that easy."

"It is after you've accepted God's gift of salvation."

Lucky nodded. He was feeling so overwhelmed that he could hardly speak.

"Are you all right?" Travis asked, wondering if he should question him concerning eternity.

"I think so. Thank you."

Travis' hand came out. "Anytime, Lucky. You know where to find me."

"I'd better get home now."

Travis walked Lucky to the barn door, the reins to Lucky's horse dangling in the younger man's hand. He swung up into the saddle and looked down at his boss.

"I think Margo feels the same way, Travis. Can I tell her that you prayed?"

"Certainly. Tell her everything we talked about. There's much more to be learned. Maybe the three of you will want to come to church on Sunday."

Lucky's eyes went to the mountains, his heart and mind busy. "It feels like snow," he commented, although it was not to change the subject.

"Yeah. You stay put if we end up in a blizzard. There's nothing pressing here right now."

"Good night, Travis, and thanks again."

"Good night, Lucky."

Travis stood still as the other cowboy moved down the road. It was hard to believe what had just happened, but Travis prayed for his friend and foreman. He prayed that God would work a miracle in Lucky's heart, just as He had in his own not too many years before.

<hr>

Snow began to fall later that night. It fell all day Thursday, through the night, and until noon on Friday. Travis went to the barn, but the men and horses all stayed indoors until Saturday. By the time the four Buchanans left that morning to find their tree, they were knee-deep in white powder. The sun was shining, however, and it promised to be one of the most beautiful Christmases they had ever known.

The boys laughed their way through the job as Travis took them most of the way in the sleigh. Then they plodded up the mountains into a dense area of pines. Coming along behind them and trying not to fall, Rebecca wondered for the first time at the fact that the boys never asked about Angel and Preston or returning to Pine Grove. But then why would they? They had all the space they could ever want, and each morning and evening they had a huge playmate in the form of their father, someone they were swiftly coming to adore.

Rebecca was doing a little adoring herself. After their meal out on Tuesday she had done a lot of thinking. The facts were simple: She could make a real marriage of this, or she could live like a stranger with her husband. It was odd. She had no more made up her mind to live like a real wife when Travis backed off. He was kind beyond description, but his demands were fewer than ever. Not that he wasn't attentive. Come dinnertime, when he was inside for the remainder of the day, he all but waited on her. And then in the evenings he always invited her to have coffee with him in the living room where he would ask her about herself and share about his own life. He still hadn't told her about his religious experience, but Rebecca thought she could wait. Things were going so well, much better than she'd ever believed they could. She didn't want to ruin it with talk about God.

"Can you make it?" Travis called down to his wife, jolting her out of her thoughts. Her concentration was also interrupted. The next moment she went down on her face. Travis' laughter could be heard echoing off the hills. He was beside her in a flash, but the merriment in his eyes belied his words.

"Are you all right? Here, let me help you."

"You don't want to help me," Rebecca accused goodnaturedly. "You want to laugh at my expense."

Travis couldn't answer, or he would have laughed again. She had snow everywhere. He brushed it from her hair, but that action only covered her face again.

"I think I can do without your help, Travis."

But he wasn't listening. He pulled her against his chest to brush off her back. It crossed through her mind that he could have walked around her, and indeed, she tipped her head back, looked him in the eye, and said as much. His own eyes were innocently huge.

"If I'd have gone around you I might have bumped you into the snow again. I had your best interest in mind, Rebecca."

She didn't want him to know how pleased she was, so she continued to remove the snow. She slipped her glasses off and gave them a small shake before getting the rest off her face. In the process she noticed Travis' hold had tightened. She looked up to find a look on his face that she hadn't seen for some time. At the same time, his head was lowering. But deciding to make a marriage of it and actually doing it were two different things. Before she could stop herself, Rebecca pulled her head back. Travis watched as she put the glasses back in place and looked at him uncertainly.

"What exactly are you afraid of, Rebecca?" She was still in his hold.

The question startled her, so she answered without thinking. "I don't want to be pregnant and alone again."

Travis no more believed that than he would believe she was unaffected by his nearness. Indeed, her face was flushed and her eyes bright. He challenged the statement.

"So you still don't think we're going to be together in the future?"

He had her, and Rebecca knew it. "I can't predict the future and neither can you," she told him, suddenly all business, straightening her glasses and putting her hands against his chest to push him away. "Now, are we going to get a tree?"

Travis let her go, but his eyes were watchful. They followed the boys up the hill to the tree they had rounded up and proclaimed to be perfect, but it didn't take long for Rebecca to see that her words had been a waste of time. Twice more she fell before they could get the tree chopped down and dragged to the waiting sleigh, and twice more Travis hauled her into his arms to help her remove the snow.

~

"There's someone coming, Travis," Wyatt said as they began to load back into the sleigh.

"It looks like Lucky's horse," Garrett added.

"I think you're right," Travis agreed. "Here, Rebecca," he turned back to help his wife get comfortable on the seat. "Let me get the blanket over you." She didn't answer because her teeth had begun to chatter. Travis was bent over her when Lucky approached.

"Well, now," the foreman smiled at the boys. "That's quite a tree. You'd think Christmas was close at hand."

"It is, Lucky!" Wyatt told him. "It's only two more sleeps."

"Two more sleeps? Wow!" Lucky winked at the boys and finally turned to the adults.

"Hello, Rebecca," he tipped his hat and Rebecca tried to smile at him. "You look a mite frozen."

"You could say that," she said with a shaky laugh and continued to huddle beneath the heavy blankets.

"What brings you out?" Travis asked him.

"Just a question. I'll ride back with you."

The boys begged their way atop the horse with him and held on tight as Lucky loped through the deep snow ahead of the sleigh. Travis carried Rebecca in through the kitchen door and came back to get the boys from Lucky's lap. The men then proceeded to the barn.

"If you'll give me a few minutes, Lucky, we can talk in the house."

"No," he declined. "Margo was a little worried about the deep snow, so I said I'd be right back."

Travis was busy leaning the tree against a post in the far corner of the barn, but he now turned and approached his foreman.

"How's Sarah Beth?"

"She's fine. To look at her, you'd never know anything happened."

"Good."

"Margo and I have been talking."

Travis nodded.

"We want to know what time church starts tomorrow, Travis."

"Eleven o'clock."

"I think we'll be there."

"The boys and I will save you a place."

"Doesn't Rebecca come?"

"No."

Lucky looked at him for a long moment. "She's changed, hasn't she?"

"Yes, but we're getting there." It was a huge admission for the ranch owner to make and Lucky well knew it.

"Well, I'd best get home," Lucky said, but hesitated. "Margo and I don't have fancy clothes."

"It doesn't matter," Travis assured him, so thankful it was true. The people of his church were more concerned with hearts than clothing.

"I'll see you."

"Great."

Lucky began to turn away.

"Did you get a tree?"

"A Christmas tree? No."

Travis went for the saw and a rope. "Take one home for Sarah Beth. Tell her it's from Mr. Travis."

"Thanks, Travis," Lucky told him and again looked at him for a moment before moving for the door.

Travis didn't move to take his own tree inside for several minutes after the other man left. His heart was indescribably full.

First Rebecca, Lord, looking at me with tender eyes. And now Lucky seeking You. I can't believe it. I'm dying to talk to Robert or run into the mountains and shout with joy, but I have to get inside. You never gave up on any of us, Lord. Never once did You walk away. Thank You for hanging on longer than I would have. Thank You for saving me. Please save these dear ones as well.

With feelings almost unbearably tender toward the people in his world, Travis knocked the excess snow and twigs from the Christmas tree and took it into his wife and boys.

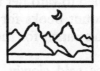

38

"You've fallen quiet," Rebecca commented many hours later. The boys were in bed, and Lavena had left them coffee and retired herself. The tree was in place, trimmed with a few wooden ornaments, but mostly green and lush. It had a hole to one side that they had tried to turn to the wall, but it smelled so good that no one minded.

Travis, whose head lay back against the chair, let his head fall sideways to look at Rebecca in her own chair. For a minute he watched the way the firelight bounced off her hair.

"I was thinking about Lucky and Margo," he admitted.

"Margo?"

Travis no longer lazed back. His head came up, and he stared at his wife.

"What is it, Travis?"

"You don't know who Margo is?"

Rebecca shook her head.

Travis' mind raced. What was the matter with him? Here he was trying to make her a part of everything, but . . . Abruptly he stood.

"Travis?"

"Just sit tight, Rebecca. I'll be right back."

Rebecca's head turned to follow him as he left the room. *What in the world was that all about?* she wondered. She didn't have long to speculate. Travis came back just seconds later, his boots loud even on the rug. Rebecca saw he had some large books in his hands. She watched as he pulled his chair close to hers, sat down, and leaned toward her intently.

"These are the account books for the ranch. Everything that's happened with this ranch for the last ten years is right here."

"All right," Rebecca said slowly. "I take it that Margo keeps the books for you."

Travis gave a small laugh as he realized he had over-reacted. "No, I'm making a mess of this. Margo is married to Lucky."

Rebecca's mouth swung open, and Travis laughed again and commented, "I have made a mess of this."

"I didn't think Lucky would ever get married," Rebecca said before he could go on. "Don't tell me they live in the bunkhouse."

"No, they live in town. Haven't you noticed his coming and going?"

"I guess I have, but I never gave it much thought. If I re-call, Lucky always had a girl in town."

Travis nodded. "I haven't started this very well, but I'll try to explain. Your question made me realize that I've been as-suming you knew everything about this ranch. Margo and Lucky have been married for several years, and I think you al-ready must have figured out that he's my foreman." Rebecca nodded, and he went on. "They have a little girl named Sarah Beth. She's only about six months younger than Wyatt and Garrett. They live in town with Margo's parents.

"Let me see, what else has changed? Oh! Biscuit is gone. Woody has been cooking for me for about five years. Race Paulson is still with me and so is Jud Silver, but the others have moved on. Kyle Strong and Chad Hartman are regulars, so is an older man named Colin North. He comes out during roundup and cattle drives and has been around a little more lately."

"And why did you bring the books out?"

"Because I want you to see them. I want you to see that every dime has been accounted for."

Rebecca began to shake her head.

"I'm not accusing you of not trusting me, Rebecca, but I want you to know that I have been careful." He stopped and sighed. "For a long time I was carried along on anger alone. I decided that if I ever saw you again, I wouldn't allow a scrap of blame to be thrown at me concerning the care of the Double Star. I no longer feel that way, but I am careful with this ranch. I've never taken for granted that one day I was a penniless cowboy and practically the next I was a husband and ranch owner. Andrew Wagner would have loved those little boys upstairs, and he would have wanted this ranch to prosper so he could hand it over to them someday."

Rebecca felt full of an emotion she couldn't define. She looked down at the books Travis had placed in her lap. "I really don't need to read these, Travis. I know now that you would do only the right thing."

"I appreciate your confidence, but the books are still an open subject. I keep them in the safe, and you can look at them anytime you want. There's also money in the safe if ever you have a need—any need."

Sighing, Rebecca set the books on the floor by her chair. "I think now might be a good time to tell you that I didn't get a chance to shop for Christmas."

"That's all right."

"No, it isn't." She looked at the fire, her face sad. "I decided on Wednesday to go into town on Thursday or Friday, but then it snowed. Now it's late on Saturday, and the stores won't be open before Monday."

"Rebecca, I was only teasing when I said you had to buy me a large gift."

"I know, but I wanted to get something. I wasn't even able to get the boys anything. Their birthday wasn't all that grand, either."

"I shopped for the boys."

Startled, Rebecca's head came around. "You did?"

"When I was in Denver. The gifts for the twins will be from both of us."

"Thank you, Travis," was all a subdued Rebecca could manage. How long had it been since someone had been there for her? How long had it been since someone was waiting to pick up the pieces when she failed? Rebecca was terrified of becoming accustomed to this new way of life, but for the first time she was even more frightened of not having it. She spoke up before she could change her mind.

"I think I need to tell you, Travis, that I won't keep threatening to leave." Rebecca kept her eyes on the fire, with only an occasional glance at her husband, but she knew she was being watched intently. "I know that the boys and I should be here now. I'm not really certain how all of this is going to work out, but I wanted you to know that we're going to stay."

When Travis didn't move or speak, Rebecca looked at him. In doing so, she couldn't pull her gaze away. Travis' eyes, tender with love, were pinned on her. Before she could think, Rebecca leaned toward him in invitation. However, she couldn't follow through. Travis had leaned as well, but just before their lips touched, Rebecca drew back, her right hand going to her neckline as usual. Travis froze, half-bent over her, his expression now sober and unreadable.

Only a few seconds passed, and before Rebecca could guess his intentions, he stood, plucked her from her seat, and sat back down with her in his lap. Unable to believe that he would actually force her in any way, Rebecca's eyes were huge as she stared up at him, literally frozen into stillness while he began to speak.

"There are a few things you need to understand, Rebecca," Travis began gently. "You see, when a man's wife wears glasses that cover her beautiful eyes, he dreams of taking them off." Rebecca couldn't move as Travis tenderly removed her spectacles and laid them on the other chair. "And when a man's wife wears her lovely hair pulled back all the time, her husband aches to take it down." A pin came loose under his fingers. "And see it . . ." two more pins gave way, "long and hanging down her back." A moment later Rebecca's soft hair cascaded around her face and shoulders.

"And when a woman keeps her dresses buttoned up to her chin, and her husband knows how soft her skin is—"

"I get your point," Rebecca whispered, but Travis heard.

"Do you, Rebecca?"

She could only nod, her hand pressed as tightly as she dared against the buttons at her throat.

"I'm not so certain." His voice was almost casual now, and Rebecca started when he stood and placed her on her feet in front of him. The fire was to the side of them, and Rebecca watched as he leaned low and bent over her. "So there's no mistaking my feelings, Rebecca, let me spell it out for you." Again her eyes were huge. "If you're pulling your hair back so tight, and wearing glasses and shapeless dresses to repulse me, then I need to tell you something." His voice dropped to an intimate whisper. "It's not working."

She could have heard a feather land at their feet. Even the fire seemed to be holding its breath, but Travis wasn't waiting for anything. He'd had his say, and he had learned that with Rebecca he had to give her time to think. The hand that smoothed the hair from her forehead was gentle, and so was the kiss he pressed to her brow.

"Good night, love," he said to her ever so softly before turning and leaving the room.

Rebecca didn't know how long she stood next to the fire in the living room, but it did nothing to warm her. She was still trembling when she climbed into bed and lay looking into the darkness for most of the night.

"Where's Mama?" Wyatt asked as the sleigh started toward Boulder on Sunday morning.

"Lavena checked on her and said she was sleeping in. You boys were very good not to wake her."

"She didn't have breakfast."

"She will," Travis assured them. "She'll get up and eat when she's ready."

"Tomorrow is Christmas." Garrett felt the need to remind him.

"Yes, are you excited about it?" Travis asked because he didn't sound it.

"I don't think Mama shopped."

"No, she didn't," Travis said. "But we still have much to be thankful for."

"The baby Jesus," Wyatt said, well remembering what Travis had been talking to them about for weeks.

"Yes, God's Son came to earth. We are thankful about that, but there are other things too."

"Like food and the ranch."

"Yes, but other things as well."

"What are they?"

"I want you to think about it."

The boys made guesses all the way to Main Street, and their list grew, but Travis was looking for something specific.

"Did we guess right?"

"You did fine, but I want you to think about your room."

"Our bedroom?"

"Yes, and even what's lying around the kitchen."

"Toys!" Quick on the uptake, Garrett guessed first.

"Yes." Travis' voice was kind, but firm. "You want more gifts for Christmas, but you don't play with half the toys you have now."

"We're tired of them," Wyatt admitted.

"Well, maybe we should give them away so someone else can enjoy them."

There had been no scolding in Travis' voice, but they looked crestfallen, and the inexperienced father felt he'd handled it poorly. He stopped the sleigh by the church and leaned over them.

"I'm not getting after you for liking new things. There's nothing wrong with that, but you need to be pleased with what you have and not always wanting more." They were looking at him, but he could tell they couldn't quite take it in. Travis tried a different approach. "Would it be right for me to ask for another horse when I have Diamond?"

"No," Wyatt said immediately.

"I wouldn't ask for two horses," Garrett told him. "I would want only one of those—honest, Travis."

Travis had to smile. He was going to have to give them more time or find out from someone else how to handle this. Nothing he said seemed to spark their understanding, and it was time to get to church.

"Are you going to spank us?" Wyatt wanted to know, and Travis knew he'd really messed up. He put his arms around them, always amazed at how willing they were for his embrace.

"No, Wyatt, I'm not. I'm not even upset with you. I need to learn to be more thankful as well, and I hope we'll learn together."

He earned sweet smiles from each of his sons before he lifted them down from the sleigh. They were just making their way into the church when Travis looked up and spotted Lucky and family making their way through the paths someone had dug through the deep snow.

"Hold up a minute, guys." While Travis waited until Lucky approached, he noticed that Margo's features were a bit strained. He only prayed as he shook Lucky's hand and kissed Margo's cheek.

"Garrett, Wyatt, I want you to meet Lucky's wife. This is Mrs. Harwell."

"Margo, please, Travis," she begged sweetly.

"All right. Boys, this is Margo, and this is Sarah Beth."

The adorable little brunette in her father's arms smiled down at the boys, and they smiled back before ducking their heads shyly. The adults shared some smiles as well.

"It's cold," Travis said suddenly. "Let's get inside."

No one argued with that. It was a little bit late for people to be milling around, so the three adults and three children slipped quietly into a rear pew. Lucky and Margo both appeared nervous, and Travis prayed that the seeds of truth thrown out this morning would find fertile soil in the Harwells' hearts.

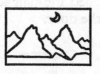

39

Rebecca stood in her room and told herself not to go back to the mirror. She hadn't emerged all morning, but now it was time: Travis and the boys would be home soon. She hadn't slept until the wee hours, so she hadn't even heard Lavena check on her, but when the housekeeper knocked several hours later, Rebecca told her she didn't want anything. She could hear the older woman grumbling as she moved back down the hall, but Rebecca had too many other things on her mind to give Lavena's moods much notice.

For the fiftieth time her eyes went downward to the rounded but demure neckline of a dark green dress she'd chosen from her wardrobe. There was nothing daring about it, but she felt naked without buttons high up her throat. The dress didn't fit as well as it used to. She was larger in the hips, waist, bust, and even the arms, than she had been before she became pregnant. But it would do, or at least that's what she tried to tell herself.

As if she couldn't stop herself, she wandered back to the mirror. If it had only been the dress, that might have helped, but with the glasses safely tucked in her dresser drawer and her hair down her back, she felt exposed, like someone who had been comfortable in the dark and was suddenly dragged into the blinding light.

"Just stop it," Rebecca spoke softly to her reflection. "He's not going to attack you, and you know it." But she wasn't all

337

that convinced. Indeed, she was trembling again as she adjusted the clips that pulled the hair loosely off her face and made herself move for the door.

$\backsim$

Travis thought about Lucky and Margo all the way home. They had clearly enjoyed the service, and he'd been thrilled at the way people had come around to meet them at its conclusion. He knew the congregation would not let him down, but he felt responsible for Lucky, and, he admitted to the Lord, he'd been just a tad nervous. The kids had done fine as well. Sarah Beth had been a bit wiggly, but the children in front of them had been more so, and negative as this was, Travis believed that it helped allay Margo's fears. Her face had been strained until the sermon began, but at that point both she and Lucky had leaned forward in their seats to hear Pastor Henley.

The message had not been on redemption directly, but on the life of Christ and the way He dealt with the many people He encountered during His earthly ministry. Pastor Henley's point had been that Christ's message had never changed. He still expected His followers to give up all for Him and pursue the peace that only He could bring. Travis wasn't certain how much of the sermon Lucky and Margo agreed with, or even understood, but he'd heard them tell Clayton Taggart that they would see him next week. Travis was still thanking God for this and praying for further opportunities for him and Lucky to talk, when the ranch house came into view.

"I'm hungry," Garrett proclaimed.

"Me too," Wyatt said.

Travis was brought up short. He realized now that they'd been talking to him and each other all the way home, and he hadn't even been attending.

"I'm hungry too," he said. "I'll tell you what. When we get inside, let's ask Lavena what we can do to help."

"Sometimes she doesn't let us touch."

"That's true, but I'll be with you and we'll ask *real* nice."

The boys grinned at his conspiratorial tone and were more than happy to double up on his back for a ride from the barn. Their giggles could be heard throughout the yard.

Lavena tried to look stern as they stomped their way into the kitchen, bringing snow in with them, but the sight of the boys laughing and clinging to their father was too much for her. She looked at them fondly even when Travis put them down and started his speech.

"We're all hungry and want to know what we can do to help with dinner."

Lavena shook her head. "Is eating all you think about?"

"We think about sleeping too," Travis told her innocently, and then laughed. "If you'll just give us a job to keep our minds off our stomachs, I'm sure we can wait for whatever—"

Travis cut off abruptly. Rebecca had come to the door of the kitchen and stood there somewhat awkwardly. Her look was guarded, but Travis hardly noticed. She had been trying to meet him halfway for several days now, but this was more than half.

"Hi, Mama," Wyatt greeted her.

"When are we going to eat?" Garrett tossed his father's warning to the wind and asked.

"You boys go ahead and help Lavena," Travis instructed his sons without ever looking at them. A moment later he started toward Rebecca. Rebecca moved sideways so he could move through the doorway, but Travis didn't want to leave the kitchen unless his wife did. He stopped in front of her, their backs to the door frame. Rebecca couldn't seem to stop herself from looking up at him. She was relieved when he only asked, "Did you sleep in?"

"Yes. It was nice."

Travis nodded, his eyes on her. The room was suddenly very warm to him.

"How was church?" Rebecca nearly squeaked as she watched his eyes drop to her mouth.

"Fine. Lucky and Margo were there."

"I didn't know they went."

"It was their first time."

Rebecca didn't know how to respond to that. Would Travis want her to go to church now? Would he take the dress as a sign that she was interested? Admittedly she was rather curious. The boys never complained about going. Indeed, they always came home in high spirits and with beaming smiles.

"I like your dress."

"Thank you," Rebecca said automatically, realizing she'd been staring intently at the string tie at his throat. She raised her eyes to his. "I've thought a lot about what you said last night, and you're right, I had hoped that you wouldn't want to touch—" When Rebecca cut off and glanced across the spacious kitchen at Lavena and her sons, Travis took her by the arm. He walked her to the study. He didn't shut the door but dropped his hand when they stood before the desk.

"You were saying?"

Rebecca's gaze flew around the room but wouldn't focus on him. "I, umm, I was telling you that you were right."

"About hoping to repulse me so that I wouldn't touch you?"

Rebecca nodded.

"And now, Rebecca?"

This time her gaze locked with his.

"I'm not sure yet, Travis."

"All right."

"You're not angry."

"I'm furious," he said with a smile.

Rebecca smiled back as relief flooded her, but then Travis' gaze became serious again.

"Shall I check with you again, Rebecca, or do you want to come to me?"

She knew well what he was asking, and also knew it was a fair question. Suddenly her mind went back to the day they had been married, or rather the night, when her father had insisted that she go to her husband's room. She realized for the first time that she'd never regretted it. Even through the years of anger and denial, when Rebecca was honest with herself, she admitted that Travis had been wonderful to her the first few days they were married. However, that had been many years ago.

"If I came to you now, Travis, I'd be welcome?"

"Very much so, Reba," he told her softly, and then forced himself to say the rest, "but as much as I'd like to see you move into my room, I know you might not be ready."

Travis Buchanan was too fantastic to be real, but the look in his eyes told her he meant it. How many husbands would hold off and give their wives room to decide?

Rebecca finally nodded. "I'll come to you, Travis. When I'm ready, I'll come."

Travis wanted very much to tell her how he looked forward to it, but she must have already known that. He'd been alone for so long—married—but living single. At times it seemed that he would never have a normal marriage, but then he reminded himself that Rebecca had been home only a few weeks. He knew his desire to have a whole and intimate marriage was normal and right, but such things could not be rushed.

"Mama?"

They both heard Garrett's voice at the same time.

"In here," Travis stepped to the door.

"Lavena says dinner is ready."

"Please tell her we'll be right there."

Garrett did as he was asked, and Travis turned back in the doorway and offered his arm. "May I escort you to Sunday dinner, Mrs. Buchanan?"

Rebecca came forward and took his arm. Travis looked down at the top of her head, his heart swelling with love and tenderness. He had always found his wife lovely beyond words, but now in a green dress that managed to make her hair look like gold, she was enchanting. He did not know when she would be ready to give herself completely, but today could not be too soon for him.

"You have to go to sleep," Travis said again.

"I'm not sleepy," Wyatt repeated rather loudly, causing Garrett to stir. Travis picked up his blond son and walked from the room. Garrett had fallen asleep almost instantly, even before Rebecca could come and kiss him, but Wyatt was fighting it tooth and nail. Travis walked him back to his own bedroom, and Rebecca, who had just come up the stairs, followed. She stood just outside the door, unnoticed by her husband and son, and watched Travis in action.

"Now," Travis spoke when he'd put Wyatt's pajama-clad form on the bed, "you're going to wake Garrett if you don't settle in, and you're going to earn yourself a spanking if you don't go to sleep. I know it's Christmas tomorrow, but you still have to obey."

The little boy looked crushed. His eyes filled without warning, and Travis picked him up and moved him to his lap.

"What is it, Wyatt?" he asked quietly. "What's bothering you?"

But the five-year-old couldn't answer.

"You can tell me, Wyatt."

But it was no use. Tears began to pour down his face. Travis tried to think back on what had happened that day but came up blank. Wyatt cried against him for a time, and then lay quietly. Travis thought he might have fallen asleep, but his eyes were still wide and sad.

"Here." Travis lay him against his own pillow. "Lie here a moment, and I'll get my guitar." Fascinated, Wyatt watched as his father moved to the closet. Travis came back to the bed, this time leaning against the footboard, a guitar across his lap. He began to play a slow melody, very softly, his fingers just brushing the strings. At one point he told Wyatt to keep his eyes closed, but other than that there was only the strum of the guitar, and the occasional mournful accompaniment of the wind outside. It took longer than Travis would have expected, but eventually Wyatt's little mouth relaxed and the hand that had been clutching the blanket grew limp. Travis finished the last bars of the hymn he'd started, and then set the guitar aside to carry his son to bed. As he'd hoped, Wyatt did not so much as open an eye as Travis tucked him in. Naturally he'd passed Rebecca at the doorway. She now kissed her sons and walked ahead of Travis to the hall.

"Too tired to go downstairs?" she surprised him when she asked.

"No, not at all."

They started toward the stairs, but Rebecca stopped at Travis' room.

"Travis, will you bring your guitar?"

Travis was surprised again but agreed. He slipped inside to take it from the bed and found that Rebecca had waited for him in the hall.

"I didn't know you played," she said when they had taken their customary seats by the fire.

"I've played since I was a kid," Travis told her, "but I haven't always had a guitar. My last one was broken, and we sold the one before that so my mother and I could eat. In fact, this one's not mine."

Rebecca's brows rose.

"You've never seen it before?"

"No, never," Rebecca told him.

"It was here, in your father's things. There's a small closet in the study, and I found it in there."

Again Rebecca looked surprised. "I've wondered at times what became of my father's things."

"Lavena put his clothing and personal effects in the room across the hall from my old bedroom, and I've even put a few items from the study in there, but most of his things are right where he had them. I've certainly added to the collection over the years, but I'm sure you've noticed most are still in place."

Rebecca nodded and looked around. "I have noticed. I only wondered about his clothes."

"Maybe you'll go through everything sometime. The boys are named after him—perhaps you'll want to find something special for them, a keepsake of sorts."

"I wouldn't have thought of that," Rebecca murmured, her eyes now on the fire. "It's a good idea."

Travis' gaze lingered on her profile for a few moments, and then he put the guitar across his lap. He played from memory, his eyes on the strings. He could feel Rebecca looking at him, but for some reason he felt reserved about this. Indeed, he was so self-conscious that it wasn't until the last song that he added his voice. Travis' singing voice was a pure, deep bass. He had nothing to be shy about, but at times his wife was like a stranger. Her question concerning her father's clothing reminded him just how long she had been away. He felt a sudden trepidation over singing and playing in front of her. He couldn't bring himself to look at her when the song ended. Setting the instrument aside, he let his own gaze rest on the flames.

However, Rebecca couldn't take her eyes from him. He was so much more than she ever dreamed. With a startling clarity Rebecca realized that she was falling in love with this man. He still frightened her a bit and confused her even more, but she was falling for him in a way that made her original infatuation seem ludicrous. The thought made her sit in quiet wonder.

It was impossible to say how long they would have sat silently before the fire, but both heard the clock in the hall as it struck 10:00. Travis sat up and stretched his back.

"I think I'll turn in," he said.

"It will be morning before we know it."

Travis smiled. "And as soon as the boys remember what day it is, we'll be expected to rise and shine."

"You did say you'd shopped for them?" She looked suddenly anxious at the empty space below the tree.

"Yes. I didn't think it wise to bring anything out until morning."

Rebecca nodded.

Travis stood and she followed suit.

"I'll lock up."

"All right. Good night, Travis."

"Good night."

Travis banked the fire and checked the doors, but his thoughts were elsewhere. He walked up the stairs, checked on the boys and then sought his own room. As he did this, he prayed.

Thank You for my wife, Father. Thank You for these boys she has given me. I can see that she's softening. Help her to that end. I might be missing something, Lord. Show me. We've talked about so much, but there are still so many things I don't know about her and she doesn't know about me. Help her to find You. Help her to see that she can't be complete without You. Give us a blessed Christmas tomorrow, Lord. Thank You for the birth of Your Son. Here Travis' heart stopped, and he remembered the day he'd come to Christ. Christmas had taken on a new meaning for him then. It was as if Christmas lasted all year long. Would Rebecca ever know such peace and joy?

I trust that You will save my wife, Lord, but before that time, touch her heart. Help her to see that I just want to love and cherish her. The new year is upon us, Father. Help us to find a new start in each other, as well as in You.

40

The boys' eyes were huge when they gained the living room the next morning. Travis had not planned to wake early, but he was wide awake before the sun rose. With great anticipation for the day, he got up, built a huge fire in the living room fireplace, and loaded the underside of the tree with the gifts he'd purchased. The twins wanted to begin tearing into packages, but Travis stopped them. He directed them to the sofa and then hunkered down in front of them.

"We have some work to do."

They looked crushed.

"This morning?" Wyatt asked.

"Yes. We have some presents to deliver."

The boys looked at each other.

"*We* have presents to give?" Garrett clarified.

"That's right. Now we need to go back upstairs and get dressed, but we need to do it quietly so your mother can sleep. Come on." Travis rose and, like a man leading his troops to battle, was followed very seriously to his bedroom. Once there Travis shut the door, and the boys took careful positions alongside the washstand to watch their father shave. They were greatly fascinated, their own chins tilting high when Travis shaved his throat. Travis glanced down often, careful to keep the smile from his face.

"Are you going to shave someday?" he asked them as he wiped the lather from his face.

Their heads bobbed in unison. Travis leaned close to their little faces.

"I think maybe you should start now," he said watching their eyes grow round. With a gentle finger, he brushed a bit of soap on each small chin. With his razor kept carefully "blade out," Travis swiped the soap from each face. The boys fingered their chins in wonder.

"Now, I don't want you to try this without me because you might get cut, but I think it's best if we're all clean-shaven for Christmas morning. Don't you agree?"

"Do we need some more?"

Travis bent again, his eyes carefully assessing his work. "I think I got it all."

"Let's show Mama."

"No." Travis' voice was deep and quiet and stopped them in flight. "We're going to let your mother sleep. You can show her later. I'm going to get dressed, and then I'll help you with your clothes."

The boys followed him into the closet, and again he fell under their scrutiny. Wyatt wanted to know if he ever shaved the hair on his legs. Travis could only laugh. He watched Garrett look at his chest and then peek down the front of his own pajama shirt. Wyatt saw his action and did the same thing. Travis decided not to comment on that at all.

"Okay, let's head to your room, but remember to be quiet."

It was a fiasco. They didn't wake Rebecca, but they were so excited about this gift outing that they tore nearly everything from their dresser drawers. Travis didn't know whether to get them out of there as fast as he could or make them clean it up. He opted to leave and hoped that Rebecca didn't find the mess first.

The three Buchanan men went down to the study where Travis retrieved some burlap bags from beside his desk.

"Can you each carry one?"

He tried to give them the lighter loads and then led the way to the kitchen where they could find their coats on the hooks by the door. They made their way outside and to the bunkhouse. The boys were quiet with their loads as they shuffled through the snow, and Travis held the door open wide to let them go in ahead of him. As he knew they would be, the hands were up and preparing to go to breakfast.

"Merry Christmas," Travis greeted them.

The men answered back, some quiet, some a little more boisterous. It helped that all the men, even those who were more prone to shyness, liked the boys.

"We have gifts," Wyatt told Race.

"Do you now?" The bearded cowboy looked pleased without smiling.

"Here you go." Travis began to open the bags and direct traffic. "Everyone gets a rope." He paused while the boys, their faces serious with concentration, handed each man a new manila rope. "Now the gloves," Travis went on, and the boys took a pair of new leather gloves from Travis for each cowhand. "And this is the last item." Travis placed small pocketknives into their palms, but the boys only stood there looking down at the prizes in their fingers.

They men had gathered around to watch the proceedings and receive their gifts, and smiles lit their faces. It was clear to all that the little Buchanans were utterly torn over parting with the knives.

"I think they're a little uncertain if we're going to like what they picked out, boss," Kyle commented. He was the bunkhouse character and regularly supplied the group with laughter.

"Can you hand them out?" Travis asked, watching them.

"Do we get one?" Garrett was bold enough to ask.

"Not until you're a little older."

This present took a little longer because each boy looked at the knife he had to give away and then at the man's face who received it. It didn't help their five-year-old hearts that the men were pleased, smiling and thanking them. Giving away those knives was torture. It took some time, but the job got done.

"Merry Christmas," Travis said to the group at large and started away. "Oh!" Travis had passed Colin's bunk. Someone had set his Christmas gifts in a pile. "Where is Colin today?"

"I think he stayed in town," Chad told him.

"I thought he said on Friday that he would be out here today and the rest of the week." Travis was sure that the older man had said as much.

"I don't think Lavena cooperated." This came from Chad. His voice was low and just a tad amused.

Travis stared at him. Had he really meant that the way it sounded? The ranch owner's eyes traveled to the others. They all had slightly amused looks on their faces. *Lavena and Colin?* Travis was thunderstruck. The men didn't say any more, although they all stood taking in Travis' surprised face. His sons were calling him, asking if they were leaving now, and Travis was forced back to the business at hand. He and the boys left a moment later.

"You'd think he would know what was going on with his own housekeeper," Jud commented unfairly.

"Don't be an idiot," Kyle said good-naturedly. "When a man's married to a woman who looks like Rebecca Buchanan, he doesn't spend much time thinking about his housekeeper's problems."

It wasn't true. Travis cared deeply for Lavena. But no one else commented. Each had his own opinion, however, most being that the boss' affairs were none of their business.

"Is there more?" Wyatt asked for the second time.

"Oh! Yes. I have some things for Woody, and then when we get back, we'll take Lavena's to her."

"Did we get Lavena a rope?"

But Travis' mind was gone again. *Lavena and Colin.* Or was it just Colin? Any way he looked at it, it was still a wonder.

Travis was half in a daze as he gave Woody his Christmas gifts, and by then the boys were more than anxious to get back to the house. Realizing that all he'd done was listen to gossip, he forced his mind off idle speculations and told the boys to head inside.

"Is it our turn for presents now?"

"I think it must be getting that time. Or would you rather we ate breakfast first?"

"No," they shouted in unison.

"Come on then. Let's see if your mother is awake."

She was more than awake. She was up and dressed in a lovely rust-colored gown that made her eyes look huge. Her hair was piled on top of her head, and the tendrils of soft curls hanging down the back of her neck were most inviting.

"Merry Christmas," Travis said, bending to kiss her cheek.

"Merry Christmas," she replied as she turned her back on the warmth of the stove. "You look like you've been busy."

The boys had hugged their mother but now were slipping through the kitchen door toward the living room.

"Leave the gifts alone, please," Travis called after them as they ran.

They didn't answer, so Travis excused himself, followed them, and made certain they understood. He was back in a few minutes, stopping again in front of his wife.

"Do you want to eat first or open gifts?"

The boys' voices, loud and excited, floated to them from the other room.

"I think we had better put them out of their misery," Rebecca told him.

"What about you? Not excited at all?"

Her eyes went down. "I would be if I'd shopped for you."

"Rebecca," Travis started, but she wouldn't look at him. With two long fingers he tipped her jaw until her eyes met his. "It's all right."

"That's easy for you to say—you shopped."

"You're stubborn; do you know that?"

"What's stubborn about wanting to give you something?"

"It's stubborn because I've told you honestly that I won't be upset."

Rebecca looked at him. The fingers that had been holding her jaw were now the back of his whole hand. He stroked down over her downy skin until he had one hand along the side of her neck.

"I knew the skin on your neck was soft."

"I don't remember your being like this, Travis," she said softly.

"We didn't have much time together." His hand still lay alongside her neck. "In fact, it will be years before we can say we've lived together longer than we did apart."

It did considerable good for Rebecca's heart to hear Travis talk about years, and especially their future. Everything had happened so fast, coming back to Boulder, being so frustrated and angry with Travis, but then realizing how wrong she had been about his motives. The realization that she did want a real marriage was a revelation so staggering that it often gave her a feeling of unreality.

"Why don't you head in and sit with the boys?" Travis now suggested. "I want to check on Lavena."

Travis had no more said the words when Lavena came from her room. She was rather dressed up, and Travis smiled at her.

"You're looking pleased with yourself," she snapped in her usual manner.

"Merry Christmas, Lavena." Travis ignored the mood. "You look nice."

She snorted and Travis, with the men's words riding him hard, needled her.

"Is there some chance that you're in your best dress for a certain cowhand?"

"Now don't you start on me, Travis Buchanan!" she rounded on him. "I've had to listen to Woody for two months."

Travis tried not to smile. "Two months! Where have I been?"

"Where you should be!" She was still outraged. "Fixing your marriage and staying out of my business. Now go with your family, or I'm not going to cook today."

However Travis went toward her. Lavena eyed him balefully but stood still. Travis put his hands on her shoulders and said, "Don't say anything."

"I don't know what you mean."

"Just keep your mouth shut because I have something to say to you. If Colin wants to take you to dinner, go with him. Close your mouth, Lavena."

She did so with a snap.

"I mean it." His voice was very firm, and the argument went out of her, her shoulders relaxing under his hands. "All you do is work and work some more. Now, go to dinner if you'd like. Colin North is a decent guy." He ended with these words and then leaned down to kiss her cheek.

She was pleased, he knew that, and he also knew that she was going to enjoy the gift he found for her. However, at the moment his family was waiting.

~

"Look, Mama, look," the boys continued to say excitedly.

"I'm looking," Rebecca told them and laughed. Never would she have guessed what her husband had bought for the boys, but he had done well. Garrett and Wyatt were strutting around in new cowboy boots that were a perfect fit, cowboy hats, and leather vests. She had never seen them look so proud. Wyatt with his blond hair had the brown set, and Garrett had the black vest, hat, and boots. Both were fair to bursting with delight.

"How did I do?" Travis asked Rebecca as he sat close to her on the sofa.

"Oh, Travis, I would have looked for toys, and it wouldn't have meant nearly as much."

Travis smiled, his own heart doing a little swelling. It was incredibly satisfying to buy things for his children and have them show such pleasure. But he wasn't through. His head suddenly turned to study his wife. A moment later Rebecca noticed his scrutiny.

"Am I in trouble?"

"No, I just hope I'm not."

Her brows rose, but Travis didn't answer. He went back to the tree and plucked a small box from one of the branches. He sat back down and placed it in Rebecca's hand.

"I hadn't really planned to buy you this, but there it was and I couldn't seem to stop myself." He hesitated. "You don't have to wear it if you don't want to."

Rebecca looked at him for a moment and then opened the box. Her hand went to her mouth. "Oh, Travis," was all she could manage.

It was a ring, a ruby ring set around with six matched diamonds. Travis had not intended such an intimate gift at this time in their relationship, but it had been under the glass at the jewelers in Denver, and he knew he had to have it. He now watched as she put it on.

"It's perfect," she breathed, her face mirroring her pleasure. "So you'll wear it?"

Rebecca looked at her hand and laughed. "I don't think I'll ever take it off."

Travis smiled and rose again. This time the box he retrieved was a little different shape. He pressed it into Rebecca's hand and then joined her again.

"Travis, surely you didn't buy more."

He shrugged but didn't apologize.

Rebecca opened this box to find the necklace that matched the ring. She was too stunned to speak. Travis reached for the fine gold chain and held it out to put on her. Rebecca leaned forward and shifted so he could hook the clasp. Her hand went to it as soon as it was settled in place against her throat.

"Oh, Travis." Her voice was soft and dreamy. "Thank you so much."

"You're welcome," he told her sincerely, sitting very still when she leaned close and kissed his cheek. She looked shy and uncomfortable, but Travis didn't let on that he noticed. The boys started climbing all over them, but Travis' mind was elsewhere. Rebecca had been delighted with the ring, not threatened by it. For the first time he knew that his marriage was going to make it.

41

"How was your Christmas?" Travis asked of Lucky the very next day. The men were sitting in the office.

"It was all right. How about yours?"

"We had a good time. How are Margo and Sarah Beth?"

"Margo hasn't been feeling the best, but other than that they're doing okay. By the way, thanks for the gifts, Travis."

"You're welcome. Single out a good-looking heifer tonight and take her home with you."

"Thank you," Lucky replied with obvious pleasure. Travis had done this last year as well, but Lucky hadn't been expecting it again. He added quietly, "Maybe Margo's father will smile a little if we have fresh meat for a time."

"He's not very easy, is he?"

"No. He thinks she could have done much better than me."

"You have a steady job, Lucky, and you provide for your family. What does he expect?"

Lucky shrugged. "I think it goes back to how we got married; you know, with Margo expecting and all."

"I remember, but that was a long time ago and you've made a real marriage of it."

Again Lucky shrugged. His face told of his discouragement.

"Maybe if you had your own place?"

Lucky shook his head. "There are no houses for rent in Boulder right now, and Margo doesn't want Sarah Beth in an apartment or at the boarding house."

"I can understand that," Travis agreed, but his mind was busy. He sat quietly for a moment, Lucky watching him.

"Do you want me to head out?"

"Yes, I'll go with you." Travis' mind had been far away.

The men walked out together, Lucky asking questions concerning business. Not until the men were on their horses, bundled warmly to spend the day in the saddle, did talk range back to the personal. Chad was with them, but he had ridden out in front for several yards, and Lucky volunteered, "We're planning on coming back to church on Sunday."

"I'm glad to hear it."

"Margo's mother might come with us."

"That's great. Is her father interested too?"

"I doubt it. He's usually hard to read, but he's made himself more than plain about church. According to him, only fools believe in God."

"But you don't agree with him?"

"I would have at one time, but not now."

"When did that change?"

"It's been coming for a time. This fall and even into the winter, I've had this restless feeling, like I was missing something. At first I thought it was Margo. I've never stayed with one woman for very long, and I thought I just might be restless to move on, but I couldn't do it. She's the sweetest woman a man could ever hope to meet. She still looks at me as if I were her dream come true."

Lucky suddenly heard himself and looked away. He felt a fool for opening up like that to his boss, but Travis surprised him.

"It's amazing how quickly we can lose our hearts. I hadn't seen my wife in nearly six years, but the moment I laid eyes on her, I fell in love all over again. It's also amazing what God uses to get our attention."

"Like Sarah Beth choking." Lucky's voice was thoughtful.

"Yeah," Travis agreed quietly and then let the matter go. Chad was dropping back to join them, and the ranch owner knew Lucky would not care to discuss this in front of the other men. However, his heart kept on.

You're doing a work here, Lord. I know this to be true. Use me. Use me to help in any way I can and to be there for Lucky and Margo. Give them a thirst, Lord, that won't be quenched until they rest in You.

When Travis came down for breakfast on Wednesday morning, Lavena was again in her good dress, the cameo pin he'd given her on Christmas adorning her neckline.

"I want to talk to you," she said before Travis could say a word.

"All right."

"You need to get that girl some clothes."

"Rebecca?"

"Of course, Rebecca! She can't keep wearing dresses that are too small."

Travis hadn't noticed that his wife's dresses were too small, and his look must have said as much because Lavena was on him again.

"And those boys. They're both outgrowing their pants, and all their socks have holes. Are you listening to me, Travis?"

"I'm listening, Lavena, but why don't you say something to Rebecca. She could get herself some clothes."

"I've said things, but she won't listen. Now are you going to take care of that girl or not?"

"Lavena, why would I insist that Rebecca needs clothes if she doesn't think she does?"

He watched her hands curl into fists at her side. She was really upset.

"She's different now. She's trying to gauge what you want. And if you don't show some interest in her clothing, she won't think you care."

"How do you know all this?" Travis eyed her suspiciously. "Has she talked to you?"

"She doesn't have to," Lavena insisted. "I just know."

Travis' hand went to the back of his neck. Things were going great between him and Rebecca. The last thing he wanted to do was mess everything up by telling her he thought she needed new clothes.

"I'm going to work," Travis decided.

"You're not going to do it, are you?" Lavena was clearly disgusted. Travis ignored her and continued toward the door. "Isn't that just like a man." Lavena was not finished. "He doesn't like the conversation so he just ups and walks away."

Travis spun back in a hurry. There were times when he allowed Lavena to infuriate him, and now was just such an occasion. He walked back to within five feet of her and speared her with his eyes. Her own gaze met his unflinchingly.

"I'll talk to Rebecca when you go out with Colin North."

He shocked her, but only for a moment. Her chin went into the air.

"Then you'd better prepare your speech. I'm having lunch with Colin today."

With her chin still in the air, Lavena turned to the stove and breakfast preparation for the twins, who would soon be rising. Otherwise she would have seen that she'd astounded her boss into a speechless stare.

"Travis, is something bothering you?"

It was evening, and husband and wife were in their usual places before the fire. Travis looked at Rebecca's hesitant expression and thought he could wring Lavena's neck.

"Not exactly," he hedged.

Rebecca continued to look at him.

"Have I done something?"

"No," Travis was quick to reassure her. "It's just that Lavena mentioned something to me, and I'm a little hesitant to say anything."

Rebecca cocked her head to one side. "You think I'll be upset?"

"I think you'll tell me I have ulterior motives."

Rebecca was overcome with curiosity.

"What did she say?"

Travis took a breath. "She said you need new clothes. She said your dresses are too small."

Rebecca blushed and looked at her lap. "They are small." Her voice was low. "I'm more filled out now than before the twins were born. You haven't noticed?"

"No. I couldn't see your figure in the other dresses, and now—" Travis cut off, afraid that if he told her a wife's curves were delightful to her husband, he'd really be in trouble.

"And now what?"

Travis hesitated. "I like the way you look."

"Why were you afraid to tell me that?"

It was like living inside a child's toy. Travis was the ball being rattled to and fro at will. Early on Rebecca was so prickly that he couldn't say a word, and now she was digging deep with serious questions. He didn't know what else to do but come clean.

"I was afraid that if I complimented your figure, you would accuse me of only wanting you in my bed."

"I did say that in the past, didn't I?"

Travis nodded.

"I guess I do need some new dresses, Travis."

"Why don't we head into town tomorrow and see if they have anything?"

"You'll go with me?"

"Sure. We can pick out some new things for the boys too."

Rebecca was so pleased that she couldn't speak for a moment.

361

"What time shall we go?" Travis asked.

She thought about it. "You probably won't want to be gone all day, but I hate to wake the boys too early."

Travis grinned. "It was Lavena's idea—let her get the boys up."

Rebecca had no problem with that, no problem at all. After deciding when to leave, Travis carefully asked Rebecca to tell him just what she needed. She did so willingly, and one more wall came down.

The next day they stayed in town much longer than they had planned, buying Rebecca a new wardrobe and many things for the boys. But along with their purchases, they were enjoying one another's company in a way they never had. Just days before, Travis had realized that they were going to make it as a couple. As they drove home to the ranch several hours after lunch, Rebecca finally knew it as well.

∽

"Robert, is that you?"

"Yes, it is," Robert called to Eddie as he came in the front door on Thursday evening.

"You're early," she smiled as she met him at the door. They shared a kiss.

"I asked David to lock up because I have good news for you."

"What is it?"

"How long ago did we decide to pray more specifically that we would see more of Travis and meet Rebecca?"

Eddie looked surprised. "That was just last night, Robert."

The banker smiled. "Travis and Rebecca were in town today. Travis brought Rebecca in to meet me. They're coming to dinner Saturday night."

"Oh, Robert," Eddie laughed in delight, "that's wonderful."

"Are you certain you're up to it?"

"Of course. I'm thrilled. What is she like?"

"Very sweet and a little shy. They had been shopping and were headed to lunch and then out to shop some more. Travis looked like a child on Christmas morning."

"Oh, Robert, I've prayed so much. I can't imagine not sharing Christ with my spouse."

Robert hugged her. "We'll keep praying. God has given us a start, and if He wants us to continue, we will."

"Shall we have anyone else?"

"I think this first time we'll just have Travis, Rebecca, and the boys."

"Do they know the boys are invited?"

"Yes, I made that clear."

Eddie tipped her head back to look at him; it was like her husband to think of everything. "Have I told you lately that you're wonderful?"

"I think you might have, but you can always say it twice."

He kept an arm around her as they moved toward the kitchen. Eddie had been feeling a little tired, but no one would have known it as she discussed with Lena what they would serve on Saturday night.

42

Friday was the longest day of Rebecca's life. The boys quarreled, and Lavena, who was cleaning at the time, had no patience with anyone. But none of those things were the reason for her restlessness. She had to talk to Travis. Much of the snow had melted off, so the men were able to cover acres of land and planned to be gone all day. Rebecca had tried to work on her mending, but after jabbing her finger several times, discarded it in disgust. She then decided to bake, but she got a few shakes of flour on the floor and was scowled at by Lavena. The old Rebecca would have cowered in fear, but since she'd come back, she stood her ground. Today, though, she wasn't up to it. She abandoned the cookie dough, sent the boys outside, and paced the living room. Her heart slammed in her chest when she finally heard the door and Travis' deep voice as he spoke to Lavena.

She hadn't counted on vying with her sons for his attention, but she hung close, even going so far as to tell the boys that they could wait downstairs tonight for their father.

"But sometimes he lets us wash up with him," Garrett protested.

"I still want you to wait down here tonight."

"No," they both defiantly proclaimed, and with that word their father was brought into the argument.

"That's enough, boys. You will not tell your mother no. Now, go into the kitchen and wash for dinner on your own."

Their attitudes still needing work, the boys went off and Travis moved for the stairs. Rebecca made herself follow him. Travis was afraid to say too much but turned to her when she came right into his room.

"You all right?"

"Yes."

He nodded. "Have a good day?"

"It was rather long."

Travis was unbuttoning his shirt now and getting ready to splash some water into the basin. He could see Rebecca's reflection in the mirror. She was as nervous as a cat.

"I moved two of my new dresses into this room today."

Travis froze for a full second and then slowly forced himself to finish lathering his face.

"Did you?"

"Yes. And a few more of my things. Not everything," she rushed to add. "I didn't want to do that yet."

"I think I understand."

They were quiet for a few moments, and then Travis asked slowly, "And do you come with the dresses, Rebecca?" He watched in the mirror as she nodded and then went back to methodically shaving his face, knowing how easy it would be at that moment to slash his own throat.

"You're a cruel woman, Rebecca," he finally said.

"I am?" She looked stunned.

"Uh hmm. Giving that kind of news to a man when he can't even kiss you."

This time he turned his head and watched as a smile pulled at her mouth.

"But there's always later," she said softly and looked up. Travis held her eyes with his own.

"Yes, later," he said softly, and Rebecca took a surreptitious step backward.

"I'll see you downstairs."

"All right," Travis agreed. He watched her leave the room. His chest rose on a huge sigh before his heart began to thunder like a runaway stage.

"Could you put the boys to bed tonight?" Travis surprised Rebecca by asking the question right after dinner. "I have some things I have to get done. We'll have coffee as usual, though."

"Sure," she agreed, but her disappointment was keen. Why did she think that Travis would put everything aside to be with her this night? A feeling of dread crept over her. This was the very thing she had feared. She was terrified that intimacy with Travis would make her some sort of possession to be used and discarded at will.

She went through the motions with the boys, but her heart wasn't there. It was with Travis who had disappeared as soon as the meal was over. The boys asked for him, but he had kissed them good-night downstairs. They were a little fussy and put out, which only put Rebecca in a worse humor. By the time she reached the living room, she was angry enough to let him have it. The fire was burning as usual, but only one lamp was lit. Rebecca didn't notice. She stormed in and was nearly on top of her husband when she noticed what he was sitting on.

Gone were the chairs that had sat before the fire. In their place was the sofa, long and inviting. Rebecca's eyes flew to Travis where he sat at one end, his legs stretched out. He was smiling at her, his eyes watching her every move. Rebecca couldn't help but laugh. She giggled from deep in her chest, a sound of delight and relief. Travis had waited to hear that sound. A moment later he snatched her hand and pulled her into his lap. He kissed her long and hard, but then broke the kiss and held something aloft. It was a simple gold band.

"Be my wife, Rebecca?"

"Another ring," she whispered.

"The one you should have had six years ago."

"Oh, Travis."

She watched as he tugged her ruby ring free of her left hand and tried to slide the band in place. She had to help him.

"Do you want this on with it, or on the other hand?"

"The other hand," she replied instantly.

Travis examined both of her hands when the rings were in place and then kissed the back of Rebecca's ring hand. He then cuddled her against him.

"Do you know what I wish?" he asked softly.

"What?"

"That I'd moved this sofa weeks ago."

Rebecca would have laughed all over again, but Travis was kissing her. She could feel the weight of the gold band on her hand, even as she was very aware of the man who held her.

His wife. I'm going to be Travis Buchanan's wife.

"I'm nervous about this dinner tonight."

Travis turned from the mirror where he'd been tying his tie into place.

"Why?"

"I don't know. What if the boys get rambunctious and break something?"

"The boys are doing great. I know that's not going to happen."

"But maybe Robert and Eddie are not used to children, and they'll—"

Travis came to her. "Rebecca, honey, Garrett and Wyatt already know Robert and Eddie. They see them every week."

"Oh, that's right."

"Do you think they'll really like me, Travis? I mean, I don't go to your church and—"

"Rebecca." He said her name only once, but his serious tone and the way he took her face in his hand stopped every word.

"Robert and Eddie Langley are my closest friends," he said as he looked into her eyes. "They were thrilled when they learned you had come back to me. You've already met Robert, and Eddie is very sweet. There is nothing to worry about."

Rebecca nodded but didn't look convinced.

"What if my dress is all wrong?"

"Your dress is almost as lovely as you are."

"You're just saying that," Rebecca told him.

Travis had to laugh and shake his head. "What am I going to do with you?" He kissed her before going back to his tie.

"Can we eat now?" Wyatt interrupted from the door.

"No," Rebecca told him, glad to have the subject changed. "You'll spoil your supper."

"What is Eddie serving?"

"Eddie? Do they call her Eddie, Travis?"

"No," Travis said easily, and then frowned. "At least I don't think they do."

This seemed to make Rebecca more nervous than ever. She had forgotten that the boys were acquainted with the Langleys. Travis said it didn't matter about church, but was that true? He felt that way, but did the Langleys share the feeling? It continued to be a worry. By the time they arrived at the Langley home, Rebecca had made herself good and sick.

"Why didn't you tell me she was expecting?" Rebecca whispered almost two hours later.

"Who, Eddie?" Travis' voice was just as low.

"Of course, Eddie. I can't believe you failed to mention that."

"I must have forgotten."

Rebecca looked exasperated. They were making their way from the dining room to the living room for coffee and had just a few moments together. Travis had thought he would need this time to ask if Rebecca was all right, but there was no need. She and Eddie had taken to each other instantly.

Not until they arrived did Travis see how low a view of herself Rebecca had. Eddie had wanted to know all about pregnancy and raising babies. At first Rebecca had been too surprised to say much, but Travis could see a change in her when she realized how much she had to offer.

"This house is beautiful," Rebecca commented as she and Travis became comfortable on the settee.

"Yes, it is." Travis' head tipped back as he looked around. "It has more of a feminine touch than our house."

Rebecca nodded in agreement.

"You could make changes, you know."

Rebecca turned to him. "At the ranch?"

"Sure. I think it will always be on the rustic side, but it would be just as easy to display teacups as guns."

Rebecca chuckled. The face he had made to accompany his statement struck her as funny. With the laugh, Travis wanted to kiss her. He was pulling her close when they were joined by their host and hostess. Rebecca's face flamed, and she took several moments to adjust the skirt of her dress.

"Where did the boys head to?" Travis asked, trying not to laugh at his wife's chagrin.

"They wanted to eat dessert in the kitchen. Robert put some old wooden toys out there. I'm sure they'll be busy for hours. Rebecca, did you say you like tea?"

"Yes."

"So do I. I put the kettle on, so it will be a few minutes. Do you want coffee, Travis?"

"If I pass, will I still get dessert?"

The question made Eddie laugh, and Rebecca saw again how close the three of them were. They did nothing to keep her out, but there was a connection among them that she couldn't quite be a part of. She couldn't put a name to it, but she could feel it.

"Were you born in Colorado, Rebecca?" Robert asked. It was the first of many questions. Rebecca asked dozens of her own, loving the romantic way Robert and Eddie had met. They talked for the next hour, enjoyed dessert, and then talked on until way too late. The boys were drooping by the time they left, and Rebecca knew they would be crabby in the morning.

"Thank you," Rebecca said to Eddie as her hostess saw them to the door. "It was a wonderful evening."

"Let's do it again."

"I'd love to. Why don't you come to the ranch?"

"Name a day."

"Two weeks from tonight?" Rebecca asked the question tentatively, but Eddie jumped at it.

"It's a date. Let me know if I can bring something."

"I'll do that," Rebecca said, sounding so pleased that Eddie impulsively hugged her. Rebecca so welcomed the embrace that she wanted to weep for Angel and the friendship they no longer shared. Rebecca left, asking herself if Eddie would ever be that type of friend. Not that Rebecca could honestly say that Angel would be there through thick or thin; after all, she had refused to take the boys. Already the letters between them had tapered off to nothing. Still Rebecca's question lingered: Would she ever feel as close to Eddie as she had to Angel?

"You're quiet."

"I was thinking," she admitted.

"Want to share?"

Rebecca thought about it. Where would she start? She finally shook her head. "No, I don't think so, Travis." She tucked her arm in his. "But thank you for asking."

43

The year 1877 arrived during a snowstorm, but by the end of the month, the snow was melting fast and everyone had the impression of an early spring. Moods were high, and romance filled the air. Travis and Rebecca fell a little more in love every day, and Colin North was becoming a regular fixture in the Buchanan kitchen. Lavena was still very much herself, short and to the point, but Colin was clearly fascinated with her. Lavena wasn't around to do as much as she had been, which meant more work for Rebecca, but she honestly didn't mind.

Lucky, Margo, and Margo's mother, Yvonne, had become regulars at church, and Margo had just recently shared with Eddie how she had taken the Scriptures to heart and made Christ the Lord of her life. Lucky still peppered Travis with dozens of questions, but his heart was tender and he continued to stay open to the truth, something for which Travis prayed daily concerning Rebecca. The Buchanans and Langleys had not seen as much of each other as they had hoped, but Travis also prayed that a friendship would grow between his wife and Eddie. He trusted God wholly for her faith.

The first Sunday of February she surprised him and the boys.

"Mama." Garrett was the first to see her.

Up and dressed in her best gown, Rebecca had come to the kitchen door. Travis left his breakfast and went to her.

He'd already pulled her close and kissed her in bed, but this was even better.

"Good morning," he said as his arms went around her. "You look beautiful."

Rebecca cuddled against him in an attempt to make her heart feel lighter. "I thought I would go with you this morning."

"I'll enjoy that," Travis said, working hard to keep his emotions at bay. He held Rebecca out in front of him and then bent to kiss her. He wanted to ask when she had changed her mind but was afraid of pushing too hard. For the most part they got along very well, but there were times she became angry with Travis and he didn't know why. The subject of God or church was rarely brought up because Rebecca did not seem comfortable with either.

"Breakfast?" Travis asked.

"Some toast, I think, and coffee."

The boys were thrilled to have their mother present for the meal, and Rebecca had a good time even though she was swamped with guilt. She knew very well what Travis' church attendance meant to him, but she was not going just to please him. Last week Wyatt had come home and talked again of the pretty lady at church. That he was infatuated was very clear. For some reason Rebecca was overcome with curiosity and jealousy. She was certain that Travis thought her best dress was for church, but it wasn't. She had worked for ages on her hair and dress in an attempt to look her best.

You're a fool, Rebecca, she said to herself. *You know Travis loves you. There is no other woman.* But it was no use. She had to go. She had to see who this woman was and whether she should be worried about her husband's attentions straying.

"Ready?" she heard Travis ask. She had been wool-gathering and barely remembered to drink her coffee. With rushed movements she went to retrieve her coat, and then she saw it. Travis had a Bible in his hand. What should have been the real reason for attending church jumped at her.

"I don't have a Bible," she said quietly, but Travis only smiled tenderly.

"You can share mine."

Rebecca smiled weakly, feeling more guilty than ever. Thinking she was nervous, Travis prayed that her heart would be calm and that she would enjoy the morning. But the tense look never left Rebecca's face, and Travis prayed for her all the way to town.

<hr style="width:20%" />

You're a fool, Rebecca Rose Buchanan. An absolute fool!

She had said the words to herself a dozen times, but it didn't stop the pain. She hadn't heard a word of the sermon. Instead she had spent that entire time looking for the woman who turned out to be Eddie's sister, Jackie. And of course there had been no mystery. Jackie had come up to them as soon as the sermon ended.

"Travis," Jackie said. "Clayton tells me your wife is here."

"That she is," Travis' voice told of his pleasure.

"Help me now." Her hand went out, and Travis reached for Rebecca in order to bring them together.

"This is Rebecca," he said to Jackie when his wife had offered her hand. "Rebecca, this is Jackie Taggart. She's married to Clayton, who teaches at the school. She's also Eddie's sister."

"Hello," Rebecca managed quietly, her hand still in Jackie's tight grasp.

Jackie's smile was beaming. "I'm so glad to meet you. I'm sorry I haven't been out to visit. Have you gotten settled?"

"Yes."

"That's great. We love your little boys," Jackie told her. "Wyatt comes and talks to me every week."

"They love you too," Rebecca told her honestly. She looked down to see Wyatt staring at her.

"They're charmers," Jackie said, laughing good-naturedly. "I would love it if the three of you could visit sometime. We live right by the school, and I'm home most days."

"Thank you." Rebecca barely remembered her manners. "We'll have to do that."

"Great. Will we see you here next week?"

Rebecca heard herself say yes but thought it must have been another person talking.

Jackie let go of Rebecca's hand when Clayton came up to meet her, but kind as she had been, it had all been torture for Rebecca.

Now the Buchanans were on their way home, and Rebecca felt as though it had all been a dream. Jackie Taggart was beautiful. But she was also married to the schoolmaster, and clearly a friend to Travis and nothing more.

"Are you all right?" Travis asked as he lifted her from the wagon and carried her into the kitchen. The snow was no longer deep, but Travis used any excuse to touch her.

"I think so."

"Did the sermon upset you?" he asked, still holding her close.

"No, I'm just thinking about the people I met."

Travis set her down. "You're sure you're all right?"

Rebecca nodded and managed to smile, but it was a relief to have Travis head back outside where the boys were waiting in the sleigh. She could let her guard down for a few minutes. The whole morning had been an awful mistake that led from one blunder to the next. She had stared at Jackie as though she had two heads, and then at her husband. To top it off, she had told them in front of Travis that she would be back the next week. Rebecca shook her head in regret, but that didn't change the fact that her temples were starting to pound.

❧

"I've worked for everything I have," Lucky told Travis halfway through February. "I think that's why I get tripped up with the free gift."

376

"I did the same thing, Lucky. There were many times even after I committed my life to Christ that I found myself trying to earn God's favor. God's grace is so huge. It's more than I can take in, but it really does cover it all. We can't outgive God or do anything to make ourselves worthy. There is no room for pride. It's so easy for a child to ask for help—for a man it's torture, but there's no other way."

The men were in the barn. The other hands always headed right to dinner when they came in from work, but since Lucky went home to Margo in town, he usually took a little time to talk with Travis.

"Margo's like a different person," Lucky shared, his voice full of wonder as though he couldn't quite believe it.

"In what ways?"

"She's not feeling at all well with this pregnancy and sometimes she has cramping. I'm afraid we're going to lose the baby, but she just says that if it happens, God knows best."

Travis nodded. "What you need to understand, Lucky, is that God never changes. Whether or not Margo had come to Him, God would still be the same. The difference is in *Margo.* She has trusted in Christ, so now He's able to open her eyes to these new truths. The question is, are you ready to follow in her footsteps? God doesn't love Margo more than He loves Lucky, but just like Margo, God is going to let Lucky decide."

It was very clear to Lucky at that moment. At least subconsciously, he had thought God had just recently become the God He was, but that was laughable. God had been there all along, the same sovereign presence for centuries, only Lucky hadn't seen Him.

"I need this, Travis," Lucky told him quietly. "I can't say as I understand it all, but I can see now that I'm lost without Him."

In the horse barn of the Double Star Ranch, Lucky Harwell, remembering all that Travis had shared with him, gave his life to Christ.

"I have run from You, God," he prayed sincerely. "I have pursued my own life and done as I pleased. I have sinned with many women and even touched my wife before she was rightfully mine. I don't know how You can accept a sinner like me, but I want Your shed blood to cover my sins too. Come to me like You have Margo. Take all of me, God, and make me the man You would have me be."

Lucky looked up to see tears standing in Travis' eyes. His own stung the back of his throat.

"It's all true." His voice was a whisper. "I've been listening to the sermons for weeks now, Travis, and it's all true. God didn't just wind up the world like a child's toy and let it go. He's here, in every place and in every heart of those who will ask Him."

A tear slid down Travis' cheek. "So many years I've prayed, Lucky. I'll be here for you. Don't forget that."

"I need to go home." Lucky was suddenly breathless. "I need to see Margo."

"Go." Travis' smile was huge. "I'll see you tomorrow, and we'll talk."

Lucky's hand came out, and Travis covered it with his own. They looked at each other, but Lucky couldn't speak. As Lucky turned and walked away, Travis stood still and poured out his feelings to God.

This is what Robert felt like. This is what Robert's heart did when I finally saw the truth. You are Savior. You are Lord. Thank You, holy Father, for showing Lucky the way. I have failed You so many times, but You've never let me down. Lucky and Margo are Your children now. Touch Sarah Beth, too, Lord. Show her young heart. Thank You that Wyatt and Garrett are so open. I know they'll find You. Rebecca too, Father. She needs You. She says nothing about the sermons, Lord; in fact she's less open to talking about them all the time, but You never give up, Lord. She doesn't even know how much she needs You, but You'll get through. You'll find a way.

Travis had no idea how long he'd been standing there, but he was suddenly chilled. It was time to go in. He lit a lantern and did a final check on the stock and doors. By the time he reached the house, his family was sitting down to dinner. The boys flew at him, and Rebecca, although she stayed at the table, looked relieved.

"I thought something might have happened," she whispered tenderly when he bent to kiss her.

He looked into her eyes. *Something did happen, Rebecca. If only I could share it with you.* Saying none of this, he only kissed her again, swiftly washed, and joined his family at the table. The evening was like many others, but Travis prayed for both Lucky and Rebecca in a new way.

44

Rebecca told herself she would not be back. It was the second Sunday in March. She had been attending church with Travis for more than a month, but today, even though the sermon was just starting, she knew she would come no longer. After the fiasco of the first week, she had listened, truly listened. Travis was so secure in what he believed, and for the first time Rebecca had opened her ears, but she simply didn't understand the draw. She wasn't interested in hearing stories about Jesus every week.

But something had been bothering her for weeks that was separate from her boredom. She had not been able to put her finger on it immediately, but she had been uncomfortable at church and even with the Langleys. Now she understood. This group of church attenders thought they had all the answers. According to Pastor Henley, there was just one way to God. Rebecca didn't believe that. What kind of arrogance was it that made them all think they had some type of spiritual understanding the rest of the world didn't have?

This morning Rebecca knew she had had enough. Travis could fall for it if he wanted, but not her. She debated telling him that the boys couldn't come either but thought it only fair that they get a taste of all religious viewpoints and make their own decision. For herself, she knew she would never agree.

"I talked to a man this week." Pastor Henley was speaking, and Rebecca, not caring to have everyone know her thoughts, tried to look as if she were interested.

"He said something wonderful to me. He said he was saved to a life."

Rebecca had come to hate the word "saved," but she also kept these thoughts from her face.

"I asked him to explain that to me, and he said that originally he believed in Christ out of need. The pastor that morning had been teaching about hell. The preacher wasn't shouting or trying to scare anyone. He was simply providing the truth of it from God's Word. My friend recognized the reality of hell and the fact that he was going there. But the preacher also remembered to tell his flock that Jesus Christ was personally able and willing to rescue them."

Pastor Henley had Rebecca's full attention now.

"That morning my friend knew a decision had to be made, and he made it. He decided to believe in Christ as his Savior," he went on, "but it was years before he understood the full import of what he had done. Saved to a life is what he now calls it. Not just saved from damnation, but saved to live a life as blameless and as pleasing to God as possible. Yes, his eternity was taken care of, but before death, for all the years he would roam this earth, he needed to commit his life daily, hourly, to God. There is nothing wrong with feeling a sense of peace and fulfillment when we finally take that step of salvation, but it can't end there.

"Look at our text today, John 10:10: 'I have come that they might have life, and that they might have it more abundantly.' Don't settle for mediocrity, my friend. God has more for you. Heaven, yes! Salvation from eternal punishment, yes! But you are also saved to a life. A life full and free when lived for Christ and not for self."

Pastor Henley continued, but Rebecca heard no more. She was stunned. Had he said this before and had she missed it? Is this what Travis believed? Did they all believe that anyone who *didn't* believe as they did deserved to go to hell? She wasn't even certain there was a hell. After all, who really knew? And beyond that, who had the right to condemn anyone to go there? Certainly not Pastor Henley, Travis, or anyone else who went to this church.

She caught Travis glancing in her direction, so she swiftly schooled her features. Now was not the time to try to figure it all out. *Just get through it* became Rebecca's battle cry for the next hour as the sermon ended, the congregation visited, and even as the Buchanans rode home. It was not the start of a wonderful afternoon or week.

Travis was at the end of his rope; Rebecca would not tell him what was wrong. She had been cold and standoffish for two days. He was at a complete loss. She had been struggling for a few weeks, he knew, but she never wanted to talk about it. He could see that she didn't enjoy church, but she seemed to genuinely enjoy the people who always came to talk with her. However, she never wanted to discuss the sermon, and she grew angry if he ever tried to press her.

Sunday, she had been quiet, short with the boys and him, and wished only to be left alone to read. Monday, Travis had worked all day, but the boys were out of control at the dinner table and Travis assumed that Rebecca had spent the day on her own again. She had no desire to sit with him in the living room but spent the evening mending by the stove in the kitchen, and was stiff as an oak board when he tried to hug her good night. He didn't know what to think as he headed home on Tuesday night, but he didn't have long to wait to find out. Rebecca did not welcome his kiss, and dinner was nearly silent; the boys were subdued as well. Not long after he had put the boys to bed, he found her in her own room, nightgown in place, legs under the covers, leaning against the headboard, reading.

"Are you all right?" he asked, keeping his voice low in deference to the children across the hall.

"Yes. I'm just turning in early."

"In here?"

"I think it's for the best."

She wouldn't even look at him.

"Rebecca, what's happened? What has gone wrong? You didn't even kiss the boys good night."

"I just can't pretend that everything is fine." Her voice was clipped.

"I wouldn't want you to, but can you tell me what's troubling you?"

The book slapped on the bed as Rebecca set it aside angrily.

"You really are incredibly arrogant, do you know that, Travis?"

It was said coldly, and Rebecca's eyes were filled with fury. Travis thought that going out to work the last few days had been a big mistake. Whatever was bothering his wife had certainly mounted in the last days and hours. Now Travis felt attacked and hated, but he managed to keep his voice calm.

"I'm sorry I've been arrogant. Was it something specific I did?"

"It's your whole church, the lot of you! What right have you to tell people they're going to hell?"

At last it was out. Again Travis kept his voice calm.

"Pastor Henley is just telling us what God's Word says, Rebecca. He isn't condemning anyone personally."

"Of course he is. You all are! You can't really know if there's a hell."

"It's talked about right in the Bible, Rebecca. I could show you."

"That's all subject to man's interpretation, Travis, even I know that. My aunt read the Bible for years, and she never believed in hell."

Travis stood there for a moment, his mind racing. Finally he said, "Everyone is entitled to his own choice of belief, Rebecca, but why are you so angry about this?"

"Because you're all so smug. What sets you apart? Do you think *you're* going to hell, Travis?"

"No."

"Why not you, Travis? What makes you so special?"

"I've learned a lot about God in the last few years, Rebecca." Travis remained calm. "And one of the things that has stood out to me is His holiness. Nothing we can ever say or do will make us good enough for God. We all deserve hell, but God made an escape—"

"Salvation," she cut him off sarcastically.

"Yes," Travis agreed gently. "Salvation through God's Son, Jesus Christ."

"What about my father?" she shot at him.

Travis had thought often about this, so he had an answer. "I never discussed things of the spirit with your father, Rebecca, but if he chose to trust God for his sin, then he is in heaven."

"And if he didn't?"

"Then the Bible is very clear." Travis' voice was soft but sure. "He's gone to a lost eternity."

"And you don't have a problem with that? It doesn't bother you in the least that you think my father deserves to be in hell?"

"We all deserve to be in hell, Rebecca," Travis repeated. "And as much as I'd like to see your father in heaven someday, I can't torture myself over not knowing. I have to concern myself with you and the boys."

Rebecca couldn't look at him. The fight had gone out of her, but she was trembling all over.

"I'm sorry you're so angry about this Rebecca, but please don't let it harm our marriage. Please come back to our room."

She looked at him, her face astounded.

"You still want me in your room, even knowing how I feel?"

Travis licked his lips. "I love you, Rebecca; that isn't going to change. We don't agree on this, but it doesn't have to tear our family apart."

Tears filled her eyes. Travis started for her, but she slipped out the other side of the bed, effectively putting it between them.

"Travis, I—" she was crying now.

"Oh, Reba." Travis' voice was tortured. "Please don't cry. Please come here so I can hold you."

But again she shook her head. "I can't, Travis. Not now—maybe never."

It took all of Travis' self-control not to go to her. She was hurting, and he desperately wanted to hold her and share the pain.

"I want to be alone now," Rebecca said in a small voice. She sniffed like a child, and Travis thought his heart would break. Somehow he needed to make her understand.

"I'll leave if you want me to, Rebecca, but nothing has changed. I'm sorry you didn't realize where I stood. It was certainly my fault for not explaining. You need to know all of it. I've believed this way for several years, before you came back to me and since. Even as we shared a room and worked at making this a real marriage, I believed in hell, and in Jesus Christ, and in His power to save. I love you now, and I'll always love you. Our differing views won't always be easy, but they won't change my love. They haven't up to now and they are not going to in the future. I hope you'll realize that soon and want us to be a real family as much as I do."

Travis looked at her, praying with all his heart that she would come to him, but it didn't happen. Rebecca dropped her eyes, and he made himself walk away and stay away, even when he heard her crying from down the hall.

Robert looked into his friend's pale face and studied the way he played with his coffee cup without drinking a drop.

"I told you yesterday something was very wrong." Travis began. "Well, it all blew up last night. She moved back down the hall." The men had met together on Tuesday, but Travis was back on Wednesday.

"It wasn't perfect, Robert, I mean, no marriage is, but we were working on it. She was asking me about my day, and I was sharing with her. Sometimes we would talk for hours. And the boys—she was getting so good at taking care of their needs. She was firm but still giving them lots of hugs and kisses. I've prayed that she would understand her need for Christ, Robert, but I never dreamed she would be so angry with me when she didn't agree."

Travis stood and paced in the Langley kitchen. "I couldn't lie to her, Robert. I don't know where her father is. I'm sure my own parents are lost . . . my grandmother too. It's too late for them but not for Rebecca and the boys. I tried to tell her, but she was so crushed."

Travis came back to the table.

"What do you say to someone who says you're arrogant because you believe you know the path to righteousness?"

Robert had listened quietly, waiting for Travis to get everything off his chest. It was a very painful place for Travis to be in, but Robert believed that God had answers for even this.

"You're certainly not in a very enviable position, Travis, but try to see it from Rebecca's perspective. Remember when Morgan Sears died? Do you recall how angry you were with me when I tried to tell you that every event was part of God's plan?"

Travis' eyes slid shut over the memory, and he nodded his head.

"It's that same way for Rebecca. She's completely threatened by what Pastor Henley said on Sunday morning. You told her you loved her?"

"Yes."

"I would keep telling her," Robert advised him. "Let her see that your love is not conditional to her salvation. She won't believe that at first, but given time I think she'll understand. Rebecca is not a combative person. I don't think she can keep on with this anger. In fact, she might be feeling differently even this morning."

Travis nodded. "She didn't even want me in the same room with her last night, but you're right. When she first came back to the Double Star she was angry about everything, but it didn't last. The kinder I became, the more she responded." Travis took a deep breath. "It wasn't that long ago, but I'd forgotten all about that."

Robert let his friend have a moment of silence and then asked quietly, "What will you do?"

"Go home. Check on the boys and see how Rebecca is doing. If she's angry I'll just hang in there and keep loving her."

"I'll cover you with prayer, Travis. In fact, let's start right now."

The men bowed their heads and surrendered Rebecca Buchanan to God. Travis left sometime later, knowing that his work lay ahead of him, and that he wasn't going into battle alone.

45

It was odd that just three days after the blowup with Rebecca, Lucky asked Travis how she was doing. Travis had to be honest and tell him that she was struggling, but the younger man had nothing but compassion for his employer.

"It must be rough, Travis, but I think it must still be easier than when the wife is saved first."

"Why do you say that?"

"Yvonne has seen the change in Margo and me. She tried to tell Freeman what she wanted to do, you know, come to Christ and all. She was even ready to pray with Margo, but Freeman got so angry that she backed right off. He threatened to leave if she brought it up again. She took a chance and still came to church on Sunday, and Freeman let it go, but I know she's afraid of him."

Travis' face showed his pain. How awful for Margo's mother. It was easy to see that he had a less complicated situation with Rebecca. She was still keeping her distance, talking to him only about impersonal business, but Robert had been right: The anger was gone. In its place was a vulnerable young woman who wanted to be loved by her husband but was afraid to let him get close.

"I ache for her, Lucky, and you're right," Travis told him honestly. "Rebecca doesn't know what to do with my beliefs. She feels threatened by them, but it's nothing like Mr. Roderick's rage." The men rode for a time in silence. "By the way, how are *you* doing?"

"Very well. It's becoming more and more difficult to live with Margo's folks, but we're getting by. I'm just praying that we can find a house to rent by the time the baby comes."

"How is Margo feeling?"

"About the same. The cramping has stopped, but she's so sick all the time. I'm thankful the baby is still with us, but August can't come soon enough for me."

Travis told him he would continue to pray, and did so as the day rushed by rather swiftly. The boys were starved for attention that evening, so he spent extra time with them, playing cowboys with toy guns. Travis died on the kitchen floor time and again, much to the delight of the outlaws hunting him.

He hadn't seen anything of his wife since supper had ended, but when he finally tucked the boys in and went to the living room, she was there. Amazed that she would wait for him, Travis noted that she had already poured herself a cup of coffee and was on one end of the davenport, seeming to be at ease. She didn't offer any to Travis, but that was not unusual. He poured his own and sat down, his long legs stretched toward the fire.

"Lucky stopped in to say hello to the boys today."

"He did?"

"Yes. I hadn't talked to him since Christmas."

Her voice was so impersonal that Travis couldn't tell whether she'd enjoyed the visit or not.

"Did you know that he and Margo live with her parents?"

"Yes."

She was looking at him, almost as if it was his fault, but Travis didn't know why.

"Is the ranch doing well, Travis?"

"You mean making money? Yes. We'll be out on roundup and then making a cattle drive in just a few months, and if everything goes well, I'll be making some repairs to the barn or possibly building another one."

"Why don't you build a few houses?"

"Build houses? Where?"

"Here at the ranch. There seems to be plenty of land."

Travis was not catching on, and Rebecca frowned at him.

"Honestly, Travis," she continued, clearly irritated. "He's your foreman, and if things continue to heat up between Lavena and Colin, they'll be looking for a place of their own too!"

Travis *had* thought of building. Months ago during a conversation with Lucky he'd asked himself why he didn't have housing for his foreman. He knew that some foremen lived with their bosses—he had and so had Grady—but that had never been Travis' style.

When Travis did not immediately respond, Rebecca began to rise.

"It's a great idea," Travis said and watched as she sat back down. "I wish I'd acted on it a long time ago. Are things really so serious with Colin and Lavena?"

"It's looking that way. She had a new dress on today."

Travis nodded. "Margo's expecting," he commented. "I know they're hoping for a place of their own before August."

"Can homes be built that fast?"

"I think so. I mean, they won't be mansions, but they would certainly be good shelter."

"So you'll do it?" Rebecca was surprised at how fast he agreed.

"I think it's a great idea. I can't say as it's never crossed my mind, but like I said, I've never acted on it. Thank you, Rebecca."

Not comfortable with his praise, she busied herself with more coffee. She was careful to keep her eyes averted.

When had it all fallen apart? she asked herself. She had been so happy at Christmas and during January, but it devastated her to think of her father in eternal punishment, and more so that Travis believed it. She was forced to ask herself why something she didn't even believe in made her so furious. She couldn't find any answers, and Travis' presence served as a reminder of all that hung between them.

"Thank you for telling me about Lavena," he commented, breaking into her thoughts.

"You haven't noticed?"

"I don't see her as much as you do. I see Colin on the range of course, but I take it he's been around the house quite a bit?"

"More so all the time."

"How is that for you? Do you ever get tired of people all over the house?"

"At times, yes, but Lavena has been going places with Colin, and then the boys and I have the house to ourselves."

"And you've enjoyed it?"

"Yes."

"Well, that settles it. Whether or not anything comes of Lavena's relationship with Colin, we'll build her a place of her own. It's time you had your house back."

"You would do that, Travis? Spend that kind of money for me even if it wasn't necessary?"

"Absolutely."

Rebecca didn't know how to handle his words. She began to rise and was on her feet when Travis caught her hand. He pulled her over until she was nearly in his lap. Travis put his arms around her, but her tears were so very close she didn't dare look at him. He was forced to speak to her profile.

"I'm not trying to buy you, Rebecca, but if I'd realized how much you needed your privacy, I'd have done something as soon as you came home."

"Maybe you should save your money, and I should just go back to Pine Grove."

Her voice was sad and resigned; Travis knew she didn't want to leave.

"I can't let you do that."

"Why not?"

"Because it would break my heart."

She sobbed. Travis shifted her until she was against his chest, and Rebecca clung to him.

"Oh, Travis," she managed, but nothing more. He didn't try to console her but held her close and let her cry until the tears were spent. When she was a little more in control and wanted to sit up, he let her pull away from him.

"Better?" His eyes were still on her profile. She was so lovely but also so very lost.

"I think so." Still Hannah Ellenbolt's niece, she pulled a lace handkerchief out from up her sleeve. She fixed her face, which was now puffy and red, and then Travis picked up her hand. It was the only part of them that touched, but Rebecca still said, "I don't know if I can do this, Travis."

"I know. You've had a lot to think about."

"I thought you would be relieved to have me go back to Pine Grove."

"Then you haven't been listening to me. I love you, Rebecca, and if you leave you'll take my heart with you."

She bit her lip, determined not to cry again. What was she going to do? Could she continue in a marriage with this man whose beliefs were so contrary to her own? How would they ever find a meeting ground? And when would she find the answers so she could stop the dozens of questions that seemed to forever swarm in her mind? The last question made her weary enough to sleep for a week. She stood, and Travis made no move to stop her.

"I'm going to turn in now."

"All right. Can I bring you something—water or tea?"

"No, but thank you."

They stared at one another.

"We'll get those houses built this summer, Reba." Travis' voice was husky with emotion. "Even if the barn has to wait. You'll have the house to yourself by fall. Lavena can still work for you if you want, but it will be under your terms."

Rebecca's heart swelled with love for him, but she pushed it down. She ached all over from the effort, but she couldn't help herself.

"Thank you, Travis."

"You're welcome. Sleep well."

He watched her walk from the room, her steps slow and weary. It was so hard not to go after her. They needed each other. Travis turned back to the fire and forced his mind to prayer. He was anxious; he was hurting; and he wanted his wife back for good.

I'm so faithless right now, Lord. It doesn't feel as if anything can repair this marriage, not even You. Help me to trust, help me to believe. And comfort that woman up there, Lord, the one who needs You. The one who means more to me than my own life.

❧

"I thought you went to church" were Lavena's first words to Rebecca the next Sunday morning.

"No," she said shortly and poured herself some coffee.

Her face did not invite conversation, and for the moment Lavena only watched her. Colin had been planning to come to breakfast, but Lavena knew she would send him away if he came in the door. Nosy as she seemed, Lavena honestly did try to leave the Buchanans to themselves. She would go hungry before sitting down to a meal with them, and never had she searched through their personal things or intruded on a private conversation. But no one could have missed the storm clouds that periodically passed through the ranch house. Rebecca was clearly on a weaving track with her emotions right now, and Lavena was beginning to think Travis was a saint. She didn't take sides, not even in her mind, but she did wish beyond anything that she knew how to help.

"How come you didn't go?"

Rebecca shrugged. "It's not for me, Lavena. Travis enjoys it, but I don't, and I'm not going to pretend that I do."

"That's certainly fair."

Rebecca looked at her. "How about you, Lavena? Do you ever attend church?"

"No. I used to, but I finally told God I wasn't interested."

Rebecca had never heard of such a thing. "What do you mean?"

"God chased me," Lavena said simply. "He chased me, but I ran."

Rebecca leaned forward in invitation.

"I was a young woman—not married yet," Lavena began. "I went to Chicago to spend some time with my cousin. We went to revival meetings, and she tried to introduce me to her God. It was a miserable summer. I ran as far as I could, but God was everywhere I looked. I finally gave up. I told God to leave me alone. I told Him I wasn't interested in turning my life over to anyone, and that included Him."

Rebecca was now openly staring.

"That's right," Lavena answered her look. "That was the end of it. God hasn't bothered me since. Not even when I was married to Frank Larson and going through those awful years did I forget that God and I had an agreement. I wouldn't bother Him, and He wouldn't bother me. That suits me just fine to this day."

"So you don't believe in hell like Travis does?"

"Not hell or heaven, either one. I think the only heaven or hell we'll ever know is right here on this earth. I guess I would say I've had a little of both. Frank was hell. Colin isn't exactly what you would call heaven, but he's mighty close."

It was all so cold and logical, but Rebecca reminded herself that she had been the one to ask. What a shock, though. As had happened before with Lavena, the younger woman would never have guessed. Someone else in Rebecca's past believed that heaven and hell were right here on earth. Rebecca suddenly remembered it was Angel.

For a moment she wondered how Angel was—wondered if she was still with Preston. Letters between them were nonexistent these days, but Rebecca had too much on her mind to worry over it.

"So you don't plan to go to church at all?"

"No."

"Well, I respect your decision," Lavena said and rose, carrying her mug to the counter before heading to her room.

She left Rebecca with a myriad of questions. Lavena believed in God. She'd even gone so far as to strike a bargain with Him. If that was the case, then where did she believe God resided? Rebecca had always believed He lived in heaven. And what if Lavena were wrong and there was a heaven, but she couldn't go because she had never believed it was there?

One thing became suddenly very clear to Rebecca. She didn't want to attend church with her husband, but neither was she ready to tell God to get out of her life for good.

46

Changes came over Rebecca in the following month. They started after her conversation with Lavena but weren't actually tied to spiritual matters. The talk with the housekeeper had made her thoughtful. She had taken the rest of the day to think about her life and decided she was not being a good mother to the boys. She had fallen back into the pattern she'd developed in Pine Grove—one where she worked more than anything, staying too busy to think all day long, and in turn wanting little or nothing to do with her children until bedtime.

Rebecca's attitude changed that day. Although not back to a good relationship with her spouse, she began taking an interest in things around her. Travis came home from church one Sunday to tell her that Robert and Eddie had had a baby boy. They had named him Robert Morgan after his father and maternal grandfather. With her new outlook toward her life and children, Rebecca loaded the boys up, driving the buggy herself, and went to visit the new mother and child.

She did something with her sons every day. For the first time in her life, she enjoyed them fully. They still whined some, but for the most part they were obedient and a joy to be around. During these outings, concepts came out of their mouths that were a surprise to Rebecca, and she didn't know how to respond.

"Look at that, Gary," Wyatt said when Travis was out of town for a few days. "Those two sticks look just like the cross Jesus died on. Do you see 'em?"

"Yeah. We should show Papa."

"Yeah. I wish he would come back." The little boy scuffed a stone with his boot. "I think he's been gone a whole year."

"It's just been two days," Rebecca said calmly as she walked beside them. "He might even be back tomorrow."

"I hope so," Garrett said with a sigh. "I hate it when he's not here to tell us stories."

"Does he tell you a story every night?"

"Yeah, well, not *every* night; sometimes we just pray."

Rebecca did not know this but wasn't surprised. Suddenly she was tired of fighting it. What did it really matter if she and Travis agreed over their religious beliefs? Was it worth the misery of holding back her love for her husband? Rebecca was beginning to think not, but she didn't know exactly what to do about it. It was time to go back to the house for lunch, and for the moment she was glad to put their differences from her mind.

Travis arrived home from his next business trip in the middle of the day. He had been too weary to come in the night before, and, in truth, these days he didn't feel as eager to be home. Rebecca was speaking to him some, and they spent most of their evenings together, but the way he had to guard every word and watch her fight against his love exhausted him.

It was already early May, and spring was coming fast to the Rocky Mountains. The boys were outside to greet him and remind him of how important it was that he be home. He had several tin soldiers with horses for them, and even received hugs along with their thanks. The boys were busy on the steps, lining up their men and knocking them over, when he went inside, two more wrapped parcels in his hand.

Lavena was nowhere to be seen, and Travis did not feel comfortable shouting for Rebecca. He moved quietly to the stairs, but she was not in her bedroom. He was on his way to the study when he spotted her. She was nearly lying in a chair in the living room. Alarm slammed through him. Not only was her position odd, but the fact that her hands were idle surprised him. Rebecca never sat idle during the day, always keeping her hands busy. As Travis approached, he could also see that her eyes were closed. She opened them a bit as he neared.

"Are you sick, Rebecca?" he voiced in very real concern.

"No," she answered, but he took in her pale features and was not convinced.

"Do you hurt somewhere?"

Rebecca shifted, but didn't answer.

"Do you want me to go for the doctor?"

"No, Travis," she said testily. "I just want to be alone."

"But your color, Rebecca. I think you're sick. Let me get you some help."

"No one can help me right now, Travis. Just go."

"I'm sure the doctor—"

"Must I spell it out for you, Travis?" she cut him off in disgust. "You're a grown man. I shouldn't think there would be a need."

Understanding hit him like a fist, and he made the mistake of smiling.

"I'm glad you find it amusing." Her voice was still irritated.

"Forgive me, Rebecca," Travis apologized, but he was still smiling. "But not being intimately acquainted with you right now, how could I know?"

She still frowned at him.

"I brought you something," he said now, his voice conciliatory.

"What is it?" she asked as he handed it to her.

"Open it."

Rebecca sat up and did so, but with little joy or interest. Her eyes widened when she saw what was inside. It was a brown split riding skirt, a beautiful cream-colored blouse, and a brown leather vest. She looked to Travis with questioning eyes.

"I thought you might like to go riding with me sometime."

"I've never ridden a horse in my life."

"I have a *little* bit of experience. I can probably show you."

But Rebecca didn't laugh. She was fighting him again, and they both knew it. Finally her eyes dropped to the other parcel in his grasp.

"What's that?"

"Just something special for the boys for the roundup."

"The roundup?"

"Yes, we leave in two weeks."

"And you're taking the boys?"

"Yes, didn't I tell you?"

"No, you did not." Her voice had gone from outrage to frigid anger, but Travis was weary of tiptoeing around her.

"Is there a problem?" he asked pointedly.

"You're taking *my* sons on a dangerous roundup, and you want to know if I have a problem with it."

She saw just a moment too late that she'd overstepped her bounds. Rebecca pressed back into the seat as Travis leaned over her, his hands on the arms of the chair, his voice low and furious.

"*Your* sons, Rebecca. *Your* sons? Did I hear you right? It wasn't that many weeks ago that you finally remembered you *have* two sons. How dare you insinuate that I would do anything to harm those boys." He continued to lean over her for several seconds, his eyes still flashing with anger, before he pushed away and strode from the room.

Her hand to her mouth, Rebecca sat trembling for several minutes before she noticed that he had dropped the other parcel. She picked it up and opened it slowly. Inside were two of the smallest pairs of chaps she'd ever seen. She had seen them one other time at Boulder's general store but not thought to buy them for the boys. Now Travis had gone for them, and she had treated him like a criminal. Rebecca rose slowly. She had some apologizing to do.

Should I tell her I'm sorry for my anger, Lord, or have I been too passive? She's so frozen most of the time that even her anger is a relief, but I no longer feel like a man when I'm with her. She won't let me touch her, and she won't let me be the head of my own home.

From his desk chair, Travis swiveled so he could see out the window and thought about the last thing he said to the Lord. If Rebecca was "keeping" him from leading this home, it was because he'd allowed her to do so. Travis asked himself what he would do if she left. For the first time he realized he couldn't let that alter his future decisions. He had to be the head of his home, and if she didn't like it she could leave. It would tear his heart in two, and he honestly didn't think she'd ever leave the boys, but if she wanted to go, he would let her.

"Travis?"

His head whipped around, and he found his wife in the doorway. So intent were his thoughts that he hadn't even heard her approach. He stood as she entered and watched as she set the boys' chaps on the desk. She looked up at him.

"I'm sorry about the things I said, Travis."

"Thank you. Did my anger scare you?"

"No. I deserved it."

Travis sighed. "The things I've said to you still stand, Rebecca. I still love you and always will, but I won't hold you any longer. If you want to leave, you can."

Rebecca could only stare at him.

"I can't imagine life without you, but it's obvious that you're miserable here. Right now I'm not certain how, but the boys and I would get along somehow."

Rebecca could hardly breathe. Was he sending her away?

"Please understand that I'm not sending you away," he went on, as if he'd heard her thoughts. "But I'm not going to tiptoe around you any longer. I'm a man, Rebecca—not some toy for you to play with and then get angry at and throw into a corner. I won't live with your sullen frowns and silent treatment any longer. I think you need to humble your heart before God. You don't believe that, but what you believe is not the main issue right now."

Rebecca, who thought all of their trouble was over religion, was surprised and confused by his words.

"The main issue," Travis went on, "is the wall you've put up between us. And it's going to stay up as long as you won't talk to me. This is not an ultimatum about agreeing with my spiritual beliefs, but it is about your anger and silence. If you hate me that much, Rebecca, I'll take you back to Pine Grove."

"I don't hate you, Travis," she whispered.

"You can understand how I would think that you did."

She nodded, more miserable than she'd ever been in her life.

"Do you understand what I'm saying?" he asked gently.

"I think so. In order for me to stay, I have to go to church with you."

"No, Rebecca, that's not what I said. But I can't live with a woman who acts like she hates me and makes no effort whatsoever in our marriage. I've done it now for months, and I'm not going to do it any longer. I thought I was good for you, Rebecca, but I'm beginning to doubt my own sanity. If you don't care enough about me to give yourself to this marriage, then you'd probably be better off on your own."

Rebecca had to force her hands to her side or she would have wrung them frantically.

"Is it now or never?" she asked.

"Not at all. I just want you to understand what we need to do. You don't have to decide this minute, nor does everything need to become perfect overnight, but the door to sharing with each other has got to be open or we might as well call it a day."

"Can I think about this for a time, Travis?"

"Take all the time you need, Rebecca. And I'll say it again in case it's slipped your mind: I love you and would love for you to come back to me."

Rebecca saw the truth in his eyes, but she was so full of emotion she couldn't speak. That, along with the fact that the boys could be heard coming from the kitchen, caused her to nod and slip out of the room. Travis heard the boys greet their mother and even heard her answer in a normal voice, but he knew she felt like dying inside. His heart felt much the same.

47

Rebecca rose early Saturday morning and dressed in her new clothing. She had spent hours thinking about her talk with Travis, and she knew that she would never choose to leave him. It would have been easy to grow angry with the way he'd laid down the law, but the thought of returning to Pine Grove, with or without the children, was incomprehensible. The amazing realization for her was that it wasn't the house in Pine Grove or the distance: It was Travis. As angry as he made her at times, he alone was the reason she must never leave. She knew that the pain and hurt between them were not going to magically disappear, but she had to stay. She had to stay and try.

With her mind made up, she went downstairs, hoping to find Travis in the kitchen. He was there, and she approached slowly. Travis, who had done little but pray since Rebecca left his office, saw a change in her face even before he spotted the clothing. However, the new outfit gave him a place to start.

"The clothes fit," he said, standing when she came into the kitchen.

"Yes."

Feeling very self-conscious under his approving gaze, Rebecca busied herself with the coffee. She even went so far as to refill Travis' cup before she joined him at the table.

"Are you very busy today?" she asked quietly.

"Nothing overly pressing. Would you like to go riding?"

"I think so. Are you sure I won't fall on my head?"

"I wouldn't let you fall," he promised her. "And beyond that, your horse is as gentle as a lamb."

"My horse?"

"Uh hmm."

"I didn't know I had a horse."

Travis looked down at his plate. "On occasion I bought things for you, especially in the first year."

Rebecca wondered when the surprises would stop. After all these years he still loved her. He wanted a marriage, but if she didn't he would let her go. She couldn't take the boys, but she could leave if she desired. When she wants to ride with him, he isn't angry, but tells her with the slightest hint of embarrassment that he's bought her a horse some years ago.

"What's his name?"

"Her name. Feather."

"Did you name her?"

"No. Her first owner did. You'll understand why when you see her. In almost the same place Diamond has a diamond shape under his forelock, Feather has a feathery shape of white hair on her face."

"Is she roan-colored?"

"Black, with white stockings."

Rebecca had run out of words, but Travis came to the rescue and picked up the slack.

"I'll make sure Lavena can watch the boys and we'll go. Did you want to have a quick bite to eat?"

"No, I'm not hungry."

Travis went to check with his housekeeper, and the Buchanans left a few minutes later. The boys were disappointed to wake and find both their parents gone, but Lavena put them to work with some cookie dough, all the time wondering how the Mister and Missus were doing.

"She really goes right where I tell her," Rebecca said in wonder, some fear still in her voice.

"Amazing, isn't it?" Travis said laughingly as he rode by her side. "Come this way now," he instructed and silently thanked the man who had trained Feather. She was a gentle mare with an easy gait, and Travis could tell she was comfortable with Rebecca's light weight.

They started out across the huge Double Star spread. Rebecca had gone very pale when she stood beside Feather in the barn, but Travis had helped her into the saddle and stayed on the ground next to her until she relaxed a little. He'd then mounted Diamond and headed them out to the east. Never moving above a walk, they rode in a huge circle and were now coming back to the ranch house from the west side. The mountains towered to the north and already the wildflowers were exploding with color.

"Right here." Travis was pointing. "We'll put the houses right here. Not too close to our place, but near enough to let the road go through and be close to the creek. Dane Wilson says he can start building next month, and the houses should be up by September. I'm not certain he was thrilled with having to come this far from town, but Robert tells me he does the best work."

"What did Lavena say when you told her?"

"She was shocked at first, I think, but then she warmed to the idea. Has she said anything to you?"

"No, but she's been in a good mood."

"I wonder how much of that has to do with Colin."

"I don't know, but he's certainly not losing interest."

"Love is a funny thing. You never know where it's going to hit."

He looked over to find Rebecca's gaze on him.

"You look good on that horse," he told her, his face shaded by his hat. "The outfit too."

"Thank you for buying it for me, Travis, and for Feather."

"Thank *you*."

"For what?"

"Do you realize, Rebecca, that you've never questioned me about this ranch? One day I was a penniless cowhand and the next I was a wealthy ranch owner. You've never accused me of taking the ranch or abusing the money."

Rebecca looked down at her lap. "I did think that for a few years, you know—about why you married me—but I can see that you haven't abused what you've been given, Travis. You don't deny us anything. In fact, you probably spoil us a little too much."

"Oh, I don't know about that," he said with a lazy smile. "Last time we were in town the boys picked out the horses they want, and I said no."

Rebecca laughed. "I think I'm glad you did."

Travis had a hard time not reaching over and pulling Rebecca from her horse and into his arms. It felt so good to talk with her and see her laugh.

She hasn't addressed the things we talked about, Lord, but could this be her way of showing me she's trying? Help me to be bold without pushing her away. Help me to know the right things to say.

"We've been spotted." Rebecca was speaking, and Travis followed her gaze. He laughed. The boys were on the front porch of the house, nearly dancing in their excitement.

"Mama! Mama! She's on Feather, Lavena. Come see! Can we ride? Can we?"

They were thronged by the boys when they got close enough, and at first Rebecca was alarmed that they would come so close, but there was no fear in either the boys or the horses. While still in the yard, Travis helped Rebecca down and then helped the boys mount Feather. Like little professionals they walked her carefully around the yard. They didn't even argue over who sat at the front of the saddle.

"You look thoughtful," Travis remarked, looking down at her.

"I'm just amazed at how comfortable they are," she said without taking her eyes from her sons.

"Look at us, Mama!" they shouted, and Rebecca turned her face up to Travis.

"Do you see what I mean? No fear."

"Well, they've been coming out with me to the barn since November, and I've told them what to watch for. But you're right; they do very well. That's why I feel confident that they'll do fine on roundup."

"Will they be on horseback?" Rebecca couldn't keep the alarm from her face.

"No, in the wagon with Woody. I'm sure they'll ride in the evenings when we're settled for the night, but when we're traveling, they'll be safe in the wagon."

"When do you leave?"

"Monday, a week."

"How long will you be gone?"

"Five days—maybe a little more."

"And after that, the cattle drive?"

"Yes. That will take several weeks, but Lucky will head that up."

"You're not going on the cattle drive?"

"No." Travis watched her face and thought he saw a glimmer of pleasure. His voice dropped, and he asked, "Dare I hope, Rebecca, that you're glad I'll be staying?"

She didn't look at him and went to the house right afterward, but he still heard her say, "I'm glad you're not going."

❧

"I'm headed into town, Lavena. Can the boys stay with you?"

Lavena speared her with a glance. Rebecca had been antsy all morning. It was so reminiscent of another morning, years before, that Lavena was afraid to let her out of her sight.

"Does Travis know you're going?"

"No."

"Maybe I should go with you."

"But if you do that, I'll have to take the boys."

Lavena scowled at her. "I'll just come right out with it—I can't take your leaving again, Rebecca. I can't do it. I'm too old for this. I can't watch him go through it all again. You can't go!"

"Go where?" Garrett asked as he came into the room.

"Just into town, honey," his mother answered him. "Here, have a cookie and take one to Wyatt."

"Thank you," he said politely and went on his way. Rebecca turned back to Lavena.

"I'm coming back, Lavena. In fact, I'm planning something I hope Travis will enjoy, but I promise you I'm coming back."

Lavena was visibly relieved. "I won't tell him or the boys, but don't you linger. Town is no place for a pretty woman alone."

"I'll be back as soon as I'm able."

Rebecca found Woody and asked him to hitch Dancer to the buggy. Rebecca was on her way some 20 minutes later, but unlike years before, leaving and not coming back was the last thing on her mind.

◦━

"How are things going?" Pastor Henley asked Travis after church. Robert was also part of the conversation.

"Better," Travis answered honestly. "We leave for roundup in the morning, and I hope when I'm gone Rebecca will have lots of time to think. We've been on horseback rides every evening this week and we've been able to talk when the boys are in bed—nothing very deep, but at least she's searching me out and sharing with me about her day."

"That is good news," Robert inserted.

"Maybe Beryl and I should visit her when you're away."

"I think that's a fine idea. It won't be that long, but she would probably enjoy a little company."

"Dinner at our house maybe?"

"I don't think so." Travis shook his head. "I don't want her coming into town on her own with me away."

"Maybe Eddie and I can have her over," Robert suggested. "We don't live that far, and I could pick her up and run her home."

"Ask her," Travis encouraged him, "but don't worry if she says no. She just might need some time on her own."

"We'll keep praying," Pastor Henley assured Travis. The cowboy thanked him. A moment later he and Robert were standing alone.

"I want to tell you what an encouragement you've been to me, Travis."

"How's that?"

"Your joy and your peace. I know it hasn't been easy, but you're still trusting and that's been a real example to me."

"It isn't always easy, Robert, but it helped to make some decisions and stick by them. I felt God would want Rebecca to stay no matter what, but she was so distant that I felt I was no longer any good for her. I think it was the hardest thing I've ever said, but I told her she could go. I found such a peace in that. I'd been so careful around her, watching my every word, but I could see later that I hadn't been doing her any favors. She found out where I stood and then was able to make her decision."

"And she told you she wants to stay?"

"No. We've yet to talk more about it, but I can tell she's trying. I always enjoy roundup, but she's becoming so receptive that I hate to leave."

"Absence makes the heart grow fonder?"

Travis smiled. "I hope it's that and not out-of-sight, out-of-mind."

Robert patted his shoulder and looked up to see Eddie coming to join them. Robert took Bobby from her arms and cuddled him close. Travis smiled down at the infant and the love and pride on Robert's face.

A short time later, Travis and the boys left the church. He found himself thinking about Bobby and his own small sons. He prayed that he and Rebecca would be blessed repeatedly with more children, children as dear as the ones God had already given.

48

"I have about an hour's work," Travis told Rebecca early Monday morning, "but then the boys and I will be back in to say good-bye to you."

"All right," Rebecca agreed calmly, taking another sip of her tea.

Travis watched her. It was easy to do since she looked wonderful in a yellow gingham gown. But he was a little uneasy. Rebecca didn't seem at all distraught about the three of them being gone for five or six days, and he didn't know if that was good or not. Not that he wanted her upset, but they had started to talk more in the last week, and Travis hated to let that go.

I've got to trust You in this, Lord. I've got to leave her with You.

"We're ready," Wyatt announced suddenly as he and Garrett came into the room.

Their parents smiled at the sight of them and went over to inspect their finery. They were fully decked out in jeans, hats, boots, long-sleeved denim shirts, vests, and their new chaps.

"Well, now." Rebecca hugged each one. "I would say you're ready to help with roundup."

"We're cowboys," Garrett said simply.

"So I see," Rebecca solemnly agreed although she wanted to laugh with delight. "Are you going to help your father this week?"

They nodded, their little faces both very serious.

"Head out, boys," Travis instructed, and the adults watched as they clopped their way to the door, both walking exaggeratedly in their new chaps.

"Are you going to be all right?" Travis asked Rebecca. He stood close to her, his eyes on her face. Rebecca tipped her head back to see him.

"Yes."

Travis seemed at a momentary loss.

"I've enjoyed our talks and rides this last week, Travis."

"I have too, Reba."

Without invitation Travis caught the back of her head in one hand and her jaw in the other. He kissed her with infinite tenderness.

"I wish I didn't have to leave you," he whispered, but Rebecca only moved closer for another kiss. Travis could have held her for the rest of the morning, but he made himself move away.

"I'll be back in a little while."

Rebecca could only nod and stand still as he walked out the door.

"Things are set, boss," Woody told him. Travis thanked his cook. He was a good man, not prone to smiling but willing to have the boys with him for much of the time and stern enough with them to be taken seriously.

"Give me about five minutes," he told Woody, and started toward the kitchen door. He had taken only five steps out of the barn when Rebecca emerged from the house. Travis froze. She was in the split skirt he'd bought her, the blouse and vest as well, but she had added to the ensemble. On her feet were heeled riding boots, and her head sported a dark brown cowboy hat. She'd banded it with a yellow scarf and had another one tied around her neck. She barely glanced at him as she came abreast of him on her way to the barn. Travis gently caught her arm in his grasp.

"Where are you going?"

"On roundup."

"*You are?*" He was thunderstruck.

"Yes."

Travis' mouth opened and closed, but no words came out.

"Is there a problem?" she asked calmly.

"Where are you going to sleep?" He voiced the first thing that came to mind.

"In the wagon."

"But I was going to sleep in the wagon with the boys."

Rebecca's brows rose, and she said softly, "Well, Travis, I hope you don't snore." The look she now sent him was an open invitation and Travis, suddenly very warm, was helpless to move when she turned and finished walking into the barn.

They didn't get away in five minutes as he'd told Woody because Travis was so rattled that he forgot what he was doing. He was half-convinced that he'd dreamed the whole scene with Rebecca but knew he was wrong when they were finally underway. The petite blonde riding skillfully on the black mare was no image. She was real, and she was all his.

○────

"I can't feel my legs," Rebecca said quietly when Travis approached. He had suspected as much when they'd made camp for the night and she didn't immediately dismount. He led Feather around to the far side of the covered wagon to allow her some privacy.

As compassionate as he felt, he still smiled when he said, "I'll help you."

"Oh," she moaned softly when her feet were on the ground. "Are you going to say 'I told you so'?"

Travis chuckled. "You just did it for me."

"I should have listened to you at noon."

"You can rest up tomorrow."

"How will I do that?"

"By staying in the wagon."

Rebecca scowled at him, but his look was mild.

"I would insist, Rebecca, but I won't have to." He leaned close and whispered, "Your bottom and legs won't let you sit in the saddle again so soon. You'll have to take it easy for a few days."

Rebecca sighed and let herself be hugged. It would have been a wonderfully tender scene, but her stomach growled.

"Come on," Travis laughed. "Let's get some food into you. That won't help the aches, but at least you won't faint from hunger."

Rebecca would have laughed as well, but she was too tired and sore to make the effort. At the moment she had all she could do to place one foot in front of the other. She wasn't certain if the next few days were going to be great fun or last forever.

"Sing the song again, Travis," Rebecca whispered to him.

"I'll wake the boys," he whispered back, casting a glance at them where they slept at the front of the wagon. His soft guitar playing and singing, after a day outside, had sent them off in minutes.

"Then just say the words to me," Rebecca coaxed. After Travis settled beside her in their bedroll, he obliged.

I want to write you a love song today,
To share all the things that are so hard to say.
And yet as I sit here with pencil in hand,
The words don't come easy from inside this man.

You are so precious, my best friend, my wife,
A constant companion through trials of this life.
So where do I start to express what I feel,
To show you a Christ-love that is strong and real.

Rebecca, my love, I say with all my heart,
You've been my true love, and have from the start.
Rebecca my love, I say with all my heart,
A treasure from God you are!

As we grow older and struggles arise,
I want to be able to look in your eyes,
And know that to you and to Jesus I've been
Committed and faithful, a strong, loving friend.

I want you to know that with God's help I'll be,
Faithful to you until my Savior I see.
So I make this promise "Till death do us part,"
I love you, Rebecca, with all of my heart.

Rebecca cuddled against Travis' chest, contentment filling her. "When did you write it?"

Travis chuckled low in his chest. "The first night we were out here."

"Oh, Travis, I love you."

By reply he pressed a kiss to her brow.

"I can't believe we go home tomorrow," she commented after a quiet moment.

"It's gone well. And you've been a great little cowgirl."

"Now that I can ride again, I almost hate to go home."

"Won't you be glad to get back to our bed?"

"Was that your way of saying you don't want me in my own room?" Rebecca asked with mock innocence.

She felt Travis' chest move with laughter. "Don't even *think* about going back down that hall, Rebecca Rose, or I will have something to say about it."

They were silent for a time, happy to hold each other. Rebecca made one more comment about how respectful the cowhands were, but Travis heard the fatigue in her voice and said no more. There was something special about camping out and being away from home. Travis could only pray that the sweetness they'd shared the last few days would continue long after they arrived home.

It was a blessed mercy that they had a cool summer. The cattle drive to Denver had been a profitable venture with no casualties or injuries for the men, and construction of the houses was well under way.

Colin had asked Lavena to marry him, but she'd said no. She told him he could ask again, but she hadn't had a home of her own for over 13 years. After having come to terms with being out of the main ranch house, she realized she wanted to experience living on her own for a time.

"I can't do that if I have a husband, now, can I?" she said to Rebecca, and the younger woman had understood her view.

Personally, Rebecca enjoyed having a husband underfoot, but then she had kept him away for so long it was a relief to let herself love again. If she lived to be an old woman, she would never forget his words to her just two days after they'd returned back from roundup.

"Are your things all moved into our room?"

"I think so," she had smiled. "Does it have to be *everything*?"

"Yes," he'd smiled back, "we need that room for the baby."

"Do you know something I don't know, Travis?"

"No," he returned, smile still in place. "Just wishful praying."

Rebecca had not commented on his words, but she had learned something in that moment. It wasn't all clear to her, but whatever it was Travis believed, he believed it with his whole heart. She was glad that she'd never tried to separate the man from his religion—it would never have worked. Although she did not agree with the teachings of his church, her respect for him grew. As the summer progressed she even attended church with him and the boys from time to time. Whenever she went she had questions. She was no longer attacking and angry but mildly curious.

"What did Pastor Henley mean when he said death entered the world through one man?"

"He was talking about Adam and Eve and the way they sinned in the garden."

"But Adam and Eve didn't die right then."

"Spiritual death, Rebecca, not physical death."

"So you believe a person can be spiritually dead his whole life, even if he lives to be 90?"

"Yes. It doesn't matter how good a person is or how hard he's tried. God has laid out the way to Himself."

"Maybe it's not for everyone, Travis," she said reasonably.

"The Bible says it is. Christ died for all. In the first chapter of John Christ is called the 'Lamb of God who takes away the sin of the world.' The world is *everyone*, Rebecca." He had stressed the word, but Rebecca was still not certain she agreed. She looked very thoughtful, however, and Travis always knew when to let the subject drop so she could think. There were moments when he felt utter despair over Rebecca's lost state, but God always reminded him that He was sovereign, and that Travis needed to remain faithful and obedient no matter what.

"Don't ever stop asking me, Rebecca," he now told her. "I love to talk to you about what I believe."

Rebecca thanked him and slipped her hand into his. They continued their tour of the houses, which were almost complete. Travis kept praying and knew great peace. He didn't think Rebecca was certain about what she believed, but she was showing interest. Indeed, God was at work in a powerful and wonderful way, and Travis believed that whatever the future held, it would be bright with the promise.

Epilogue

Late Summer 1877

"As soon as the subject of hell comes up, she backs right off," Travis shared with Robert during their regular study.

"Is it fear?"

"I'm sure that's part of it. If she admits there's a hell, then she'll have to face where her loved ones might be if they chose to trust in themselves over God. Even her own eternity would be in jeopardy."

The men fell silent for a time. As always Travis' heart was serious about his wife's salvation, but not heavy. Their relationship had become sweeter and more precious than he ever dreamed it could be. Travis had much to be thankful for and didn't hesitate to share with Robert.

"I'm also thankful for Margo," Travis added.

"Are they all settled?" Robert wished to know.

"Yes, and Rebecca honestly enjoys her company. Sarah Beth and the boys are having the time of their lives, and Rebecca adores Mary Ann. All three of the older kids start school next week, so I'm glad the women will have each other. I just wish I could do more."

"Be careful with that attitude, Travis. Do not take Rebecca's sin on yourself. Morgan Fontaine has been surrounded by the truth for years, but he still believes he can do it his way. Addy

421

writes and tells us that he seems more sensitive at times, but it may take years."

Travis nodded, his face sober.

"Don't let that discourage you, Travis. I just want you to see that it's her choice. You stay faithful, you keep giving out the truth, and God will take care of the rest. Don't ever forget, my friend, that God loves Rebecca much more than you do."

The words were precious to Travis, and he carried them in his heart for the rest of the day. Indeed, he was awake in the night, not able to get comfortable on the mattress, and the words were still on his mind.

The moon was shining off their balcony, and Travis rose, opened the glass door, and slipped out. Feeling the cool night air, he stood in awe as his eyes roamed the majestic shape of the mountains. He was praying, his skin growing cold, when he heard his wife stir.

"Travis?"

"Out here," he said softly and came to the door. "Come and stand with me in the moonlight."

She rose and went into his arms.

"You're cold," she said as she wrapped her arms around him.

"Not anymore," he assured her, and thanked the Lord again for this wonderful woman in his life. She was so dear to him, and he praised God that He had restored their marriage.

"I love you, Reba."

"I love you, Travis."

And it was so true. They did love each other.

Being confident of this very thing, that he who hath begun a good work in you will perform it until the day of Jesus Christ. The verse came suddenly to Travis' mind, and he saw how far-reaching his confidence in God could be. His heavenly Father had started a work in him that He was still completing. And because it had begun in the first place, Lucky, Margo,

Yvonne, and even his dear Garrett and Wyatt all believed in Christ.

Travis pulled the woman in his arms a little bit tighter against him. The moonlight reminded him of the way "heaven shine" might be if there were such a thing. It made him feel special, like the cherished child of God that he was. He led Rebecca back to bed with a prayer in his heart. *Continue the work in me, so we will be set apart for Your glory alone. Set us apart, holy Father—not just me, but both of us. Amen.*